Maggie Cartwright was born in Birmingham and now lives in Cambridge with her husband, Martin. Their two sons live nearby. From a very early age she always had her nose in a book, but latterly even more so with crime being a particular favourite genre.

Death of Dreams had been swirling around her head for years, but not feeling terribly confident that her lifelong ambition could be achieved, it was thanks to her husband Martin who inspired her to take it to the finishing post.

This book is dedicated to my husband, Martin, and my two sons, Philip and Richard.

Never forget you can achieve anything if you believe in yourself.

Maggie Cartwright

DEATH OF DREAMS

AUSTIN MACAULEY PUBLISHERS™

LONDON * CAMBRIDGE * NEW YORK * SHARJAH

A CIP catalogue record for this title is available from the British Library.

ISBN 9781035812974 (Paperback)
ISBN 9781035812981 (ePub e-book)

www.austinmacauley.co.uk

First Published 2024
Austin Macauley Publishers Ltd®
1 Canada Square
Canary Wharf
London
E14 5AA

Prologue
Two Years Earlier

With the white bulbous clouds billowing deep within the blue sky, the vans marked with the name of the construction company, 'David Sheehan & Partners' were now in convoy to start the renovation of the old, abandoned pub that had taken them a long time to get their hands on, even though they bought it almost two years earlier.

The men shouted and whooped for joy at finally getting all the papers signed, including most importantly, the rubber stamped planning permission, which seemed to have been bounced back and forth from one official to another just like an inflatable beach ball.

Opening the back doors of the vehicles, men were busily unloading machinery of all shapes and sizes. Reels of electrical cord which would spark power and life into tools that would cut away rotting debris, wood sanders that would restore majestical beauty to timber with its fine grains and knots running through, and lastly the heavy iron bolt cutters that would give them access to what they all anticipated and hoped would result in other big contracts following a successful restoration of the concrete derelict ruin.

Trudging over the neglected car park whilst battling with all the over grown shrubs, dangling branches of disease infested trees, as broken glass shattered into tiny shards underneath their steel-toed work boots, they were all inwardly dreading the state of the inside, if the dismal state of the outside was anything to go by.

Despite evidence of the ten foot high fence guarding the ruin, it obviously hadn't dissuaded dependent alcohol and drug users from feeding their habits in this abandoned corner of Upper Stanton, as there were hundreds of cigarette butts, discarded needles, empty cans and bottles strewn around the abandoned property, destroying any possibility of nature being born, or able to survive, around this once popular, up market suburban gastro pub.

Finding the sign of the pub that had been destructively torn apart into two portions, and thinking that it would be a good idea to have a before and after photograph, two of the men each picked up a piece, as another pressed the button on the mobile phones photo app. All the men raised an index and middle finger in a victory sign, as the name "The Tanner House" towered above their heads.

Making their way to the main front doors which were secured forcefully with a heavy, rusted metal chain, and after some brute force and with the aid of bolt cutters, the chain finally gave up the fight and clonked loudly to the ground. 'Okay lads, let's get moving, we're in,' declared Liam Rafferty, the burly red haired Scottish site manager. 'Let's see what we've got in here shall we?'

They filed in one by one with orange hard hats, and heavily pocketed army styled combat trousers where belts with small pouches wrapped themselves around thick set waists, with every tool enjoying its own little compartment.

With axes and heavy duty saws in hand, and with unleashed stored up energy, the inside was quickly torn apart. Burly workmen with Hi-Vis jackets armed with old termite infested wooden furniture doused the pile with a fast working accelerant and watched as the funeral pyre became awash with orange flames. Piled up high, somewhat resembling a funeral pyre, the oxygen fuelled fire soon turned the termite infested wooden furniture into ashes.

Nothing could be heard amidst the loud, thump thumping of bass sounds emanating from the speakers of the paint splattered radio, and the deafening sounds of power tools ripping apart anything that needed to be destroyed as Liam spread the approved plans on the top of the bar.

Not renowned for being the most observant of people, he was taken aback somewhat as he noticed that there was no dust on the dark, badly stained mahogany bar, and staring into the wide mirror on the back wall he saw what looked like a tape deck as well as several empty discarded plastic bags sluggishly strewn on the floor. As the windows had all been barred up like prison cells since the pub's closure, it would have been virtually impossible for squatters, or anyone deciding it would be a great place for an illegal rave or any other excuse to get in, but to Liam it was obvious that someone had recently been inside the desolated building.

Looking around the place further, he found the outdated but serviceable kitchen, a small office, cleaning cupboards but very little else, until he came to a door right at the back of the bar. He found it quite bizarre that, unlike the rest of the doors that he'd stumbled upon, this one was padlocked with exactly the same thick, heavy chain that secured the main external door. Picking up the cutters once more and with flexed, bulging biceps he managed to unleash the door where spiders and dragonflies scurried off to find a new refuse from the light that now invaded their privacy. Groping around the walls on the left and the right for the switch that would cast light into the darkened abyss, he switched it on with some trepidation as to what he might find.

Treading gingerly down the creaking, wooden steps laden with flies who failed to escape the interwoven silvery strands of webs, he had to cup his mouth with his hand as the smell that exuded from the darkened emptiness was too much even for the Scotsman who, being an ex-soldier, had borne witness to the most barbaric of atrocities. Now that he'd reached the basement of the building and the almost deafening sounds from upstairs had been reduced dramatically, he thought he could hear the slow, strained tap tapping of something on a metal surface, perhaps an old, creaky pipe. Not knowing where he might find any overhead light, he removed a torch from the inside of his work belt and shone it all around.

There was an old green leather couch, a few bits of old furniture, which over the years, the owners probably hadn't got the heart to part with, and then there was another partially opened door, and that's when the blood pulsated around his heart so fast he thought it would explode.

Lying side by side along a wall where plaster and paint had been mercilessly stripped, either due to physical forces or because of temperatures that would never rise above freezing, were three beds, each with a body on top.

Desperately trying to keep his phone in his hand without letting it crash to the ground, he punched in the three digits alerting the emergency services, which would unfortunately halt the renovation indefinitely, but would inevitably give him the answer as to whether they were alive or dead.

Chapter 1
Present Day

He wasn't asleep, just staring at the bumps and cracks hidden in the depths of the ceiling which was crying out for a little attention. The dagger of light from the early morning sun proudly and piercingly dazzled its way through the slit in the hastily drawn curtains forcing its way into the darkened room.

Lying there as the long day lay ahead of him, with no set time to be anywhere or with anyone, he picked up his phone that sat motionless on the bedside table and quickly scanned for any messages that may have somehow found their way through the technological stratosphere magically ending up on his number. None.

Detective Inspector Mark Jarvis often felt as though he had probably made the wrong decision in retiring at the age of 57, and this morning was certainly one of them. Staring at the photograph of his wife on the chest of drawers in front of his bed, taken on their magical wedding day, he remembered amusingly shedding a tear at her sheer beauty, but sadly now he had to be content with seeing her eyes shining like marbles, and her unmarked, smiling face permanently ensconced in a Georgian frame.

Jarvis dragged his fingers through his mousey blonde hair which was longer now than it used to be whilst he was still working as a Detective Inspector, but he was rather enjoying the freedom of getting it cut when he wanted to, not when some high ranking official raised his eye brows and constantly harangued him with belittling comments as to how he had a duty to maintain not only to his uniform, but also to junior members of the force, and that it wasn't befitting for a senior member of the investigating team to be seen with hair, which in his opinion, was downright unkempt.

Shaking his head with a hint of a smile on his face as he remembered this rather outdated regulation, he decided that there was no point lying there any longer, so he sluggishly swung his legs to the edge of the bed, gazed around the room where clothes were lazily and unlovingly dumped, and made his mind up that today he would have a bit of a blitz and do a few domestic chores, which he admitted to himself he loathed, but also knew that no one else was going to do them for him.

Throwing on a T-shirt that was ready for the wash, he made his way down the bedroom hallway, and as there was no one but him living in the house now there was no need to poke his head around the empty rooms. He passed the daffodil yellow walls where beautiful woodland and rugged highland scenes were on display, which his wife had painstakingly and lovingly painted, bringing life to the otherwise soulless upper floor.

Heading into the kitchen, he turned on the television that was set in a small alcove within their old Welsh dresser, and using the remote control tuned into the BBC world news station, and whilst not diverting all of his attention to the important news bulletins he was still able to get the gist of what was going on in the world.

Filling the kettle ready for his cup of tea, and searching through his fridge for something to eat, he realised that this was something else that he needed to take more notice of, as there was only one slice of wholemeal bread that had curled at the edges and was speckled with blue and green spots, but he wasn't that bothered as there was no butter anyway, so he figured he'd eat later, but in the meantime would just have to settle on the injection of caffeine.

Waiting for the kettle to do its job and getting the teacup ready for its infusion of boiling water, Jarvis focused on the wearied tone of the broadcaster clearly saddened as her facial expressions expressed shock and heartfelt condemnation of the report she was about to give.

'At around eleven p.m. last night emergency services were called to Lansdale Road in the east London area where a 13 year old boy was found dead, stabbed outside of his own home. Local residents have said that they heard loud noises and shouting at around ten pm., but they said that this was a common occurrence and so didn't pay much heed to it.'

A reporter at the scene commented, *'Time and time again residents have voiced their anger within the immediate vicinity, who are fed up and disgruntled at the way the police are ignoring their pleas for help, as the knife crime around the streets continues to disintegrate and young lives are being lost. We can now hear from the mother of a local boy, who sadly lost her own son a year ago under similar circumstances and the assailant has still not been found.'*

Holding the long, furry microphone in front of a black lady, possibly in her early forties, clad in a scarlet red polo neck jumper and black leather jacket, Adam Jamieson the reporter with furrowed brows asked concernedly, *'So, Mrs Hutchinson, thank you for talking to me…'*

Details of this recent attack was exactly why he had made his mind up to quit the force, with the increase in crime rates in general, murder, rapes, attacks on the elderly in their own homes, and drugs being passed around the streets like sweets at a children's party, but it was the harsh reality that knife crimes in the country, especially in parts of London had gone completely out of control.

Having heard enough of this depressing news, Jarvis picked up the remote control and flicked through the channels until he found something lighter, and chose Channel 4, and even though he had watched the DVDs over and over again, he still got a kick out of Frasier.

He decided on showering before he got on with his chores, so he grabbed the small Bose portable speaker and headed on up the stairs. He chose a playlist on Spotify that he listened to on a daily basis, and chose Daily Mix 2, this being a compilation of some, if not most, of his favourite tunes from the 70s up to the present time. Supertramp's infamous 'Logical Song' started to pound its way through the circular speakers as he opened the shower cubicle doors and turned the taps on ready to get the temperature right before he stepped in.

One of Eleanor's treats to both her and Jarvis had been the installation of a state of the art shower with classy looking sliding double doors. Even though it was a luxury that they really couldn't afford, once it was powered into life, jets would fire water at both an incredible force and speed from all angles making it impossible not to feel its massaging effects both inside and out.

With a towel wrapped snugly around him, he stepped across to the wash basin mirror and with his hand wiped the steam away with circular movements until his reflection stared back at him. Even though he'd put a little bit of weight on since retiring, his angular face was still lean and his light blue eyes still held a brightness, despite the deep circles underneath. With toothbrush held loosely over a white porcelain oyster pedal basin he squeezed out a pea sized amount of paste, pressed the 'on' button of the brush and let the swirling action of the brush do its job.

Clearing the splodge of pure white paste left at the side of the basin with both hands, and whilst holding onto the side of it whilst combing his straight mousey blonde hair, he realised that every day seemed to begin with exactly the same ritual, and that's when peering at his image he knew that the time had come to start making plans once more before life became too dull when he'd loathe even getting out of bed in the mornings.

Maybe get a part time job somewhere, do a bit of volunteer work, anything that brings a bit of structure to his life again. Perhaps it was time to go out dating again, but that was something that he didn't think about for very long, 'cos he knew Eleanor could never be replaced, but what if he found someone that would just like to go out for drinks or a dinner with him, perhaps even a trip somewhere? I mean, he thought inwardly, whilst stepping into his dark blue jeans, and pulling the black T-shirt over his head, 'I don't need to start a physical relationship, now do I?'

Grabbing all the laundry he could hold between two outstretched hands he made his way down the stairs once more to the laundry room that was next to the kitchen. Loading everything into the machine, he looked in the cupboard underneath the Belfast sink for detergent tablets, only to find the box empty. 'Shit,' he complained to the empty room, and at that point he knew that the next hour of his life was sorted, and not for the first time, the rest of the chores would have to be put off while he did a bit of an essential shop, but he also knew what that meant, he'd wander off somewhere, lost in his thoughts and end up walking for the best part of the day.

***

Before leaving the house, Jarvis picked up his mail, and there was only one letter which he placed on the hall table, the rest were flyers advertising pizzas, curries, even burgers seemed to be delivered these days and, he silently wondered, that as there was a plethora of houses on the market, why did estate agents bombard house owners with promises that their property could be sold within a matter of weeks, even though the owners had no intention of selling whatsoever. He grabbed the useless flyers and left them on the table ready to put in the recycling bin when he returned.

Taking his black waterproof jacket from one of the many coat hooks that lined the wall closest to the front door, and pocketing his keys, wallet and phone, he stepped into his laceless black trainers, and whilst patting his trouser pockets he was silently convinced that he'd remembered everything, and was now ready for whatever the day held in store for him.

13

Unlocking the door from the inside to the outside world revealed that autumn was playing its part by laying a carpet of newly abandoned crisp, orange and brown leaves broken into shards of dried parchment at his feet.

Jarvis had been living in this quiet, leafy suburban village of Upper Stanton for almost fifteen years now, but it never failed to amuse him that when he closed his front door, no matter what time of the day it was, he could feel the prying eyes behind the twitching of net curtains from nosey neighbours, who having nothing else better to do, decided to ease their boredom by checking on people's comings and goings.

He sauntered past his battered old Peugeot, which was parked on the roadside, and decided he'd walk to the shops which were a couple of miles away, deciding that the exercise would do him good. Walking at a steady pace, and in no particular hurry, it once again struck him that it didn't matter how many bins the councils provided in public places, some people really couldn't be bothered to use them for whatever unfathomable reason.

It was a well-known fact to the local residents that at the top of Hewlett Road, adjacent to the main road leading into the town was a honey trap for teenagers not old enough to go into pubs unaccompanied, but this is where they all congregated leaving behind their debris of ground down cigarette butts, cans, empty liquor bottles, presumably taken from homes where alcohol wasn't under lock and key, or bought on their behalf by someone who was going into a local Spar who was over eighteen.

Jarvis made his way, with hands deep in coat pockets, along a fairly busy suburban road lined with small trading shops, a pub, chemist and the usual suppliers of essentials which small communities heavily depended upon. A couple of nearby cafes decorated lifeless footpaths with tables and chairs, surrounded by upright ornamental trees housed in terracotta planters emulating the fashionable continental life style whilst instilling the air with titillating aromas of freshly baked bread and coffee, bombarding the culinary senses of hungry shoppers. Having missed breakfast, he made his mind up that he would do the shopping after he lined his stomach with an early lunch, mind you, as he checked his watch, it wasn't that early, it was, after all, almost midday.

**

Walking past a little Italian restaurant, called quite simply 'Ciao' with its garlic scent infusing out of its doors, he decided he'd sate his hunger and eagerly strode through the red and green chipped painted wooden doors with its name carved on the glass panels set within its frame.

He didn't quite know why he liked this place, particularly as it wasn't furnished with what you would call vibrancy or high quality furnishings, and the atmosphere with its sparsely decorated walls, lacked warmth or indeed any sense of welcoming.

Jarvis knew, from his previous visits, that the restaurant was owned and run by a husband and wife, with the latter being in charge, and the husband more or less keeping a low profile. As he entered through the doors and stood beside a wooden stand where a plastic based sign instructed patrons *'Please wait here to be seated'* was embossed in rose and gold colours, he was greeted by Anna the owner with her usual flat, unreadable expression, 'Good afternoon, Mr Jarvis.'

He answered with a quick glance towards her and muttered, 'Morning to you too, Anna.'

'Where would you like to sit, Mr Jarvis?' Anna asked, smiling with embarrassment, 'As you can see, there's plenty to choose from.'

Once seated, he glanced around at the unusual, mismatched ensemble of tables and chairs standing in anticipation on an old lino floor, with its undulating bubbles and cracks that would be a welcoming playground for all sorts of crawling, invisible guests. Walls were scantily adorned with prints from a seemingly forgotten age without any Italian connection, or indeed any thought as to why they were hung in the first place, probably only there to service as a screen to hide some embarrassing disfigurement that lay underneath them. With only two other tables occupied, the retired police officer was confident that there wouldn't be long to wait for his much needed food and drink.

After having scanned the menu, Jarvis decided that he would have the Ravioli with a portion of garlic bread and a bottle of Peroni.

With nothing really to arouse his attention, he looked over at one of the adjoining tables where he could see two middle aged women who were animatedly exchanging no doubt hidden secrets, with the agreed promise of 'Don't tell anyone, but…' as they surreptitiously cupped their hands around their mouths, whilst turning around to make sure no one was listening.

The retired detective decided to scan through latest news items on his phone as he quietly waited for his fare to arrive when out of his peripheral vision he noted the arrival of what appeared to be a young family. With phones at the ready, they sat down without as much as a glance at each other, or any discussion as to where they would sit, they almost robotically sat at the nearest table closest to the door, still completely transfixed at the brightly lit screens where their thumbs skittered around deftly at alarming speeds.

They each gave the waitress their order, barely raising their heads from the laminated sheets encased inside a synthetic leather cover, still not diverting their attention from their phones just in case a ping went unnoticed.

The former police officer's food arrived with tiny parcels of neatly packed Ravioli adorning a brightly coloured plate bearing pictures of popular Mediterranean food where a small translucent container was ensconced in the middle, bearing the jewel that gave the dish its authentic Italian taste. Whilst savouring his eagerly awaited food, he could feel a slight breeze as the door to the restaurant was pushed open announcing its newest customer.

He appeared to be in his late thirties or early forties, dressed casually but smartly in khaki coloured chinos, denim blue Oxford shirt, light brown suede jacket with a cross body bag over his right shoulder. The man chose a table adjacent to Jarvis, removed his jacket and with almost obsessive precision placed it on the back of the wooden chair, which seemed unworthy to adorn such an exquisite, elegant garment. It appeared to him that this stranger had almost strategically placed himself in a position where it would have been difficult for either man not to acknowledge each other, even if it was just spontaneous eye contact, or a nod of the head, in acknowledgement of one another's presence.

The finely attired man, whilst strategically placing his cutlery from a haphazardly folded napkin, was the first to break the silence whilst smiling awkwardly, 'Hi. Food any good?' he asked.

Jarvis paused, and then nodded, 'Yeah, not bad at all. You get what you pay for, but good enough when you've got nothing in the house to eat I s'pose.

The sound of a scraping chair could be heard as the stranger stood up and made his way to the retired officer's table, stared at him with his proffered outstretched hand and announced 'Hi, my name's Noel Deacon,' as Jarvis studied the man for a moment, smiled awkwardly and replied, 'Mark Jarvis.'

'Yes, I thought I recognised you from the various newspaper reports about the great things that you've done in the police force.'

'Well, I seem to be at a disadvantage then,' interjected the detective inspector peering curiously at the stranger.

'Oh right, of course, I'm sorry,' Noel replied courteously, whilst dragging his fingers through his stylishly cut blonde hair. 'I'm a reporter for the Warwickshire Standard, and I have, to put it mildly, been following your career over the years with much interest, as you have erm…quite the reputation of being a fellow who can get the job done, but get it done honestly and without breaking the rules.'

'Is that so?' Jarvis remarked, with an almost flat, unreadable expression on his face.

'Listen, do you mind if I join you, but I understand if you want to be left alone?' Noel asked rather timidly, as he jiggled with coins in his deep, trouser pockets.

'Well, I've already eaten, but sure, be my guest.'

Having seated himself opposite Jarvis, Anna approached him with slight curiosity and asked whether he was ready to order.

Noel paused momentarily then answered, 'Yeah, I'll have the Salmon with steamed vegetables, and a Peroni for me and for the gentleman, if that's OK.'

Whilst they were waiting for Noel's order, the retired police officer briefly refocused his attention on the family of three as they were preparing themselves to leave, with the male mimicking the new modern way of asking for the bill by scribbling in the air with an invisible pen. He knew that it wasn't a rarity for families to sit in a public space and never talk or laugh with each other, thanks to modern technology, but nevertheless it still made him feel quite sad as he remembered with fondness the many meals that he, Eleanor, and his two children would have together, where there were always tales to tell and listen to, and much laughter.

Even as they'd opened the door to leave, they once again checked their phones, and in single file sauntered past the outlandishly large neon signed window, without a second glance as to where they'd just spent an hour of their lives.

'I'm not keeping you from anything urgent am I?' Noel asked, somewhat meekly.

'No, but my natural inquisitive disposition is, to be honest with you, a little in overdrive as to why you would want to sit with a complete stranger, and more questioningly eat at the same table, especially as it's obvious that I've already eaten,' replied Jarvis with a hint of sarcasm.

As Noel ate in silence, the ex-detective used this time to check his phone for any messages, one of which brought a broad smile to his face lightening the tension at the table somewhat.

'Some good news I hope?' Noel said, putting down his knife and fork, wiping his mouth with his napkin.

'Well, it's a message from my younger son, Andrew. You see, he's rather got it into his head that he feels as though he needs to check up on me to make sure I haven't left the gas on, or failed to turn the taps off when I leave the house, and he always ends the message with a stupid bloody emoji. It's become part of my day, and it's just a silly gaff, but harmless, and of course it means he doesn't have to physically pick the phone up and talk to his old man. He also keeps going on and on that it would be a good idea if I got a dog so that he could come and play with it, whilst I fed it, paid the vet's bills and cleared up his shit when we went out for his daily constitutionals, and he even offered to look after it if I wanted to go away for a weekend!'

'And are you?' Noel asked as he smirked, whilst pushing food onto his fork.

'Oh…that's a long way off yet, I'm just used to having the day all to myself. I can get up when I like, go to bed when I like, so I guess I'm becoming a rather selfish bastard, but I'm loving it and I'm not ready to share it with a four legged animal.'

'Good for you. I mean…pets are great, don't get me wrong, but they're time consuming, vet's fees are enormous unless of course you invest in some kind of pet plan with an insurance company, then there's the money for injections, flea powders, but I think the worst part is that their bowels and bladders don't always keep to the schedule of waiting till they go out for walks. Believe me I know, we've always had a dog even as a young child, but when she eventually died, I decided I wouldn't have another one for a while, and it wasn't just about walks, bills, etc., it breaks your bloody heart when they eventually go, it's like losing a member of the family,' as Noel raised his glass in the air with a silent 'Cheers.'

'May I call you Mark?' The journalist quizzed, as a coy smile paraded across his face, patiently waiting for a response.

'OK, I can still see that you're uneasy with my being here so I will explain if you'll let me.' Noel spoke in a quiet voice watching Jarvis carefully.

'Well, as I'm here, and you've bought a relative stranger a beer, then you can call me Jarvis as this is what most people call me. I'm not entirely sure why, because I think that Mark is a very easy name not only to pronounce but also to remember. But, put that to one side for now as there's one thing you can tell me, how did you know where to find me and, as I'm not working on any newsworthy cases, and am not likely to be again, why the sudden interest in me?'

'Well, as journalists, were hum…pretty adept at getting information, so I called the station and asked whether there were any senior detectives who were about to retire, or indeed have recently retired and would be willing to speak to me. When they gave me your name I knew I recognised it, but I wasn't sure why, so I decided I'd use the good old Internet to find out some stuff about you. The sergeant at the front desk at Stockfield Road Police Station was most helpful, he wouldn't give out any phone numbers or your address or anything, he just told me that you could occasionally be found eating here, and bingo, I guess I struck lucky. Mind you I have to tell you that I'm sure the owner here thinks I'm some kind of stalker or maybe even worse, 'cos the amount of times that I've walked past lately, it's a wonder she didn't come out and threaten me with the bloody Mafia.'

With elbows resting on the table and with fingertips forming a triangle Jarvis responded guardedly, 'Oh, so it was our big, mouthed sergeant was it? Actually, I'm not mad at him because you could have found my address in the electoral register I suppose, saving you the time and embarrassment of standing outside here all times of the day and night!'

'To answer the second part of your question will take me a lot longer, but the upshot of it is, is that at present the stories that I'm asked to pursue are, to put it bluntly, boring the crap out of me and, quite honestly, are nowhere near newsworthy, and I think mostly they're an insult to the readers, almost to the point of, well…I honestly feel insulting their intelligence. I absolutely, categorically feel that the majority of the pieces that I foolishly put my name to should never get to print, and unless I do something about this soon, I think my chances of being critically acclaimed as a reliable journalist are doomed.'

Jarvis shrugged with seeming disinterest, 'And, what's that got to do with me?'

'OK, each year there's a journalist award, a bit like the Emmys, Golden Globe that sort of thing, and of course it goes without saying that it could be something big for the recipient. You know, recognised amongst the well-known tabloids, broad sheets, possible openings on TV, and radio broadcasting, amongst other things.'

'Still don't get why you're sitting opposite me though, especially as you already know I'm no longer a member of the club.'

'Another Peroni or coffee perhaps?' the journalist requested in the hope that he could entice the man opposite to sit with him for longer.

'No thanks I'm fine, I really need to be going 'cos well…you won't believe this, but the only reason I'm here is that I ran out of washing detergent, and boring as it may seem and a bit wussy I suppose, but this was my day to sort out my house a little, because suffice to say, I've become a bit of a slob.'

After a lengthy pause, noting the earlier quiet confidence ebbing away from Noel, Jarvis added with a reluctant sigh, 'Ten minutes tops, then I'm off.'

'OK, it's a deal. Right, my idea is that its high time that instead of the police being vilified, albeit by a small minority of the general public, cases need to be published that not only end with a positive and just outcome, but also ones that have wrecked the lives of others, other than the perpetrator of the crime. I needed, therefore, to search for a detective who was noted for his humane conduct, not only for excellent results achieved, but for his renowned fairness and treatment of not only the victims but also someone who finds it difficult to understand why a suspect did what he did, especially if it was a person with no known history of violence, who've perhaps never even received a parking ticket. I guess that the angle that I'm looking for is what sent the person over the edge to do what he or she did. So…I figured that guys like you need to share with the public, a case or even more than one, that have given you huh…sleepless nights, and to some degree, you wish in the depths of your soul that they'd ended with a different outcome,' explained Noel, as he poured water from a jug placed within easy reach on the table, whilst peering at Jarvis nervously.

The retired officer, whilst clasping both hands around the back of his neck, leaned back in his chair and sighed, 'So, if I agree what's in it for me?'

'Apart from proving to the tax payers who paid your salary, that you're not all pigs the way that they say you are, and apart from seeing your name in headlines, if I win of course, then sorry to say nothing.'

'You're definitely very convincing Noel, and as your profession would suggest a man of many words. You also certainly seem very passionate, not only about the subject matter of the piece that you're hoping to submit, but also in trying to make a name for yourself, which I guess in your profession isn't that easy. So, I guess the only answer that I can give you is yes I'll give it a go, and hopefully you'll get something out of it, well…if you say some good things about me of course.'

Noel drew a deep breath, lowered his head in silent acknowledgement and replied, 'I don't quite know how to thank you.'

'No need, so…when d'you want to make a start? Now that I'm out and it's such a lovely autumn day, and as I really can't be bothered with bloody household chores, how about we get out of here and get some fresh air, stretch our legs and after what I have told you, then you can decide whether it's the pitch that you're looking for. I'm not promising that I'll get everything chronologically correct, but it'll be as near as dammit, and I promise you I'll be as objective as I can.'

Noel quietly put down his knife and fork, wiped his mouth with his napkin and beckoned Anna for the bill, whilst Jarvis' thumbs busily tapped out a message on his phone.

***

The two men left the restaurant and turned left away from the hubbub of the lunch time shoppers and after strolling down leafy roads and side streets they found themselves walking across a bridge that had been designed by someone who felt that the area deserved something beautiful and meaningful, leading into a sanctuary, cast away from traffic, shops and the everyday noise pollution which almost takes away the ability to think freely and allow minds to wander aimlessly.

The billboard adjacent to the wooden overpass announced with majestic grace that they had now entered Stanton Park whilst acquainting its users of its history, routes of beauty, natural habitat and inhabitants that could be found, and information to be followed as to safety for both the users and its wildlife.

As they passed dog walkers and children busily kicking and playing in the debris of the autumnal leaves, Noel asked, 'Can we start by you giving me some background as to where you were born, what your childhood was like, your family, you know that sort of thing. This will give the readers some insight as to you the person, and not just the job that you used to do, oh and any objections if I tape the interview, 'cos it'll probably be better in the long run as my hum…shorthand can be a bit sketchy, and I'd hate to get anything wrong, or miss anything out?'

21

'Well, I was born in North Easton, a sleepy little place which is about fourteen miles north of Stratford, I've got two brothers and sisters and I'm number four in the pecking order. I went to a catholic primary school and then to the local comprehensive where I did okay I guess but nothing special that's for sure. Went on to do 'A' levels and then straight on to become a police cadet and worked my way up the ranks, and that's it pretty much in a nutshell.

'Except to say that I suppose I was a bit of a social nightmare, if I'm honest, quite shy and introverted, which at school was taken to mean that I was some sort of snob, which of course I wasn't, as there was nothing for me to be snobbish about, because let's face it, as children we had the bare essentials but nothing fancy. In fact, we used to wear hand-me-downs, so it was the eldest boy and girl that got the new stuff and the young 'uns had to make do with what they were given.

'I was a bit overweight and would be teased as I walked past the bust stop and to the shops with piggy noises echoing through the streets, so I pretty much kept to myself, apart from school trips which I was forced to go on. So, for me to have met and married my first teenage girlfriend was an absolute miracle I can tell you, and we've had a great time together ever since.'

Noel paused momentarily pondering as to whether he had the right to ask the inevitable question, 'Erm…are you still together?'

Finding a wooden bench with scratched hearts and initials embossed through the central veins of its fibres, both men sat down as the retired detective began his narrative, 'Let's leave that to one side for the moment if you don't mind, and let me start with me telling you about what had to have been one of the worst years in my career, and I can honestly say it feels like a lifetime ago, but d'you know what…it was in fact only a couple of years back.'

Chapter 2
Two Years Earlier

Denton Heights sits on the edge of an estate where empty tower blocks were left derelict with graffiti covered walls, windowless, lifeless, where shards of glass lay beside abandoned cars, children's playgrounds dominated by youths of all ages at all times of the day and night, as worried parents had no choice but to refuse their children the freedom that they once enjoyed in this former safe haven.

Waiting for the long awaited renovation plans to be approved, life went on with escalating unemployment figures, drugs and prostitution becoming increasingly more dangerous.

With police presence sporadic at best, it was felt by the higher echelons within the metropolitan police force that this was, for the time being, the best course of action as heavy handed intervention may cause the numbers of major crimes to soar, with murder, theft, muggings, and rioting to rise out of control.

With pockets of diehard residents staying put, even though they knew it was a ticking time bomb where drugs and their users would eventually take full control, they made their minds up that until the wrecking ball had attacked the high rises first, they preferred to stay with the friendly Asian corner shop with its displays of fresh fruit and vegetables sitting in their wooden crates on the pavement, and the all-important newsagent, where adverts were still being displayed in the windows.

Barbie dolls, small boxes of Lego bricks, could be bought in a hurry when a birthday had been missed, and an array of magazines ranging from the up-to-date fashion editions to fighter planes raging through white skies, and old steam trains billowing out white clouds. Cards for all occasions and daily local and national newspapers were all attainable together with the all-important weekly lottery ticket. No need for getting on buses, or walking miles, the things that these residents needed were all to be had within a spitting distance of their front doors and they weren't leaving until there was nothing left for them to stay for.

On the edge of the estate, hooded youths would congregate on street corners, answering calls from cars hooting their horns, where on a whim of a nod of the head another of the gang would scurry away on a bike lifting the front wheels up in the air as they went in search of their supplier. With careful passing of both money and goods in a silent handshake the deed is done until the next car or passer-by comes along.

Prostitutes used to work safely around the streets, but after a number of nasty incidents they had been forcefully driven indoors, mainly to an old white and black mock Tudor three floor residence. It used to be a hotel when the area enjoyed a suburban calmness and modest affluence, then as trade moved to newer, updated hostelries, it was sold off and now it's quite simply known as Cinders where its name is neatly and succinctly displayed on a black canopy with smaller letters underneath advertising that it is legally licensed to sell alcohol.

As the black Range Rover with its black tinted windows drove up and parked immediately outside of the establishment, a doorman sporting a close-cropped hair style and a dark but speckled grey beard, clad in a black suit coupled with a white shirt and maroon dicky bow tie appeared.

He opened the driver's door where its owner slid out effortlessly, moved his hands down the front of his shirt and jacket, ironing out invisible creases, handed the keys to the man charged with guarding the entrance, and sauntered up the slight incline to the entrance.

Being a regular patron, he never bothered to stop and gaze at the portraits of the famous blondes of years gone by as the likes of Marilyn Monroe, Diana Dors, Jayne Mansfield gazed down on the ensemble of guests who sauntered in with a confident swagger, strutting their self-importance and leaving behind in their wake the over powering scent of expensive after shave.

Entering the main area where the bar predominantly held centre stage with a myriad of varying coloured optics suspended in air, being reflected in the mirror lining the entire back wall, as red leather Chesterfield sofas dominated the main floor space, with small mahogany-coloured tables and chairs dotted around. On seeing the new arrival enter into the club, the owner rushed over and proffered an outstretched right hand over exaggeratedly, with his left hand seizing the other man's shoulders and announcing, 'Well, hello there my dear friend, so wonderful to see you here tonight. Can I get you the usual Mr DaCosta? Would you like your usual table, sir?'

Inwardly flinching at the over embroidered welcome, the guest casually strode over to the corner booth with its red leather sofa, black onyx lamps sitting aloft glass side tables, and removing his mobile from the inside of his black bespoke jacket he checked it for unread messages, before finally placing it onto the seat beside him. The red-headed barman known to all as 'Nate' approached the new guest with a colourless liquid floating around a balloon glass where the ice and a slice of lemon bobbed around and placed the drink on a coaster in front of him, together with a small white mini ceramic dish hosting green and black olives with a supply of cocktail sticks standing upright in a small holder.

Glancing around at the occupied tables and with a nod of the head whilst raising his glass off the table as a form of acknowledgement to certain individuals' presence, he noted at the far end of the bar, which was partially concealed by a pillar obstructing a full view, a girl with a black shiny halter neck top and beautifully thick strawberry blonde hair styled in a shoulder length bob. Picking his glass and mobile up he swankily manoeuvred his way to where she was perched on a black leather bar stool with chrome legs.

'Anyone sitting here?' The olive-skinned man asked with his fashionable top knot, and chic, expensive looking clothes.

'No, go right ahead.'

'Can I get you something to drink, perhaps a glass of champagne?'

Looking sideways in a rather flirtatious manner at the attractive man beside her, she dreamily replied, 'Ah…a girl never says no to a glass of bubbly, well…not when she earns so little that she can only dream of the stuff.'

'So, all the more reason then that the girl's dream comes true,' uttered the man, as he swivelled his bar stool around so that he was face to face with her whilst peering into her green eyes. 'So, not wanting to sound corny or anything but what's a beautiful girl like you doing here all on her lonesome. Are you perhaps waiting for someone?'

'The answer to the second question is no, and to the first well…I just didn't fancy another night in front of the telly and decided I needed a bit of company,' she answered rather seductively.

'I haven't seen you here before, but I have to say I'm rather glad that you decided to give the remote control a rest tonight,' replied the man whispering into her ear.

As the champagne was released of its cork with, characteristically, frothy liquid oozing over the top, the well-dressed man ran his finger up the girl's left arm until he rested it at the spot where etched on her lily white skin in dark black ink was an eye, wide open with long, curling lashes surrounding it.

'So, people tell me that when they have tattoos they normally choose something that is symbolic to them, so what's the meaning of this one then?'

'Ah…well it kinda reminds me that someone's watching out for me, you know? I suppose I like to think of it as a bit like a crucifix warding off the devil,' she replied, dabbing at a droplet of the light gold liquid with a folded napkin that had escaped from the corner of her mouth.

'Oh, you won't need anyone peering over you tonight, not when you're with me. So…what d'you say we take this bottle of champagne and get ourselves comfy, eh?'

'Sure, why not, edging herself off the stool,' as DaCosta gave the nod to the bar tender, as he quietly scrutinised his latest conquest who was garbed in leather skinny trousers made even more sexually alluring by her stiletto heeled ankle boots, zipped up at the back, as she headed almost panther like in front of him towards the stairs.

Nate, the bartender, was busily holding up glasses to the light whilst painstakingly checking for water marks or fingerprints, picked up the phone.

Within minutes another security guy dressed in the accustomed black attire arrived and took the champagne, ensconced amongst huge chunks of ice in a metal bucket, and holding two fresh glasses upside down by the skinny, long stems headed to the stairs.

The stairs to the upper floors were closed off with an emerald, green barrier rope with brass hooks either side, and as it was removed, DaCosta informed the bouncer, 'That's okay Jimmy, I know the way.'

'Very well, here's your key sir,' replied the man, handing the man the wooden key chain with the number three on it, and strolled back in the direction of the bar.

The room was at the end of the rather long, narrow corridor and with the key in his hand DaCosta opened the door wide for his guest to enter first. As they both entered into the small but serviceable room, he placed the champagne on a carved wooden ash dresser where a matching mirror reflected a double bed draped in white, crisp looking Egyptian cotton bed clothes, and two bed side tables each bearing a cheap looking crystal lamp and very little else, but he thought inwardly, everyone has to slum it once in a lifetime.

'D'you mind if I play a little music? It helps me to relax a little, you know,' muttered the young lady, as the man pulled her towards her and started to nuzzle against her thin pale skinned neck.

'If it makes you happy, and we can enjoy ourselves more, then why not? Just not heavy metal, 'cos that just wouldn't be sexy now, would it?' He grabbed hold of both of the glasses and poured champagne into both of them. Stepping quietly over to where the young lady stood with her phone in her hands looking through a playlist from Spotify, he put his arms around her waist sliding them upwards towards her breast, and as far as she was concerned, timing couldn't have been better, as the Four Top's 'Do What you Gotta Do' started to resonate around the room.

She never liked this kind of work, and she was certainly not a natural in the art of seduction, in fact she loathed it with every fibre of her body, but she knew she had to do this to pay her rent, and to well…survive. But, she thought, looking at his reflection in the mirror he wasn't as bad as some of the loathsome old, fat, drooling poor excuses of the male sex, and in fact, she silently confessed, she found him to be incredibly dishy. His look definitely appeared as though he could well be from South America or Southern Europe, and one with considerable wealth, or so she hoped.

He, however, was certainly no amateur in lustfully trying to remove her glitzy top as he even managed to undo the tiny almost invisible hook and eyes at the back of her small figure-hugging top. As she always did, she acted out the role and tried to forget she was there but to get the money at the end of the night she knew she had to play seductress and respond to being sexually aroused.

Whilst alluringly removing each other's clothes, their foreplay was intense, and even though her eyes were closed throughout, with her mind focusing solely on the bank notes at the end of the night, he surprised her by swooping her up in his huge muscular arms gently but passionately and laid her on the bed. He removed her arms from around his body and stretched them upwards behind her head, as his tongue probed all over her body, and whilst straddling on top of her put his erect penis inside of her where he pushed and thrusted when a roar of loud satisfaction erupted from his long, muscular throat as it jerked upwards to the ceiling.

Climbing off the young, slim girl and swinging his legs to the edge of the bed where he sat, grabbed his black Calvin Klein underwear and pulled them on. He sauntered towards the champagne and pouring two glasses, handed one over to the young girl who was lying prone on the bed. As she sat up to take a sip, he placed his on the night stand where he had placed his phone, and wallet and moved towards the bathroom.

'I'm taking a shower, humour yourself while I'm, gone,' announced the self-confident, olive skinned, man whilst glancing across at the outline of the body sprawled out under the now wrinkled covers. 'Unless of course…you'd like to join me?'

Stifling an imaginary yawn, the strawberry haired blonde stared up at him with her penetrating green eyes and sleepily murmured, 'Ah…I think I'll pass and just enjoy these gorgeous soft sheets, well, if it's alright with you?'

Not responding, the Latino looking man simply turned his semi-naked body and headed into the bathroom, turned the shower on and stripped his body of the last hour, the only remaining evidence he had which couldn't be washed away was her cheap perfume which seemed to have seeped through his blood stream.

Meanwhile, the young lady, refusing to refer to herself as a sex worker simply lay there looking around the room and it didn't matter whether they were furnished well, or whether she earned her money in a tip, she had to keep reminding herself that it was simply a job, and as long as she went for regular testing at the centre for sexual transmitted diseases then she should be okay for the time being, but she swore to herself continually, the day that she was debt free she would walk away from this squalid life, and hopefully would never return.

As he re-entered the room, the infamous melodic sounds of Otis Reading's 'Sittin' on the Dock of the Bay' was playing, as he was rubbing his hair roughly with a towel, questioning her whilst bearing a sarcastic grin on his face, 'Don't you ever listen to any up-to-date music, these tunes you're playing are far too old for one so young?'

Perched on the edge of the bed, stroking the pale blemish-free skin of her arm which was lying across the pillow where he'd been previously, she quietly responded, 'Well, I grew up with these songs, you know. My mum and dad loved this type of music, and obviously Motown, so I guess it kinda sticks with you.'

Sipping at a half full glass of the intoxicating liquid and walking over to where his trousers had fallen to the floor, he reached inside for his Marlboro and a lighter, where with one cigarette perched inside pursed lips he offered one to the flaxen coloured figure, 'Huh…no thanks, but are you sure you're supposed to be smoking in here? I mean, there's enough *'No Smoking'* signs in here ain't there?'

Stubbing the flame out of his cigarette in the dregs of the liquid lying in the bottom of the glass, the punter slowly but meticulously re-dressed in his wrinkle free clothes, taking out of the inside jacket pocket a roll of notes, and throwing five twenty pound notes beside her, sighed heavily and muttered, 'Here you go, erm…never did get your name, but see you around perhaps.'

The quiet, rather ordinary girl who didn't stir from that same position on the mattress reached over and picked up the notes one by one and announced rather sheepishly, 'Ah…thanks, but I'm not sure that's enough 'cos I spent longer than an hour, so we could well…round it off to an hour and a half. It's just that I've got a lot of bills this month what with my rent, and tuition fees, so…well you're a business man, you understand, right?'

DaCosta well known for his short temper and one who would never take kindly to being questioned or told what to do, which in his mind questioned his power, slowly picked up his cigarette packet, removed another one, and whilst staring at himself in the mirror making sure that his clothes were free from any loose threads, removed his green cylindrical shaped Bic lighter, and showed the white tipped drug a yellow flame, and exhaled the smoke upwards.

Sauntering confidently towards the bed once more, and again casually seating himself on the side where she lay, he leant over and pierced her back with the lit cigarette over and over again, and as she tried to turn herself over to fight back, he held her neck with his left hand and continued piercing her lily white skin descending down her back and the backs of her thighs, smiling sadistically and oblivious to the savage screaming that filled the room. Not content with the brutish attack on the back of her body, he turned her body over, but this time he covered her mouth with his free hand, as he didn't want to alert any of the other club members what was going on, especially as he was enjoying himself so much, and repeated the act all over her chest, arms, legs and even her genitalia.

Leaning over to his glass that was resting on the bedside table he tossed the butt into the glass that she was drinking out of, and to stop her screaming loudly he bent down to retrieve the thong that she'd been wearing, and stuffed it into her mouth. She was in too much pain to fight against the beast that had got what he wanted from her but then had used her as some kind of ash tray, but in her wildest of dreams she could never have imagined what the next few minutes would throw at her.

Whilst still lying supine, he decided to use his fists which he used to hammer against her face, over and over again, and then sliding his fists down almost calculating where his next hit would be, pounded down over the rest of her body making the red welts from the burns almost invisible, with blood coursing its way down her body, and the puffiness of her bleached white skin made her unrecognisable as the young girl that had lain there just five minutes previously, and almost in an unconscious state, she neither cared nor wished that the bombardment would end.

Rubbing his knuckles to ease his discomfort, he leant over the silent, damaged body and uttered in her ear, 'No one, but no one ever tells me what to do, and when I invited you to take a shower with me the answer that you should have given was 'yes' because no one refuses anything I ask them to do. And finally, no one, but no one, tells me that I owe them anything because that's a word I don't like to hear. I take whatever I want, and like it or not that's a fact, and if you know what's good for you won't ever forget it, and erm…don't forget to tell your friends about how I was probably the best fuck that you've ever had.' She never moved. No sound came out of her mouth. But he didn't care, as this was now someone else's problem.

Moving almost panther like towards the door he stopped and glanced across at her, threw another note on the bed, and casually but acidicly boasted, 'I always pay for a service, but I only give what I think its worth. This is a bit extra, not that you've earned it, but let's just say…as you won't be earning anything for a while then maybe this will help with the bills eh? Take it or leave it, whore,' and with that he let the door slam behind him.

The squeaks on the carpeted floor boards upstairs could be heard as the confident, arrogant man approached the wooden staircase, and whilst strutting down one tread at a time, he made sure his shirt was smartly nestled within the waist band of his trousers, that the collar of his shirt was sitting neatly within his designer jacket, and piling his hair back into its original top knot secured it with a hair tie.

Not wanting to upset his regular client, the owner Barry Cronin nervously loosening the collar around his throat with his index and middle fingers, coughed nervously, as the sound from the upstairs had not been stifled, but now there were no sounds from room number three, only a deathly silence.

'Ahem, is everything alright, Lenny? Was she no…' interrupting, DaCosta gestured towards the room with a thumb pointing upwards, and before opening the door to the outside world, coolly and smilingly announced, 'Huh…there's a bit of cleaning up to do upstairs,' and before exiting through the door, he turned around abruptly and stared directly at Cronin, and urged with a degree of malice, 'Make sure this goes away, d'you hear me old man?' and with that the door slammed closed, as he stepped into the outside world with an air of imposing superiority.

Cronin signalled to his second in command with a flexed index finger in the air wriggling at speed, delivering a message of 'Come here.'

Jimmy Malone scurried to his boss's side, and with a furrowed crease in his brow demanded curiously, 'What the fuck's going on boss, I swear I'm sick of cleaning up his shit. If he's hurt that poor girl, I swear I'll…'

'You'll do what exactly, stop talking crap and let's go up and see just what's been going on up there,' the owner of the club appeared dwarfed as he and his trusted bouncer made their way to the stairs.

Standing silently outside room number three, Cronin adjusted the cuffs of his navy blue pin striped suit as if he were meeting some kind of dignitary, stared down at his black shiny patent leather shoes with a two inch heel, because he was fed up with the jokes about him being a victim of the so called short man syndrome.

Rubbing his fingers through his straight, greasy looking grey hair which was tucked behind his ears, Jimmy used a two knuckled rap on a scarred, dirty white painted door.

As he opened the door wide, and with no movement visible from the partially naked body lying on the bed, the shock of what they witnessed was palpable as the two men covered their mouths with closed fingers and shook their heads slowly in reverent silence. Checking to see if she was still alive, Jimmy crouched beside her kneeling on both knees, and checked her wrist for signs of a pulse. He quietly announced to his boss, 'Thank God for that, anyway. I don't know how, but yeah she's…still alive. So…what do we do now boss, any ideas, 'cos we either call an ambulance or we get her to a hospital ourselves? But either way, she's gonna need treatment and damn quick before we end up with a corpse on our hands.'

'Well, there's no bloody way we can call for an ambulance because we'll have the fuzz all over us, and then before you know it, they'll be searching for drugs and anything else they can find to shut us down once they see the state that she's in,' retorted Cronin pointing an index finger towards the stretched out body.

'So, you're suggesting we take her in that state in a car, and how the hell do you propose we get her down the stairs then, as she ain't gonna be walking anywhere tonight, that's for sure?'

'Okay, let me think. Right, first of all we gotta cover her up, because as you can see, there's no way in hell we're gonna be able to get her clothes on. Can you search the rooms and see if you can find a dressing gown or something that perhaps one of the other girls left?' Barry queried, as his thumb and index fingers ran along his chin stroking it in quiet anticipation.

Standing there glancing around the room whilst ruminating as to how they were going to sort this mess out, he heard the sound coming from his phone as it signalled a muffled ping within his trouser pocket. He stepped cautiously to the bathroom and whilst standing in front of the mirror he found himself reading the words to himself whilst looking down at the floor which was strewn with wet towels. The bold lettering of the message succinctly hailed a chilling order,

'You'd better make this go away, Mr Cronin, because you don't want anything happening to your club now do you?'

Wiping his imaginary sweat from his brow, Barry returned to the bedroom and covered the girl with a towel that hadn't been used, in the hope that she'd be able to tolerate having anything against her skin, as he'd read somewhere that the body could go into some kind of shock after a major trauma, so he wanted to keep her warm.

Jimmy entered the room quietly and slowly carrying a rather large dark blue overcoat, holding it in the air, he looked at the club's owner who now stood in the corner of the room, with his two arms folded heavily against his chest.

'This is all I could find boss, but it'll do the job in getting her out of here unnoticed, I s'pose,' as he carefully draped the used coat over the young girl's battered body.

Cronin peered over at his accomplice and with a questioning tone pleaded to the other man, 'We've got no choice have we but to get her to hospital, but erm…how the fuck are we going to even get her down the stairs? I mean, there's practically a full house down there, we're not going to be able to just quietly slip past, and what if she wakes up, what're we going to do then, eh? I could kill that son of a bitch for what he's done, and between you and me, I've always known there was a satanic side to him, something about his eyes, they're like pure evil, know what I mean?'

Jimmy, still staring at the lifeless, battered figure with blood oozing from her wounds and almost being able to see the bones beneath her once perfect ivory skin where the burns had deeply penetrated huddled under a used overcoat, clapped both of his hands together in sudden euphoria and exclaimed triumphantly, 'I got it, I know how we can sneak her out without making spectacles of ourselves. Here's what you do, you go down with a smile on your face and making sure that everyone hears you, you tell them that you've just had some wonderful news and that you're going to stand everyone the price of a drink. Then, you walk over to the alcove, the one furthest away from the doors, and get Nate to set the drinks up there, and that's when I'll help this little thing out through the door. While you're with the punters, I'll ask Bob out front to bring the car around to the front, and he can help me get her onto the back seat.'

'Yeah, that could work. But you're forgetting one important factor in your plan, how're we gonna get her down the stairs?' Barry quizzed, pinching the bridge of his nose with his thumb and forefinger.

'Well...look at her, she's only a snippet of a thing, I'll just pick her up and carry her down the stairs. I just hope that when I touch her she doesn't scream the place down. To be honest with you, I'm getting the heebie-jeebies, I mean look at her. I just hope we ain't left it too late. So, may I suggest to you as politely as I can, that you get a bloody move on before we're banged up on a fuckin' murder charge?'

Cronin moved cautiously over to the door, opened it and walked through when at the same time Jimmy was figuring out how to pick the fragile body up from the bed.

Not stirring as she nestled against the strangers chest, it was better than he could have imagined, and gently swept up the small, battered and bruised body in both of his arms, grabbed her clothes off the bed that he had laid there before scooping her up, and simply piled them on top of her, unaware of the crunching twenty pound note that lay on the floor where it had been dropped.

With the door already open, he teetered through it with the wrapped up body carefully ensconced within his arms, and gingerly made his way down the stairs taking one step at a time, not wanting to drop or inflict any more pain on the young woman who just so happened to have been in the wrong place at the wrong time.

Reaching the ground floor, he could see that Barry had in fact cleared the bar area to the far corner of the room as planned, and hearing the echoes of laughter, light-hearted chatter, he made his way unnoticed to the front door, gave the order to Bob the doorman to bring Cronin's car around, which he did and almost in an instant it miraculously appeared.

With the silver Mercedes now sitting idly outside and with Bob's help, Jimmy managed to guide the body onto the back seat, grabbed a pillow from the back shelf and laid it tenderly underneath her head. With slight groaning noises gurgling out of the victim's mouth, Jimmy started to panic, so rushing back in to find Cronin who was luckily already making his way to the front doors, they both headed for the car and started the short but yet gruelling journey to the local hospital.

'Just drive, Jimmy and let's get this over with,' ordered the boss as he slid the seat belt across his chest and slotted the metal clip into place with a securing click.

'I can't believe we're left to clean up his fuckin' mess, but I tell you now, this is the last bloody time because we ain't doin' it again, and I don't care what he threatens to do to me, or to you for that matter.'

Jimmy, not looking across to the man in the passenger seat, simply shook his head responding quite sharply, 'Have we figured out yet what we're gonna say when we get this poor gal to the hospital? I mean, if we take her in to the accident department, they're gonna think we did this to her. Have you thought about any of this, like the implications that could fall on our shoulders, you know…we could go down for this, and by the looks of her for a very long time? You damn well know that that bastard DaCosta ain't gonna be taking the rap for this don't you, and I'll bet you everything I own he'll deny ever having laid eyes on her.'

Cronin, as if suddenly remembering the reason why they were in the car, turned around to the girl clad in the oversized coat, and he knew then that the words his co-conspirator had spoken were true. There was absolutely no way they could escort her to the emergency department, they would simply have to find another way of getting her in there. Turning right at the roundabout as the lights turned green, they followed the signs to A&E and parked as close as they could to the closed automatic doors, where a wooden bench was strategically and conveniently placed either side.

Both men opened their respective doors, and whilst moving slowly but with purpose, opened the rear passenger doors. Barry removed the victim's belongings, whilst Jimmy scooped her up into his arms once more being careful not to smash either his or her head against the door panel as he diligently led her out to where the noisy sounds of sirens could be heard blasting out through the brightly lit star speckled sky. People could be seen rushing around in dark green paramedic uniforms pushing gurneys as the newest arrival was all but hidden beneath scarlet red woollen blankets, apart from the plastic-coated mask across the face, giving the patient oxygen that he or she were obviously unable to take in themselves.

Once the mayhem had died down, the two men laid the girl down on the wooden bench with a brass plate nailed on the back paying tribute to someone who was sorely missed, 'Jane Simpson 1987–2012 taken from us too soon.' Both men stood over the swollen, bloodied, unrecognisable face but knew they couldn't stay long for fear of being seen, and worse, accused of the atrocity that they lay witness to. They hurriedly returned to the car and drove off at such screeching speed, warding innocent bystanders off the road and onto the nearest sidewalk.

Slumped on the hard, wooden bench with her clothes strewn across her mutilated body, passers-by glared at her in disgust and loathing as her near nakedness began to reveal itself where the coat gaped open.

Chapter 3

Not quite believing what he was seeing, he couldn't resist the temptation to photograph the event. As the light momentarily flashed into the face and body of the badly beaten young lady, the man waved his phone into the air trying to get a good WIFI connection so that the photograph could be sent. Underneath the caption he typed quickly as his two thumbs danced around the screen of his phone, 'Looks like someone had a bit of a rough night!' Send.

'Pat, you didn't post a picture of her on Facebook did you, 'cos man that's just sick,' demanded the lanky, pock marked youth.

'No, I did not. As a matter of fact, I've sent it to Instagram, Twitter, Snapchat and Facebook! It's not every day you go for a crafty fag while you're a patient in a shitty hospital having a bastard operation and find a totally nude woman lying outside on a bench now, is it? Come on Sean lighten up for fuck's sake, this shit happens once in a lifetime and so I've just made the most of it that's all,' exclaimed Pat excitedly, as he began scanning his phone to see whether he had any hits.

'Got twenty likes already, see…' showing the electronic device to his not so elated buddy. 'Not everyone's a bloody boring bastard like you, and it's obvious that these people can't see the harm in seeing some naked bitch that's probably had it coming to her. It's called life my friend, and it's time you grew a pair, know what I mean?'

'You're sick, and I ain't sticking around here any longer, I'm off. See you around, may be when you get to go home.' Sean left his friend scrolling through his screen with his thumb deftly sliding up and down and stopping when he'd come across a reply that he found interesting.

'Hey, Sean, listen to this. There's a reporter from The Herald who saw the photo and he wants to know where it was taken, and could he meet me. Think this could mean a few quid for me, what d'you reckon? Shall I tell him?'

'Do what you want,' Sean shouted as he neared the bus stop that would take him away from the guy that he once was proud to call a mate.

Two people clad in green scrubs, who'd just come off their fag break, ran towards the body lying on the bench as the female employee knelt down and said quite loudly but clearly, 'Hello…hello…my name's Carrie and I'm a nurse here at the hospital, can you hear me?' Quickly her training kicked in as she held onto the victim's shoulders and started to shake them lightly in the hope of trying to get her to open her eyes, and to be able to try and assess her state of consciousness.

She looked at her male colleague who said quite matter-of-factly, 'You stay here, and I'll go get a gurney and some help to get her inside.'

Whilst he was gone, Carrie poked underneath the old shabby coat for the girl's wrist, and using fore and middle fingers sighed in gratitude as the weak but palpable tap tapping sounds could be felt radiating through her digits. Yes, she was weak, but yes, she was alive. Staring down at her ravaged body, it was hard to tell whether she'd been hit by a car, or beaten half to death, but whichever; they needed to get her in to the warmth and fast.

As the double doors to the emergency room glided open three males rushed through pushing the gurney as fast as they could with only the noisy sound of the squeaky wheels to ease the silence of the night. One of the men was a doctor, 'Hi there, I'm Dr Kerrigan, we're going to help you onto this bed, and get you inside where we can take a look at you. Is that okay?' Crouching on one knee and glancing up at his fellow workers, he voiced his thoughts out loud, 'We don't know if there's been any neck or spinal injury, so we need to be very, very careful how we move her. On my count, Carrie you and Jonathan take her legs, and me and Tony will take the torso, ready, one, two, three…okay, lift.'

Once she was safely inside Carrie and Jonathan, the other nurse who found her outside, discussed how they were going to get the coat off her as it was too thick to be cut with the standard hospital scissors.

The six feet, well-built male nurse with short army-like haircut smiled at the patient, as he pushed the black framed spectacles back into position as they had slid down to the end of his nose, and quietly stated, 'Hello there, its Jonathan here. Me and Carrie are going to roll you a little bit to get this big overcoat off you, so if you can hear and understand me could you nod, or raise a finger or thumb to let us know that this is okay?'

Nothing. No response. Both experienced nurses, having done the log manoeuvre more times than they'd like to remember, managed to roll her to one side removing one half of the garment, and then to the other side to remove it completely. They covered her up with a lightweight sheet whilst the on-call Dr Kerrigan began to examine her injuries and finding a blank prescription chart started to jot down various medications that he felt she would need as a matter of urgency.

'Do we know anything about this young lady, a name even?' Quizzed the thirty-something years old doctor where a raspberry birthmark was etched deeply, bearing the shape of a spear, into the left side of his forehead, cascading down into the top of his eye lid. 'Well, whoever dumped her on that seat outside left her belongings, and I think there was a bag as well. Carrie opened the blue curtains with the words, '*Do Not Enter'* embossed across them, and went in search for the only evidence that they had, which could lead them to some clues as to who she was.

She found clothes, shoes and a small, gold coloured clutch purse, but before she touched it she pulled on a fresh pair of blue latex gloves, just in case the police needed to remove prints from it.

In a small zip within the small, but dressy evening bag with its tiny diamante beads glimmering even under the powerful fluorescent lighting, she found what appeared to be an identity card with a photograph which revealed a very pretty young lady, with dark hazel eyes, and a well-cut hairstyle which emphasised not only her flawless complexion but a distinctive oval-shaped face.

As she held the small card with the embossed picture of her on it, in between thumb and forefinger in the air, she re-entered the curtained cubicle, announcing with subdued excitement, 'Ah, here we are, she's called Eva…Miss Eva O'Connor, and according to this, she's twenty six years old, and is currently studying at Colston College,' whereupon she replaced the credentials back to where she found them.

It was good that they could refer to her by name, but they desperately needed to find out what, if any, medications that she may be allergic to, but unless they got some sort of response from her soon, the doctor would have to just go ahead and prescribe what she needed urgently.

'Hi Eva, its Dr Kerrigan again, you're in hospital and you're very safe,' and at the same time Jonathan entered the secured area pushing a small metal, two tiered table on castors, and on it was an assortment of medical equipment including bandages, and packets marked sterile wound dressing pack, a tourniquet, cannula, a giving set to administer intravenous fluids and drugs, and two bags covered in plastic, one containing saline, and one ready to give in case she required sugar, namely dextrose.

Trying to find a bulbous vein in her right arm to insert a cannula seemed to arouse Eva where barely audible groaning sounds could be heard, but as Carrie sat next to her on a stool which she found in the corner of the cubicle, took hold of her left arm and gently stroked her forehead quietly, and gently soothed her with calming words which seemed to have the desired effect.

With the intravenous needle securely inserted and covered with a bandage, Dr Kerrigan entered the cubicle, and seemed much relieved that the patient had at least woken up, so that treatment could begin, and expressed with a degree of importance in his voice, 'Okay guys, let's get this bag of fluids up and running, as she's terribly dehydrated, and whilst you're at it, can we get some blood via the cannula to test her glucose levels. Carrie, I'm going to leave you and Jonathan to clean up the wounds, and I'm sure you'll agree that she'd be best lying on her side where the monster hasn't stubbed out his cigarettes. I'm going to order some x-rays as I'm worried that she's got internal injuries, and I'm particularly concerned that she may have a pneumothorax, but it'll be no surprise if she hasn't got a few broken ribs. Oh, and I'll get in touch with the police while you guys carry on here, as we've got to let her next of kin know that she's here. Do we know whether the order has gone through to the pharmacy yet for the Morphine, because let's face it; she's not going to respond to any treatment unless we get her pain controlled? Right, thanks you guys, I'm going to leave her in your capable hands, but I'll be around if you need me so just holler, and in the meantime, I'll contact Pharmacy and find out where the meds are that I ordered.'

The young doctor flung his stethoscope around his neck as he marched with lengthy strides to the nurses' station at the front of the department where he found a phone that wasn't being used.

***

'Honey I'm home!' announced Jarvis, as he closed the white PVC door and peering through the diamond shaped glass to make sure that he'd not left the interior light on his old Peugeot which he was perpetually accused of doing, repeatedly having to call out roadside services the next morning, because he'd got a dead battery.

'Ellie…where are you, darling?' he asked, having removed his shoes, and putting them neatly side by side on the wooden shoe rack that lay underneath the row of brass coat hooks, hung his jacket up using the sewn in hoop, and deposited all of his loose change, keys and badge in the colourful ceramic bowl that used to be a home for fresh fruit, but now had more of a less glamorous task.

Jarvis meandered through to the kitchen, but there was no sign of the customary array of pots and pans lined up on the Aga with the sights of steam diffusing in the air, and the sound of water bubbling as the infusion of herbs and spices dissipated from the culinary delights being prepared. To his surprise there was not even a light on, no sign of anyone now or indeed anybody having been in there recently.

Looking upwards towards the mahogany staircase with its gold runner and brass carpet rods whilst calling out her name, it was only the sound of his own voice echoing around the walls that could be heard. The door to the sitting room was partially closed, and through the crack of the door frame, he could see beams of light flashing on and off from the television, and as he entered the medium sized cosy lounge he spotted his wife under a small blanket that she used to put across the boys when they were babies, keeping them warm as they were taken out for their daily stroll in the push chair.

Jarvis knees groaned as he knelt down beside her, and he felt quite taken aback as to how small and innocent she appeared, curled up into a ball without a care in the world whilst clutching onto one of the many scatter cushions, almost as if it were a childhood favourite teddy bear.

He tiptoed out of the room, and quietly made his way to the kitchen where he decided for once he'd put a meal on the table for Eleanor. Not sure where the boys were, he looked at the whiteboard that was perched on the outside of one of the cupboards, where each member of the household was encouraged to insert a tick or a cross if they would be home for dinner on each designated day.

He and Eleanor had agreed with the boys that this would give them both independence, but mainly it was because that there was nothing worse than cooking for people who weren't going to be there to eat it, and morally it was plain wrong to see good food being thrown out.

The younger of the two, Andrew, being a sporty fifteen-year-old, usually came home around 8:30 in the evening, dashing up the stairs ready to shower from whichever muddy, sweaty field he'd been kicking or throwing around a ball in. Alex, the elder who was now seventeen, and deep in the throes of getting ready for his all-important A levels would come home after revision nights either at school or at a mate's house and would re-heat something up in the microwave when he got home, which was usually around 9:30, or the latest on a school night, ten o'clock.

Rummaging through the fridge, Jarvis found a container with fresh minced beef, and as his culinary skills were scant at best, decided that he couldn't go far wrong with Spaghetti Bolognese, which he was of the firm belief that a blind monkey could cook.

Trying to make as little noise as possible, he removed the frying pan from its upside-down position on a hook which was hanging alongside all the other brass coloured pans held on a rustic country hanging pot rack over the central island. He poured a little olive oil into its base, set the flame underneath it and heated it a little. As the smoke began to emit from the base, he removed it, and using his right hand grabbed the meat from the cellophane covered container, gingerly fed it into the oil where it spat and hissed, depositing miniscule spatters of fat onto nearby surfaces.

Not really sure which spices Eleanor used in the concoction, he made an educated guess, and chose a couple which he really liked the smell of, Turmeric and a hint of garlic, and was rather pleased with himself as the smell didn't seem that offensive. He then opened the cutlery drawer where he found a cork screw, and from the wine rack which was cleverly built into the base of the oak dresser chose a bottle of Rioja, which both he and Eleanor were partial to.

Removing a couple of wine glasses from a cupboard next to the hood of the Aga, the door opened slowly and there she stood rubbing both eyes with knuckles from her index fingers in an almost childlike manner, and stifling a yawn, remorsefully expressed, 'Hi babe, aww…I'm so sorry I was asleep when you came in. Here let me carry on with that.'

Jarvis paced quickly towards where his wife was standing, held her in his arms, stroked her hair and planting kisses on the top of her forehead expressing sincerely, 'Don't you worry about anything, I'm alright in here honestly, and anyway it's about time someone cooked for you don't you think? So off you go and sit down and I'll pour us a glass of red, okay.'

Eleanor sat down on a bar stool at the island in the centre, held the glass to her lips as he enquired concernedly, 'Are you alright love, you look a bit pale, have you eaten anything today?'

'Nah I'm fine, I've just had one of those stinking headaches that won't go away and makes you feel really lethargic, you know. I honestly think it's purely and simply down to me staring at canvases for too long. It'll pass soon not to worry.' As she sat there sipping from the skinny stemmed glass, he could see her rubbing her abdomen and wincing at the same time, almost gasping for breath.

He came around and stood behind her draping his arms over her shoulders, 'I thought you said that you had a headache, but it's not just that is it? How long have you been feeling like this?' Bending his head so that his right cheek was resting against her left one, he carried on, 'Sorry…no more questions, but I'm slightly worried, 'cos this just isn't like you, sleeping at this time of day, but more importantly you look as though you're in a lot of pain.'

'Oh, really this is nothing, you know how I sometimes feel a bit bilious after eating peppers, well I ate some with dinner last night, and I think that's what's causing this bloody pain. I'll take something for it honestly, but d'you know what Mark, I'm erm…not sure I could eat a thing. I'm so sorry after you've gone to all the time and effort, especially after being at work all day, but I think I'll just take this wine up to bed and just curl up with a good book, and I promise you I'll be better in the morning.'

'Okay Ellie, I'm not going to force you to eat, and I'll be up to check on you a bit later. I'll put some on a plate for the lads and when they come in they can shove it in the microwave, so it won't go to waste don't you worry. You know what gannets they are,' he replied, as they both lovingly embraced.

Not wanting to wake Eleanor up with his music, he decided to put the television on that was housed quite neatly in an alcove within the pine dresser and surfed the channels. Not an avid soap opera fan, he decided to settle for Channel 15 which usually had a fairly decent movie at this time of night and carried on cooking.

Mopping up the rest of the bolognaise sauce with a piece of bread, he rose from his chair and started to clear the table and load the dishwasher amazed at how many pots and pans he'd used for this simple meal, and chuckled to himself that all this fuss and work was for only one person, when actually a cheese sandwich would have been more than enough to feed his hunger.

Jarvis, satisfied that he'd tidied up, avoiding being chastised by Eleanor in the morning, he decided that he'd go through to the sitting room and load up a DVD and settle there for the rest of the evening as it was far too early for him to go to bed, even though he quietly knew that he'd probably fall asleep half way through watching it, which he normally did. Kneeling on two knees whilst searching through the little drawer that was underneath the TV stand, he heard the front door closing together with the thud of a heavy bag being dropped, and the clinking of keys as they were being dumped into the ceramic bowl that stood on the hall table. He stood up whilst holding the selected DVD case in his hand and moved towards the hallway where he was greeted with a carefree salutation of, 'Hey dad, what's up?'

'Hi Andy, good day, yeah? So, what did you get up to after school this evening? Sorry I missed you last night, but we're busy on a pretty heavy-duty case at the moment.'

Andy removing all of his outer clothing, obediently hanging them on one of the brass hooks on the adjacent wall next to the front door, kicked off his shoes and not bothering to put them on the shoe rack, left them lying on top of one another exactly where he'd removed them. He picked up his rucksack once more that was straining heavily at the seams with the buckles struggling to stay closed, and headed to the kitchen, 'Yeah, not a bad day at all ta. We had a swim meet after school, and then I went over to Jack's house where we got most of our homework done, and then we played a few games on his X Box. Where's mum by the way?'

'Ah…she's gone upstairs for an early night as she's not feeling brilliant this evening. D'you want dinner? I've saved you some Spag Bol,' asked the young lad's father, as he made his way back into the kitchen to follow his son.

'Mum's not well again? She went to bed early last night too, and all she said was that as you were going to be late home from work then she'd make the most of having not to cook a huge meal. You two aren't keeping something from me are you; I mean…you would tell me and Al if there was a problem, yeah?' pleaded the fifteen-year-old, as his dark blue eyes penetrated into his father's, demanding an answer.

'No, honestly, she's fine, and it goes without saying that if there was a problem then we would discuss it with you and your brother, well within reason of course. She reckons that she's eaten something that hasn't agreed with her, so she's taken a tablet which should help her get rid of the wind that's probably giving her the pain, and then she'll let rip a monumental burp, and after a good night's sleep I'm sure she'll be as right as rain tomorrow. So…dinner or what?'

'Nah, I'm fine ta dad, had something over at Jack's. I'm a bit knackered so I'm going up, night pops.'

'Okay, night son, might not see you in the morning, 'cos I've got an early start again. Any idea what time your brother will be in?'

'Haven't got a clue, but I expect he won't be much longer, 'cos I think he's got mocks in the morning, I'm sure that's what he said anyway.'

With his bag slung over his shoulder, Andy moved slowly towards the stairs, and with tired looking strides, went up to his room.

Jarvis decided he'd stay and wait for his elder son Alex to appear before calling it a night, but he didn't have to wait for long. So, the DVD that he was looking forward to watching was put on hold again once more, not that he minded at all, as he relished the time he had with his sons, because with everyone in the household having busy schedules, he didn't get to see or spend much time with them.

Once again, the thud of removing shoes and the thumping of a heavy laden bag echoed through the hallway. Seeing that the kitchen was in darkness and light was emitting from the sitting room, the elder of his two sons poked his head around the solid oak varnished door and found his dad stretched out on the comfy, yet rather worn sofa, with a half empty glass of red wine perched on one of the walnut side tables.

'Hey dad, are you okay? How come you're sitting here on your own, where's mum?' enquired Alex as he perched on the end of the arm of the sofa, opposite his father, obviously not wanting to make himself too comfortable before it was time for him to head up towards his bedroom.

'Yeah, I'm fine thanks Al, and your mum's just gone to bed, she's just a bit tired that's all, so she's having an early night,' his father replied, 'Andy tells me you've got a mock tomorrow, is that right? Are you confident you've done enough revision?'

Combing his dark, floppy hair through with his fingers, and quickly glancing at his wrist, 'Oh, yes in eleven hours thirty minutes to be precise, and its history, one of my better subjects I have to say. That's where I've been, we had a late revision session with our teacher, you know…going over things that we're probably gonna see in the paper. He's a really good guy is our Mr Adams, really wants us all to do well. He's got no favourites and he treats us all the same, which is more than I can say for some of the teachers at that place, that's for sure.'

'That's great to hear kidda, well, all me and your mum want is that you try your best, and if you get a good result then great, but if it's not the result you expected, then promise me you won't beat yourself up about it. You know…we're here, and you can talk to us about anything, okay. You look a bit pooped son, perhaps you should try and get some rest, and hey…no more revising before you go to sleep,' as he reached over to the side table and calmly picked his wine glass up and upended the remaining few sips.

As Alex rose up from where he was seated and making his way to the door, Jarvis chuckled mainly to himself but loud enough that his son would hear, 'Did I ever tell you that that's what happened to me, I mean…I revised so much each night before every exam that when I sat in front of the paper that was staring me in the face, I literally froze, forgot absolutely everything, couldn't even remember my bloody student number for God's sake, it was all a…a…blank. It was my own fault, I s'pose, but I just wanted to do well and get a good job and everything. I mean, I wasn't a book worm or anything, but in those days getting the right results to do 'A' levels and go to university was a big deal. My dad used to turn the light out at night before I sat an exam so I wouldn't be able to read any more, and when I heard him snoring, I'd turn it on again and carry on till the early hours of the morning. The moral of the story? Your brain can only absorb so much son, just remember that, but also remember that whatever the outcome; it's not the end of your future.'.

'Ahhh…thanks dad, and yeah you've told us that story a zillion times,' sniggered Alex as he stood over his dad, patted his shoulder and uttered, 'Night pops, love ya.'

'Oh Al, forgot to say, there's some left-over Spag Bol left, d'you want me to heat it up for you?'

'Nah, it's all good, but thanks anyway. Later dad,' and with that his son left the room and headed for the stairs, leaving him once again in the room with his own thoughts. He loaded the DVD into the player, picked up the remote control and pressed play.

***

Having slept through most of the film, as he suspected he would do, removing his phone from the side table ready to plug it into the charger, he shuddered slightly as the phone pinged in his hand and opening up the message read the few words that Detective Sergeant Javid Das had posted. Leaning against the back of the sink with both ankles crossed at the front as he read, '*Sorry to disturb you guv but need a word.*'

DI Jarvis called his colleague knowing that he wouldn't have bothered him if it wasn't something that couldn't wait.

'Hi Javid, what's up my man?'

'Er…sorry to bother you boss, but I thought I should let you know that we've just had a report in from The Hamilton General that a young lady has been admitted with severe lacerations to her face, torso and has sustained other injuries which are…,' the young detective cleared his throat before continuing, 'well…oh shit, bloody hideous. Some arsehole stubbed out his cigarette all over her body, beat her to a pulp, and if that wasn't enough, the bastard dumped her body outside of the hospital, naked apart from a bloody old overcoat.'

'Oh my God, who the fuck would do that to someone? Okay, let's get over there, because the sooner we interview staff at the hospital before they go off shift the better, you know…they might be going on leave, or might not even work in A&E permanently and could be agency staff.'

'Yeah…I totally agree, d'you want me to come and pick you up?' asked Javid.

'If you don't mind that would be great as I've had a couple of drinks. I'll see you when you get here, and I'd better go and have a chat with Eleanor and tell her where I'm off to.'

'Okay, see you in five.'

Jarvis climbed the stairs to their bedroom and found his wife sitting up in bed clutching a book against her breast with her eyes closed. He tiptoed around to her side of the bed and leant down and kissed her forehead before removing the book and turning off the bedside lamp.

He closed the door behind him, and went towards the boys' rooms, knocked on his elder son's door, and when there was no reply he entered, as he knew he would be doing something with his headphones in. Alex being quite surprised to see him again so soon removed them in a hurry and asked, 'You okay?'

The boy's father stood in the doorway with his hands deep in his pockets as he glanced swiftly around the room, silently wishing had had this start in life with every electronic gadget that was going, his own choices of what to read other than school text books, his own music centre and collection of records, and not being constantly shouted at to '*Turn that bloody noise down.*'

'No, everything's fine thanks Al, but I've just had an urgent call from Javid, so I'll be out for a while. Mum's spark out, so if she wakes up and wonders where I am could you tell her I'll see her sometime tomorrow. Oh, just before I go as Javid will be here in a minute, good luck for tomorrow.'

'Okay, thanks dad. Don't worry I'll write her a little note letting her know where you are,' responded the tall, gangly teenager lying prone on his bed with his head resting on his hands and his earphones lying beside him.

Jarvis retreated out of his son's room and did the same to his younger son, knocked lightly with a knuckle rap on the door and like his elder brother no sound came from the other side of the closed door, so he merely turned the brass knob slightly, peered in and this time there were no headphones, only the sight of his dark hair peering over the top of the duvet. Closing the door, he made his way down the stairs as his phone once again pinged, announcing his colleague's arrival.

***

Chapter 4

Jarvis opened his front door, stepped out onto the front door step where the automatic security light sprang into life announcing the detection of body heat. He strode across the brick paving that led to the garden gate passing a neat lawn area on the left, surrounded by evergreen shrubs, a beautiful cherry tree that energised the whole neighbourhood when its bloom notified passers-by that spring had arrived, together with a perennial border which never failed to offer a variety of colour.

Jarvis spotted Detective Sergeant Javid Das' dark blue Audi across the road, as there was no room outside of the Inspector's house, and so he strode over at a hurried pace as the driver re-started the engine on his approach.

Opening the passenger door, Jarvis stooped to avoid hitting his head as he climbed in, and whilst sitting on the beige-coloured leather seat where his knees were hunched up to his chest, laughingly joked with his colleague, 'So who was the last short arse leprechaun who sat here then?' Having found the lever underneath his seat to push it back, he then secured his seat belt around him where it clicked swiftly into position.

Das leant across to the dials on the dashboard to turn the music off that was vibrating through the speakers on the side panels of the doors, but Jarvis put his hand on his arm and declared with light-hearted enthusiasm, 'You don't need to switch that off on my account, you know. Who is this by the way, I'm sure I know it but can't quite remember the name?'

'It's Elbow, and they're a favourite band of mine,' responded the driver as he checked both the rear view and the wing mirror whilst cruising along.

'So, what do we know about this poor girl then that was dumped like an old sack outside of the hospital?' enquired the Inspector as his hands rested with palms down on his navy-blue chino trousers.

'My notes are there on the back seat, but if I remember her name is Eva…something, d'you want to get them so you can refresh my memory?' The senior officer reached back and found a buff-coloured file with just one sheet of paper inside.

Opening it up, and reading the information from the white unlined notelet, he found himself squinting slightly from the more or less undecipherable words scrawled in black ink, 'Well I think it says here that her name's Eva Oc…O'Connor, yeah that's it, and she's twenty-two, and presently the only other thing that we know of her is that she attends a Colston College. How on earth did we manage to get that last bit of information, I mean, it's not something that's posted on a driving licence now is it?'

'Ah, that's because the only identification that she had on her was bizarrely her security ID for the college. There was nothing else, a few quid and a couple of keys on a key ring, that was all she had, not even a mobile phone, which presumably had been stolen from her bag, but we'll know more when we see her I expect.'

Jarvis looking sideways towards D.S. Das, questioned with a furrowed brow, 'Do we know if she was raped, or do we have any idea if she's conscious or not?'

The driver still staring ahead as the rain had now started to come down heavily and was concentrating hard not to let the hypnotic swishing of the wiper blades send him into a state of sleepiness, answered with a muffled sigh, 'Sorry, sir I don't know any more than that I'm afraid, as that was the only information the desk sergeant could give me. The hospital won't give details out over the phone about rape or what state a person's in, which is why I felt we should see for ourselves exactly what happened to the poor woman as a matter of urgency.'

***

Hospitals used to be a maze where people would run around in circles trying to find whichever department it was that they were looking for, but the last decade has seen the advent of decent signage that not only saves the public time, but also quenches the need for rage when in times of urgency. So, it was a pleasant surprise that the officers managed to find the Accident and Emergency department without the need for constant stopping, interrupting and questioning an already overworked population.

Approaching the reception area where rows and rows of red soft backed plastic chairs stood empty, Jarvis and Das showed the lady sitting behind the main desk their ID badges, who was shielded from the public by a Perspex screen, that ran along the entire length of the oak coloured wooden counter, and explained to the middle aged, short haired receptionist that they needed to speak to a member of the medical team regarding a recent admission under the name of a Miss O'Connor. Non-smiling and non-committal, she quietly picked up the beige-coloured phone, pressed a single button which would presumably automatically lead straight through to the treatment area, which is sealed off from the outside world, and began repeating their request.

Both detectives separated whilst waiting for the appearance of someone with a stethoscope around their neck who was looking worn out. With hands thrust deep into pockets, they found themselves staring at various posters on the walls, giving rather graphic, but easy to understand information to the public as to what to do when feeling short of breath, or when to seek help if pain in various regions of the body becomes too painful. Gory pictures of the effects of tobacco on the lungs, enlarged livers due to excess alcohol, and the biggest and boldest of them all was the one warning of drug abuse.

'Ahem…I'm Dr James Kerrigan. I hope you haven't been waiting long, but well…that's just the way it is, I'm afraid.'

'Thanks for taking the time to speak with us Dr Kerrigan. We've been advised by someone in your department about a new admission, a Miss Eva O'Connor, I believe that's her name, who had recently sustained severe injuries, and well…we need to find out what happened, so do you think it would be possible to speak with her?' the elder detective asked the man who was sporting green scrubs, with arms folded whilst studying the two men before replying quietly, 'Yes, that's correct, we have seen this lady and yes, she has received some severe injuries. However, it's far too early to say what damage has been done internally, and obviously we can attend to the wounds on the outside, but let's just say whoever did this to her has left her in a right state, I can tell you. When she's medically stable, I'm going to arrange for the Plastics team to have a look at her, and not ordinarily being a betting man, but I would stake everything that I own that this young lady will need to have some kind of psychiatric evaluation. I'm sure you'll agree that the scars that she'll unquestionably be left with will not just be visible on the exterior for a very long time, but how she'll cope with re-living the scene is the million-dollar question, because in my humble opinion an attack of this kind will take years to erase from her mind. And even then, will she ever be the same person again? I very much doubt it, detectives.'

'So…do you think she'd be up to seeing us, and we promise we won't take long and overtire her,' requested the Inspector, as he ran his hand through his hair trying to keep his dark blonde fringe from falling into his eyes.

'Oh, I'm afraid that's not possible at just now as she's having her wounds assessed, and we're awaiting medication from pharmacy to arrive to ease the pain, which must be unbearable. We're also in the process of setting up intravenous fluids and antibiotics because it's imperative that the wounds don't become infected. I'm waiting for her to go to our x-ray department for urgent pictures to see whether she may have a punctured lung. So, as you can see, not only are we busy fixing her up, but I'm afraid I don't think you'd get anything out of her anyway, because she's pretty much been out of it since she got here. I'm hoping that once we get her stabilised and hydrated, we'll be able to find her a bed on a ward fairly soon where her journey of recovery will begin. I'm sorry I can't be of any more help.'

'No, no that's absolutely fine and understandable. Have you any idea who found her, even where she was found?' muttered the senior detective.

'Yes, thankfully for the victim, she was found by two of our nurses who were just returning from their break, and they're the ones who are actually assisting with her treatment now. Their names are Carrie and Jonathan,' smiling outwardly and rubbing his chin in slight embarrassment he admitted, 'D'you know I don't even know their surnames, as we normally only address each other by our first names.'

'Any idea what time their shift finishes, or would it be possible to speak to them after they've finished with Eva's treatment? I mean…we certainly wouldn't keep them long, but it's important that we start to paint some kind of picture as to what happened to this poor girl. Oh, and one other thing, is it normal in cases like this for photographs to be taken, not necessarily by you of course, but someone from another department perhaps?'

Dr Kerrigan, lifting his wrist up and glancing swiftly at his watch, hurriedly replied, 'No we certainly don't, but the specialist Dermatology and Plastics teams will most definitely take some, purely as part of the healing process, you understand. Now, gentlemen, I rea…'

'Of course,' interrupted Jarvis, 'we're sorry to have taken up so much of your time. We'll wait over here until the two nurses can find a few minutes to come and speak with us. You've been very kind doctor, thank you.'

Both men took a seat in the waiting area, and searching through pockets found enough coins between them to insert into the hot drinks machine where Javid chose a hot chocolate, and his boss chose a black coffee.

'Blimey, coffee at this time of the night, guv?' asked the Asian detective as he was ripping open the sachets of sweeteners between his teeth and shaking them into the already sweet drink.

'Well, let's put it this way, I don't think there's much chance of any sleep tonight, do you? So, I'll need this injection of caffeine to keep me awake,' added Jarvis whilst removing his outdoor lined waterproof jacket and laying it on the empty seat next to him.

'So, what d'ya think sir, any chance that these two nurses will be able to give us any leads?'

'Not sure, if I'm honest, but you never know they may have seen something that might be useful to us. We'll just have to wait, I guess.'

With Gardeners World, National Geographic magazines having been flicked through to pass the time away and replacing them neatly on the small white table found next to the drinks machine, two nurses with lengthy strides approached the two detectives.

Nervously standing in front of the two police officers, the male nurse broke the silence with, 'Hi there, I'm Jonathan Sterling,' who proffered an outstretched hand, whereby both detectives shook it in turn and introduced themselves.

'And I'm Carrie Calder,' she too shook hands with the two officers.

'Shall we sit down at the back over there where no one will be able to hear us?' the Inspector suggested, as he pointed to the back of the room, which was devoid of any human presence, and provided the secrecy which they all welcomed.

Following each other in single file, and arranging chairs forming a circle, making it easier to see and hear each person, Jarvis then opened the discussion.

'Right, firstly both myself and Detective Sergeant Das are so grateful for you taking time out of your busy shift to speak with us. We just wonder whether you could run us through everything that you saw and did when you found Miss O'Connor. But first, I'd like to remind you that it doesn't matter whether you think some things are just too trivial to mention so please don't worry as that's part of our job to determine which information is useful and what isn't. Both me and Detective Das can reassure you that over the years we've been able to build substantive evidence on material that witnesses feel are too trivial to divulge, and yet it's these small snippets of information that usually help us to get to the bottom of a case. So, in a nutshell anything you can give us which may help us to unravel the reasons as to why this lady is here will be greatly appreciated.'

Both nurses glanced at each other earnestly wondering which one of them would be better at relaying the night's events.

Carrie, clearing her throat nervo…y began, 'Okay, so I and Jonathan were on our break that would have been at 11:15 pm that's right isn't it Jon?' she glimpsed towards the male nurse for confirmation that this was correct, to which he simply nodded. 'Anyway, we'd been for a quick fag, well…that's why we always go together now as it's not safe in the smoking area for a female on her own at night, and even though Jon doesn't smoke, he's such a sweetheart he always comes with me. I digress,' nervously giggling, whilst making a steeple with her fingers. 'Sorry…so we were just walking back onto the hospital grounds as there's a strict no smoking policy anywhere on site, and if you're caught well…it's a hanging offence,' the black nurse with her well contained Afro hairstyle once again sniggered at her own little jibe, and continued, 'erm…I'm so sorry, there I go again.'

'Cas, d'you want me to do this, otherwise these poor detectives will be here all night at this rate, and don't forget this is officially our break,' interrupted the male nurse apologetically.

Carrie, even though she was tense crossed one leg over the other and folded her arms underneath her breast, 'No, I got this. Anyway, we'd had our break and just making our way back to the department, and I remember hearing the loud screeching of tyres and then people staring at a bench, but of course from where we were we couldn't state what was on the bench, 'cos we were too far away, but when we approached it was obvious that the car that had driven off had dumped the poor young lady outside. Mind you, at least they gave her a bit of dignity by laying her on the bench and covering her up, you know.'

'Ahem…' coughed the Inspector, both out of sarcasm and incredulity at the idea that the monsters who did this even knew what the word dignity meant, never mind show it, and continued, 'So, neither of you got a good look at the car, its colour, make, number of people inside, nothing, is that correct?'

Jonathan, whilst removing his glasses and massaging his eyes with both index fingers, stated calmly but unfalteringly, 'You have to remember Inspector that we hear the sounds of cars roaring off at high speed all the time, you know when…for instance when someone's dropping off a patient and needs to get the car parked, so that they don't leave the person alone for long. Mind you, most people just dump the car in the ambulance bays, and quite frankly they couldn't give a toss. Well anyway, I certainly didn't see anything, apart from the poor young woman with her clothes and bag lying beside her, never seen anything like it before.'

'Right,' voiced Jarvis, 'if that's everything, and believe me we're sorry to have taken so much of your time, we won't trouble you any further. Needless to say, if you think of anything else, then don't hesitate to contact either one of us.' Both detectives removed contact cards from their respective wallets and handed them over to the two nurses.

Both detectives watched the female nurse walk alongside the six feet tall, well-built male with his military style haircut, silently heading back to the mayhem behind the double doors.

Javid stood up and resignedly said, 'Oh well…that's it then, nothing much to go on, but there's got to be CCTV around where she was found as there usually is near an A&E department, don't you think, guv?'

'Yeah, absolutely. Come on.' Jarvis stood up, and grabbing his jacket off the chair, headed off to the sliding doors marked, 'Exit,' as Javid followed.

Striding out from the electronic double doors, they both found themselves staring up at the cold, dark red brick walls in search of the tell-tale signs of security cameras, they both stopped and stood underneath a red-light emitting rays of light from a cylindrical mounted camera, where their figures were being scrutinised behind closed doors by uniformed security officers.

The detectives would need to find out how they could get to see the images on the camera and went back inside to speak to the receptionist that they'd spoken to earlier, to find out whether she knew which department or office they should go to.

Entering through the emergency unit once more, it was surprising how much busier it was than when they'd previously arrived, so they merely sat down again and waited until they were called.

Having explained to the receptionist the information that they needed, she once again picked up the phone, and spoke with a member of staff from the switchboard.

'Right, you need to go to the porters' offices which are on level 1, but as this is a restricted area to staff only, so I'll ask Tony who's around here somewhere to show you how to get there. If you'll wait a minute, I'll go and find him,' the receptionist, whose spectacles were hanging on a neck chord removed them from her face and let them dangle around her chest.

A bald, muscular male, whose lower arms were heavily tattooed, and clad in a light blue polo shirt with navy blue combat trousers arrived to escort the men to the porters' rooms, and without any exchange of words, the detectives hurriedly followed the lengthened strides of their guide.

Both detectives made their way through the endlessly, long white walled corridors, with stone grey lino floors marked with red tram lines, with no indication given as to what these signified, or what might happen if a person crossed out of the boundary.

Javid, whilst walking in haste with his hands in his pockets, glanced across at his boss, and curiously asked, 'Why is it d'ya think that receptionists are always like that? I mean man, they never smile and it's almost as if you're an imposition and that they've got better things to do, and that we're simply wasting their time. D'ya know what I mean?'

'Yeah, I get what you mean. The one at our medical centre, blimey, you'd think you were asking for an invite to see the Pope for Christ's sake. She wants to know bloody everything before she decides whether you get an appointment or not, so d'you know what I do…I always make something up, like stabbing pains in my chest. The funny thing about that is though, when I tell her I've got something that's possibly life threatening, well she can't do enough, and once she asked if I needed an ambulance to pick me up and take me to the centre or whether I should go straight to A&E. Can you imagine me on the other end of the phone? I honestly thought I was going to piss myself laughing.

'Mind you, when I got to the centre, the doctor that I was booked in to see, having been informed that I'd got chest pains, gave me a right bollocking. So, I said to him that I didn't think it was right that a non-medical person has the right to determine whether I get an appointment or not, and that if I needed to see a doctor, then an appointment in two weeks' time was just not acceptable. I also pointed out to him that I was in the job of saving lives too, and that my time was as precious as his. But before I left his office, he clearly stated that he wouldn't tolerate this behaviour again, and he even wagged his finger at me like I was some petulant child. It was really bloody funny actually, and I know that I was wrong, but it was this power that she thought she had over whether or not I get to see a doctor, and well…she just really pissed me off.'

As they'd passed a sign marking the route to their destination, Javid chuckled and asked his boss, 'Bloody hell, did the receptionist ever find out about that stunt you pulled?'

'Not sure,' as the door was held open for them by Tony at the top of a stairwell ready for the descent down to level 1, 'but let's put it this way, I was never put through the Spanish Inquisition again, that's for sure. The odd thing is though, she never looks me in the eye again when I'm in the surgery. Odd that don't you think?'

'Okay, we're here,' announced Tony.

'Thanks very much for your help, it was really kind of you,' responded both detectives.

As the door was already open, the two detectives waited to be invited into the room.

'So, how can I help you guys?' enquired the man seated behind a computer screen also clad in a light blue porter's uniform, sporting dark unruly curly hair with a full, dark, mottled beard.

Both police officers once again removed their ID from inside their wallets, and introduced themselves, 'Hi, I'm Detective Inspector Jarvis, and this is Detective Sergeant Das, and you are…?'

Showing the senior police officer his small passport sized photograph with his name embossed underneath hanging from a lanyard nestled around his neck, he answered with a hint of caution in his voice, 'I'm…Mr Ingram, but just call me Justin.'

'Right Justin, we were wondering if we could take a look at some CCTV footage that was taken outside of the A&E department this evening, if that's possible. We're not sure of the exact time that we need, so somewhere between 9:30 pm and 11:30 pm would be great. I realise that you're probably busy, this being the night shift and everything, but it is really important that we get this recording as soon as possible,' remarked Jarvis as he held onto the back of the office chair with two hands.

'No that's not a problem, I'd be happy to help, but as you can see, the tapes still running so I don't need to remove the tape, we can just rewind it to the time that you're looking for, and if you need to take a copy with you, then I can organise that for you.' Rising from his seat he moved to the other side of the room where the monitors were in full view, and moved two black, PVC leather chairs that were on castors, so that the officers could sit in comfort whilst searching through the camera footage.

Jarvis, pulling his chair closer to the screen asked without focusing his attention directly to the man in charge of security cameras, 'Is this part of your job description Justin, or is the hospital merely trying to save a few quid? I mean, normally large companies usually use outside security companies to deal with crimes either internally or externally, and don't get me wrong, I think you guys are all amazing, irrespective of the uniform that you wear, but don't you think it's a huge responsibility?'

'Nah, not really. If it saves the NHS some money, then why not? We're all trained, and it goes without saying we know what we have to do when the need arises, and to be honest with you well…we kinda like doing it as it's a bit different from pushing hospital beds and wheelchairs around the hospital all day. The best of it is though that you get to sit down for a while, which in our job, as I'm sure you're probably aware, we don't get many opportunities.'

'Oh well, that's alright then. Just needed to satisfy my idle curiosity, I suppose.' Both detectives now had the screen all to themselves and obviously were able to use the monitor without any assistance, whilst Justin turned away from them in search of a phone to answer his bleep.

With beady eyes and deep concentration, both men scanned through the film without much to arouse their attention until the sight of a silver Mercedes S class drove onto their screen. They watched in earnest as events started to unwind before their eyes. The time on the monitor registered 22.58, and it saw the driver's door being opened first where a male came into view, possibly middle aged, sporting a ponytail, and who appeared to be well dressed in a dark suit and a bowtie. The passenger door then opened more cautiously, revealing what appeared to be a slightly older man. The driver of the car opened up the back door, leant in and lifted something up from the back seat. The package that he removed was then laid on the wooden bench which was about four metres from the car. The second man, who was wearing a baseball cap, removed some items from the back seat and hurriedly dropped them to the side of the perfectly still, wrapped bundle.

Both men rushed back to the car, and with a heavy foot on the accelerator sped off at a speed which was certainly higher than the designated 15 M.P.H. speed limit.

'Well, we've got 'em that's for sure. Can we rewind the tape, I mean it's obvious it's a Merc, but we need to get the model and registration plate. Javid, I'll leave you to do that, while I go and find Justin and find out whether he can make a copy of this for us to take away.' Jarvis pushed up from the arms on the black office chair and went in search of the man in charge of the office.

***

Javid drove his boss home, and as it had been a particularly long day and night, very little conversation passed between them, until that is when the younger of the two announced that he would get the registration plate traced with the Driver and Vehicle Licensing Agency (DVLA) first thing in the morning.

On closing the passenger door for the last time that night, the Inspector nodded and patted his hand on the roof of the car in a salutary bid of farewell. Opening the front door and locking it on entry, and after depositing his jacket and shoes in the obligatory resting places, he decided he'd make his way up the stairs and climb straight into bed. Sleep was, however, denied him, as he couldn't get the image of the body dumped mercilessly like a worthless sack on a bench out of his mind. He certainly wasn't looking forward to meeting the woman who would more than likely be scarred both inside and outside for the rest of her life, through no fault of her own.

Having given up the ghost, he woefully turned and glimpsed at the bedside clock which signalled that it was 5:45 am and rather than tossing and turning any longer he decided he'd make an early start.

Taking care not to wake the family up, he made his cup of coffee and took it up to the family bathroom, rather than using his en suite as the noise of the water gushing out and the internal fan would most definitely have woken up Eleanor. Showering quickly but fastidiously, and leaving the bathroom in a fairly neat state for the next occupant, donned his boxer shorts, and took his clothes down the stairs where he dressed in the quietness of the kitchen, allowing the warmth radiated by the heat of the efficient Aga to stimulate a bit of warmth.

He talked himself out of making breakfast, again not wishing to stir the family so early in the morning as he could pick something up from the cafeteria at the station. Before leaving, he searched through the odds and sods drawer in the quaint oak cabinet where he found a yellow post-it pad and wrote three messages, one for each person in the house, and placed them side by side so that they would be difficult to be missed.

In stockinged feet, he made his way to the hall, removed his black woollen jacket from the brass hook, pulled his brown lace up shoes off the shoe rack, and found his keys, wallet, and ID from the ceramic bowl on the bow legged, veneer table, which was nestled idly by the front door.

On opening the front door, he patted his jacket and trousers to make sure he'd got everything, stepped outside, turned around and quietly pulled the door shut.

Chapter 5

With sounds both old and new emanating from his favourite radio station whilst driving to Stockfield Road Police Station, he eventually climbed the two flights of stairs that would lead to his office located on the second floor of the building. As it was still fairly early, there weren't many of his officers around to which he found himself immensely grateful, as this gave him time to think both silently and out loud.

He made his way to the kitchenette at the far end of the office and made a cup of coffee and found a couple of custard creams that had been left behind in the packet that had been ripped open down the middle, and began to munch on them as he made his way back to his office. Pushing the door to his office open, he was unsurprised to see everything in exactly the same place as he'd left it the night before and placed his cup on one of the existing white rings that had been left as a legacy from one of the many occupiers prior to his arrival.

He removed his jacket and hung it on the wooden coat stand and emptied the contents of the now shabby, khaki green laptop bag onto the wide, scratched and heavily stained mahogany desk, and awaited news as to what the new day would bring. Undoubtedly, this would be another day when a member of the public would report that they'd lost or had something stolen, or worse someone had died mysteriously.

Journalists would take photos of yet another pointless slaying of an innocent victim, large headlines on the front pages of both local and national newspapers would be in big, bold lettering displaying contempt that offenders were repetitively smashing windows and helping themselves to things that didn't belong to them, because well...they needed a fix, or wanted a new watch, or perhaps a diamond ring, and didn't see any reason why they should have to earn a living to get them, when a brick and a balaclava would give them what they want.

The paperwork on his desk seemed to be piling up at a ridiculous speed, so he made the most of the quietness to begin ploughing through it.

With a quiet two knuckled rap on the side of the door, Jarvis looked up and saw a body slouched on the door jamb to his office, 'Got a minute, guv?' questioned DS Das, with a surprising sense of eagerness, especially at this time of the morning when the quotient of caffeine wouldn't have kicked into his blood stream yet.

'You got the driver then eh? That quirky smile on your face tells me that you struck lucky?'

'That would be a big fat yes, boss. It belongs to a guy by the name of a Mr Barry Cronin, and the address that he's given to the DVLA is that of a joint called Cinders and it's on Norwood Road, which is off the main Wellington Road, not far from the infamous Denton Heights.'

'Well done, Javid. Any news on how our Miss O'Connor is this morning, because the sooner we get in to see her the better? We don't want her mooning over this and somehow blaming and convincing herself that she deserved it.'

'Yeah, I'll get on to the admissions office and see if I can track down which ward Eva's been admitted to. What time d'you want to pay our Mr Cronin a visit then as I can re-arrange some of the non-urgent stuff?'

The senior detective glimpsed at the face of his leather strapped watch and replied, 'What about eleven thirty? There's bound to be someone there then, even if they are cleaning the khazis.'

Javid turning slightly towards his boss, nodded and responded, 'That sounds fine.'

***

Realising that he hadn't spoken to his wife since the previous evening, Jarvis decided he'd give her a call on her mobile and he almost ended his attempt when finally, she answered, 'Hi honey, what's up?' Quizzed the lady on the other end of the phone. 'Why do you always assume that there's something wrong? Can't I call my wife in the middle of the day and say hello, eh?'

'No, don't be silly, you know I didn't mean that, it's just that well I wasn't expecting a call from you that's all,' replied Eleanor with her distinctive nasal Brummie tones.

'Are you alright sweetie, you don't sound like your normal happy go lucky self, you haven't got a fella in the house, have you? You wouldn't be having a

61

quick how's your father while the old man's at work now, would you?' quipped the Inspector jokingly, whilst emitting a vibrating, thunderous belch.

'Charming, I'm sure. And if that's the kind of bad manners that you're exposing me to over the phone, well it'll be your fault if I fall into the arms of a secret lover. Okay, all joking aside what time d'you expect to be home?'

'Honestly, haven't got a clue at the moment honey, gotta couple of scum balls that I and Javid have got to go and visit. So, no just go ahead without me, and I'll warm something up if I need to.'

'Okay, if you're sure. Actually, that works well with me as I might have another early night because I think the lads are doing their own thing again. And don't you think you should go out and have a pint with the lads as you haven't done that for so long?'

He couldn't see his wife, but as she was speaking to him, she was reading a letter at the time, flinching inwardly at the words as they leapt up at her from a crowded piece of paper.

'Nah, I'll get something, don't worry about me, and you go on ahead and have an early night, but hum…are you sure you're alright, because you seem, oh I dunno, a bit vacant. You're not worried about anything are you? I know the boys have got exams going on at the minute, but they seem happy enough and don't seem overly bothered.' The detective rubbed his free hand against a furrowed brow and enquired further, 'How's the painting you're working on, is it nearly finished or what?'

'Oh, it's going alright, I suppose. There's nothing wrong, I'm just a bit tired that's all. I think I could be a little anaemic, so I'm going to get some vitamin B12 tablets from the chemist this afternoon and see whether that'll help. I'll be fine in a day or two, so stop bloody worrying and get on with your job of catching the bad guys.'

'Well, if you're sure you're okay, then I'll love you and leave you.'

As Eleanor put the phone down, she put her arms around her abdomen and groaned loudly.

The Detective Inspector retrieved his jacket from the stand behind the door and went in search of his colleague. Passing by a myriad of bodies at overloaded desks who were all holding onto phones, whilst balancing them dubiously on a tilted head and raised shoulder, firing questions down a mouthpiece, and with their free hand searching for pen and paper, DS Das stole up behind him.

'Ready to go boss?' he asked, checking his pockets for his car keys and phone.

'Yep, let's do this,' gaining pace to the door marked 'Exit,' Jarvis declared to any of his fellow officers who may have been in ear shot, 'I'll be contactable on my phone if anyone's looking for me,' and with that they strode swiftly across the badly worn, grey carpet tiled floor, and left the Incident Room.

Making their way through the main double doors and to the car park where they found Javid's Audi which was parked in between two squad cars, as the doors unlocked with the pointing of a fob, Javid got in the driver's side and his boss the passenger's side, seat belts were clicked securely into place, as they made their way to make a couple of lives extremely uncomfortable.

'Remind me again what that shithole club's called,' requested the senior detective whilst checking messages on his phone.

'It's called Cinders and I know exactly where it is, so don't worry, and it's not the first time I've had to pay a social call there,' declared the young Asian detective rather waspishly.

Without the good natured banter that the two men usually enjoyed especially whilst driving somewhere, the unlit sign of the licensed but seedy hostelry signalled that the road trip was all but over, as the driver indicated right to pull into a vacant parking space that was about a hundred yards from the venue's front door.

'Well, from the outside, it doesn't look too bad does it, you know. I mean considering they're pulling most of the area down, this kinda looks well…I hate to say it, but rather upmarket. Having said that, considering where it's located, you hum…don't need to be a genius to figure out what sort of low life come here, eh?'

Both detectives got out of the car and surreptitiously glanced around as if in fear of being mugged, or someone sneaking up behind them brandishing a knife, as they paced with lengthy strides towards the entrance. The premises seemed to have been locked but they rang the bell anyway that was found underneath a brass plate bearing the name of the proprietor, *'Barry Cronin.'*

With cupped hands around the sides of his face, Javid attempted to peer through the gap of the sleazy looking maroon coloured velvet curtains that didn't quite meet in the middle, but they knew that there was indeed life behind those closed doors.

Trying to attract the attention from within once more, the young detective used a clenched fist and started pounding heavily, whilst Jarvis simply left his index finger on the door bell.

People meandering past stopped and glared at the two men as they saw and heard the sheer determination to gain access to whatever it was they were looking for in this now sparse community, and they remained rooted to the ground until their curiosity had been satisfied.

Eventually, as the detectives cast a sideways glance at each other, they heard the sliding of locks both at the top and the bottom of one of the doors, and with the sound of jangling keys, they were about to step across the threshold into the entrails of the well-presented, fake Georgian structure.

The figure that appeared before them didn't appear threatening, and didn't hurl abuse at them for halting whatever it was he was doing that prevented him from answering the pleas for entry.

Being the wrong side of fifty, he certainly wasn't shy at showing off the long, black venomous snake tattoo slithering down his arm, or the hairy spider whose legs wrapped around the man's large, thick neck. Teamed with his T-shirt of Jimi Hendrix and a black leather waist coat, the man before them resembled more of a roadie than a bouncer of a night club.

'Ahem…guys, we ain't open yet, but if you'd like to come back we open again at seven p.m. unless of course you're here to read the meter, or have an appointment to see the owner.' The expression on the bouncer's face made it difficult for the two detectives to read.

'Actually,' Javid removed his black wallet from his jacket pocket and opened it up to reveal his identification, 'I'm Detective Sergeant Das, and this is my colleague, Detective Inspector Mark Jarvis, and we'd like to ask you a few questions if that's possible?'

The burly, greying, pony tailed figure started to close the door, but the young Asian detective was too fast for him, as he swiftly and firmly planted his right foot in the partially opened doorway, and stepped up onto the threshold, pushing the door and the man behind it back, so that the door stood wide open.

People thronged outside found this highly entertaining, as they nudged each other, with some even applauding the two policemen, with repeated parroting of, 'Cor, did ya see that?'

'Wonder what's going on there then, reckon its time they shut that place down.' 'Yeah, nothing but trouble from that place, and the noise at night time with people drunk and fighting, and blokes revving up their engines, it makes yer sick.' 'Me and the missus have complained to the council about this place so many times, and the buggers well…they never wanna do nothing about it 'cos I reckon they're too bloody scared to, or someone's paid 'em like you know…when the Mafia bribed all of them New York cops and stuff, remember?'

They all laughed heartily at this latest comment, where an elderly man in a dark brown puffer jacket piped up, 'Awww Geoff, sometimes you don't 'arf talk a load of crap.'

DS Das slyly looked across at the senior detective with a grin etched on his face as it was impossible not to hear the remarks being made by the locals.

'I said, we only wanted to have a word with you, why are you so twitchy, got something to hide have you?' demanded the younger detective, as he stared unblinkingly at the gatekeeper. 'Why don't we start with your name then, eh? And just for the record, we aren't leaving here until we've got what we came for, so you might just as well answer the questions. Right, this isn't an audition for Mastermind, so once again I'm going to ask you…name?'

'I don't think you've got any right to be here and ask me anything, but I can be a good citizen when I've got a mind to it, so its Jimmy Malone, no James or Jim, it's Jimmy, so you can jot that down in your bloody stupid little notebook.'

The bouncer stood there with his arms crossed, and leaning his back against a wall, enquired of the Asian detective, 'So, what is it that's just sooooo important that you've gotta practically knock the bloody door down, huh? 'cos let me tell ya now, I ain't done nuffin wrong.'

'Okay, good, well that's a start. Is there somewhere that we can go that is more erm…private?'

Pausing for a moment, not wanting the two detectives who were encroaching his space to think that he was some kind of pushover, he casually swaggered ahead of the men through a plush looking entrance hallway, with slate grey flooring and black and white prints of famous blonde, curvaceous superstars who would have turned in their graves to see images of their perfect faces and bodies adorn a club with such a notorious reputation.

The plainclothes police officers were led to the bar area where optics of colourful liquids lined the wall behind the bar together with glasses of varying sizes hanging upside down on glass shelves brightly lit by hidden strip lighting underneath.

Beer mats were stacked in neat piles either side of the beer pumps, and kiln jars contained juicy green and black olives, slices of oranges and lemons all ready to adorn the simplest and the most complicated of liquor filled concoctions.

'This'll have to do,' declared the tattooed man, pointing the two visitors to the black swivel barstools.

Both men sat, whilst the third man stood behind the bar trying to find things to keep him busy so that he didn't have to give them his undivided attention, thus making it difficult for them to scrutinise his facial expressions when faced with questions that he knew undoubtedly would come, and of course he knew deep down why they were here.

'Right then Mr Malone, can you tell us where you were yesterday evening after ten p.m.?' questioned Das, with both hands clasped together resting on the bar.

'Well, that's easy enough, I was here from seven in the evening till we closed at around two in the morning, when we thr…huh, I mean asked the last person to leave. What d'ya wanna know for anyway?'

'So, you weren't anywhere near The Hamilton General Hospital last night then, is that what you're saying? No customer was taken ill and instead of you calling for an ambulance you drove them, perhaps? You know, you being a good citizen and Samaritan and all.'

Malone heaved his large frame from a squatting position to standing upright and rubbing the small of his back as he frowned and squinted whilst shaking his head at the same time, 'Officers, I honestly haven't got a clue what you're talking about, I mean I do know where the 'orspital is but I ain't been there for years,' touching the side of his head with his finger, 'touch wood an' all that, eh?'

'Are you absolutely sure about that, Mr Malone? You see, we have reason to believe that you were parked outside of the hospital, in fact the Accident and Emergency Department, at around eleven p.m. Also, you weren't alone, there was another gentleman in the passenger seat, so tell me, now do you remember? No bells ringing yet, hum…?'

'What the fuck's going on in 'ere?' demanded a balding, sixty something year old man sporting a pair of dark blue jeans and white shirt opened at the neck.

'I said, what the fuck's going on, Jimmy, everything okay?'

Malone answered with a quick glance at the two officers of the law, 'Yeah, everything's fine Mr Cronin. Don't worry, I've told these two gentlemen here everything I know, which is nothing, so I expect they'll be on their way, isn't that right gents?'

'Oh, so that's it then Sergeant, s'pose we'd better get off then, right, 'cos if Jimmy here says he doesn't know anything, then we've got no choice but to believe him,' quipped the Inspector, with an unhidden air of sarcasm.

'Mind you guv, our Mr Malone did say that the other gentleman here is a Mr Cronin, even though he hasn't introduced himself. So, I'm thinking he might know the answers to our questions, what d'you think, worth asking him, you reckon?'

'Now that is what I call good police work Detective Sergeant. Mr Cronin what car do you drive, hum…just as a matter of interest you understand?'

'Why didn't you say you were police officers? Has Mr Malone even offered you the chance to partake of a beverage?' asked the club owner, using a false voice that really couldn't be taken seriously, considering the barrage of abuse they'd heard being emitted from his mouth earlier.

'No, we really don't need anything, but thank you. Now, if you'd just answer the question, we'd be very grateful, and we can then be out of your hair.'

'Yes, well you see my car is insured for all my employees so that if a member of staff needs a lift home, or indeed, if there's an emergency of some kind, then there's always a set of wheels available, because, as you can appreciate officers, I'm not always around to help when these needs arise. Now, I know it costs me a bloody arm and a leg, but it works well, ain't that right Jimmy?'

'Oh yeah that's absolutely spot on, and I can 'onestly say I don't know what we'd do without it, I 'onestly can't Mr Cronin. As a matter of fact, I think me and the lads drive it more than you, and d'you know what, I can't for the life of me remember you havin' driven it for, oh blimey…let me see now, well it's got to be a couple of months at least.'

'Right, so that's settled then. Anything else we can do for you good people?'

The senior detective stated quite seriously whilst glancing towards the young Asian officer, 'I don't believe we asked you about who drives the car Mr Cronin, I think the question was quite simply, what make of car do you drive? So, once again, could you please answer the question, or of course, we could do this down at the station, if you prefer. Your choice.'

'No, that won't be necessary Inspector. I drive a silver Mercedes, and it's a rather classy looking S class, and really expensive too, with real leather seats, and not the synthetic cheap shit that your regular poor man has to put up with, you know the kind that sticks to your backside in the summer and freezes your arse in the winter. Now, if you'll excuse me, now that we've given you the information you came for, I'm a very busy man, as I'm sure both of you are. You must have better things to do like, oh I don't know…getting the real villains off the streets and finding the fuckers who steal little old ladies' handbags, eh?'

Reaching into the inside of his jacket, Javid pulled out a picture on A4 sized printing paper, and handing it over to the owner of the club asked with a measure of brusqueness, 'Would this be the classy looking Mercedes that you've just described, Mr Cronin?'

'I er…well, I don't rightly know, if I'm honest. It certainly looks to be similar to mine, but you see detective, without a number plate it's impossible to tell.'

'Would this be the registration plate you're referring to by any chance?' the younger detective handed over a second photograph of the car, but this time it exposed black letters and numbers which were settled neatly on a white metallic background.

'Wh…where did you get this, detective, and what's it supposed to mean? I can assure you I'm up to date with tax and insurance, and I don't even have a penalty point, or a parking ticket, so I wish you'd come straight to the point and tell me why you're showing me pictures of my car.'

'Well, well, well, aren't we an upstanding member of the public,' voiced Jarvis, as he gave the slow hand clap, 'So just to be absolutely clear, am I right in thinking that you've just identified this as your car, and this time just a 'yes or no' answer is all we need?'

With both the accused and the accuser staring at one another, the former declared quite openly, 'yes,' and threw the two pieces of paper on top of the polished wooden surface of the bar.

DI Jarvis, retrieving the picture, and pointing to the figure underneath the CCTV camera, requested of the owner of the club, 'Am I right in thinking that this is you in the photograph, Mr Cronin?'

'I suppose it is, but you have to admit that there's a lot of fellas who look like me in the world, so it might be me, or it might not. Let's face it, that picture's not very good after all now, is it? But let's say for argument's sake it is, you haven't even told us where it was taken for fuck's sake, and what it is that we're meant to have done. If we parked on a yellow line for a few minutes, then we'll pay the fine and be done with it, but isn't it time you levelled with us and tell us what it is you think you know that we may have done eh, what do you say?

Because well…if I'm totally honest with you, this is all getting to be a bit boring, and I really have to get on as I have a club to run, just in case you hadn't noticed, and this is my bread and butter. I mean let's face it the state don't pay my boys' wages now do they?'

'Well, if nothing else, it's good to see that at least you're a little bit intrigued as to how and why we've got proof that the car in the picture is yours. You see, here's the thing, you didn't do a very thorough job of making sure that the girl that you beat up to a pulp got medical attention. I mean…' Jarvis chuckled in the hope of igniting some kind of reaction, 'you have to appreciate that when both Detective Sergeant Das and I first saw the footage we had a good old laugh, it was better than some of the comedy sketches you see on the telly. You know, what idiots after smacking up some poor defenceless girl so bad, leaves her on a bench right outside an Accident and Emergency Department right underneath a CCTV camera? I tell you, we both wish that all criminals were as kind as you two were, leaving all of the evidence right before our eyes, we didn't have to look or interview hundreds of suspects, no…you hum very kindly gave it all to us on a plate. It really was incredibly generous of you. In fact, I think we should nominate you for some kind of badge of honour, what d'ya think of that?'

Taking the remaining picture off the bar, the Inspector repeated his question, but this time he aimed it at the bar tender, 'Now then Mr Malone, please take a good look at this other photo, now would you say that this is an exact likeness of you? Or, to put it more accurately this is you in this frame, isn't it?'

As the silence ensued, Jarvis continued, 'Okay Detective Sergeant I've had enough of this, read these two their rights, would you please?'

'You can't arrest me, I ain't done nuthin, you ain't got no proof, none at all,' protested Malone.

'Jimmy, enough! I'll get my lawyer and he'll see that this is all a load of nonsense which has been drummed up by these clowns. I know what you lot are up to, you've been dying to close my place down for years, and now you think just because you've got a couple of photographs of us, you can intimidate us. Oh, believe me, you'll have to do much better than that Detective Inspector.'

'Mr Barry Cronin, I am arresting you on suspicion of causing grievous bodily harm…' as D.S. Das continued with the declaration, Jarvis stared at the other man who was stationed behind the bar, loudly clinking bottles into a uniformed line behind the bar, feebly protesting his innocence.

'Hello, this is Detective Inspector Jarvis, and I need you to send two patrol cars around to Cinders which is on Norwood Road, off the main Wellington Road. Yes, right away please.'

***

As the squad cars arrived to escort the two arrested men to Stockfield Road Police Station, both investigating detectives made their own way back in the dark blue Audi with once again very little conversation exchanged between them.

With the Custody Sergeant having booked both accused men in to the system, finger prints taken, personal details divulged, and with their personal property placed into huge brown envelopes that were sealed, both Das and Jarvis discussed quietly in one of the vacant interview rooms who was going to question who, and which other detectives they wanted in there with them.

'Well, it's obvious that Malone isn't going to take much of a going over before he spills the beans, but I think when Cronin's lawyered up, he'll be the one that'll dig his heels in, even though we've got enough photographic evidence to nail their sorry arses. I mean, even if it wasn't them that caused the injuries, which is probably the way they're going to play it, they're still going down with accessory charges. So, how about we get this thing moving? You take Malone and get D.S Carmichael to go in with you, hopefully his hard nut exterior might put the frighteners on him, and I'll take Cronin and get DS Turner to sign up with me. If I know our honourable club owner, I think he'll be on edge that we'll have a big, hard man in the room which will, no doubt, get him nicely worked up, which is the way I want him…stewing nicely.'

Jarvis took Interview Room 3 which was of a medium size, probably around 8 x 10, bare walled, and with four chairs strategically placed along a rectangular, grey metallic table where a tape recorder was evident. Cronin was brought in together with his solicitor, known as a Miss Ryan, whom Jarvis had had the pleasure of meeting many, many times before, so they were both aware of each other's stoic, professional attributes when it came to finding out the truth.

The senior detective began the proceedings by cautioning the accused once again, but breaking each point down step by step to ensure that the defendant knew what his rights were. Cronin looked across at his solicitor for some kind of reproach or to squash the procedures altogether, but she simply sat there looking straight ahead at the narrator, soaking in every word in the hope that he'd make a mistake or erroneously miss a word that needed to be spoken, as she crossed one leg over the other, picked a pen up in her hand, and found a fresh ink-free page on a lined legal pad placed in front of her, ready for the attack.

'For the record, this interview is taking place on 8th April at 11:30 am in Interview Room 3, Stockfield Road Police Station. Those present at this interview are, Detective Inspector Mark Jarvis, Detective Sergeant John Turner, Miss Jocelyn Ryan, legal representative for Mr Barry Cronin, who is also present.'

'Ahem…' the Inspector cleared his throat before commencing, 'Mr Barry Cronin that is your real name?'

'No comment,' declared the man resolutely.

'Do you understand the charges that have been brought against you?'

'No comment.'

Placing two photographs flat on the table in front of both the man held for questioning and his legal advisor, the senior detective continued, 'This photograph was taken outside the Accident and Emergency Department at The Hamilton General Hospital on Tuesday 7th April at 22:47. We traced the vehicle here through the Driver and Vehicle Licensing Agency (DVLA) and they were able to track the owner of the registration plate to you, Mr Cronin.'

'No comment.'

'For the benefit of the tape, I'm now going to show CCTV coverage for the night in question as given to the police department by the aforementioned hospital as evidence in support of the charge brought against the defendant.'

Josh Turner, the thirty-eight-year-old black detective sergeant stood up from the table and stepped slowly but with conviction to the recorder and inserted the tape that had been copied from the original.

Staying in close range in case the tape needed to be rewound, stopped or fast forwarded, he continued to set the scene for all members in the room. 'As we can see from the tape the silver Mercedes, S class model, registration plate BC1 X23 is seen approaching the A&E department of The Hamilton General Hospital at 22.39. The vehicle parks up a…'

'We don't need a bloody running commentary, we've got fuckin' eyes, you know. So, why don't you go and rebraid your hair or something, or just shut the f…' Cronin was halted by a hand being placed on his forearm by the short, blonde-haired attorney.

'I think what my client is trying to say is that he and I would much rather just watch the footage for ourselves, and then we'll be in a much better position to answer any questions you might have officers.'

'Very well,' remarked the Inspector, as DS Turner sauntered back to his seat with a quirky smile on his face, knowing that his tactic had worked. The smugness that had previously reigned over the face of the middle aged man had quickly evaporated as he was witnessed finger combing his greying, greasy hair around the back of his ears nervously, as the monitor was busily laying bare the true facts that one of the men staring through the glass screen was indeed the man who had not only been seen getting out of the car, but who had also sworn himself into silence in the hope of trying to vindicate himself from any crime committed.

The youthful looking, well-dressed legal representative requested of both police officers, 'I wonder if I might have a word in private with my client?'

Inspector Jarvis smiled inwardly and spoke directly to the tape, 'This interview is being suspended at 11:50 pm as legal counsel wishes to speak with her client in private.' Click. The recording was halted, and as both detectives left the office, a uniformed constable was summoned to stand outside the door.

'Let's be clear about something,' Miss Ryan declared. 'You can go no comment all you like, but you've got to tell me the truth about what happened to that poor girl. You can't escape that it's you on that bloody tape, and they've got evidence that you own the car, so how can I defend you when they've got all this hard evidence. Now, before I walk out of this room, I want to know the facts, because from where I'm sitting, you're facing a conviction unless you can tell me what really went on.'

Groaning loudly, Cronin replied haggardly, 'Okay yeah, well…I s'pose I don't have any other choice now do I?'

'No, you don't. So, let's not waste any more of each other's time, agreed?'

'Right, it was on 7th April, when was that, shit…it was only yesterday, anyway it was about half past nine in the evening, and one of our regular punters came down the stairs a…'

'Mr Cronin, I want to know every detail, I don't know where these supposed stairs are, so perhaps you'll enlighten me. I need for you to tell me names, places, everything because that's the only way were going to get you out of here. Do I make myself perfectly clear?'

'Yeah, I got this. So, as I was saying, last night at my club, the er…Cinders on Norwood Road, it was around nine thirty in the evening when a regular client of ours made his way down the stairs from one of the rooms on the first floor which we rent out so clients can, huh…invite female company and have a quiet drink and a chat together, you know in private without anyone interrupting them.'

The man was halted abruptly again from continuing his accounts of the night in question. 'I thought I made myself very clear Mr Cronin, I want the truth, because if this goes to trial before a jury, you're going to be asked questions which will require you to go into full detail as to what your club offers. So please, spare me the blushes,' lamented his counsel.

'The rooms that we rent out are there so that our clients can scr…I mean have sexual relations with whomever they so wish.

'So, last night, as I tried to tell you earlier, a regular client of ours comes down the stairs, and he was like some sort of cock of the walk, all pleased and proud of himself, it was then that I got a bit, oh I dunno…a bit ashamed and disgusted with myself for what I'd done. I'd turned my club that I'd worked hard for years and years, into a fucking knocking shop, and I felt as if I just needed to get out for a while and clear my head. So, I bought a round of drinks for the regular members who were dotted around the downstairs bar and the cosy booths, exchanged a few pleasantries with some that I've known for a long time, and then I saw Jimmy, who was just kind of standing around, 'cos it really wasn't very busy. I asked him whether he could drive me around for a bit as I really needed to get some air, to which he said that he would love to, as he was a bit bored himself.

'Anyway, Malone brought the car around and I got in, and we'd gone about oh…I s'pose a mile or a mile and a half from the club, and I looked across at Jimmy and told him to stop the car as I could swear I saw something lying on the footpath. We opened the car door very slowly, 'cos well…you never know do you in these sad times, and the area doesn't exactly score very highly in low crime rates, know what I mean? Anyway, stepping towards her, we scouted around the um…immediate area before we well…bent down to look at the figure who was just lying there. We didn't know if she was dead, but then Jimmy remembered watching a film once, he absolutely loves murder and blood thirsty films…' the aging club owner chortled at this so-called humorous recollection

73

of his buddy, 'and so he removed a handkerchief from his pocket and put it to her mouth, and lo and behold the small piece of cloth moved.

'We were well made up I can tell you as it meant she weren't dead, know what I mean? And then Jimmy said that he'd always wanted to do that and oh my God he was so pleased with himself, you'd have thought he'd just performed bloody major brain surgery.

'Anyway, you can understand our fear and well…pity for this poor young thing that had been battered and bruised from God only knows what, and we did what any respectful human being would do, we took her to the Emergency Department that was closest to us,' Cronin applauding himself inwardly at his sterling performance, wiped an imaginary tear from his eye, and held his head down towards his chest.

'I can arrange to get you some water, if you would like.'

'Nah, I'm good thanks.'

'So, can you tell me what sort of a state she was in, were her clothes stained, did she have a bag with her, a phone, or what? You need to give me the ingredients for the whole cake Mr Cronin, not just the butter and flour,' remarked Miss Ryan as she was swiftly guiding a pen across a lined page.

'Ah…now, well…she appeared to be completely naked, apart from as I said earlier, an old co…'

'Excuse me again for interrupting your account of what you believe you saw, but here's the thing I don't understand. You see, unless this so-called coat was buttoned up to the neck completely, then you'd be able to state whether or not the victim that you alleged was lying on the side of the road was indeed naked or not. Now, I have to advise you, as your legal representative, that if you want the police to take your story seriously then give them a plausible account of what you saw.'

'Well then, the answer is yes, she was naked apart from the old navy blue overcoat that was covered over her.'

'Now, I need you to answer the other part of the question which is, did her attacker or attackers leave her clothes or any other belongings, and was there any evidence of anything that they might have used when they did this act of violence near where you found her, like a bat or a piece of metal piping, anything like that? Think Mr Cronin, this is very important as I'm sure you'll agree.'

'Yes, her clothes were left neatly in a pile beside her, with her bag lying on the top. I remember that bit well, 'cos I put them in the car exactly in that way so that we didn't lose or drop anything.'

'So, some guy or guys beat the crap out of a young lady, and then they politely assemble all her clothes and lay them tidily beside her battered body. My oh my, violent people are becoming much more respectful of their victims these days, how very touching and commendable I must say. This act of generosity needs to go in the newspaper, and the journalist writing the story should ask for the perpetrators to come forward urgently so that they can give them a reward for being so unbelievably kind.'

'There's no need to be so sarcastic,' rebuked the accused, feeling regretful that his imagination to tell a good story was somehow lacking credibility.

'Okay Mr Cronin, dare I ask what you did next?'

'So anyway, Jimmy being a bit fitter than me 'cos I hum…well struggle with me back you see, leant down and cradled up the young lady in his arms, and then very carefully placed her on the back seat of the car, but he made damn sure he didn't bump her head on the way in, as he didn't want to inflict any more pain. We used her clothes as a kind of pillow, but obviously not the spiky heeled boots, 'cos we didn't think these would be very comfortable, you know…?' Once again, Cronin found the words that came out of his mouth to be highly amusing, as he snorted at this last remark he'd made.

'On the way to erm…dropping her off at the hospital, well me and Jimmy decided that the best way to play this would be to just…ahem…leave her somewhere where she'd be found by someone, like you know, a nurse or a doctor or someone, and of course it goes without saying that we made sure that she was covered up and as comfortable as we…well, as well as we possibly could, under the circumstances.'

'And that's the whole story, is it? So, let me get this straight. You were somehow criticising yourself for becoming an upmarket pimp by letting your premises become a glorified brothel. You then decide to buy everyone in the club a drink, and then…to somehow satisfy your conscience, you ask one of your bar tenders or bouncers, or whatever you'd like to call him, to take you out for a drive in your car, and then by sheer coincidence you come across a half-naked body on the side of the road? Mr Cronin, do you honestly expect me to believe these shenanigans really took place?

'I mean…the one question, which I for one, am dying to know, and it's my guess that the investigating officers are going to want to find out is, why didn't you call for an ambulance or the police, eh? That's what I would have done if I'd found a beaten-up body on a pavement near to my place of business. Oh, and you never said what time all of this happened by the way?' as the defending councillor sat opposite the man whom she had asked the question, crossed one leg over the other and with a rigidly tense body, folded her arms.

'Well, that's an easy one to answer, it was about…oh, I guess if I was a betting man, I'd have to say it was about ten o'clock, something like that. The reason that we didn't call for an ambulance is because we didn't know how long she'd been lying there, and…we didn't know how much blood she'd lost, so we figured time would be lost if we waited for either the police or ambulance services. Being God fearing, good, honest people we felt as though we acted in the best interests for the young lady, and at the time we thought we'd done the right thing.'

'That's very commendable, Mr Cronin, but why didn't you take her inside the A&E department into the warm. I mean, the double doors were only a few feet away from where you left her on that cold, wooden bench. So, surely, if you'd been so worried about her state of health, the least you could have done was for one of you to have gone inside, alerted a member of staff, while the other one stayed by her side to make sure no more harm came to her. Now if you'd done that, then it goes without saying that she would have been attended to earlier, and I'm sure you'll agree that this would have been the best cause of action in the circumstances?'

'Oh, hindsight is a wonderful word, don't you agree Ms Ryan? But you see here's the thing, if we'd taken her inside the building in that state, you can imagine that the police would have been called, and let's face it, me and Jimmy would have been accused of slapping her up wouldn't we? I mean…it's not rocket science, is it? Also, let's not forget that as soon as they'd discovered that I was the owner and was in charge of the day to day running of Cinders, they'd simply put two and two together, and they would have been like judge and jury all in the space of five minutes, and the next thing you know we'd both have been thrown in the slammer. Oh, and don't go blarting on about honesty is the best policy and all that, 'cos call me anything you like, put any label on me that you think I may or may not deserve, but don't think for one minute that I'm stupid, 'cos that I ain't.'

'That's as may be, but…even if they do believe your story, which if I'm perfectly honest with you is doubtful, they could still try and pursue a case against you for negligence, and where life is at risk this could mean jail time. You had a duty of care towards that poor young woman, I mean…how do you know when huh…Jimmy picked her up that she didn't have spinal injuries, eh? That's why in cases like this one, people normally call for paramedics, because even though, to use your words, you were doing what you felt was the right thing, you may have caused her permanent damage. So, I guess what I'm saying is, that even though you can't see an obvious injury, neither you nor Jimmy are qualified to assess that, because you see the fact of the matter is that you're not medically trained, are you?'

Clasping his hands behind his back he declared rather defensively, 'Well, now that you put it that way, it does kinda seem a bit dumb that we didn't call the cops I s'pose, but you know, it all came as a big surprise to us finding her there and everything, and I guess we panicked. There's no law against that now is there?'

'Right,' uttered the impeccably attired solicitor as she stood smoothing the wrinkles out of her grey, pencil skirt, 'it's time for you to stop with the no comment, and tell the detectives everything you've just told me, and pray to any god that may be listening, that they believe you.'

***

With both sets of interviews having been taken, and the accused now back in their respective cells, the four detectives met in Jarvis office for a de-briefing. The senior detective started the proceedings with, 'So, what've we got? Our Mr Cronin said that they found Miss O'Connor about a mile away from the club and the reason they didn't contact us guys or the ambulance was because they didn't want to be accused of beating the shit out of her themselves. What did our mastermind Malone have to say for himself, then?'

'Pretty much the same guv, except he said that they found her on the edge of the Denton Heights estate, but like you say, he's not exactly the sharpest knife in the drawer, is he?' offered Javid as he massaged and squeezed the back of his neck.

'I've been in touch with Tim Slattery from the Crown Prosecution Service who has said that there's not much that we can hold them on. Yes, we've got footage from the CCTV, but we've got nothing to say that it was them that did the damage to our victim, and to be honest with you, I can't see them doing this to her. For a start off, what would be their motive, and I don't know, they just seem to be…well not violent men, I guess. And let's not forget, who in their right minds would dump a body of someone that they'd just pulverised in front of a sodding set of cameras, for fuck's sake,' everyone in the room sniggered lightly at this, as the Inspector continued, 'but nevertheless, I do think they know who did it, but for now we've got nothing else, so I suppose we've got to let them go, and see whether the coming days will bring us anything new.'

Detective Carmichael who'd been sitting in with the interview of Malone added, 'Gotta agree boss. I think our Jimmy boy couldn't do that, you know. I agree that he's meant to be a big, mean bouncer and that's what their profession expects them to be, but I can't see it, he ain't got it in him. No way. I also agree with you that these two turtle heads know who did this to Miss O'Connor, but I think whoever it was has put the heebie-jeebies up the two of them and it's my best guess that they were told to get rid of the evidence somehow, and this is the best that they came up with.'

'Of course, there is a caveat to all of this, and that is if Eva should die from her injuries, then we could get them on a gross negligence manslaughter charge. So, all we can do for the time being is to sit it out and wait to see how she's getting on, I s'pose. But this isn't the end, we've got to find the bastard who did this, so for now, what d'you say, shall we set 'em loose?' commented Jarvis as he pinched the tip of his nose with his thumb and forefinger.

As all members of the team arose from their chairs ready to depart the office, the familiar face of the attractive thirty-three-year-old, Detective Sergeant Donnelly from Galway leant against the door frame. She tossed her black mane of curly-hair out of her eyes and announced 'Sorry guys to break up your little boys' club, but I thought ye'd like to know that we've just had a call from the local fire brigade to say that a club just outside of the Denton Heights estate has had a match set to it.'

Whilst all the detectives simply gazed at each other, Jarvis broke the silence with a simple question, 'Which club Sergeant Donnelly?'

'Cinders.'

'What d'you reckon guys, coincidence or what? How badly damaged is the club, do we know yet?' demanded the senior investigating officer.

'The fire fighter who made the call said that the damage had been mainly in the back of the building, the office and the kitchen area, and it was all thanks to an anonymous caller who said that they'd seen smoke as they were out walking their dog, and it was thanks to him or her that they were able to save most of the building without too much damage,' answered Donnelly.

'Well, isn't that dandy? We don't have anything to do with that place for years and now out of the blue we have two separate incidents where somehow or other that bloody club is concerned.'

'Could be someone is trying to send a message d'you think?'

'Right, let's get 'em out of here and back to what's left of that shithole. Can one of you get a couple of squad cars to take them back please? And guys, we've not been out for a sup in a long while, so…anyone fancy having a pint, and well I know it's only Tuesday, but I've got a serious urge for alcohol?'

Chapter 6

Jarvis suggested that they go to their favourite jaunt, The Merchant of Venice, a quaint little pub, and apparently as rumour would have it, where Shakespeare would indulge in his writing skills, but regulars would always chuckle when they heard this story because they knew damn well that the building was only about a hundred years old. Its décor is filled with framed prints of sixteenth century England with narrow cobbled side streets with children dressed in rags running over uneven terrain, presumably in search of food or a dropped coin.

The pub was an easy choice for everyone who worked at Stockfield Road cop shop as it was literally on a side street about a quarter of a mile away and was tucked away nicely from the hosts of hen and stag nights, and evenings when pay day brought out all the revellers in their droves, puking up from over loaded livers, and blocking up the drains even more.

Shortly after eleven o'clock, Jarvis found himself paying the taxi driver, threw the empty foam polystyrene container that held his burger in the blue recycling bin sitting outside of the front door, and made his way into the stillness of his home.

He grabbed a glass of cold water and made his way up to bed, and just in case he woke up with the mother of all hangovers, he went in search of some Paracetamol because he couldn't bear the thought of feeling groggy the next morning which he usually did when he'd had one too many.

Not wishing to disturb Eleanor, he looked inside the off white, mirrored cabinet in the family bathroom but there was not much there only a couple of spare packets of razor blades, half used tubes of toothpaste that had been brought back from school trips and never either been thrown out or finished. Closing the door quietly and turning the light off, he sauntered his way to the bathroom off his bedroom and opening the cabinet doors underneath the oyster shelled wash basin, he was surprised to see the array of white folding cartons containing capsules sealed inside foil, and on closer inspection revealed the name, 'Mrs Eleanor Jarvis, dob 14/5/1974.'

Taking just one of the boxes into the hall where one of the wall lights gave off sufficient light for him to read what the name of the drug was, 'Gabapentin' and reading a brief description as to why it was prescribed, the typed words laid bare their function, 'Take two tablets for pain control, but do not exceed the stated dose.'

He certainly wasn't going to go through all the containers now as he would most certainly make too much noise, but after finding the blister pack of Paracetamol, he popped two out and washed them down with a long swig of water.

Sleep was almost instant, thanks in the main to a fun, relaxing night out with the lads with no talk of work, but silly nonsensical jokes and much piss taking of the two bozos they'd interviewed earlier on in the day.

DS Carmichael got an explosion of laughs as he amusingly related his conversation with the owner of Cinders regarding the fire where he was greeted with a barrage of verbal abuse to which the officer had no idea whom Cronin was directing it to.

'He can't fucking well do that to me, after all I've done for that sonofabitch,' said Cronin, as his comrade in arms, Jimmy, whispered rather coyly, 'Is everything alright, Mr Cronin?'

'Oh no, everything's just fucking brilliant.'

'Yer don't sound very 'appy even if I say so meself.' suggested the older man's right-hand man.

At this point Carmichael interjected, and asked the club's owner, 'Mr Cronin, do you know who set fire to your club, because if you do, it's your duty to notify us, as arson is a very serious offence. as you must be quite aware?'

'No, no this has nothing to do with that, this is a message about something entirely different, believe me,' he responded, whilst shaking his head and mumbling under his breath, 'So you wanted to send me a message did ya, after I've spent the bloody day in a nick for something that you did, you evil conniving bastard.'

Detective Sergeant Carmichael had no choice but to simply make his report stating that the club's owner had no idea what had happened to cause the fire and had apparently not the faintest idea as to who may have wanted the premises torched to the ground.

***

Jarvis punched the button of his alarm clock with force, and quickly decided he not only needed, but came to the conclusion that he'd earned an extra ten minutes or so, and when he eventually woke up he was stunned that his so-called add on of a few minutes had turned into an hour and a half. He jumped out of bed, and with even more haste showered and dressed in his customary smart, but informal apparel of a blue pin striped shirt with beige coloured Chinos, and made his way down the stairs to the hub of the house where he was expecting to see all members of the household in heavy debate about something that they'd heard on the news, or more usually whose turn it was to take out the rubbish.

Silence from the nucleus of the home, which was ridiculous but glancing at the circular clock above the fridge with its Roman numerals displaying the time, he now discovered the house was void of sound, well of the boys anyway.

Calling out for his wife and checking the downstairs rooms and the shed which had been converted into an artist's studio for her, she also was nowhere to be seen. Re-entering into the kitchen, he found next to the coffee percolator a note which was in her usual neat, printed script informing him that she'd got an appointment at the dentist and then she was going to visit her sister, so she'd be away for most of the day. At the end of the note, she'd drawn a heart with an arrow piercing it through the middle.

Taking his coffee back upstairs, he decided to have a look through the medicine cabinet once more, but this time more thoroughly, as his recollection as to what he'd done once he got home last night refuelled the concern that he clearly felt last night. There were at least six different sets of pills and he had definitely never seen them there before, and they were all dated 25th March, so what the hell was she holding back from him?

He knew that there'd be a perfectly good explanation and, as they'd never kept secrets from one another, he felt as though he had entered uninvited into a part of her world which she wanted to keep private for reasons which only she knew.

Grabbing his keys which were stashed ready for a quick getaway by the front door, he made his way out of the front door and climbed into his burnt orange coloured Peugeot.

***

He made his way to the station, and on entering the second floor, which is where his office was located, he called everyone to gather around the white boards in the incident room to have a catch up on recent events, and discussions as to how they were going to proceed.

'So, as we all know from the interviews yesterday is that we didn't get a match for the attacker of Miss Eva O'Connor, but we subsequently found out about an attempt to burn down the club where one of the suspects in the enquiry is the owner. Any thoughts, anyone?'

DS Das cleared his throat a little before replying, 'There's got to be a connection to all this somewhere, but not sure what. I don't think it would hurt for one of us to lean on those guys again, but this time focus more on the fire and not the attack. Maybe our Mr Cronin will be so angry about the arson attempt that he may just let something slip.'

'Yeah, I agree, so whoever's got the balls to go and visit our two angels of the night, let me know how you get on. Meanwhile I'm going to The Hamilton General to see if I can get in to see Eva, well if she's well enough that is, and I suggest that Donnelly you come with me, because I feel that having another female in the room might help her to open up you know, rather than having two males gawking at her.'

'Boss, have we arranged for any house-to-house calls to see if anyone saw or heard anything, either for the assault or the fire, because from where I'm standing someone must have seen or heard something. And if the goings on in that place are to be believed, I bet there'd be a few locals who wouldn't mind shopping them in a neighbourly bid to have the place shut down for good,' queried Detective Sergeant Pettrini, who up until this point had been assigned the job along with a few DCs to try and find out who was responsible for the sudden spate of increased muggings and car thefts.

'Javid did you find out which ward she's on or is she still in ICU?' asked Inspector Jarvis as he hurriedly made his way to the exit followed by the Irish detective.

'No, she's out of there now and in a general ward, called the Angela Ashby Ward.'

***

Jarvis, feeling confident that both he and Detective Sergeant Donnelly would find Eva without much difficulty marched along lengthy, light blue, rubber-like flooring where their footsteps were cleverly silenced. They passed by sterile, whitewashed walls where colourful prints were hung, perhaps in the hope of breaking down the monotony of such institutionalised dullness, or in the hope that whilst stopping to gaze at their vibrant colours and hidden meanings, they would somehow bring a brief period of respite from hidden fears.

Both officers arrived at the ward at ten thirty a.m. where Eva O'Connor was being treated, and seeing the slender chrome door handles on the fluorescent blue door, immediately pulled on them in an attempt to enter, however, both detectives failed to see the notice on the side of the wall adjacent to the doors that entry would only be gained by pressing the black rectangular button on the grey intercom perched on the wall. Pressing the buzzer, they then waited patiently until they heard the response emitting through the little, but effective grey round speaker. 'Sorry, but the unit isn't open for visitors until eleven o'clock.' Click.

'Bloody hell, that's a bit rich wouldn't you say so sir? I mean to say now, half the day is almost over,' remarked the female police officer.

'Rules is rules, Kelly. C'mon let's go and get a cup of coffee, I don't know about you but I'm gagging. The good thing is at least we know where she is and when we've finished our drink it'll be opening time.'

Rather than make their way back to the concourse area where there was a myriad of shops, and famous purveyors of coffee and eateries, they tried their luck with a dispensing machine which was located within a hundred yards from the ward. As the coins clunked into the back of the huge vending machine, Jarvis entered both his and his colleague's preference on the keypad and taking sugar and plastic stirrers from a half filled white foam cup, they went in search of two empty plastic seats. 'So, sir how d'you think we're going to play this then? I mean…what if she doesn't want to talk to us, or give him up to us, what will we do then, d'ya think?' asked Kelly, as she stirred two sweeteners into her dark coloured coffee.

'Ah…let's just enjoy the quietness for now, speculating isn't going to give us an answer, is it? But I tell you what though, I want to nail the sorry bastard who did this to her. So, I guess for now, the whole point of this exercise is to get her to trust us.'

Instead of idle conversation, both detectives decided to check messages on their phones wondering whether there was anything pressing that they needed to take care of.

With only five minutes to the allotted entry time, both officers stood up, pocketed their phones, and headed in silence once more in the direction of the now familiar blue doors, in both anticipation and foreboding, not knowing what sights they were about to witness.

The door clicked open this time, and almost immediately they spotted a nurse dressed in a blue pin striped tunic, royal air force blue trousers, who told them where they would find Miss O'Connor.

'She's in a side room, but not for any infectious reasons you understand, but erm…simply because she's very, very emotional at the moment and can be incredibly tearful. So, her consultant felt that for her mental wellbeing, it would be better for her to be in a room on her own. She's not had any visitors so far, you're the first, but I must insist that you don't stay long. May I ask if you're friends or family perhaps?'

Both officers removed their IDs that were lying neatly inside a plastic see through compartment from black leather wallets and held them in front of the proficient, smart looking nurse as she led the way to room eleven.

The patient's door was closed, and on receipt of the third attempt at arousing someone from inside, the stifled mumble of 'yeah' could be heard, and so Jarvis gingerly pushed down on the door handle.

On entering the sparsely furnished room with its off white coloured bare walls, and a bedside cabinet placed beside the bed, the only other feature that could be described as a 'home comfort' was a high backed, olive green coloured plastic covered chair, and if it wasn't an inanimate object and could talk, it would be able to relay many a sordid story as to its occupants over the years. A huge benefit to having a single room was that, unlike those unfortunate enough to having to share a bay with as many as ten patients at a time, at least this occupant had the benefit of the privacy of a bathroom all to herself, which lay hidden behind the blue door within the room.

Smiling awkwardly, the Inspector tilted his head to one side and said to the woman lying in the bed, 'Good morning, it's Miss O'Connor, isn't it? I'm Detective Inspector Mark Jarvis, and this is Detective Sergeant Kelly Donnelly. May we sit for a moment, and…as we both realise what you've been through, we promise we won't take much of your time? Would it be alright if we were to ask you a few questions?'

Each detective picked up a chair by its arm rests and positioned them so that they were close enough so they would be able to hear what she had to say, but not too close that their proximity might instil a sense of fear, thus forcing her into a state of silence. With her body being shrouded by hospital bedding, the only part of her body that they were able to see was her face, revealing tiny strips of white tape, presumably in the hope of stopping blood from oozing from the cuts, and partially to assist the skin in the healing process.

Red deep welts dominated her youthful features, and it was obvious that she was unable to open her eyes as they looked almost glued together, her lips swelled almost twice in size as though she'd had a massive allergic reaction to something or had recently received cosmetic fillers that seemed to have gone horribly wrong.

Not wishing to frighten or, more importantly, intimidate the lone figure, Jarvis continued to speak in a controlled but serene tone.

'I know from the medical team who attended to your injuries, and even though they are considered severe, you are not considered to be in a critical condition, and they're also extremely confident of a positive outcome. So, whilst that's very encouraging news, the reason that we're here is that it should never have happened in the first place, and we need to get this person or persons who did these atrocious things to you.'

The young victim held her head towards the window even though she would fail to see the hundreds of red linear bricks peering back at her. She fiddled with a button on a small, grey pump lying on her bed where a plastic looking tube taped to the back of her hand delivered the Morphine to a body invaded with pain.

With the visible rise and fall of her chest, the relief must have been instantaneous as she lay her head back on the pillow and uttered the weakest of sighs.

Not quite knowing what to do, whether to stay or leave, the two detectives glanced sideways at each other, as they sat there whilst waiting for some kind of signal from the injured victim. Stirring slightly underneath the plain blue hospital covers, the senior officer figured it'd be a missed opportunity if he didn't re-start the conversation.

'So, Miss O'Connor, if you could answer just a few questions, where you're able to that is, then that would be most helpful to us.'

'Mm-hmm, yeah,' gently murmured the young lady as a strand of her strawberry blonde hair dangled across her face. 'Do you know whoever it was that did this to you Miss O'Connor, or…can you remember where it was that it took place, anything at all that you can give us? Why don't I ask you first of all if it was a man?' asked the senior detective in a soothing tone.

The wounded victim groaned as she ever so slightly nodded her head.

A rap at the door, and as it opened, a familiar head popped its head around apologising profusely, and suggested, 'I'm so sorry to disturb you Eva, but I think you need some rest now. These officers will have to come back some other time.' She glimpsed shyly at the two officers and quietly closed the door.

Jarvis initiated the departure from her room as he stood up to leave and lifting the chair up with both arms and replacing it back to where he found it, as Kelly removed her chair and stored it underneath the window. He crouched down so that his and the victim's eyes were at the same level, thus making it more personal, and chastised himself inwardly at not being fitter as his knees moaned loudly, 'Thank you so much for your time, Miss O'Connor but I agree with the nurse that we've perhaps tired you out. Would you agree if we came back, perhaps tomorrow or the day after, and carry on our conversation?'

Eva offered no response as they closed the door quietly behind themselves and made their way back to the car park in a sense of compassionate silence.

***

'Gather round everyone. Are there any new developments, any news on the house-to-house calls? Give me something, anything, somebody, anybody,' appealed Jarvis as he stood in front of the white board with both of his arms splayed outwards.

'Well, we've got an eye account from a seventy-nine-year-old man, a Mr Fred Wrightson who seems to…spend his time sitting in his bay widow since his wife died and to quote him, '*I've got nowt else to do now 'ave I?*' Anyway, he said that on the night in question, he saw someone carrying something over his shoulders, well to be more precise he said it looked like a body covered in a blanket or something and that he was carrying it like in a fireman's lift, and when I asked him where this was, he was proper shirty with me, and he said, and I quote, '*Well where else would they be coming out of except that dump of a bloody club.*' I asked him if he would give evidence in court, and he laughed out loud and said he'd be more than happy to if it meant that the place would get shut down. I have to say, I think I made a very lonely old man's day, you know like…something to tell his grand kids or his mates when he goes down to the local.'

Detective Sergeant Carmichael gave out a beaming smile as he relayed the last bit of testimony.

'That's great news, well done Dean. Did he say what time this was?'

'Yeah, he reckoned it was around ten fifteen, and he's absolutely sure of this as he normally gets his hot toddy ready at that time, plus he claims he doesn't even need to look at the clock anymore because he knows when it's time for his snifter.'

'Okay, so as you know, me and Kelly went to see Eva O'Connor in the hospital today and to say she's in a sorry mess would only be stating the blindingly obvious, but well we couldn't really get anything out of her apart from a definitive nod of the head to say that it was a man. Too early for anything else I'm afraid, so we'll just have to follow the lead from the neighbour and push the owner of the club and his sidekick as hard as we can.'

'So, shall we get round there now guv? Mind you, I wonder whether it's shut down since the fire, as I have to say I didn't see much action there when I went past it earlier' Javid remarked.

'I don't give a rat's arse whether the place is open or not, we need to speak to those two clowns again, and I mean today. So, get out there and bring them back in. If they don't come in voluntarily, then simply tell them that we have got a positive ID for both of them on the night in question. That should be enough to scare the shit out of them,' announced Jarvis as he strode briskly towards his office.

'Dean, you and me, eh?' asked Javid, as he picked up his mobile and his jacket from the back of his chair.

***

Two squad cars reached the club at eleven am., and like before, it wasn't going to be easy to gain access. Persistence is a word that comes with the badge and not one of them was going away until they'd got what they came for.

Obviously, the club wouldn't have had a full complement of staff at that hour of the morning, so there was no surprise when the familiar raspy voice of Jimmy Malone greeted them in the open doorway, recoiling from the sight of the four officers. 'What the piss do you lot want now? I and the boss told you everything you wanted to know, so can't you go and fu...I mean, leave us alone. This is 'arrassment this is, I ain't lettin' you in till I speak to Mr Cronin and well, he erm...ain't 'ere like. So, it was very nice to see you again and we'll be in touch,' and with that the very naïve bouncer, this time clad in a T-shirt with an enormous pair of pinkish lips on the front, with the words, *'I Can't Get No Satisfaction,'* turned his back on the officers and started to close the door.

Carmichael, being closest to Malone, swiftly jammed his foot in the doorway, chuckled and mockingly stated, 'Aww...Jimmy, don't be like that, we just want to have a little chat. I thought we were like mates, especially as we spent sooo much time together the other day. Now, this ain't how good friends treat each other now is it? So, let us in, and if you know where your boss is, you can give him a quick bell and let him know we want to talk to him. The sooner you do this, the quicker we'll be out of your hair. Now be a good fella and go find Cronin.'

'It's Mr to you. But look...there's no need to be like that, I'm not trying to be difficult it's just that well...things ain't been that good lately, 'cos well you accused us of beating up a bird, and then we get back 'ere like and the bloody place has been torched, and it ain't right, and it ain't good for business, know what I mean? Don't you think you'd be better off talking to some other dude, and find out who did these things to us, 'cos honestly, we ain't done nuffin wrong and I don't know how many bloody times I 'ave to tell you.'

'Of course, we understand you're upset about everything, but believe me once you get hold of your boss, we'll nip back to the station so you can answer a few questions, and hopefully that'll be the end of it,' Carmichael continued his calm approach until the ageing rock fan acquiesced to the officer's demands.

'Right, come in then. I don't s'pose I've got much choice anyway, 'ave I?' Malone left the detectives to meander around whilst he apparently went in search of his boss, insisting that he didn't have a clue as to his whereabouts.

All four men sauntered towards the back of the building where the fire had been. 'Could have been worse I suppose but I can't help wondering why they did a half ass job of it. I mean...why not set a match to the whole place instead of just this part?' enquired Josh, as he jiggled coins around in his trouser pockets.

'Ahem…gentlemen, what can I do for you this time?' enquired Cronin with a slightly haggard look on his face, 'As you can see, there's a lot to be done here, so with all due respect, I have very little time for small talk. So, if you'll get to the point, I'd be very grateful,' remarked the club's owner.

This time it was Javid who was quick to respond, 'Hi again Mr Cronin, and once again, we as members of the Metropolitan police force, are extremely sorry to have to bother you, but also once again we'd very much like it if you'd accompany us to the station to answer a few questions in connection with the young lady that you claimed you found lying on the side of a road, and then very kindly dropped her off at The Hamilton General,' responded the Asian detective in a heightened tone of sheer sarcasm.

'But we've told you all we know about that, and I thought it was agreed that me and Jimmy were innocent. So, really officers, if it means we're just going to be going over the same old crap again, I'm afraid that the answer is going to have to be a no, unless of course we're being arrested.'

'At this stage in our investigation, we aren't arresting you, but there has been a development in this case, and so things don't seem quite as cut and dried as you appear to think they are. So in light of this new evidence, it would most certainly be in your best interests if you would accompany us voluntarily, and that goes for you too Mr Malone.'

'Why 'ave I gorra go? I keep tellin ya I ain't done nothin, and anyway I ain't 'ad me breakfast yet,' whinged the ponytailed bartender.

'Huh…are you a diabetic, Mr Malone?' Dean requested whilst maintaining a straight, humourless face.

'Nah, I don't fink so, should I be?'

Dean cheekily grinned towards the club's employee and responded dryly, 'I tell you what, if you get a bit peckish, I'm sure one of us can rustle you up some bacon and eggs as we wouldn't want you passing out now would we? So…how's that sound, have we got ourselves a deal here?'

Mr Cronin glanced slyly at each of the four hovering detectives and realised that he'd got no other choice but to agree, stating almost as if he were granting them an interview out of the goodness of his heart, 'Okay, we'll come with you, but I won't be able to stay for any longer than an hour, 'cos I've got some workmen and builders due to arrive to sort out the shit that I've been left with. And it goes without saying that you'll bring both me and Jimmy back here, yeah?'

'Mr Cronin, you'll be coming with us,' reported Javid, as he and Dean led him to the front door and to the waiting car, as the Asian detective nestled himself behind the steering wheel with Carmichael keeping a close eye on the club owner in the back seat. Meanwhile, Jimmy briskly marched behind his boss and got into a separate car with DS Turner and DS Pettrini.

With both men being escorted towards the rather dull, grey building, signposted Stockfield Road Police Station, with its bright blue framed sliding doors where the nearby Beech and Chestnut trees reflected their long, wiry, leafless branches into the numerous, large windows, they made their way towards the lift as Javid pressed number two on the inside panel which would lead them to the interview suites.

Jarvis decided he'd sit in with the interview of Cronin and placed himself at the back of the room by the doorway, whilst DS Das and DS Carmichael sat at the table in front of the club's proprietor and Carmichael commenced the interview formally.

'So, Mr Cronin, you came here voluntarily to answer a few questions. The reason that we asked you to come here today is that we have gained new evidence regarding the attack of a young lady whom coincidentally you so kindly took to The Hamilton General Hospital. Firstly, we have information that confirms that someone was seen leaving your club, Cinders, with what appeared like a body thrown over his shoulder in the manner of a fireman's lift at around ten fifteen on the evening of 7th April. And, having spoken to residents along the street where you claimed that you found the victim, there wasn't one person, including a few dog walkers out on that same road at the same time, who saw a beaten-up young lady lying in a near unconscious state. They also said that if they were witness to something so terrible, they wouldn't have hesitated to dial 999. So, you see the dilemma that we face ourselves with now, don't you? It leaves us with the all-important question and that is, do you still maintain that you found this poor lady on the side of the street, or do you want to change your story?'

'I er…don't understand what you're saying. I thought this was all sorted out. I told you everything you wanted to know, and I really don't know how else I can help you. That person who said he saw something is lying, or perhaps he's got dementia or something and sees things. Like I said before, me and Malone only took her to hospital 'cos we were worried about her, and if she was to lie out in the cold all night, well…who knows what might have happened, she may have been accosted again, or wild animals may have got to her, 'cos you read about this sort of stuff in the newspapers all the time, don't you?'

'What you mean like wolves or coyotes, those kinds of vicious animals? No Mr Cronin, the only wild beasts out there that night was the bastard who pulverised her into a pulp. Look we know you didn't just find her, because she was found in a residential area and not everyone goes to bed at ten o'clock at night. So, the best thing you can do for yourself is to tell us what you know.' Dean could feel his anger rising as he banged his fists so hard on the table that he startled the now quavering bar owner.

'So, let's cut the bullshit and tell us the truth, because you're not leaving here until you give us something. And, well…let's face it, I'm sure we can find something against you about what actually goes on in your club which would, more than likely, be deemed as illegal, and I'm pretty sure that even if we didn't, somebody just might actually find something and with a phone call to the right person well…you'd probably end up shutting the place down. Now you wouldn't want that would you?' taunted the detective with his trademark shaved head.

'Look…you don't understand, this bloke's a nutter, he'll fucking kill me. Torching the club is nothing compared to what he'll do to me if he finds out I'm a snitch, so no I can't and won't do it, and you've gotta let me go 'cos I'm innocent, which I keep telling you and to be perfectly 'onest with you I'm fed up with the whole fuckin' sorry story.'

'So, let me get this straight, we all understand that you're a bit pissed off with being asked questions about a young lady who was severely beaten up, and her wounds could have been fatal, and that you'd rather we disappeared out of your lives and you go about your business, but you claim that you didn't violate her, and yet in the same breath you're also telling us that you know who did this to her?' Javid queried with furrowed lines appearing above his hazel eyes.

'I ain't saying any more about anything, and you've got nothing on me and all the blackmailing in the world about planting things in my club won't wash, 'cos I'll tell my lawyer everything about your threats, and that won't look good for the police now, will it? Can you imagine the headlines?'

'Well as we're here and you won't give him up, then we'll need to see CCTV coverage for the night in question. I'm right in assuming that you do have camera security installed?'

'Nothing would give me greater pleasure than being able to provide you with the evidence of that night, because then I'd get you off my back and then you'd be able to see for yourselves that neither me nor Jimmy had anything to do with it, but here's the pissin' bummer, he made sure that there wouldn't be any, because it got destroyed in the fire. So, I guess we're back to shittin' square one, ain't we? I think it's time to get my lawyer back in again if you're going to hold me for any longer,' remarked Cronin, with an air of undeniable agitation and helplessness.

Jarvis arose from his desk and jerked his head to the side as a silent request for Javid to meet him outside. 'We've got mug shots for both him and Malone, don't we? So, here's what I'm thinking. We show them to Eva, and we'll keep them here until we know for sure whether it was them or not? I can't honestly see them as violent blokes, crooks yeah, but not beating people up to near death and especially not women. So, I'll take Donnelly with me again, and you do what you need to do with the pair of them but keep the frighteners on them for now at least.'

Detective Sergeant Das re-entered Interview Room number three, and sat down in the same chair as before, re-commencing the conversation with, 'So now Mr Cronin, here's the question you seriously need to think about before you give us your answer. Are you now ready to co-operate, or do we need to get a search warrant and see whether we can get any evidence of illegal drug use, which as I'm sure you're aware is a crime, and one that you could go down for. Oh…and just in case you're wondering, we've got trained dogs that could sniff substances out of the most incredible so-called airtight hiding places. Trust me, you won't believe some of the most bizarre and ridiculous places we've found hidden stash.'

'I, I, I…want protection, guarantees, otherwise it's a no deal,' stammered Cronin, as his hand rubbed anxiously backwards and forwards across his bristled chin.

Both Carmichael and Das glanced surreptitiously at one another and bearing a grin, Dean casually remarked, 'So what you're asking us for is that you'd like a safe house, a new identity, passport that sort of thing, is that what you're implying Mr Cronin?'

'Yeah, that's about the gist of it I guess, otherwise I'm keeping schtum.'

'I think you've been watching too many American cop shows mate, and the point that you're finding it difficult to grasp is that huh…I'm not sure you're in a bargaining position, with respect…sir. You see, we either get you and your sidekick for this offence or you give up the name of the arsehole you claim did this crime. It really is that easy, and as the saying in the famous advert with the Meerkats in, says, '*simples.*' So, what's it going to be then, eh? But listen, I've got an idea, why don't we leave you alone for a bit so you can have a ponder and erm…reflect about how you should do the honourable thing, and let us into your little secret?' Both detectives stood up and pushed their chairs away from the table with the backs of their knees, and as they left the room, a uniformed officer entered and stood to attention in front of the closed door.

***

Jarvis and Donnelly used the Inspector's old burnt orange Peugeot to get to the hospital and decided on keeping dialogue away from the case and focusing predominantly on each other's social lives.

'Got any holiday plans?' asked Jarvis as the blades swished backwards and forwards across his windscreen, in an attempt to rid it of smudges and stains that were hampering his visibility.

'No not yet anyway. I wouldn't mind going on one of them river cruises to see the fjords, and if I had the money Iceland sounds bloody amazing, but I guess I'll just have to make do with looking at the pretty pictures in the brochures. What about you then, would ye be going away somewhere?' asked the curly-haired Irish detective with hints of her native brogue.

At the roundabout on Kildare Road, Jarvis signalled left where the signs to The Hamilton General would lead them to their destination.

'Not right now. We've got nothing planned as the boys are in the middle of exams and I'm not sure whether Ellie is feeling that brilliant at the moment, so we'll wait a bit longer until we make our minds up I s'pose.'

Finding a car park that had spaces was more difficult than when they were here before, but finally they managed to find one which was adjacent to the Neurology unit. As this was at the opposite end of the hospital from where they were previously parked, they needed to follow the blue signs to the Angela Ashby Ward which would afford them an increase in their daily step counter which they both lauded themselves as a positive achievement. 'Ah ha…that's me at 9,367 not bad for an old timer. That means I can have a couple of beers tonight, without Ellie having a go at me about my pot belly.'

'I think you'd have to do a few more than that before you hum…get rid of it, sir,' chuckled Kelly.

Taking the stairs up to the third floor to the area where they would find Eva, the senior detective pushed the button of the intercom and waited patiently until someone finally answered. Not being fobbed off this time by not allowing entry because it was too early, and with suggestions that they come back at a later time he was more than ready with his professional response.

'We only want to visit with her for a couple of minutes so that she can verify something for us, and as this is an urgent police matter, I strongly suggest that you let us in.'

'Hold on a minute, and I'll see whether she's having urgent medical care and whether she'll even agree to seeing you.' Click.

After a spell of a few silent minutes passing, the door was opened by some electronic device inside the ward, and as they heard the clunk of the unlocking system, Jarvis pushed the door open and proceeded to room 11 where the young victim was to be found.

Gently knuckle rapping on the door and waiting for a response before going in, he finally pushed down on the metallic handle and entered the room. There didn't seem to be much difference in the appearance of the twenty-two-year-old, and she'd obviously had a few of the Steri-Strips removed from around her eye sockets, but her hair was still stuck to her head most likely from dried blood and sweat as the room was unbelievably hot.

He kick-started the conversation, 'Hello again Miss O'Connor. We're so sorry to bother you again, but there's a couple of photographs that we'd like to show you, and if you're up to it we'd be more than grateful if you could take just a couple of minutes to look at them.'

Kelly removed the plastic wallets from her black leather shoulder bag, and approached the bed where Eva was ensconced with her bed clothes neatly arranged around her obviously petite frame.

Seating herself on the chair already placed beside the bed, she leant across to Eva and showed her one of the two mug shot pictures of both Cronin and Malone.

'Do you recognise this man, Miss O'Connor?'

With a simple nod of the head, Kelly proceeded, 'Is this the man who did this to you? Take a good look.'

Eva holding the picture, and squinting intensely at the owner of the night club, shook her head, managing a one-word response, 'No.'

'Okay, very well. Now, I wonder if you could look at this second picture, the same questions as before, do you know him and was he your assailant? Once again, Miss O'Connor, take as long as you want.'

The victim, clad in yet another hideous garment courtesy of the NHS, but this time it was an unflattering pink nightdress with tiny little flowers dancing around the fabric, glanced towards the female detective and once again shook her head.

'So, Miss O'Connor, you're absolutely sure that the two men in the photographs were not the men who attacked you?'

'Yeah.'

'Right, fine, erm…thank you very much for your time, Miss O'Connor, and if there's anything that you can remember about what happened to you, and you know it doesn't matter how small or insignificant you may think the information may be, we'd like to hear about it. And believe me when I say that we're going to find the monster that did this, of that you have our word. It might not be today, tomorrow, or even next week, but we'll get him.'

Eva turned her head to the window as they left the room.

***

Walking past the mayhem in the reception area with cries of 'I ain't dun nuffin it weren't me,' recited the rather bedraggled forty-something-year-old man, who was finding it difficult to stand in one spot without swaying from side to side whilst trying to remove a broken cigarette from a crumpled packet out of his back pocket of his badly stained dark blue jeans.

Jarvis and Donnelly sniggered, and both stuck a thumb up in the air towards the duty sergeant, who in turn, raised his eyebrows and shook his head slowly in a manner suggesting, 'What am I going to do with this joker, for fuck's sake?'

Entering the second floor and heading to the white board in the Incident Room, the senior detective summoned his fellow officers to gather around.

'So, we've just had it confirmed from the victim, that our guys were not the ones that attacked her. Now, I'm sure none of you will be surprised by this news, I know I'm not, so now we've got to find out who the real bastard is. We all know that the key to unlock this question, of course, lies with Cronin and Malone. Have we still got them here by the way?'

Javid, whilst casually perched on the edge of a table, reported, 'Yeah, they're still here boss, but neither of them is giving us anything and we haven't even got any CCTV to give us a bit of help as that evil piece of fuck made sure of that when he started the fire. I really think they're shit-scared of this dude and what he's threatened to do to them if either of them talks.'

'I think we've got no other option but to do round the clock surveillance on the club, and see if we get any clues that way,' suggested DS Turner.

'We also need to find out who was manning the front door on the night and lay a bit of weight on him as he probably won't know that the motherfuckers got Cronin and Malone by the balls,' interjected Carmichael, as he lazily slouched in his chair with legs outstretched and both feet crossed.

'So, anyone fancy some overtime if I clear it with the Super?' asked Jarvis scanning around the room waiting for some reaction.

Chapter 7

'It's your turn to get the coffee, I got it last time,' quipped Carmichael as he was heavily slumped in the front seat of the unmarked people carrier whilst peering lazily out of the tinted windows.

'Alright, alright keep your hair on. Just bloody make sure you don't fall asleep like you normally do and miss something. You know you can't be trusted on these jobs – you'd soddin' well fall asleep standing up if you could,' scoffed Turner as he opened the door carefully and closed it with even more vigilance.

'Just go get the fuckin' coffee.'

Checking his phone intermittently whilst remaining focused on the doorway to Cinders and the surrounding area, everything remained eerily quiet, as it had done for the preceding three hours, but then he spotted a single set of head lights cruising up the main road where a single amber light flickered on and off indicating that the driver was turning right towards the club.

Carmichael picked up the expensive police issued Canon 700 from the floor of the vehicle and with lens at the ready, he was in a good position to get a clear shot of both the black Range Rover with its tinted windows, and the man who was about to open the driver's side door.

He prayed that his buddy Josh wasn't going to come sauntering around the corner from the pub where he went to buy the coffee and perhaps attract attention from the man who was about to enter the premises.

Carmichael managed to get the registration plate and at least five shots of the man getting out of the vehicle from different angles, thus making it easy for identification purposes. The door of the club opened and out came a smartly clad man dressed in a smart pinstriped suit and shiny black shoes, and peering closer through the small but effective lens, it revealed the unmistakeable characteristics of the owner.

As good as a camera is at visual recognition, unfortunately, it's not much good at deciphering what people are saying to one another, but it has to be said, sometimes no camera is needed as body language will tell its own tale.

It seemed to Carmichael that the infamous Mr Cronin was not best pleased with the newly arrived visitor, and it appeared as though the security man who had been manning the main doors seemed to have blocked the doorway, in what can only be described as a way of prohibiting the man from entering the premises.

There was a lot of finger pointing, shaking of heads, and finally before the man got back into his car, he bent down towards Cronin and whispered something into his ear, and without another word escaping from his lips, the owner with head bent retreated back into his safe haven. The driver of the prestigious looking Range Rover slammed the car door shut as the rest of the shiny black metallic body shuddered in response, and in attempting to turn it around, he managed a very hasty three point turn before speeding down the same road that he had confidently cruised along some ten minutes earlier.

Carmichael could see Turner through his wing mirror carrying the two polystyrene cups of coffee, and so he thought he'd pull a fast one.

Opening the passenger door, the black detective gasped and swore heavily at the sight of his colleague slumped over the steering wheel and placing the two hot cups of caffeine fuelled liquid in the cup holders attached to the dashboard, he prodded and poked the man he left in charge of surveillance as part of the deal.

'You…f…'

'Whoa there, big boy, I was only kidding man. It's been quiet, apart from the odd taxi drop off, but then the last five minutes have been rather interesting shall we say.'

'Oh yeah, how so?'

'A bloke just arrived in a black Range Rover and it looked as though he and our Mr Cronin had words, he was refused entry and the old man sent him away with a flea in his ear. So, there's definitely some kind of history between them that's for sure, and you never know we just might get lucky. So, all we got to do is run the number through DVLA and see where it takes us.'

'Trust me to miss all the fun, perhaps I should do the coffee run more often eh? So, what do you say to us sitting it out until the joint closes for the night? Best drink it up before it gets cold though, and I never thought I'd ever say this, but I guess you've earned it.'

'Bloody hell, high praise indeed.'

'I'll call one of the guys and get him to do a check on the reg plate and then at least well have something to report to the boss tomorrow, and perhaps he'll be pleased that his overtime wasn't totally wasted,' Turner started flicking through his contacts page on his phone, whilst Carmichael blew and sipped on his hot coffee.

***

Having slept for a few hours, both Carmichael and Turner arrived at the station at around eleven in the morning, seemingly alert even though they'd only had a few hours shuteye. Passing by colleagues enclosed within their little cubicles with phones held in one hand and pen in the other as the click clicking of keys on keyboards reverberated around the metal desks where they sat, Carmichael enquired, 'Hey guys, what's up?' as he led the way to Jarvis' office.

As the door to their boss's office was always open, officers didn't need to knock, but out of respect for the highly admired Detective Inspector they both tapped the wooden door frame.

'Morning boss. We struck lucky last night, and it was confirmed by the photographs that we had developed earlier this morning that the guy trying to gain entrance to Cinders was none other than our Latino friend, Mr Lenny DaCosta. Cronin was there to meet and greet him and then he had him thrown off the premises after a bit of a shouting match, and when he left DaCosta looked really pissed, so it's my gut feeling that Cronin hasn't seen the last of him. To be honest with you, I think the boss of Cinders has just given us the name that we've been looking for, don't you?'

Turner placed the photographs from the night before in front of the senior detective in the chronological time order in which they were taken. 'Well, well, well. So, our paths cross again, eh? Well done you guys. Okay, I'm going to pay Eva another visit and show her these, but I reckon you're right lads, this is the evil son of a bitch that we're looking for, because we all know what this sick fuck is capable of, perhaps even worse than what he did to that poor girl.'

Detectives Jarvis and Connelly made the sojourn to the grim looking medical institution once more and found themselves re-treading the steps that they'd made twice before.

They were automatically allowed entry this time without needing to proffer any explanation as to why they should be allowed in to see the lady in room eleven once more.

Even though visual recognition was instant as the two officers entered into her room, the lack of facial expression on her face indicated one of two things, one that she shouldn't use all or any of her forty two muscles designed for scowling, laughing, eating, drinking, kissing, licking, or that she was still in a state of shock, denial, hatred, disgust, self-loathing, or most probably a drip, drip infusion of them all.

Jarvis showed the badly beaten young lady the photographs from the night before at Cinders and at long last the two officers were shown a flicker of recognition as she glimpsed briefly at the sight of the face on the latent images which were sitting side by side on the bright blue counterpane covering the bed.

'Miss O'Connor, have you ever seen this man before?'

Whilst trying desperately to make herself comfortable in the bed, it was obvious that any slight movement caused her considerable unease as the pain ransacked her body viciously, as she squirmed and grimaced.

Not quite knowing what to say, and feeling the ever-growing tension in the small hospital room, Jarvis broke the stifling silence with a humbling plea, 'I know what you must be go…' And for the first time, they actually heard her speak.

The words that flowed were slow and at times weren't clearly vocalised, but both officers certainly understood the gist of what she had to say.

'No, you don't know what I must be going through, because you've never had cigarettes put out on you like you were an ashtray or being able to smell your own skin burning like a piece of frying meat, so please don't insult me by saying that you can possibly understand what I'm feeling, either inside or out.'

Scrunching up a sopping tissue, and clutching it in between a clenched fist, the senior detective apologetically interjected, 'I'm sorry Miss O'Connor, it was very insensitive of me, and you're absolutely right, I haven't got the remotest idea of how you are managing to cope with all of this. Both I and Detective Donnelly just want you to carefully look at the photographs and tell us if you know the man.'

'*Yeah, I've seen him before,*' she reported, as she turned her head towards her sanctuary, the empty view outside the cold sheet of glass.

Jarvis leaned forward in the cheap, high-backed chair and quietly commented, 'I know this is going to be hard, but we have to ask you anyway, is this the man that viciously beat you, because if it is, we will need you to tell us your story and let us arrest him?'

'*No, I'm not going to do it, I can't. He'll get me; I know he will, so I hum...think it's best we just let it go.*'

Donnelly then took the lead, presumably in an effort to enforce female solidarity and a common understanding of the psychological impact that females had to tolerate as their bodies were constantly violated, 'Eva, is it alright if I call you by your first name?'

The woman in the bed nodded briefly, but still staring into oblivion, 'No one, but no one should have to go through what you suffered, and we both know that you're scared, but don't you see that what he's done to you he could do exactly the same to someone else, except the next time she might not be so lucky, and she just might, might...not make it.'

Responding to Donnelly's appeal, Eva directed her eyes towards her and her alone, '*I hear and understand what you're saying, and I s'pose I'm one of the lucky ones, because I've seen girls on the telly and in the newspapers when they've had acid chucked at them, and it used to make me really angry and sad, you know. But, well...if he did this to me when all I did was say something that he didn't like, what on earth do you think he's going to do to me if I hand him over to you? It won't be just his fists or cigarette ends, oh no...I think the next time he'll make sure I don't say another word to anyone ever, because d'you know what he'll make sure that the breath is sucked out of me for good. Is that what you want me to sign up for?*'

The Irish officer, determined to keep the dialogue open, pronounced empathetically, 'We hear you Eva, and you've got our word that well do all we can to support you, no matter what it takes, we'll keep you safe. But first, we need you to formally identify the man as your attacker.'

Shaking her head as much as the pain would allow, Eva responded with nothing but fear in her pale blue eyes, '*I don't know, I mean I know it's the right thing to do, but you've gotta understand, he, he...was just like a wild animal, and I think he'll stop at nothing to find me, and I'll bet you anything he's got people who are, more than likely, worse than he is who'll do anything he asks of them. Then what, huh...I ain't going to be able to help you guys get him off the streets, so…you tell me, how are you going to make sure that I'm safe eh, 'cos I don't think you can?'*

'All we can ask is that you think about it. Kelly can stay here with you to talk about everything in more detail if you wish and believe me when I say she's a good listener, so rest assured you can ask or tell her anything. Whereas I, in the meantime, will be speaking to higher ranks in the force to see about getting an officer posted outside of your house, apartment, wherever it is that you live, for when you return home. I'm sure whatever decision you arrive at will be the best for you, and I have to say its good to see you looking so much better than when we first met.'

***

Approaching car park marked D where their car was stationed on the fourth floor, the sound of Black Sabbath's 'Paranoid', made famous by one of Birmingham's favourite sons, Ozzy Osbourne, resonated from a shuddering mobile within the depths of the lining of the Inspectors black woollen jacket pocket.

'Jarvis,' announced the detective through the hidden microphone of the small, handheld device.

It was the sound of the Italian officer, Detective Sergeant Nico Pettrini, who quite alarmingly declared, 'Guv, we've just got a report of a man who seems to have gone missing, well…when I say missing, he's kind of not where he should be, which is with his other half.'

'Go on, Nick,' encouraged Jarvis opening up the driver's door of the burnt orange coloured Peugeot.

'I know it all sounds a bit barmy sir, but it's really weird this. See, this woman arrives at the station and says that her brother Robin, who's a senior physiotherapist, went to some kind of symposium and he's not returned. I went through all the usual spiel, how…you know some people may stay a few days longer at these sorts of things, because they may want to see more of the town or surrounding area or may have met up with someone they knew or have found something really interesting to visit, to justify them staying longer, that sort of thing, you know. Well, she wasn't having any of it, so guess what…she's still here, and she's insisting on seeing whoever's my senior officer, and she's not leaving until she does.'

'Right okay, but well…tell me this, how long's he supposedly been missing in action then?'

'She claims that he's not been seen for almost three days now and has not been contactable by phone either, or that's why she's got her knickers in a twist.'

'Alright Nick, I'll see you in my office when I get back.' Click. Silence.

I decided that I needed to start the ball rolling if I was going to see this thing through, and make them pay for what they'd done, or more importantly in this case what they didn't do.

I've got it all worked out you see, it's just a case of whether I can keep my nerve and not give in to my real feelings and kill them on the spot. The first one will be mine soon. I'm sure he's gay, not that I care a fuck about that at all, but if he'd only done his job properly then he might not be getting what's coming to him.

I knew how to contact him, that was the easy part, as I already knew his name; boy did I remember that, so…all I had to do was use the Internet, simple as that.

I didn't choose the particular day for any special reason it was just that the process had to start somewhere, so why not today?

The phone was answered by a friendly receptionist, 'Good morning, The Hawthorne's Physiotherapy Practice, how can I help you?'

'Good morning to you too, I was wondering do you have a physio there by the name of Hackman…yes, I'm sure that's the name that's been recommended to me?'

'Why yes, we most certainly do,' replied the pleasant, well-spoken lady, 'could you tell me what it's in connection with?'

I put my best woebegone voice on, and I even managed to sniffle loudly as if I was in some kind of distress, 'you see I need someone to come out and see my son, Simon, as a matter of urgency. He, he…well he suffers severely from multiple sclerosis, and I've been helping him with his exercises you know…so that his legs don't seize up, and normally he does alright, what with the medication and everything, but well you see, I can't get him up out of bed this morning as he's just so listless, and I've tried to ring the G.P but the line's always busy, you know what they're like, you can never get through, and I…'

I was doing so well before she interrupted me, 'Oh, I hardly think Mr Hackman is the best person for your son to see, as I honestly feel that the best place you could take him would be to the Accident and Emergency Unit at The Hamilton General. I'm not sure whether you're familiar with the area, but it's just on the outskirts of Upper Stanton. It's quite easy to find and I could give you the address if you wish.'

'Ahem…' blowing my nose hoping that she would hear my despair, 'sorry about that, but you don't understand. You see, my wife sadly passed away last

year, and the thing is, Simon hates hospitals because he associates them with losing his mother. So, I guess I'm begging you, would it not be possible for me just to speak to this Mr Hackman as I've heard about some of the marvellous things that he's done for people with Simon's condition. I mean, maybe he'll be able to find a slot for him, and if you're worried about payment for the appointment, let me assure you that I don't have a cash flow problem, and in fact I could pay in advance if that's what you want. But, before you give me your answer, let me just say this…if I lost the only thing that I have left in this world, then I really don't know whether my life will be worth living.' Not a bad performance at all, even if I say so myself.

Before she could respond to my request, I could swear that I heard a bit of sniffling and if I'm not mistaken her voice quivered ever so slightly, 'yes, yes of course, I'll put you straight through, but first could you give me your name?'

'Of course, it's Mr Finnegan, Declan Finnegan.'

'Okay, give me a few minutes and I'll see if he's in his office.'

Not long after, the man himself answered the phone, come on now…keep it together, as it's not long before he's all yours. 'Hello Mr Finnegan, how can I help you?' asked the rather serious man, with the merest hint of a Mancunian accent.

'Thank you for agreeing to speak with me Mr Hackman, I really appreciate it, especially as I know how busy you must be, fixing peoples legs, backs and other bits that aren't working properly,' I sniggered as I said this, but then apologised, 'sorry about that Mr Hackman, but I guess I'm a little nervous and excited at the same time that finally I may have found the help that I so desperately need. Anyway, I don't know whether the receptionist told you about my seven year old son, Simon's his name, and well…he's been struggling with M.S since the day he was born, and I really could do with your expert help and soon, because I'm really, really worried that if we don't get help then I'll lose him. And believe me when I say this, but I'll pay anything, anything just for him to live.'

'I understand, but I'm not really sure why you've come to me Mr Finnegan as there's a lot of physiotherapists out there who work in the community, and I'm sure if you went to see your G.P, then he'd make sure that you got to the top of the list for him to be seen, if you think that his case is urgent that is, and you wouldn't have to pay for treatment either. Or, as Mrs Paul our receptionist

may have advised you, that if you took him to A&E, he'd more than likely be admitted, and a physio would see him as a matter of urgency, because they don't want people staying in hospital for long, as they're desperate for beds. So, I guess all I'm saying is that I'm not saying that I won't see this young man, it's just that you do have other options and far cheaper ones.'

'Thanks for being so honest Mr Hackman, but as I explained to the lady on the phone, Simon really hates hospitals and normally he's such a sociable little fella but when he's in those kinds of environments he just kind of shuts down and won't answer the doctors or nurses when they ask him questions. Also, he refuses to take any medication when they offer it to him, so you see it would hum…really be a pointless exercise and one that could prove fatal.

Now, you asked me why I chose you, well it's simple, your name cropped up when I was talking with a very close friend of mine who told me that you treated his mother for quite a long time who has the same condition, and that you're nothing less than a genius when it comes to treating people with neurological disabilities. So, if your answer is yes, then I'd rather not waste any more time, because if he doesn't get up out of bed soon, then I'm worried about the long-term effects this may have on his condition.'

'Okay, Mr Finnegan let me look in my diary and see whether I can come and take a look at him some time this afternoon or perhaps early evening,' I could hear him flicking pages of his desk diary and sighing deeply, 'I guess I could come and see Simon at around 4:30 this afternoon. Now, all I need is an address where I can find you.'

I had my answer ready, 'That's very kind of you to squeeze us in like this, I won't forget it, ever,' again clearing my throat slightly and pretending to blow my nose, I uttered, 'I think the best thing is if I come and collect you, because the thing is well…we kinda live in the sticks, and I'm not exaggerating but you'll never find the house, especially at this time of the year when the trees are beginning to wake up after the winter, meaning the house really is hidden by all the foliage, and even if you were the greatest map reader in the world, I doubt very much if you'd find us. Of course, rest assured that afterwards I'd drop you either back at your practice, or even at your home address, if that's what you'd prefer.'

'I see, I suppose it'll be alright. I hope I'm right in assuming that you live around this area and that we haven't got to drive for hundreds of miles to get there,' he responded rather flippantly.

Punching the air with my fist as my face lit up with the broadest grin, 'I really can't thank you enough for giving Simon the help that he's desperate for, and I understand that you might be feeling a bit hum...how shall I put it, apprehensive as to where we live and everything, but if you'd rather well...then you could follow me in your car, I mean...I don't want to force you or anything?'

'No, and even though I've never met you, there's something about you and your voice that is somehow trustworthy, especially with the lengths that you'd go to for the sake of your son. And anyway, I'm really not the greatest driver in the world as I find that I cope better on roads that I'm familiar with and knowing me I bet I haven't got a lot of petrol left in the tank. Right let me see now...my last patient is due at around 3:15 pm so it all works out perfectly well. You never actually told me where you live, just so that I can jot it down in my diary for future calls, if I'm needed that is, and for billing purposes.'

'I guess I didn't, did I? We live about six or seven miles from the centre of Upper Stanton, so I guess it would take us about twenty minutes at the very most, and you'll get the correct address when we arrive 'cos I'd better be getting back to Simon now. See you around 3:30 then, yeah?'

Now all I have to do is wait. I've waited for this moment long enough, and now it's time for you to pay for what you did, or more importantly, for what you didn't do.

Chapter 8

Detective Sergeant Pettrini bopped his head up from his screened cubicle like a turtle gasping for air in the dark blue ocean, as he heard the arrival of his boss and Donnelly into the office suite.

Jarvis approached him on the way down to the interview rooms where Pettrini re-iterated what he'd been told by the anxious and seemingly pissed off sister of the so-called missing man.

The detective sergeant, not wanting the senior detective to believe that he hadn't taken the lady's concern seriously, rolled out her name, 'she goes by the name of Andrea Littlejohn guv, and she's in room nine.'

Approaching the designated room, Jarvis knocked lightly and without waiting for a reply strode into the room and seated behind a worn out, badly stained, dark wooden table was a well-dressed, forty-something lady, who sported short, auburn hair and on first glance, bore a rather portly figure.

'Ahem…' as the Inspector cleared his throat slightly to diffuse the deathly silence in the room, and continued, 'good afternoon, I'm Detective Inspector Mark Jarvis,' whereby the woman rose from her chair as they proffered an outstretched hand to one another in a customary manner of salutation.

'Please take a seat.'

The woman ran both of her hands down the back of her skirt before she sat down and stated matter-of-factly, 'Good afternoon to you too, Inspector. My name is Andrea Littlejohn and I am the sister of Robin Hackman, and that is the reason why I'm here.'

'This is Detective Sergeant Nico Pettrini, whom I believe you've already met. Can I interest you in a drink of some sort, but I feel I need to pre-warn you though that the coffee is disgusting, but we make a rather nice cup of tea, or if you prefer, I'm sure we can rustle you up a cold drink from the dispenser?'

Outwardly showing signs of nerves, the sister of the man who hadn't been seen for three days declined with a definitive shake of her head and continued to tap her fingers on the hard, wooden surface, almost as if she were practising on a keyboard, 'No thank you Inspector, I just want to get this over with.'

'So, hum…Mrs, have I got that correct?'

'Yes, that right.'

'Right, Mrs Littlejohn, can you tell both me and Sergeant Pettrini here what's got you so worried about your brother?' Jarvis queried, whilst keeping a fixed gaze on her round, pleasant face.

'Well, erm…I got the distinct impression that your Sergeant didn't seem to think there was anything for me to be concerned about, but I'm afraid I can't get it out of my head that there is something not right about all of this.' As she spoke, she became very animated and gesticulated with her hands dancing in the air in every direction possible, 'I'm sorry if it came across to you that I was disinterested, but I can assure you that we take each and every report of the possibility that someone has gone missing extremely seriously. What I was trying to do was to assuage your obvious worrying by telling you that your brother may have wanted to spend a bit more time in the area where the symposium was.

'And, as I'm sure Inspector Jarvis here will agree, we have over the years seen cases exactly like this where someone has been reported as missing and it turns out that he or she just wanted a bit more time to themselves, and the usual outcome is that normally the person always returns home when they're ready. That is, of course…those that want to go back home. You see, and this may be difficult for you to hear, but some people simply want to carve out new beginnings and they don't want to hurt the people closest to them by knowing that this is what they want, so they simply leave without telling a soul.' Pettrini side glanced towards his boss searching for confirmation that this indeed could be a plausible possibility, thus rendering some kind of reprieve that he had somehow dismissed the woman's fear that something had happened to her brother.

Jarvis acquiesced by reporting, 'Sergeant Pettrini is absolutely correct when he says that we take every case very, very seriously, but it is equally true that perhaps eight times out of ten, some people just don't want to be found, but that's not what we're saying about your brother, you must believe that. Now, how about, Mrs Littlejohn, you tell us everything you know, so that we can start joining the dots and try to figure out where Robin is?'

'Well, apparently, he didn't show up for work on Wednesday 6th April and according to Dominic, his partner, he received a text from Robin, and all it said was, *'Gone to a symposium.'* And that was it, that was all the information that he gave, no address, no mention of what the conference was about, nor when he would be home, we don't even know how he bloody erm…sorry, how he got there. That was six days ago, and I know my brother really well and let me tell you that this is completely out of character. He's not the sort of person that sends a text the same day that he's going away, because he's like an excited kid, he crosses days off the calendar, that sort of thing. And he would always have his clothes neatly pressed and piled on the spare bed ready to go into his suitcase days before he was even due to leave.'

'I see,' muttered Jarvis pinching the bridge of his nose with thumb and forefinger.

'And that's not all,' continued the interviewee excitedly. 'He's so meticulous with details, and normally if he was going to be gone anywhere for more than one night, he would let both me and Dom know all the specifics, absolutely every detail. We used to joke with him about it saying that we didn't need to know everything about his whereabouts, and that he was a grown man after all and free to do what he wants. I mean…it's not as though he's got any children to worry about. But d'you know what his reply was every time, *'You never know, something might happen, and you'd be the fools when speaking to the police that you didn't know where I was or where I was supposed to be, now wouldn't you?'* But, don't you see, this time he didn't tell us anything, which as I've just described, is just not him. Ironic, don't you think?'

With pen in hand, and note pad in front, Pettrini still gazing at the woman who was displaying higher levels of anxiety now that she'd convinced herself with even stronger evidence that her brother had somehow mystifyingly disappeared off the planet, suggested quietly, 'How about you give us some details first, is that alright? You say his name is Robin Hackman.'

'Yes, that's correct Sergeant.'

'Very well, so now if you could give us details as to his home address and where he works that would be of great help. And you previously told me that your brother's partner goes by the name of Dominic, and his surname?'

'Thurston, Dominic Thurston, and they've been together now for the best part of seven years, if I remember correctly. He's really lovely and they're such a perfect match, and I believe that they're already talking about going the full hog, you know, tying the knot, and quite frankly, we all couldn't be more excited and happy for both of them.'

'Now, I suppose what we really need to know is, huh…why is it that you've come forward reporting these concerns and not his partner, whom you've just admitted is extremely fond of your brother. Not that it makes it less important, but don't you think it's well, how can I put this sensitively, huh…slightly unusual for a sibling to raise the alarm, rather than someone who Robin is in a serious relationship with? You have to agree, especially to an outsider, that it does sound a bit strange, but then it's certainly not within our remit to sit in judgement on whether something that's either done or said is conventional or not.'

Whilst sweeping away a strand of hair from the side of her face, she looked at the officer and responded rather concernedly, 'Yeah, I totally understand why you would find this very difficult to grasp, but…you see the thing is that Dom well…to put it bluntly, doesn't seem to think that there's anything to panic about, and that he'll come home in his own good time. But see, here's the other thing, Dom as, huh…well become so withdrawn lately since Robin left, he doesn't answer my phone calls, well, he'll text but he won't speak to me. I won't say that that's what drove me to come and see you, but it all seems to be out of the ordinary, bizarre even, and as I said, completely out of character for both of them.

'You see, Robin and I have become even closer since the death of our father, and this strong relationship is so important for the sake of our mother's health, as she kind of gave up on well…everything if I'm honest with you. She didn't want to go anywhere, wouldn't cook, stopped meeting with her friends, and she just…hardly ever bathed, and she was just content to sit in the armchair all day staring at the bloody door as if she was simply waiting for him to come home from his short strolls to the shops, or from his days out fishing. And all of this was due to nothing more than complete and utter grief. We made appointments for her to go and see her doctor, but she refused to go, so that's when I and Robin stepped in, to see if we could instil a bit of life back into her bones.

'So, we started on the long road of rehabilitation I suppose you know, helping her with the mundane things like shopping, making sure she kept her appointments at the doctors, picking up prescriptions from the chemist, a bit of cleaning, mowing the lawn, well pretty much everything really. So, we've got a sort of rota going on between us, and it's been like that for the past three years, and neither of us has failed to keep our set days, and it's pretty much set in stone. But more importantly, it goes without saying that if either one of us is going on holiday, or is unwell, then we immediately notify each other, and this is another reason why I know that something isn't right.'

Both officers noted the intensity rising in her voice, and so it was with an air of calm resonating in his voice as Jarvis responded, 'We're so sorry for everything that you're going through at the moment, as it must be increasingly difficult for you to make any sense of what's going on, what with your mum and everything, but would it be okay if I were to ask you about the last time that you saw or spoke with Robin?'

With a heavy sigh, and with a slight but noticeable knocking sound of her foot against the leg of the table, she openly declared, 'Oh, I remember it well, it was March 31st and he'd just been around to mum's, as it was his day you see, and as I was within spitting distance I decided I'd pop in and see her you know, I couldn't not, now could I, as well….it just wouldn't have been right, and anyway he was just closing the front door as I walked up the garden path. He huh…said the usual, that mum was fine, and listed a few of the jobs that he'd managed to get done, and that she was dressed ready for bed, she'd had her tea and that he'd left her quite content, watching her favourite soap, Coronation Street on the telly. I remember I asked him whether he was going to come back in with me for a quick cuppa, but he declined and said that he needed to get home as he and Robin were going out with a couple of mates. So, we gave each other a quick hug, and I let myself in through the front door, and he drove off in his Mini, and that's the last I saw or heard from him.'

'Ah I see. So, when was it that Dominic got in touch with you?' noting that there was no hint of a profession for Robin's partner, Jarvis enquired, 'Is Dominic employed?'

'Gosh yes, he's a pharmacist at the chemist on Caldman Road, it's just off the High Street in Upper Stanton. I'm sorry, you must know it as there aren't many in our little town are there, and they're all so friendly and completely professional. So, to answer your question Inspector, it was Robin's turn to take mum to the doctors and I had a call from the receptionist at the surgery to say that she had failed to turn up for her appointment and that they'd tried to contact my brother, but he wasn't answering his phone. I called Dom on 3rd April, which was the date of the appointment, and it was then that he told me that Robin was out of town at this so-called symposium.'

The lady sitting opposite the two officers wrestled with a tissue passing it from one hand to the other, when the younger detective asked, 'One other thing that I think we need to know is, have either you or Dominic been in touch with his office, and have you any idea as to whether they were aware that he was due to go, or indeed, if he actually went to this conference? And perhaps even more importantly, was it jotted down in his diary? I mean…I…I'm assuming that if he hasn't got his own personal secretary or an assistant, then there must be, oh, I dunno…a receptionist that sorts out his appointments and knows where he is or isn't supposed to be, you know that sort of thing?'

'Well…when I first approached Dom to say how worried I was, he said that he'd do it, but I honestly hand on heart couldn't tell you whether he did or he didn't. I don't know what's got into him, he just seems to be, oh I don't know…off at the moment, certainly with me anyway, and he's really evasive almost to the point of not actually being that bothered. I even went around to their apartment because I wasn't getting anything from him apart from bloody texts, and I could tell that he didn't want me to be there, as he kept going on and on about how I was making too much of it, and that he was perfectly safe, and basically, that…I was making a mountain out of a molehill. And that's when I told him that if he wasn't prepared to take this thing seriously, then he gave me no choice, and that I was going to come and speak to you, because I'm at my wits end worrying about him. I can't sleep at night, and I've run out of lies to tell my mum when she asks me why he hasn't been around very much.'

'I can imagine this is all very difficult for you, Mrs Littlejohn and we thank you for all the information you've given to us. The next thing that we need to do is get one of our detectives to go around and speak with the receptionist or partner at Robin's office and then well take it from there. It's easy for us to sit here and say don't worry, but there's no question about it, its early days you know, and please rest assured that well do everything in our power to find out where your brother is. May I ask you, before you leave that is, have you got an up-to-date photo that we could have, perhaps on your phone, and also could you give us the address of his office, if you'd be so kind?'

Crouching over the desk whilst adding the address to the other snippets of information that had been garnered, each of the three people in the room stood up simultaneously, glanced at each other and bade farewell with promises that they would keep in touch.

With Mrs Littlejohn having been escorted to the stairwell and eventually the exit to the building, Jarvis returned to where Pettrini had obviously been hoping for a quick getaway as he pushed the hastily rolled up cigarette behind his ear.

'What d'you think guv?'

'She's worried that's for damned sure. I have to admit though that I think her partner's reaction seems a bit weird, if her suspicions that something has happened to her brother are correct. It could be that he and this Dominic fella have had a massive lovers' tiff and Robin's gone off to cool off a bit and his partner hasn't got either the balls or the nerve to tell his sister that this is what happened. It's all very peculiar.'

'D'you want me to go and talk to Thurston then?' enquired Pettrini tucking the manila folder underneath his armpit as he headed for the exit sign and down the two flights of stairs to get his nicotine fix.

***

I parked on the main street away from the centre and waited outside for him far enough away from windows and doors so no one would be able to see me.

I saw the figure approach me, and as he started to look around, presumably for the stranger that had successfully begged him for help but who remained only the man with the voice on the other end of the phone. As I gingerly approached him away from any secret eyes that may have been perched high on doors, gutters or any other surface that would reveal the identity of anyone entering the car park or the actual building, and offering an outstretched hand as an act of simplistic introduction, he asked curiously, 'You must be Mr Finnegan?'

'Hello Mr Hackman,' leading the way with purposeful strides to my van before he changed his mind, I turned around slightly making sure that he was following me and remarked with an infusion of animation, 'and can I say thank you so much for helping me and my little Simon. I wasn't sure whether I was allowed to park on the actual car park as I wouldn't be using your facilities so to speak, so just to be on the safe side I dumped it just outside here,' where the red van sparked into life on the silent command of an over eager thumb triggering the fob as it emitted the quick successive beep-beep sounds, as small orange rays pulsated swiftly from the head lights.

As my sacrificial lamb was now opening the passenger door, a quick flicker of light headedness swept through me, but not until the engine roared into action could I show any signs of overindulgent optimism.

Turning my head slightly to the right and left whilst steering the van, the man peered rather cautiously at me and reflectively asked, 'Have we met before Mr Finnegan, because from this angle your face seems very familiar?'

Pushing the fake, powerless, black rimmed glasses with his index finger from the bridge of his nose, he sweetly replied, 'Oh no, you must be mistaken Mr Hackman, I've never seen you before in my life. Mind you,' I theatrically guffawed, 'I bloody well get that all the time. There must be an unfortunate soul out there who resembles me big time. Poor sod.'

'Yeah well, I guess we all get mistaken for someone else sooner or later eh, just another case of mother nature having a good ole laugh,' sniggered the physiotherapist seemingly momentarily to cast away any doubts that previously had nagged away at him. 'Anyway, let's get back to the reason why I'm sitting in a stranger's car. I need to know everything about the treatment that Simon's

had since he was a toddler, and in particular details as to what medications and treatment worked and of course those that didn't.'

Staying perfectly zoned in on driving and deliberately not looking sideways at the passenger, I inwardly confessed that I hadn't banked on a barrage of bloody questions about a condition that I knew sod all about.

'So, the poor wee thing was diagnosed when he was around two and a half, and of course me and Veronica, that was my poor wife's name, we um…took him to see consultant after consultant because I s'pose we didn't believe what they were telling us, or it maybe it was a classic case of not wanting to hear the truth. Anyway, he was put on all sorts of medications, and they took scans, MRIs and they kinda said finally that his condition was irreversible, and that both he and we had just got to learn to live with it and manage his condition with the regimes and the programmes that they'd set out for us. That's about it in a nutshell, I'm afraid to say.'

'Mr Finnegan, what medication is he taking at the moment? Perhaps it might be that it needs reviewing again and that's why he's unable to move very well this morning? Have you got a number of the specialist nurses that you could call, because that's what they're there for is to help in cases of emergency and believe me there's not much that they don't know about the conditions they treat. Oh, and don't forget, the reason why they're employed in the first place is so that patients like little Simon don't have to be hospitalised and therefore, potentially take up a bed that someone else needs more urgently.'

Keeping my hands on the steering wheel in a clock position of ten to two and accidentally turning the radio on full blast so that my answer would be muffled, making it difficult for him to hear me, '…And he's been on it for about oh eighteen months now, and he's never had any difficulties since. So, no…I erm don't think it's got anything to do with the drugs that he's on.'

'Sorry, what was the name of the medication again, I didn't quite hear you?'

'We're almost there now, it's just around the bend here and then you can see all the bottles of pills for yourself,' as I smugly steered the van to turn right in the direction of an old estate that was destined for demolition which can't be seen from the main Paget Road due to, over grown trees, bushes, weeds, and was to all intents and purposes known as the dumping ground of anything and everything.

'You erm…live around here or is this some kind of short cut?' asked my passenger in a rather concerned voice.

'I guess it looks a bit slummy I have to admit, but I've managed to keep my property because I refused to give way to the high-flying developers. I gave them one hell of a fight, and well you'll see that I made the right decision when we get inside. It's got massive potential.'

'Is it much further, because I've just remembered that I haven't got long, I erm…have an appointment at five o'clock, you see?'

'We're almost there now Mr Hackman, and don't worry we're definitely through the worst of it, and I'll make sure that you get to your appointment in plenty of time. Simon will be so relieved and grateful that you've agreed to see him.

'I almost forgot to ask, who…who's looking after him now, as you said that your wife is no longer around? I mean, I don't remember you mentioning that you had any other children who could perhaps mind him whilst you were out.'

I almost felt sorry for the bloke as he rubbed his sweaty palms up and down his black jean clad thighs.

'Here we are then,' pulling the hand brake on and hearing the clatter of the keys against the dashboard as I turned the ignition off and glanced swiftly to the rather bemused man in the adjacent seat.

I could see him looking at the boarded up windows, with the roots of nearby trees having sought a way of finding a way out of the underground by ripping up the tarmac of the car park, and the old sign that had obviously been ripped off its prime position and hacked in two, leaving a picture of an old six penny piece on one side of the driveway and a house on the other, pieced together read, 'The Tanner House.'

'You, you…live here with your seven year old son?' he asked whilst running his fingers nervously through his mop of unruly dark, wavy hair speckled with a dusting of grey, 'See here Mr Finnegan if this is some kind of joke then I'm sorry, but I've got better things to do with my time, so if you don't mind, I think it's best if you drove me back to my practice.'

'Mr Hackman I can assure you that the outside is only a ruse, because well…if I do the place up, then the money grabbing council bastards will know that someone's living here, and then I'll be slammed with all kinds of bills. Then they'll demand to see certificates for this and certificates for that, have I *got planning permission, names of builders and architects that sort of thing, so you see this way…well I get to live here free, so to speak. You'll be pleasantly surprised when we get in, believe me. It's really quite comfortable, and I must admit I'm rather hurt to think that you could even suggest such an idea that I'd let my little man live in some kind of squalor.'*

I led the way to the back of the property as the rather reluctant physiotherapist grudgingly followed.

Fighting off the vicious tendrils of white flowered bramble, stinging nettles and the sticky weeds that weaved their way covering most of the ground whilst hiding any traces of pathway, I glanced over my shoulder and commented, 'This used to belong to my grandparents, well…they didn't own it or anything, they were just the licensees. When they died, the brewery were going to do it all up into some kinda swanky place you know, but then of course the thieving bankers caused that almighty crash years ago, and so there simply wasn't the influx of cash any more to do the place over.

'And now of course it's ear marked for an early death so to speak,' flailing his hands and arms around to rid himself of being stung by unwanted scrub, and by inhabitants of nests unused to being disturbed from their adopted homes, Hackman finally asked, 'Why are you living here then if it's due for demolition? I mean…it can't be safe, and then there's the question of gas and electricity. How do you keep the place warm, or cook meals for you and the lad?'

'It's quite simple, me and Simon live here because I was due to take over the place, and it had always been agreed with my gran and granpops even though I'm still not sure whether they agreed it with the brewery, but I just figured what the heck? I'd always had my own keys you see to help them around the place, and I was never on the payroll, so I guess no one really knew who I was. There were never any National Insurance payments made, no tax was ever declared, I was purely and simply someone who just came and went. So when the recession hit in 2008, I decided that I wasn't going to have what was mine taken away from me, so we all moved in and nobody has bothered us since. It was, I have to say, bloody easy to siphon off power, 'cos my mates think of me as a bit of a Del Boy, so don't you worry you'll be nice and warm when we get inside,' as we approached the back door, I slid the key from my key chain into the heavy cast iron padlock where the door screeched loudly, and opened.

I'd already cleared away most of the cobwebs, junk mail and squirted a bit of an air freshener around the inside a couple of days ago, so it wasn't too bad and my guest was following me every step of the way.

'Tada', theatrically outstretching my right arm to the inside of the once popular watering hole where a mahogany wooden bar and bar stools sat empty of life, with only the etchings of memories to keep them warm, 'So what d'ya think, cool eh? I mean there's no booze here or nothing, but well it's not everyone that gets to live in a pub where there's no customers.'

'Yeah fine, but erm…as I said I'm in a bit of a hurry, so why don't we go and see if Simon's any better, and then we'll be able to decide what sort of treatment is best for him, wouldn't you agree?' questioned the overly nervous man as he ran his hand across his forehead wiping away the fine beads of sweat that had gathered in the fine lines nestled above his dark, well-shaped eye brows.

Moving swiftly away from the bar I continued, 'I've transformed the basement into living quarters, and it's just down here, so…come on then, Simon will be wondering where I've got to.'

After freeing the locked door of its padlock and feeling around the wooden beams around the doorway for a switch that would emit sufficient light on the dusty staircase and the spiders' webs trapped with prey.

As we both descended the bare wooden staircase, the door slammed shut and it would be impossible to open it from the inside without a key, and this was tied to a cord and hung around my neck both day and night.

There was an old battered looking but serviceable green leather sofa which I pointed to and suggested amiably, 'Why don't you sit there while I go and fetch my son?'

Mounting the creaking treads and unlocking the door once more, I found the plastic carrier bag with the carton of orange juice that I'd bought a few days earlier sitting on the floor behind the bar. Digging deep into the worn out pocket of my black joggers, I took out the folded piece of tin foil and gingerly plopped both pills from the shiny, crinkly paper into the orange liquid and watched them swirl and fizzle into nothingness.

With both glasses in hand, I made my way back down to the basement where a voice exploded loudly into the silence, 'What the fuck's going on here Finnegan, and where is your supposedly sick son? If this is some kind of sick, sordid joke then let me tell you that I for one don't find it fucking funny. So, *just get me the hell out of here and get me back to my practice,' whilst prowling backwards and forwards like a caged panther.*

'Oh, come on now Mr Hackman, calm down. I've got us an orange juice each because I'm afraid that I forgot to buy fresh milk so we can't have tea or coffee.' I started sipping from the half pint beer glass and patted the leather cushioned seat stating calmly, 'I'm not going to hurt you I promise. I mean do I look like some mass murderer?'

'Just tell me…what is it you want from me? I…I've got money, you can have that and I won't tell a soul, I promise. Please…I beg you, just let me go and I'll call a taxi and well…we need never mention this little episode again to anyone.'

'Just come and drink this, and we'll have a chat and I'm sure we can sort something out. Here you are,' cautiously peering at me whilst slowly surrendering to his impossible plight. Perching on the edge of the cold sofa and staring blankly into space, he finally picked up the glass and drank almost greedily, whilst I continued, 'Right, where to begin. You said when you got into the van that you thought you recognised me, well I'm a bit angry with myself about that because you weren't supposed to, but yes you're quite correct Mr Hackman, our paths have crossed before now. You see, the reason that you're here, oh and by the way as I'm sure you've guessed by now, there is no sick Simon.

'You're here to be taught a lesson and to somehow, oh let me see now…make amends and perhaps reflect on what you did, or in your case, what you didn't do for the most important person in my life,' making no obvious reaction apart from a series of thick furrowed lines which suddenly appeared across his brow the beleaguered looking man lay the empty glass on the bare concrete floor and simply cradled his head in his hands.

After what seemed to be an incredibly lengthy pause he finally pleaded with outstretched arms in the air, 'I really still don't understand what it is I'm supposed to have done. If you tell me that I made an error in judgement over some treatment to someone in your family or close circle of friends, then I'm really sorry and I promise I'll try and fix whatever it is you think I've done. Please just give me another chance to prove myself and nobody, I swear nobody need ever know about this. Ever.'

'You had your chance Hackman and I watched you with your so-called treatment, and you made her a laughing stock. I followed you from the gym in

the hospital where you'd had a session with her, and you were with a student or a bloody assistant and without even bothering to look around to see if anyone was in earshot, or even to speak quietly, you leant into her and casually remarked, 'Bloody hopeless case, she's absolutely FUBAR, and then d'you know what you did, you fuckin' well sniggered.

'The young lady that you were with asked you to explain what the letters meant, and you replied, and believe me I heard it quite clearly, 'Quite simply it means, fucked up beyond all repair.' You swaggered along as if you were some kind of a god and put your arm around the young trainee as she was sniggering away at your so-called pun. Well, it's not so fucking funny now, is it? So, you see hum…now it's your turn to feel what it's like to rely on someone's compassion and empathy in the hope that they have a fighting chance of getting their life back. Your failure to help the love of my life shattered all of the dreams that we'd made. So, my friend, you'd better start praying that you're gonna be able to live out your dreams,' no longer listening, the man beside me suddenly slumped back as the Rohypnol had at last started to flow through his veins.

It took me a lot longer than I thought it would, and he was certainly heavier than he looked as I dragged his sorry arse over to the bed and with high levels of adrenalin now, I was able to haul him onto it. Having done my research as to the benefits of zip loc ties as a form of restraint I tied both his right arm and leg to the metal frame on the side of the bed.

Grabbing the phone out of his jacket pocket and seeing the face of another dimwit fuck on the screen which was obviously his gay lover I opened his messages and reading the last one from some geezer called Dominic I figured this was Hackman's nearest and dearest and typed out four words, 'gone to a symposium,' pressed send and flung the phone at the wall.

Chapter 9

Pettrini, after attempting and consistently failing to contact Dominic Thurston by phone at his place of work, residence or even on his mobile phone, decided to pay him a visit at his home. He knew where he could find the chemist as his home address was given to him by his partner's sister, Mrs Littlejohn. So, punching in the details he finished the latest instruction with the postcode, and satisfied that the system had accepted the information, he let the satnav do the rest of the work.

Nico arrived at the rather elite looking apartment complex at 19:45 pm, and whilst standing outside the closed security doors, he found himself running his forefinger down the aluminium front door panel affixed to the wall, and having found the right name, leaned close to the speaker on the entry system, where after a couple of minutes a voice emitted out of the mouthpiece.

'Good evening, Mr Dominic Thurston?'

'Yes, who wants to know?'

'This is Detective Sergeant Nico Pettrini, and I'm sorry to bother you Mr Thurston, but I wonder if I could have a word?' The young officer always hated these speaker systems as it was impossible to know how much the person on the other end was able to hear, but he figured he'd spoken clearly enough to be understood.

'What's it to do with, because I'm rather busy at the moment, as I've just got back from work. Is it something that can wait until tomorrow or another day?' replied Thurston irritably.

'I'm afraid this is rather a sensitive issue, and I don't think it's one that should be discussed in shall we say…a public place.'

On receipt of that information, a clunking sound resounded, and magically the outside doors to the apartments were opened, granting Pettrini access.

Nico climbed the stairs to the second floor, and with a few footsteps found himself looking at a solid oak door, adorned with brass numbers delineating the number twelve with an impressive lion headed door knocker which, he chuckled, seemed to engulf the wooden frame. Rapping loudly with two knuckles on the door, Pettrini announced his arrival. The apartment owner must have already been behind the closed door as it was opened even before the rapping had time to penetrate through the wooden panels.

Holding out his identification badge in front of the blonde, spiky haired man, who was sporting a goatee, clad casually in denim and barefooted, he peered at the stranger in the tiny rectangular card being held out in front of him and muttered matter of factly, 'Well, I suppose you'd better come in then, hadn't you?'

'Thank you for agreeing to see me, Mr Thurston, and I'm sorry to disturb your evening, but hopefully this shouldn't take long.' closing the door behind himself Pettrini noticed a helmet and hoping to diffuse the obvious tense situation declared somewhat with an air of optimism, 'Ah, I see one of you is a cyclist. I love it too, great feeling with the fresh air against your face, and that great sense of freedom, don't you think?'

The short, but rather curt reply, certainly set the tone for what was undoubtedly to be a formal meeting with no exchange of idle conversation, 'That's not actually a cycling helmet, it's the one I use for my Kawasaki, Sergeant.'

Being escorted to the living area, Pettrini couldn't help but admire the chic pieces of furniture that lined the small, elegantly neat hallway, with its stone coloured, bow legged console table bearing a pewter looking dish where keys, and loose change were deposited at the end of the day. Synthetic lilies perched in a vase of the same dull looking metal, and stone white walls were adorned with old fashioned, almost antique looking lamps which shone brightly on the plethora of portraits of both men.

Entering the sitting room, the detective was invited to sit on one of the dark brown leather chairs in a room that was defunct of evidence of anyone ever having lived there, no books, magazines, newspapers lying around, no used coffee cups, nothing but organised emptiness.

'Officer, can I offer you a drink of some kind? I can only assume that the anecdotal phrase of never while on duty to the invitation of alcohol applies, but perhaps I could interest you with a cup of coffee, tea or a glass of boring old tap water?'

'No thanks, I'm fine, but you go ahead, don't mind me. I know what it's like after a hard day's slog,' chortled Pettrini. 'Sometimes it's just seeing the booze in the glass that really relaxes you, without even needing to taste it. Anyway, I'm going to get straight to the point, Mr Thurston, I'm here regarding your partner, Mr Hackman. Oh, by the way, any objection if I record this conversation on my phone?'

Thurston nodded and muttered, 'Go right ahead.'

'Thank you. Anyway, we've had a visit from a Mrs Andrea Littlejohn who says that her brother Robin, has, according to her, not been contactable for the past six days; no one has seen or heard from him since he went to a medical conference. So, I guess what I need to know is this, firstly, aren't you concerned about where he might be, and secondly, have you managed to get in touch with him?'

'Huh…well, I'm not sure I can tell you anything more than Andrea's already told you.'

'Ah you see that's where most people are wrong, there's always something that a person will inadvertently forget to mention, and you'll be very surprised when I tell you that, research has proved over the years, that no two people will remember the same things, even though they've been at the same place at the same time. Hard to get your head around that statistic, isn't it? So, why don't you tell me what you know about the day that he failed to come home, which erm…I believe I'm right in thinking was 31st March?'

Running his fingers through his short, gel infused hairstyle, Thurston was quick to remonstrate, 'As I've said over and over again to Andrea, he's quite safe, of that I'm absolutely sure, and maybe he just needs a few days on his own, you know, without me constantly nagging at him to tidy his clothes, and give him a subtle nudge when it's his turn to do the cooking. Actually if I'm honest with you, I'm a bit of an old woman when it comes to having everything done by the book, so to speak. Yeah…now that I come to think of it, and of course it makes sense, that he's just gone away for a bit of a breather from me,' outwardly displaying an unconvincing grin at the very idea that this was what he actually believed.

'Forgive me for saying this Mr Thurston,' remarked Pettrini, 'but that last comment that you made almost sounded as though you were convincing yourself that he was safe. I have to repeat sir that if you know anything at all, then it's your duty to report it to me here and now.'

Lowering his head in silent acknowledgement and crossing one leg on top of the other with his ankle lying on top of his thigh he reluctantly commented, 'I don't know why I said that actually, I guess I'm just not used to having a copper in my home. Call it nerves if you like, but I just have to re-iterate that I know he's safe and well, and he'll be back in no time and I've got every confidence because he knows when he's on to a good thing, what…well I mean to say, he's got me hasn't he, so why would he throw that away? And anyway, he absolutely adores his mum, so nah…he's not gone far.'

'I hear what you're saying, and it's comforting to know that you're so confident that nothing's happened to him. But, let me ask you this…have you any idea where this symposium could be held, for instance, is it in a convention centre, hotel, hospital?'

'Huh…no I haven't, because quite frankly he never mentioned a word about going to a convention of any description, so why would I check on details that I know nothing about?'

'So basically, we have nothing to prove that there even was a conference, is that what you're implying Mr Thurston? I mean, to all intents and purposes, he may have left the country and gone on a holiday. Have you even checked whether his passport is where you'd expect to find it?'

The thought of checking for this vital piece of evidence never entered into the pharmacist's mind, so he rose from the chair, and as the weight was lifted from the seat the leather groaned and creaked, and as Thurston entered into an adjoining bedroom, Pettrini could not fail to hear the sounds of drawers being hastily opened and banged shut.

'Well, we know for certain that he hasn't boarded a plane,' energetically waving the burgundy booklet where the royal coat of arms was emblazoned on the front in gold at the young Italian detective, 'Look what I found.'

'At least we know that he's still in this country then, so that's something I suppose. Now, another thing I need to ask is…have you been in touch with his office? Have you checked how much clothing he took with him, toiletries you know…that sort of thing.'

'Well, no I haven't, because I didn't realise that I needed to spy on my soon to be husband that I've known for six years, and for what…that he hasn't been home for six days. Sergeant, you've got to realise that even though we're romantically involved we're not chained to one another, and the sooner Andrea realises that the better. She's taking this to another level and there's really no need, because he'll be back when he's good and ready, which is what I've been trying to tell her and you, so now I'm really hungry and I need to start getting my supper ready.'

'That's all very well, but I would still like you to go and check whether you can see how much of his personal possessions have gone, if you wouldn't mind, Mr Thurston.'

Shaking his head negatively and pointing his right forefinger towards the detective he snarled bad temperedly, 'Have you any idea how many clothes your wife, girlfriend, male friend has? How should I bloody well know whether any of his stuff is missing? And let me tell you that man has so many jars of cream for dry skin, normal skin and bloody oily skin, not to mention the bottles and bottles of nonsense that he's got piled up high for his mop of unruly hair, that it's an absolute miracle that there's any room in there for my gear. So, once again, no I wouldn't have a clue whether he's got his deodorant or not, or a clean shirt, or even clean bloody boxers, because it's quite simple, I…DON'T…KNOW.'

'Alright, one last thing and then we'll call it a day for now. At what time did you receive the text message to say that he'd gone on a symposium?' Pettrini glanced across at the man who was flicking through the screen on his mobile with his thumb to find his partner's last message.

'Three thirty in the afternoon of March 31st and that's the last message I got from him.'

Nico made his way to the doorway with Thurston following closely behind when the young detective stopped to look at one of the many photographs lining the walls, pointed to one and remarked admiringly, 'Ah…this is a really good photograph and such lovely views, erm…where was it taken, can you remember?'

Losing his patience, the other man barked angrily, 'No, I can't…. now if you don't mind?' hastily grabbing the door handle and pulling it open with such force sending the security chain loudly clattering on the doors cold, wooden surface.

Thinking that he'd seen the back of the detective he was about to slam the door shut when Pettrini barred the action of its closing with his foot, and issued one last request, 'Oh, just one more thing, Mr Thurston. We don't seem to have a photograph of Robin, which is why I stopped to admire the one in the hall, so is there any chance I could have one now? I'll wait here if you like, that won't be a problem, will it?'

Nico tut-tutted to himself, shaking his head in disbelief as he overheard the denim clad male swearing and cursing, and once again noisily opening and banging shut drawers in the pursuit of the requested photograph.

Handing the picture over to the officer, Thurston quipped sarcastically, 'Hope this one will be okay, and sorry that you can't see his feet, but I'm right in assuming you'll be able to imagine what they're going to look like, eh?'

'Looks alright I s'pose. When was this taken Mr Thurston? Or perhaps more importantly could you tell me has he changed much since he posed for this?'

'Oh, for fuck's sake man, I haven't got a bloody clue, but I suspect it's probably about two years old, and no he hasn't changed, he hasn't got older, fatter or thinner since then. Now for the last time, if you'll excuse me I need to have some dinner.'

Scratching his scalp whilst still hovering at the half-closed door, Pettrini asked, casually perusing pensively at the other man, 'There's just one other thing I forgot to ask you, which I guess is kind of important, well I think it is. Did Robin take his phone charger with him, and I know you're probably going to say that they're easily replaced these days, but if I was going anywhere, and I mean anywhere, I would always make sure this was the first thing to go in my bag. So, is it still here or what?'

'Are you serious? How the hell should I know if he's taken his damn charger with him? I mean…I know where he usually charges it up, but like every other normal human being, he may have one, two, or even as many as three stashed away. Like I said before, we may be in a relationship, but I don't know everything about him, and he certainly doesn't know everything about me. Satisfied?'

Attempting to close the door finally, Pettrini's foot once again barred the apartment owner from escaping his final question, 'Did you and Mr Hackman have an argument or a …disagreement the day or night before of March 31st?'

'Not even going to answer that. I think I've put up with enough from you this evening, Sergeant Pettrini,' and with that, the man walked back towards the living area, leaving the door to slam shut under its own volition.

No point staying around any longer, the detective slowly descended the metallic staircase and made his way through the leafy suburban street to where his Volvo was parked. Magically unlocking the doors as the fob was pointed at the car, Pettrini got behind the steering wheel and listened to the gentle purr of the engine as the wheels started to move.

As he drove along in the darkness of night with the well-lit streetlights helping him to steer his way, he couldn't help but notice couples going out for a late-night stroll, dog walkers eagerly trying to keep up with their four legged friends where excitement at the idea of a final walk led them to high energy levels. Youngsters dressed in fashionable gear, eagerly striding in haste towards their favourite hot spot helped to change the young detective's mind from not returning to the station but to a nearby pub so he could get himself something to eat and a much-needed drink.

Sitting there mulling over his half pint of bitter and savouring the gravy filled steak pie, his mind wouldn't or couldn't let go of his suspicion that Dominic Thurston was holding something back, and his behaviour in answering the most basic, simple questions about his forthcoming betrothed was, to say the least, baffling.

***

Pettrini messaged his good pal Josh Turner to say that he would be late in as he was going to the offices of Robin Hackman and that they would see him at some point.

He arrived at the offices of Lime Acre Private Physiotherapy Practice, which was situated on Lavender Road, Middleton just shy of ten in the morning. The car park was virtually empty, and he climbed the two steps of the well-presented entrance with its large, grey containers housing healthy looking, ever green plants, of which he was ignorant of the name. His body heat announced his arrival as the automatic doors whooshed open displaying a clean, bright and impeccably tidy reception area.

He approached the desk of the middle-aged lady who appeared business like in her black trouser suit brightened up by a red polka dot blouse, which seemed to be the same shade of red as the frames of her glasses.

Holding his ID badge in front of the woman seated at a pine-coloured desk he issued a salutation, 'Good morning, my name is Detective Sergeant Nico Pettrini and I would just like to ask a few questions in connection with a Mr Robin Hackman, whom I believe is a partner in this practice.'

Noting from the badge which was secured to the lapel of her jacket he learnt her name, 'Why, yes of course. As there's no one here and I'm not expecting another patient for the next fifteen minutes, would this be okay right here, and then I'll be able to answer any incoming calls. Or we could sit over there where it's more comfortable, if you like?'

'I think over there might be better,' pointing to a seated waiting area which housed a glass topped table hosting an array of differing magazines from the popular glossy variety to Gardeners World, National Geographic and of course copies of sports medicine and one simply entitled, 'Frontline' which prided itself as being the voice of physiotherapy.

'So, Miss Paul, may I ask if you've had any communications with Mr Hackman since 31st March?'

The short, wavy-haired lady responded as she nervously turned her wedding band around and around her ring finger, 'Well, the answer to that is simply no, we haven't heard or seen Robin since the 30th actually. We obviously thought he was poorly, so we didn't think too much about him not turning up to the practice, you know. Mr Findlay, the senior partner, always believes that when someone is not well, then…it's only proper that they're left alone so that they can get well, and he also knows that no one who works here takes time off just for the sake of it, and he's absolutely right we're just not like that here.'

'That's fine. Well, we all know now that Robin wasn't ill, he was apparently at some kind of a symposium. Have you had any notification of such an event taking place, and that perhaps everyone just forgot to jot it down in the diary, because that can happen. You know, *'Ooh I must remember to note that date down when I get a minute',* and then the hours in the day just fly by and the moment's gone, and the message doesn't get passed on. And please Mrs Paul don't think for one minute that I'm suggesting that you're incompetent, because that's the furthest thing from my mind, so I hope I haven't offended you, but if I have, then I apologise profusely.

'You see, according to his sister, Mrs Littlejohn, Robin used to get so excited about going on trips that he used to cross dates off in the calendar, and he would always take days to get his clothes and personal stuff ready, all neatly laid out on the bed, that sort of thing you know, but this time, well…there was no mention of any trip and none of the hype that he would usually go through. No excitement, no post it notes to remind himself to do this, or take that, in fact there were no clues to suggest that he was going anywhere, so you see Mrs Paul, we're in rather a bit of a quandary.'

'Can I ask you to please call me Lorna? It really is a bit of a muddle isn't it, because you see detective, the only time that we heard that there was any suggestion of Robin being at a symposium was when Andrea called, who was frantic to know why Robin hadn't contacted either Dominic or her, after I think it was about five or six days, and she insisted that this was most unusual. She really was in a bit of a state, talking about her mother's doctor appointment having been missed, and I know she wasn't accusing me that I wasn't telling her the location, or even what the so-called conference was about, she just thought that both I and Mike, erm…Mr Findlay, were keeping his whereabouts secret for some weird reason. I tried to reassure her of course that I didn't know anything about any conference, but then she blurted out that if I or Mike weren't going to give her the address, then she would have no other alternative but to go to the police. So, I guess to sum up detective sergeant, I have no information whatsoever to give you, which I'm desperately sorry about.'

Pettrini stood up silently and made his way to the water cooler, pulled out a plastic cup from the bottom of the dispenser and poured himself a cold drink, 'Can I get you one Lorna?'

'No, thanks I'm good.'

Approaching the seating area whilst gulping the refreshing colourless liquid, he calmly commented, 'We've been in touch with all of the local hospitals, and so far, he's not turned up in any of them, which is encouraging at least. Is Mr Findlay in today by any chance?'

'Yes, he's here, but I'm afraid that he's having to see all of Robin's patients as well as his own, so he's really back-to-back the entire day and in fact the whole week, well…until we can get a locum in, or even better, when Robin returns to us.'

'I wonder if you could tell me Lorna whether you or Mr Findlay are aware of any enemies that Robin may have. You know, maybe a disgruntled patient who thinks perhaps they're not getting value for money, or that their problem hasn't been fixed, that sort of thing? Has he received mail through the post that he may have found distressing, well…that you're aware of I mean, as I'm assuming that, as you're a relatively small practice that you'd chat about things like that, perhaps in the staff room over a cup of coffee, or at the pub at the end of the day?'

The lady sitting opposite simply shook her head politely, as Nico scrunched the plastic cup up with unintentional fierceness, aimed it at the wastepaper bin, missed, and had to get up reluctantly once more and drop it into the receptacle.

'We've got a really good rapport here with one another, but sorry detective, Robin's never mentioned anything nasty, or…ugly that's been said or sent to him. I'm absolutely certain that if he had, he would have mentioned something, and knowing him he would probably have found it amusing.' Lorna chuckled momentarily, as she uttered this last sentence.

'Well, how about billing then? Is there anyone that's not paid their bill and is mounting a huge debt to your firm, and huh…perhaps polite reminders have been sent, to which the recipient may have taken umbrage to? Anything like that happen lately that Robin may have been made aware of?'

'Of course, detective, we do send reminders out when a client hasn't paid for two months or longer, but mostly all they need is a slight nudge in the right direction, and then payment usually arrives within a day or two. So, I'm afraid, that that line of enquiry won't be of much help to you, but what I could do is go through all of Robin's case notes, and see whether there's anything untoward, you know like a post-it note saying something or other that he doesn't necessarily want me or Mike to see.'

'Have there ever been any patients that wish to change from having Robin treat them in favour of Mike, purely for the fact that Robin's gay? I know in this day and age probably nobody really gives a damn what sexual persuasion a person is, well…so long as they're getting the treatment that they need, and that it's the right one for the diagnosis, but we don't live in a perfect world do we? But sadly, there are still ugly people out there that feel that it's okay to be homophobic, know what I mean?'

'I'm so sorry detective but once again I can offer you nothing, as I've personally never heard of any slurs or insults that have been directed towards Robin, and he's not said a dicky bird about it either. So, I guess that's a no then as well.'

'Not to worry, we cops need to ask all sorts of questions which could be plausible in this kind of unusual situation, because in our experience it's usually someone that the person knows who's behind cases of this sort. Now I was just wondering, if when you're going through his clients' files, well…if you find anything, it doesn't matter how insignificant you may think the information is, then would you do me a favour and call me?'

'Of course, not a problem,' responded the receptionist, arising from her chair and extending her hand to wish the detective farewell.

'Oh…I almost forgot, could I have all the names of his clients that he's currently treating, and has treated within the last oh, I suppose…twelve months, and a copy of all appointments for the previous six months?'

'Yeah, I can get that to you within a day, or two, at the very latest.'

Moving towards the automatic exit doors, Nico turned and suddenly remembered, 'Just one more thing, and then I really will leave you to get on with your work. Does he hum…only treat patients here, or does he go into people's homes, care homes, hospitals, you know…that sort of thing?'

Lorna moved casually towards where Pettrini was standing and gliding her hands in her trouser pockets she answered excitedly, 'Oh my goodness, yes well…both he and Mike go all over the place, but it's mostly Robin that does the travelling around, because he says it gets a bit boring being here all of the time. He actually does a lot of locum work at The Hamilton General Hospital just outside of Upper Stanton, you must know it.'

'Know it well, but I don't suppose you know which wards he covers? I mean…are they always the same, or are they kind of picked at random? I guess what I'm saying is, does he get sent anywhere to cover for staff shortages, that sort of thing?'

'Well, he specialises in neurology disorders, for example, motor neurone disease, Parkinson's Disease, then there's the head traumas you know, like after car accidents which leaves the patient with poor balance both sitting and standing but his main passion is with getting patients to be able to get back to some kind of normal life. He is so passionate about these victims, as he so rightly calls them. Oh, my goodness what a silly bloody fool I am for not remembering before now,' she exclaimed by banging her forehead with the palm of her hand. 'You see a couple of days before Robin failed to come to work, a man called up and insisted that he speak with Robin, and only him mind you, and when I asked what it was in connection with he said it was regarding his son who, if I remember correctly, suffered from multiple sclerosis, and that he couldn't get him out of bed, as his condition had seemingly deteriorated. I tried to tell him that the best place for him to go would be to The Hamilton General, or to his local G.P, but he wasn't having any of it, simply saying that the seven-year-old didn't like hospitals as he associated them with his mum dying. I put the call through to Robin, but then you know what it's like with constant telephone calls and general admin duties, I simply forgot to ask Robin what the outcome was.'

'Lorna, this is really important can you think of any details that he might have given you as to where he and his son lived. For instance, when you asked him to visit the hospital or G.P. did he say that he couldn't because he wasn't in the area, anything like that? Take your time, there's no rush.'

'Honestly, well…thinking about it now, he really seemed a genuine, nice guy and I could tell by his voice that when I wasn't going to put him straight through to speak with Robin his voice kinda wobbled, as if he were going to cry or something. And when he told me about the death of his wife, he really did seem like a broken man, but no he never mentioned anything about an address and stupidly, I suppose, I never asked either. But surely Sergeant you're not suggesting that this man had anything to do with Robin not having been seen for a few days are you?'

Flicking the top of his ballpoint pen into the off position, he pushed it into the spine of his spiral notebook and pocketed both inside his jacket whilst reporting, 'Oh no Lorna, I couldn't possibly speculate at this stage that that phone call had anything to do with Mr Hackman going off the radar, and let's face it we don't yet have any definitive proof that he hasn't gone off somewhere just for a change of scenery, that sort of thing. As I'm sure you're aware it's very early days, and rest assured that somewhere along the line we manage to find the smallest of jigsaw pieces, then this gets slotted into the rest of the puzzle and bingo we find the answer to the mystery.'

'Well, thank you for being honest with me Sergeant, and if there's anything else that I can be doing to help speed things along then please don't hesitate to let me know.'

Standing up from the quiet seating area, Pettrini clutched his keys from the inside of his trouser pocket and finding the one he needed, cocked his head to one side and politely suggested, 'Actually Lorna if you could check recent billings for the past six months to a year say for patients that Robin has treated absolutely anywhere, that would be much appreciated, and it would be helpful as far as work that he's done at The Hamilton is concerned, whether the hospital could give you details as to the specific wards which he was working on, as I'm sure you'll agree this would hum…save an incredible amount of time, you know rather than checking with each individual ward.'

Strolling side by side towards the main doors the rather diminutive receptionist once more proffered an outstretched hand to the police officer and reported, 'Not a problem officer, I'll get that information over to you electronically as soon as I can, and I'll put a hard copy in the post for you.'

Delving into the inside pocket of his navy-blue jacket, Nico removed a couple of business cards and handed them over to her, replying gratefully, 'Thanks very much, and I look forward to receiving them, and well if you'll excuse the cliché, but if you think of anything, you and Mr Findlay can call me day or night.'

'Rest assured detective I will.'

The Italian detective made his way to the car park, and the receptionist returned to her desk where she immediately set to the task in hand of trying to find anything that may lead them to the whereabouts of her friend and colleague.

***

Arriving at Stockfield Police Station once more, Pettrini mounted the external steps to the entrance, greeted the duty officer with a friendly nod of the head, and a raised hand in the air.

Having reached the second floor he decided before attending to a mountain of paperwork that he knew would be waiting for him on his desk, he'd head straight for Jarvis's office and report on what he'd found out and perhaps more reluctantly, what he hadn't managed to find.

No need for knocking as the door was already open, and Jarvis had already looked up as Pettrini approached, 'What's up Nic?' asked the Detective Inspector, removing the black framed glasses from the bridge of his nose, and gently rubbed both of his upper eye lids in circular movements, 'Got anything?'

'Well…'

'Sit Nic, take a load off.'

'Oh okay, cheers guv. So, I want to just keep you in the loop regarding the case of Robin Hackman. I went to visit with his partner, Dominic Thurston yesterday evening, and this morning I went to the physiotherapy practice where Robin works.'

'Get anything?'

'So, I met a really helpful receptionist at The Hawthorne's, that's the name of the private practice that Hackman works at, and she basically had no idea that he went, or was even supposed to attend a symposium, and the only reason that she knew that there was a problem was when Mrs Littlejohn called the offices.'

He never mentioned anything, he didn't ask her to put it in the diary or to cancel his appointments, and let's face it, that would have been totally unprofessional, and well a bit weird as it's hum…it's his livelihood after all's said and done, as I'm assuming that he'd only get paid for the treatments that he gives. Could he really afford to lose his clients and all the locum work that he does by simply forgetting to ask the receptionist to re-schedule their appointments?

'She also told me that, like his sister, even if he had a few days off he'd tell her and the senior partner,' flicking through his note pad, he was able to find what he was looking for, 'a Mr Mike Findlay, everything that he was going to do, where he was going, and they used to take the piss out of him as they reminded him that they didn't need to know absolutely everything. I then asked her whether she was aware of anyone that may have had a grudge against him, but according to her, Robin was Mr Nice guy, and there's no way he'd ever have enemies, just hasn't got it in him. But now here's the thing, she was able to tell me that some random guy called out of the blue to see whether Hackman would go and see his son at his home, who apparently has severe multiple sclerosis and was unable to get out of bed that morning due to deterioration of his disease.

'This guy also categorically refused to take his son to a hospital or to a GP surgery, and that it had to be Robin and only him. Mrs Paul said that he sounded very sincere and downtrodden as his wife had died recently, which was the main reason that the little boy refused to go to A&E because that was the last time that he'd seen his mum. Anyway, she relented and put the phone call through to Robin, but she never found out whether or not he agreed to see the youngster. She couldn't tell me where he was phoning from, whether it was out of jurisdiction somewhere, so the call could have been made any bloody where. And of course, she hasn't seen hide nor hair of her colleague since. So…what d'you reckon, coincidence or what?'

Leaning back in his black, faux leathered, office chair with both hands clasped around the back of his neck, he smiled and mockingly commented, 'Doesn't matter whether we think it's a legit cry for help or not Nico, because we've got no way of finding out, have we? I mean the receptionist didn't get an address, and even if Hackman did write it down on a scrap of paper, he would either have pocketed it or trashed it. The best we can hope for is that we get a list of his patients pretty damn quick and pray that this is an isolated incident.'

Pettrini sighed heavily, crossed one leg over the other and continued, 'You realise it's going to take a shit load of man hours to go through and visit all his patients from let's say the last six months, but I suppose unless he turns up of his own free will, we've got no other choice but to just get it done I s'pose.'

'So, how did you get on with Hackman's partner? Please tell me he was able to give you something?'

'Yeah…I spoke with him alright, but he's a bit of a cool customer that's for sure, and I have to admit that I reckon he's holding something back, you know. He's just so totally weird about the whole thing, says that there's nothing to worry about, and that Robin's just gone off on a jolly for a couple of days. He said that his sister is worrying unnecessarily and that he's tried to convince her that her brother's fine and having a great time all by himself.

'Also, when I asked whether or not Robin had taken many clothes, or whether his passport was missing, talk about having a fucking hissy fit, he almost lost it. And you don't even want to know what his reaction was when I asked whether he'd taken his phone charger with him, so…no, there's something going on here, and considering they're supposed to be formalising their partnership, well…if only Robin knew about his couldn't care less attitude, then I think he'd be wise to run for the hills.'

Jarvis, smiling wryly, glanced towards the younger detective and enquired 'So what do you suggest, keep an eye on him?'

'Well, the uniforms are checking hospitals around our local area, and we're getting photographs circulated to all police stations within a 20-mile radius, but don't you think it's time to go national and issue a press release.'

Jarvis stood up, and with both hands on the small of his back, gave his spine a much-needed stretch, responding with, 'Once we've checked the hospitals, then I guess we'd better release something low key. So shall we give it another twenty-four hours?'

'Yeah, sounds good. Meanwhile, I think I'm going to see what our Mr Thurston's hiding, so that's where I'll be, okay?'

'Take as long as you need, and I'll let the rest of the team know.'

***

Chapter 10

With everyone around the white board in the Incident room, Jarvis informed the detectives who were present about the lack of information, and as yet, the unknown whereabouts of Robin Hackman.

'So, with Nico doing a bit of a stake out at Weldon Pharmacist, there's not much for us to go on apart from checking on all of the hospitals, medical centres, educational institutes who specialise in physiotherapy, sixth form colleges and schools in the area, as we've no idea as to the reasoning behind the symposium as it could, to all intents and purposes, be nothing more than a recruitment drive. It's a long shot, but there's sod all else for us to be going on with. Anybody got any worries, concerns about any other cases, oh…and how are we getting on with the Eva O'Connor case, anything to report Kelly?'

'She identified DaCosta from the photo that Josh and Dean gave us, and she's agreed to press char…' before the raven-haired detective had chance to finish her sentence, there were whooping cries with fists being punched in the air.

'Great work Donnelly. So, what are we waiting for, go and get that Latino bastard. I'm sure he won't have gone far at this time of the morning, well…it's not as though he's got a job to go to, has he, apart from narcotics distribution and beating up defenceless girls that is. And when he comes in, I want to be notified, and even if I'm in a meeting come and interrupt me, because it'll be worth it to see him squirm his way out of this one.'

***

Pettrini nestled within a short distance from Weldon Pharmacy which was tucked away off the High Street in Upper Stanton, and arriving well before the official opening time of 09:00 enabling him to get a pretty good parking spot, one that was close enough to give him a good sighting of the shop, but not too close that his presence would be easily observed, and quietly acquiesced that this was going to be a boring old day.

Nothing of interest happened for the best part of the morning, but all the local shops seemed to have an impressive footfall including the chemist, and wondering whether the overworked pharmacist would ever take a break, he finally spotted him. It was obviously time for his lunch as he left the pharmacy and crossed the road to the local Spar supermarket exiting with what looked like a pre-packed sandwich and a red stringed mesh bag filled with small tangerines. So, chortled Nico inwardly, obviously not the greasy chips kinda guy.

With the young detective wishing that he'd offered the assignment to somebody else, even though he knew no amount of cash would ever entice any of them to sit in a crammed car for the best part of a day, he didn't envy his partners, Turner and Carmichael, who went in search of the scumbag DaCosta.

***

Of course, they knew where to find him as he'd been in and out of police stations for most of his adult life, and yet no one had ever found him guilty of anything as he managed to buy himself out of any charge that was ever brought against him.

With the black detective Turner driving, Carmichael, who was desperately trying to give up the nicotine habit chewed noisily on the drug injected gum, peered across at the driver and casually asked, 'Wanna have a bet that he's not there?'

'Yeah, I'll take you on. I say he's there and if I win you buy me a pint.'

'You're on. That's a pint of beer right, not hum…whisky, brandy or some other expensive shit?' snorted Turner.

The Pines, where DaCosta was holed up, well that's the last address they had for him courtesy of the DVLA, was on the outskirts of Upper Stanton in a very exclusive gated neighbourhood, where access was only granted after identification through a series of intercom systems.

Dean sarcastically commented after they were allowed entrance on the first security check, 'Thank fuck I'm not a delivery man or dustman, who the shit do these people think they are? I mean…it's obvious they're either bankers, and that's with a 'b' by the way, stock brokers or fucking gangsters.'

'Okay, big boy, calm down. They can't all be bad ass dudes here, know what I'm saying?'

Having reached the gold spired, black metallic gates, there was yet another intercom that they were to be scrutinised by.

'Yes, what do you want?' came the curt reply to the rather piercing sound of the buzzer.

'We're from the police, and we'd like to see Mr Lenny DaCosta,' informed Detective Turner in his equally no-nonsense tone.

'I'll see if he's available to receive you. Wait there.'

'Huh…I think you misunderstand me man. We're not here to see if he'll have morning tea with us, we're here on official business, so there'll be no asking him if he's available, just go tell him that we'd like very much to speak with him. Now do you understand?' No more words were exchanged.

It wasn't a long wait, it just felt like it, as both detectives' tempers were rising, when on receipt of a click through the intercom, the gates slowly started to swing open.

Carmichael decided he'd stride with kick ass confidence across the neat block paving to the front entrance, whereas Josh drove the short distance and parked right in front of the front door. Even though they'd announced their arrival previously, they still had to go through the formality of either knocking or ringing the bell.

'These really are a bunch of mother fuckers. Leave this to me,' having been goaded just a little too far, Carmichael used the black wrought iron anchor shaped knocker so hard it's a wonder the wood of the door didn't fracture, and he refused to stop until there was a face in front of them.

Eventually the door opened, and it wasn't the lithe, deeply tanned, Latino man that they were expecting to see, and on hearing the terse, coarse voice, it revealed it to be the man who had spoken to them on the intercom system.

He moved away from the heavy, wooden, oak door to bid them entry, where the two men were frozen to the ground as they stared in awe at the sheer wealth and opulence that they'd just stepped into. The black and white tiled floor, together with the marble heads of lions and busts of possibly Greek philosophers, and with the heavy presence of hanging chandeliers the hallway definitely had a southern European feel to it.

'So where is he then?' enquired the bald, heavy set, Carmichael.

'He'll be down in a minute, when he's good and ready,' replied the black, dreadlocked man sporting a fashionable but obviously expensive Nike track suit, with equally top of the market trainers.

'Okay, Josh why don't we just have a nose around the joint then while we wait for the coming of the fucking Messiah. Tell your lord and master that we'll just be in one of the rooms down here, when he's huh…good and ready.'

'You ain't allowed to go anywhere unless Mr DaCosta says you can. So, you'd better wait here, otherwise the boss is gonna be real mad, know what I'm sayin'?'

'Awww, he's going to be mad at us, is that what you're saying brother? Well, that just plain sucks man, we wouldn't want to upset him now, would we Carmichael?' and with that both detectives pushed past the so-called minder and made their way to a heavily furnished room which they assumed was one of the sitting rooms. 'Nice here ain't it Josh?' As they picked up dainty objects d'art and without replacing them on the polished surfaces without the due diligence that they should probably be afforded, they both commented mockingly 'These are alright, but not my cuppa tea, how about you pal? I mean…I wonder how much they cost to replace should one of them accidentally fall to the floor.'

'Kindly put those down where you found them, and let me tell you if there's any marks, chips or any trace of your filthy fat fingers on them, then your department will find themselves with a hefty bill on their hands.'

'Well, well, well, if it isn't our Mr DaCosta finally honouring us with his presence. No seriously, we know just what a busy man you are, and we are so humbled that you could find the time,' continued Carmichael with his unrelenting use of deep sarcasm.

'So, you know who I am, who the fuck are you two jokers then? I'd like to know, before I have Kadeem here throw you out,' the handsome, olive skinned man with his piercing hazel eyes, clad in white sweat pants and a black towelling robe bearing a gold crown emblem, opened an onyx cigarette box, took one out and lit it with a lighter made from the same gemstone. Scanning the photographs of both detectives he uttered as the cigarette hung loosely from the corner of his mouth, 'So, what can I do for you detectives Turner and Carmichael?'

'We'd like you to accompany us to Stockfield Road Police Station for questioning regarding a serious allegation. Now, you can come willingly, or we can caution you. We'll obviously give you some time to get dressed, but I have to tell you one of us will be accompanying you to your bedroom while you do this.' Josh stood waiting for a response as he placed one hand in his trousers pocket and the other on his hip.

'If this is some kind of a joke, then I'm not finding it very funny. So, what is it I'm supposed to have done this time then? It seems to me as though every time you guys need to find a…what's the best word to use Kadeem, ah yes, I have the right one I think, huh…a fucking scapegoat you come knocking on my bastard door,' and almost with noses touching, DaCosta was eye balling Carmichael, and was about to finger prod his chest when the detective removed his hand roughly, and angrily remonstrated, 'Go ahead make my day asshole, and you'll have another charge of police assault on your rap sheet.'

Josh felt he needed to take control of the already overheating situation that was now unfolding in the elegant, but overly opulent sitting room, with its chic white sofas, heavy, red velvet free standing lamps, and art depicting the owner's love of both contemporary and historical importance lined every square inch of the room.

'We have reason to believe that on the 7$^{th\ of}$ April you beat up a young lady at an establishment called Cinders, which is located on the Norwood Road. As I mentioned earlier, we would rather you come in to the station voluntarily, or we can arrest you. So why don't you save us all a lot of time, because the sooner we get this done then the quicker you'll be able to return to your huh…business of making money, doing whatever it is you do to earn it, so what d'you say bro?'

DaCosta nudged past both officers, peered across at his henchman, and nodded his head towards the stairs whereupon Kadeem almost telepathically knew what his master wanted.

'Right detectives, I need a quick dose of caffeine while my man sorts me out some clothes. You see, there's no way in hell I'm letting you up my stairs and into my private quarters, that privilege is for invited guests only, get my drift?' He then moved slowly towards the kitchen with both men following in pursuit just in case he'd got the notion that he'd make a quick escape, although deep down they knew he never would, because as they both knew only too well, he didn't need to because he'd find a way of escaping the noose.

Dressed in dark brown leather trousers, a pin striped, brown shirt with the black iconic image of the polo player on a horse stitched onto the breast pocket, with the top buttons undone showing his hirsute chest. Standing tall after zipping up his dark brown ankle boots, DaCosta turned towards his faithful lackey, held him by both shoulders and staring directly at him, wearing a huge grin, confidently declared, 'I'll be back sooner than you know, man, and tapped him playfully on the side of his cheek, as he marched out of the front door.'

'By the way, Carmichael, you owe me a pint,' sniggered Josh.

'Look here mate, if we manage to nail this son of a bitch, I'll buy you a bloody pub.'

Both back doors and driver's door of the Volvo banged shut.

***

Having gone through the rigours of booking the accused in at the duty desk, and with the relevant questions asked as to whether he was feeling medically well, did he have any mental issues, and did he know why he was being detained, the man about to be held for questioning turned seductively, and with panther like slinking grace followed the officers to interview room number five.

It was obvious, as the three men entered the room, that there was already a fourth man seated at the dark grey metallic table, and that DaCosta had managed to call his lawyer from the house, or he'd got his gofer to make the call, after having instructed him to do so in the likelihood of such an event happening.

The fourth man in the room stood when his client entered the room where they both acknowledged each other's presence with a slight nod of the head, as DaCosta seated himself next to the silver fox haired man, clad in a light grey suit, white shirt and scarlet red silk tie.

The whole routine of recording the interview, naming those present, the date, time, room number and the name of the police station, and finally reading out the charges were all explained to the defendant, with the lawyer nodding his approval that all guidelines had been met.

Detective Turner started the proceedings, well aware of course that in an adjacent office sat Jarvis who was watching the proceedings on a computer screen, and who'd said that he wouldn't miss DaCosta trying to get out of this one, even though he was about to miss a meeting with the DCI and would more than likely get a right bollocking over it.

'As we mentioned earlier at your home, we have evidence to prove that you were guilty of causing grievous bodily harm to a lady whom we believe you have met, a Miss Eva O'Connor, on the night of 7th April at approximately 10:15 pm and that this assault was committed at Cinders, which is a club situated on Norwood Road, and is also not far from the Denton Heights Estate, which we can all assume you know very well. The lady in question was beaten up so badly that you left her body black and blue, she was also unable to see or eat for a while

143

because the swelling was so bad, and she was forced to spend time in the Intensive Care Unit at The Hamilton General. But that wasn't the extent of her injuries, as you very well know, because you'd decided that she needed to be given an even tougher sentence, so you decided to burn her young skin with cigarettes leaving her with 33 permanent scars. Have you anything to say to this charge?'

Not fazed by anything that had just been reported, the accused leant back in his chair that not only contained handcuff bars, but was also bolted to the floor, and casually folded his arms behind his head, responding with, 'I have no idea what you're talking about. For one, I've never even heard of the club and to accuse me of knowing that sink estate, well…that's not only an insult to my character, but severely damaging to my family's respectable name. And as for this tart, whoever she is, I've never heard of her,' the flamboyantly dressed Latino man, glanced towards the man who was representing him, who simply stared blankly at the detectives opposite him.

'So, you deny knowing Cinders and a Miss O'Connor? What about a Mr Cronin, who is the manager of the club or a Mr Jimmy Malone? Ring any bells?' enquired Detective Carmichael staring intently at the brown eyed man opposite.

'No, as I've just told you, I've never heard of this damned club. Detective, do you think it's time to get your hearing checked perhaps, or have you got something more seriously wrong, like a degenerative disease of some sort? The reason I'm asking is that, well…I know there's no clock in here, but even I can estimate that it can't be longer than what…a minute, since I told you this?'

Carefully removing an A4 photograph from a manila folder and sliding it in front of the defendant, Carmichael continued, 'Mr DaCosta, would you say that that is a photograph of you getting out of a black Range Rover, license plate LD1?'

'I suppose it could be, but you see it's not always me that drives my car. It has to be said, that sometimes out of the goodness of my heart, I often let members of my staff drive it around, you know. They rather like the tinted windows you see, so that they can get up to all sorts of stuff, well…I guess you know what I'm getting at, huh?'

'Is that so? You really are a decent chap, and as the saying goes, they must have broken the mould when you were born. But you see, here's the one thing that might blow your last answer right out of the water, because we had a funny feeling that you might pull that stunt, so we contacted your insurance company, and guess what…that vehicle, and just to repeat the registration plate of LD1, is only registered in your name, so even out of the goodness of your own heart, as you so nobly put it, it would be highly illegal of you to allow any other person to drive it. Now, I'll repeat the question again, is that you in the photograph in front of you?'

Both the accused and his lawyer, Jeremy Kerr bent heads towards each other where words were exchanged as DaCosta responded with a smirkish grin, 'I'm not sure whether you've got knowledge as to how insurance policies work detective sergeant, but anyway let me play devil's advocate. What if it was me driving the car, which it wasn't? There's nothing to say that even if I was there, that doesn't mean that you can accuse me of slapping up some whore, now does it? I mean, well…where's the proof? Have they got CCTV in that joint, because I heard there was some sort of a fire recently, shame that was, and I'm not sure but…I don't think they found out what really happened, or could I be misinformed?' grinning as he spoke, and to emphasise his relaxed, devil-may-care behaviour whilst still slouching in his chair, he crossed one leg over the other, rested his ankle on his thigh and admired his footwear.

'So now, you not only agree that you know not only the whereabouts of the club, but also the club itself, and that the vehicle in the photograph is indeed yours, but more importantly that it could be your face that's printed on the laminated paper? So, for the benefit of the tape, could you confirm that this is the case, Mr DaCosta?'

'Yes, I guess so. But I'm sure my attorney will agree that you've got no right to hold me here, on what…mere suspicion that I attacked some silly girl? Once again, I think you owe me the courtesy of providing both of us who're sitting this side of the table, exactly where your hard evidence is, especially of me being guilty of a crime, because quite frankly this…' picking up the photograph from the table and childishly throwing it on the floor, 'proves absolutely bull shit nothing.'

'Oh, we're getting to the good stuff, don't you fret Mr DaCosta,' both detectives knew that they'd been instructed tactically to leave the room after showing that first photograph, so with a tap on the door, Jarvis stuck his head around it and beckoned both Turner and Carmichael to listen to what he supposedly had to say to them. Turner spoke into the recorder, 'Interview suspended at 11:13 am.'

'Let's leave him to stew for a bit eh, lads? We got him to agree to at least knowing the club, and even though he saw right through our claim that he wouldn't be able to allow his mates to use the car, all we gotta do is hold onto our trump cards, and then we can read him his rights. Shall we go for a quick coffee and leave those two in there to get really rattled, and I guarantee DaCosta will come up with one hell of a story which, in itself, will be well worth listening to.' Jarvis led the way out of the corridor leading to the interview rooms and descended the stairs to the station's cafeteria.

The three detectives chatted about football, the latest Six Nations Rugby scores, and then after about half an hour, they all decided that the two men that they'd left in Room number five would be getting really hot under the collar by now, so after tidying their chairs and replacing them back underneath the table, they made their way back up the stairs.

The uniformed officer standing outside of the interview room stepped aside to allow Turner and Carmichael entry.

Retrieving the seats that they had previously vacated, Josh turned the tape recorder back on and clearly and authoritatively spoke into the microphone, 'Interview reconvened at,' raising his right wrist in the air scanned the time quickly and continued, '11:45 am Now Mr DaCosta we previously managed to ascertain that you in fact know the club named Cinders, and that it was you getting out of your car on the night of the 7th April. You never responded when we asked you whether we are correct in ascertaining that you do in fact know the club owner, a Mr Barry Cronin. So, which is it, yes you do know him, or no you don't?'

'I might know him to look at, but when I go there, which is very occasionally I have to say because it's not really my kind of place, if you know what I mean, well…I tend to just have a quiet drink on my own. You see, I'm not really a sociable kinda fella, and I actually prefer my own company, rather than making idle conversation to some of the people that go there, 'cos well, most of them are…how can I put this without sounding rude, huh…they're simply not in my league, know what I'm saying, bro'? So, to answer your question if I perhaps saw a photograph of this dude, I might be able to give you an answer. Does that satisfy you, detective?' responded the man oozing with self-confidence.

Carmichael responded with a wry smile, 'So what would you say if we told you that Mr Cronin knows you quite well in fact, and that you indeed had quite a lengthy conversation a couple of nights ago, and well…it seems as though he didn't want you entering his club. Have you got anything to say about this claim then?'

'Oh…so that was the owner, was it? I had no idea. He wouldn't allow me to go into the joint because,' DaCosta sniggered slightly, 'the tosser said that there were already too many in the place and that he would be breaking fire regulations if he went above the specified headcount. But I can tell you this, he huh…wasn't very pleased when I reminded him that perhaps he was a little late in worrying about that now, what with the recent fire an' all.'

Carmichael glanced sideways to his colleague and continued with an air of exasperation, 'D'you know what, we're getting pissed off with your playful, merry go round of lies, DaCosta. We have evidence to say that you were in the club on the night of the 7th April, and we've also got evidence that it was you that beat up your accuser.'

This time the defendant's lawyer spoke up, with, it must be said, unequivocal steadfastness to his client's plight. 'So far, detectives, you've caught my client out on a moment of absent-mindedness. I mean let's face it, we all forget things sometimes, but you've not offered either myself or my client here, who came here out of his own volition I might add, one piece of evidence that puts Mr DaCosta either in or near the club on the night in question. My client has not been read his rights, and as far as I'm concerned you are holding my client without any legal reason to do so.' The arrogance of both the lawyer and the man of South American descent, simply astounded both officers, but neither officer was going to afford the two men seated opposite any outward signs of sheer disbelief as to the lies that they were being fed.

'Believe me, we haven't got to the good stuff yet, so may I suggest that you both sit down again?' The last three words were said not as an invitation but an order.

Detective Sergeant Turner provided a statement from the manila folder and pushed it gently towards the attorney and his client, stating with alacrity, 'For the benefit of the tape, I am now producing two sworn statements, one from a Mr Fred Wrightson, and the other one from a Miss Eva O'Connor. The first account states that Mr Wrightson saw a person being carried out in a makeshift fireman's lift on the night in question at approximately 10:45 pm and bundled into a silver Mercedes. The second statement declares that Miss O'Connor has identified you as being the man that beat her up and put her into the Intensive Care Unit on the same night in question. Anything to say to this Mr DaCosta?'

Mr Kerr, the attorney pulled at the cuffs of his pristine white shirt and pronounced quite succinctly, 'Officers, I need a word with my client in private.'

Both officers stood and pushed their chairs away from the table with the backs of their knees, and Josh spoke once more into the tape recorder, 'For the benefit of the tape this interview is suspended at the time of 12:02 pm.'

With the detectives' absence being replaced once again by the same uniformed officer standing to attention outside of the door, Josh not wanting to appear too elated muttered softly towards Carmichael, 'Well we didn't have to give up Cronin and Malone, at least for now that is, so what d'you think?'

'I think that shit ball will try his luck with some cock and bull story, and his dumb ass lawyer will believe him and knowing his record of never going down for any of the crap that he pulls, this will just be another feather in his bow. And when this goes down, you know what that means, don't ya, it'll be a classic case of his word against hers.'

'Has anyone been in touch with the dudes from the club lately?'

'Not sure, but the last I heard from the boss was that they're staying put and not running anywhere anytime soon, as they reckon they've got enough muscle power already on tap should they need it.'

Turner and Carmichael returned to the 8x10 room after an interval of about thirty minutes which they figured was enough time to allow Kerr and DaCosta to come up with, in their opinion, a laudable and credible story that only they themselves actually believed.

Both officers seated themselves once more, recorded on tape that the interview had reconvened as Turner re-commenced the previous line of questioning.

'I believe we terminated the meeting at the point where you, Mr DaCosta, was asked to read a statement provided by the lady whom you attacked. So, for the purposes of the tape we would like to hear what you have to say about the witness statement.'

'My client agrees that he was at The Cinders club on the night of 7th April, but he has no recollection of any events other than having a drink at the bar, which he now puts down to the fact that his drink must have been spiked. He has no idea how long he was at the club for, or indeed how he got home that night. So, this woman who claimed that Mr DaCosta severely brutalised her is very much mistaken. And, as there is no photographic evidence to prove that my client is guilty, then it's obvious that there is no legal reason for you to detain him any longer,' declared Kerr, as he started packing up his brief case in readiness to leave the windowless room.

'No, you're quite correct we don't have photographic evidence, but we do have a sworn statement that the doorman saw Mr DaCosta leave the club at approximately ten minutes after ten in the evening, and for the benefit of the tape the accused is being provided a copy of the document in question.'

'Who the fuck signed this. I can't read his signature?'

'Oh, sorry about that Mr DaCosta, but if you look here,' Dean leant across the fairly wide table, and even though the document was upside down he was able to track the name with his forefinger, where he with a measured pinch of sarcasm pointed it out to the man opposite, 'See here, huh…it reads, a Mr Sean Coughlin, and it also states that he opened the club doors for you to leave, and he drove your black Range Rover to the front of the building, and then handed the keys over to you, whereupon you simply drove off. I think I've got it right I mean…it's not easy when you're having to read it the wrong way up, know what I'm saying bro?'

'Like Mr Kerr said, I do remember going to the club that night, but he must have got the wrong man, 'cos I wouldn't have been in a fit state to drive the car, no way man. D'you know what I think? This is a glorified stitch up, so you're going to have to do better than that.'

'Oh, we can, we also have a statement by two other persons who have stated that they saw you leaving an upstairs bedroom at approximately 10.10 pm., but they are at present under protection due to fears of witness intimidation, so we will not be providing you with their names at present. If the case goes to trial, then your attorney will be apprised of both of their names. Now, have you anything more to say before we formally charge you?'

Not showing any emotions one way or the other, and with his attorney also showing an unruffled façade, Josh began reciting one of the famous passages from the police bible, 'I am arresting you on suspicion of causing grievous bodily harm on the night of 7th April this year…Anything you do say may be given in evidence.'

As all men stood up, DaCosta was duly handcuffed and taken into custody. Before he exited the doorway, Kerr strode up behind him and murmured, 'I'll make sure you get out on bail.'

'Fuck you,' was the reply.

I know exactly what she looks like, so all I've got to do is persuade her bosses that I need to speak to her urgently. I did it once before, and he's tucked nicely away, so this should be a piece of piss.

Making sure that the price tags were off the cellophane that held the brightly coloured stems upright, and zapping the car locked, I stood in front of the offices of the Phoenix Specialist Nursing Agency.

Staring at the red brick building it was somewhat surprising how it looked like a normal detached house which could have been a home to the most typical of hard working families, and it was only the light blue lettering set on a rather impressive dark blue back drop canvas with three words written boldly and in italics 'Award Winning Care' that would alert the passers-by that this was actually a place of business.

Pushing the buzzer on the outside wall and announcing my arrival in the grey, steel intercom, the door eventually clicked open.

Waiting for the receptionist to finish the call that she was on, and idly perusing around the room where the walls were lined with photographs of smiling people, both old and young, with quotes expressing gratitude for being given a second chance to lead a new life, as others enunciated to the world that this agency's nurses were the best in the land. The Indian lady dressed in her native garb peered over the top of her gold framed glasses and asked, 'Hi there, can I help you?'

Cradling the bouquet of as yet unopened lilies whose heavily perfumed scent was still locked away, I glanced coyly at the raven haired lady behind the desk, 'Hum…this may sound a little unusual but I erm…I bought these flowers for one of your nurses who was so kind to my mother while she was in The Hamilton General, and I just wanted to show my appreciation, you know.'

Pushing the chair back, the lady stood up and the only sound that could be heard was the jangling of her bracelets that danced around her wrists, 'My goodness, that's so kind of you. If you tell me her name, I'll make sure that she gets them.'

'To be honest with you, I'd rather give them to her myself, as I've not had the chance to thank her in person for everything that she did for my mum,' removing a tissue I movingly wiped the side of my eyes, 'you see even after all the good work that the nurse did, mum didn't make it, and I know that she

thought very highly of her, as she mentioned her all the time after she had the operation.'

'I'm afraid that I'm not able to give out any details as to where any of our employees either work or live, so no, that would be out of the question.'

'Look, I don't want you to give me her address or anything, but couldn't you just let me know where she's on shift today, because well…otherwise these babies will die, and that would be such a shame wouldn't it? Please…as a dying wish for my mother. I mean, what harm could it do, and imagine the surprise that she'd get after working long and hard all day to get one of the greatest gifts of all…a nice thank you from one of her patients. And let's face it, it's not every day that these overworked people even get acknowledged, let alone receive a beautiful bouquet of flowers, is it?'

Even though it was clear there were only two of us in the room, the Asian lady, clad in a deep purple sari, slowly turned her head to the right and the left as if she were fearful of being overheard, before finally uttering, 'This really is most irregular, but you're right, what harm can it do? If you give me the nurse's name then I'll check where she's working today.'

'Her name is,' removing the small yellow piece of paper torn from a post it pad from a back pocket, I handed it across to her, 'I know how to pronounce her first name, but I erm…seem to struggle with her surname as it's a bit of a tongue twister.'

As ringed fingers danced across the keyboard, she finally peered over the top of the screen and pronounced rather proudly, 'Ah…here she is, Rosario Baluyot. She's working at Long Acre Care Home which cares for people suffering from chronic neurological disorders. According to her schedule she started at seven this morning, and as it's a twelve-hour shift, she finishes at seven thirty this evening.'

'Thank you very much, you've been very kind. As I don't know this area very well, could you tell me where I can find this place?'

'Of course, not a problem Mr erm…sorry but I didn't catch your name.'

'It's a Mr Derek Quinn.'

'Very well Mr Quinn, you'll find Long Acre at Overton Road, in a place called Little Sheridan which is around three miles outside of Siddington. Just go down the main road here and find the B263 and it practically takes you all the way.'

Sniffing the unscented flowers, and clutching them to my chest I started to make my retreat and halted at the main reception door before turning around and acknowledged gratefully, 'Thanks again, and I'm sure between us we're going to make someone a very happy lady today.'

The door slammed shut, as I made my way to the red transit van where my next guest would be invited in.

I remembered what she looked like, quite short, shiny raven coloured hair, deep brown eyes, always wore bright red lipstick and a bit on the podgy side, but always appeared very smart with each strand of hair tucked away into the pony tail that swung jauntily with each step that she made.

I parked on a side road and walked to the main entrance doors and patiently waited for her to step through into the outside world.

At seven thirty on the dot the automatic doors seemed to go into over drive as the night shift entered and the day staff would finally ease their minds into a semi state of calm whilst trying not to worry too deeply about things that needed to be done but, sadly, never got around to it.

Weary males and females some in uniforms, others in civvies seemingly struggling to put one foot before the other clambered tiredly onto push bikes, others scrambling to catch their bus whilst others made their way to the overly priced car parks, and that's when I saw her. With a rucksack lodged cosily on her back, and hands thrust deep inside the pockets of her maroon puffer jacket she made her way rather energetically to the bike shelter, almost as if she'd got a hot date or something, or perhaps just going for a few drinks so that she could forget about the day that she'd rather like to forget about.

Waiting until she'd got a few yards head start, I made my move, and pretending to be out of breath when I caught up with her, I lightly tapped her on the shoulder as I asked her in between breaths, 'Hum…I erm…sorry…but can I…speak to you for a minute?'

'Get your breath back, you must have run a long way to be so short of breath,' she jokingly tittered.

'No I haven't actually, I guess I'm not as fit as I thought I was, or at least as I should be, I should say. The reason I wanted to talk to you is that I have these flowers for you, well they're not from me actually but from my mum,' handing them over to the young Asian girl as she removed her hands from the inside warmth of her jacket to receive them.

'Are these really for me? And are you absolutely sure you've got the right person? I mean you look fairly familiar, but I work at so many places nowadays, and it goes without saying that I see so many family members and friends of patients, that it's not easy for me to remember them all.'

'Oh it's you alright, your name is Rosario yeah? Well you looked after my lovely mum…' glancing briefly at the diminutive young lady whilst looking down at my feet in an attempt to show that I was finding it difficult to talk to her about my non-existent mother, and after a brief pause, I continued, 'Listen I don't normally do this, but can I buy you a cup of coffee and then I can tell you all about the brilliant things that you did for my mum, 'cos well…it's getting a bit parky out here isn't it?' exaggeratedly rubbing both hands together in an effort to keep warm and flicking a thumb towards the entrance of the care facility whilst suggesting, 'There must be a nice little café in there, so…what d'you think?'

'I suppose a quick cup wouldn't hurt, but actually there's a nice little pub not far from here, and it doesn't have well…you know, the usual hospital smells, know what I mean?'

Pulling the keys out of the side pocket of her backpack ready to unlock her girlish pink bike from the black metallic bike rack, I took a couple of steps and stood in front of her, and with my head cocked to one side I smiled and suggested coyly, 'Look my car's just on the other side of the road, and well…I'm sure you've had a bloody long day, why don't I drive us? It's big enough for you to put your bike in the boot, and then when we've finished, I can drive you home. I can treat you to a bit of supper if you like, and then when you get home you can crawl straight into bed, how's that sound?'

Scanning her phone quickly, as if a sudden message might make up her mind and scupper my plans, but then she simply slid the phone into her pocket looked into my eyes and cheerfully responded, 'D'you know what, that sounds absolutely amazing but I really can't be out long 'cos I've got to be up at half five in the morning.'

Chuckling rather too loudly I picked up the feather weight bike and rested it on my shoulder as we made our way to the van.

Having loaded the two-wheeler into the back I opened the passenger door for the young Filipino nurse and made my way to the driver's side. Starting the engine where the main headlamps fired into life as great beacons of light shone on the black tarmac, and taking my foot off the brake, the car started to slowly accelerate.

Perusing shyly sideways towards me, the young lady released her shock of jet-black hair and put the elastic tie around her wrist and finger combed her hair so that it hung loosely, accentuating her round face as she giggled and remarked, 'This is weird that I've got into someone's car and I don't even know his name! My folks back home would kill me if they knew. So…what is it?'

'Oh erm…its Derek, Derek Quinn.', 'Pleased to meet you, Derek. Now, tell me about your mum, is she fully recovered? I have to tell you though, as I explained earlier it's impossible for me to remember all the people that I've nursed. So, I'm afraid you're going to have to give me a few hints, you know like which hospital, or care home she was in, and what was wrong with her, and then I might be able to put a face to the name.'

'Her name is Dotty, well actually Dorothy and she was in The Hamilton General and I think she was in the ward G3 to have gall stones removed, but there was a complication and she ended up with a severe infection so it was touch and go for a while and that's when she said that it was you and only you that helped with her full recovery. So, as I said, a cup of coffee is the least that I can offer you for helping her through her massive ordeal.'

'By the way, how did you know that I'd be working at the Rehab Centre today? I mean, I work all over the place and sometimes not even my best mates know where I am unless I message them, or was it pure fluke?' *looking out of the passenger window waiting for a reply, she turned towards me with a startled look in her face and rather nervously stated,* 'That's the pub I told you about, the Merrymakers Arms and you've just driven straight past it.'

'Oh, don't worry, I didn't tell you in advance, but I've got somewhere else in mind. It's another pub where the people are really friendly and it's one my mum goes to for cheap fish and chips in the early evening, 'cos she says that it's cheaper for her to eat there than if she cooked it herself, and at this time of night its known as the 'early bird deal' for pensioners. So, you see this way you'll be able to see her for yourself and see if you recognise her, and then you can ask her how well she's doing.'

Hesitating momentarily clutching her backpack to her chest she finally responded, 'Oh okay that should be alright I suppose, but it's not far is it?'

'No, no not far at all. In fact,' *scanning quickly at the clock on the dashboard, and glancing towards the young nurse I replied,* 'we should be *there in about five to ten minutes or so, unless of course there's some kind of road accident or something.'*

Turning the local channel on the radio, the D.J announced that it was now the beginning of the Tamla Motown hour, as Diana Ross's voice erupted through the sound waves, with her infamous song 'Ain't no mountain high enough.'

'Brilliant song, don't you think?'

'Dunno never heard it before. Look, is this pub much further, 'cos to be honest with you I'm a bit tired and hungry? Perhaps it might be better if we did this on one of my days off, you know what I mean?'

Still tapping with my thumbs on the steering wheel and staring straight ahead as the overhead streetlamps shone brightly on the darkening road, whilst muttering quietly, 'Nearly there, and it'll be worth the wait, you'll see.'

Left hand down on the signal lever into Homersham Road, and then a sharp right into Meadway Close leading them to The Tanner House, and as the car finally stopped the young lady sitting next to me let out a stifled shriek, 'This isn't a pub, where are we?'

'Yeah, it is, it's just not one that's serving to the greater public at the moment that's all. I'm doing it up you see, and wait till you get inside, you'll be amazed at what I've done already. Actually, I'm really chuffed with meself if I'm honest with you. Anyway, out you get now, time for that cup of coffee I promised you.'

Opening the passenger door gingerly, she silently followed me around the side of the abandoned building where only the sounds of old debris crunching underfoot could be heard in the stillness of the rapidly darkening sky.

Leading the petite Asian woman into the unlit interior, I searched for the light and when she saw the state of the inside, she stifled a screech by covering her mouth with her hand. Trying to get out of the door quickly I beat her to it and picked her up as she futilely kicked and lashed out with flailing arms, 'Look you're here now, so you might as well calm down and I'll get that coffee, well if I've got milk that is, but if not then we'll have to have something cold. Come on and I'll show you around. It's really quite peaceful here don't you think, and the absolute beautiful thing about this place is that not a soul will hear us or know that we're here. So, you see we have absolute privacy.'

Sobbing quite loudly now and grabbing her mobile encased in its pink protective shell from her inside pocket, but as her tremulous hands couldn't hold onto it, it fell to the concrete floor shattering the screen into what resembled a spider's web.

She was quite submissive as I led her way down to the basement where Hackman could be heard shouting, 'Let me out of here! Help!'

Trembling all over now, the Filipino nurse ran to where she heard the cries for help.

'Well…I was going to introduce you two myself a little later but now's a good a time as any. Rosario meet Mr Robin Hackman, Mr Hackman meet Miss Beu…sorry still can't pronounce your surname, meet Rosario. You see, one of the reasons that I've brought you here is that you're going to look after him while I'm not here, because as you can see, he can't move either his right leg or arm,' turning slightly towards the nurse and the shackled physiotherapist, I smiled broadly with a somewhat inner sense of achievement.

'Wh…what the bloody hell…who the fuck are you anyway?' she demanded in a loud controlled voice, 'Look, I'm not taking any more of this shit so I'm off, and you'd better let him go too,' and with that she clomped heavily up the wooden stairs, and started pulling heavily on the door handle, cursing at the top of her voice as if she were in some football ground and her team was losing in the final minutes.

I slowly removed a shiny metal blade from the inside of my jacket pocket and silently followed her up the stairs, grabbed her ponytail and jerked her head back and placed the cold, jagged tip against the warm, sweaty skin of her throat. In terror, she slumped and gave up as she realised I would kill her unless she stopped resisting.

'Look you'd be far better off just calming down, so get back down here and learn to accept that we three are going to get to know each other really well.'

Reluctantly, she had no choice but to obey me and joined my other captive downstairs in the makeshift prison from which there was no escape.

Standing there with a sheer look of despair she demanded, 'Answer me one thing why me? I mean you say that I was kind to your mother but quite frankly I don't believe a fucking word that comes out of your mouth. And exactly what is it that I'm meant to be doing to help that poor man over there?'

'Being a nurse, you're going to have to see to his erm…how can I put this, his toileting habits, 'cos as you can see, he's not able to go to the loo, as he's kind of tied up at the moment. Now, over there in the corner you'll find a bag of stuff that you might need to help with this huh…dilemma. Or, as you did

with the most important person in my life, you can leave him in a wet and dirty bed and end up with pressure sores. *Your choice Rosario. Now I gotta go, and I'll probably be back with some food and stuff later, or I might not. Again, neither of you two gave a flying fuck whether she was able to eat or drink, so now I guess you'll soon find out what it's like to be treated as though you weren't important, and that you're just another hospital fucking number on a plastic wrist band. You see, the reason that you two are my guests shall we say, is that you need to be taught a lesson on how to respect and show compassion to the people that you're being paid to look after, get it?'*

This time the physiotherapist announced defensively, *'Look here, I…I've told you before if you tell me what it is you want me to do, then I'll do it. Holding me here isn't going to do anybody any good is it? Come on man, give me a second chance, and her, and we'll do everything you want, won't we erm…Rosario?'*

'Too late for that MAN, you had your chance two fucking years ago, and you didn't give a shit then, so why the hell would I trust you now?'

With keys in my hand, I started to climb the stairs when a shrill voice bounced through the air, *'You're gonna just leave us here, with nothing to eat or drink? You're a bloody animal, and if this is the way you treated your friend then it's no wonder she ended up the way she did.'*

'There's a jug of water on the windowsill and you'll just have to make do with that. And after that little outburst of yours, young lady, then let's put it this way…I just might not be able to come back with food. So, what d'ya think of that then, still want to hurl abuse at me?' and with that with her mobile in my hand, typed the four words again, *'gone to a symposium,'* pocketed it safely and unlocked the bolted door once more.

The last I heard was Hackman deriding the nurse, *'What the bloody hell were you thinking, pissing him off like that? You must have known that he'd get back at us somehow, so well done. If I'd got the use of both hands, I'd soddin' well clap.'*

'Screw you,' was her reply.

157

Chapter 11

At the usual time of nine in the morning on the second floor at Stockfield Road Police Station, Jarvis's team of hard working, non-complaining officers met around the partially covered white boards which showed photographs of people missing, or dead, with red and black arrows leading to a maze of possible names of places, dates and times where they were last sighted.

Jarvis greeting the team with his usual salutation of *"hi everyone,"* announced that Lenny DaCosta was awaiting a date set for his bail hearing, and that thanks to everyone's hard work it was at least a start. He then directed the question to his crew as to whether anyone had anything to report on the case of the so-called missing physiotherapist.

'Ahem…' replied Sergeant Pettrini as he cleared his throat softly and almost shyly, clearly not comfortable with public speaking, as he reported on his findings, 'there was definitely nothing going on for the first couple of days, but then 'as it 'appened, last night there was something that wasn't quite right, well not to me anyway. Thurston had been leaving the pharmacy, known as The Beacons, which is situated on Weldon Road at about 5:45 pm, and he'd always lock the place up himself, and meticulously did a security check, prior to heading home. In fact, it became ridiculously boring, if I'm honest. Last night though was different, very…different as he still hadn't closed up at six o'clock, and then at around 7:15 pm a fella dressed in dark clothing, well to be more precise a black hoodie bearing a large Adidas logo on the back, and what looked like sweatpants and dark trainers arrived outside the premises on a push bike.

So, when he gets there, he takes his phone out of his trouser pocket, and obviously sent a speedy message because no sooner than his thumbs had stopped flitting around the bloody screen when the side gate suddenly opened, and there was our Mr Thurston allowing the man waiting outside to enter through it. The stranger didn't seem to be in a hurry, but slowly and with short steps made his way towards the pharmacist. Not locking the gate, I was able to take a few photographs from across the road where there was a side alley in between the sandwich shop and a Betfred betting joint.

Within minutes of their meet, Thurston handed over a rather large package in a white bag bearing the name of the pharmacy to the hooded man, whereby he placed it in a black rucksack, secured it on his back, and mounted his bike, which incidentally he hadn't bothered to lock up, obviously assuming that he wouldn't be off it for any length of time. During the short interval that they were seen together there didn't seem to be any words exchanged between them, no friendly common courtesies of handshakes, or back slapping and neither seemed comfortable in one another's company.

Anyway, the fella rode away, leaving Thurston to lock everything up and go home, which is where he went, with no stops on the way. So that's it, but you have to admit it's all a bit bizarre.'

The dark-haired Irish detective Kelly Donnelly was the first to cite a response, 'Could be he was handing over prescribed pain killers in exchange for a few quid. We all know that its feckin illegal, but I don't think he'd be the first eejit to risk his license for the sake of a few drugs sold on the side, know what I mean like?'

Carmichael swivelled around on his chair to face Kelly, as he'd previously been heavily engaged on the phone during the latest hand over, having lost interest to what the person on the other end had to say, but he was well aware as to what they were all talking about, 'Nah, not buying that Kelly, no one in their right mind would risk their livelihood, for the sake of a few Oxys.' I mean, you've gotta agree it would be much easier and safer to tell the guy go fuck himself and go find a street corner like most junkies do. No, that's not the reason. But here's the burning question, what are we waiting for, why don't we just get him in and ask him? 'Hum...yeah, I'm still here Mrs Whittaker, and I take the loss of your cat very seriously indeed.'

With eyebrows raised in the air, he swung his chair back round to his desk to continue hearing about the missing feline.

Jarvis concluded, 'Nic guess you'd better bring him in. It may be nothing, but we've still got no sightings as to where Hackman is, hospitals are showing no results, and there doesn't seem to be an institution that's been tracked down that had his name on any list of any symposium. So, I reckon someone knows something about where he is, and if this is the only lead we've got then so be it, because I'm giving it another twenty four hours and then we've got to give something to the press.' His phone erupted with the heavy plucking of guitar strings, 'Detective Mark Jarvis.'

'Huh…this is DI Geoffrey Mathers from Siddington Police Station, and well sorry to bother you, but…I got a feeling you're going to find this bit of information well, rather interesting I suppose. Obviously, we know about the man, the erm…physiotherapist that's gone missing, but we've just been alerted that we now have a missing person, and she was last seen on the 13th April. Here's the funny thing though, or should I say coincidence about this missing lady, she's a nurse. Anyway, like I say it's interesting, because check this out, we were informed about her disappearance by a Philippa Nugent, who's a close buddy as they both belong to the same nursing agency, and the reason that they're close is that they, more often than not, have shifts at the same hospital, nursing home or whatever, so they swapped numbers. It was her that showed us the last text that she received from her which simply read, '*gone to a symposium*' so now you see, Inspector Jarvis that's why I thought you'd be interested in this missing person case.'

'Well….it seems as though our two cases are most certainly connected, don't you agree? What's the info on the misper anyway, where's she from, how long's she been with the agency that sort of thing, and perhaps more importantly, did the young Filipino say anything at all to Philippa that she was going to a conference? I mean if they're quite close wouldn't she be the first person that Rosario told?'

'Okay, she's a twenty-six-year-old Filipino lady known as Rosario Baluyot, that's spelt B A L U Y O T,' the detective slowly tiptoed around the alphabet, giving Jarvis the time to note each letter down correctly, 'and she works for a company which goes by the name of Phoenix Specialist Nursing Agency Group, and she's been there for the best part of eighteen months. To answer your third point, Philippa said that if her friend was going anywhere then she'd always message her straight away, because Rosario got so excited about everything, which is why she's surprised to have received the text. We got her address from the agency, and not knowing whether her next of kin spoke English or not, we managed to get hold of a translator, who eventually touched base with her mother, known as Maria, and she informed us that they were speaking on Facetime on the 11th April and Rosario was very happy, enjoying her work in the U.K, and had made quite a few friends.

'Also according to her mum, she never mentioned going to any symposium, or in fact any upcoming trips that she was likely to be going on, which I find a bit strange, because well…if she'd been talking about work, wouldn't it be perfectly natural that she'd mention about going somewhere perhaps new, and wanting to show her excitement with her mum, knowing that she would probably be so proud of her, you know. Not sure if this is connected, but three days ago a fella appeared at the Agency who employs Miss Baluyot, and the receptionist said that he had some flowers for Rosario as a thank you for what she did for his mother whilst she was in hospital, and well…he was so adamant that he wanted to give them to her personally, so she caved in and told him where the young nurse was working.

'Of course, she's gutted that she made this decision now, but at the time she didn't feel as though she was doing anything wrong, because the man seemed so sincere. We're arranging for her to meet with one of our sketch artists to see if we can get some kind of photo fit picture as to what he looks like, but I'm not holding my breath, because when she was asked for any details as to his appearance she couldn't give us very much, just that he had died peroxide hair, and wore a track suit. But as you well know, this scant description could match at least two thirds of the male population. Who knows though, our guy may well be able to jog her memory a little bit, 'cos he really is good at his job.'

'This is a long shot I know Inspector Mathers, and I know the answer before you even give it, but well…the text that was left on her friend's phone, it didn't by any chance say where this symposium was did it?'

'No, nothing I'm afraid. Anyway, we went around to the young lady's place of residence, which is a house that she shares with two other people, and they both claim that they hadn't seen her since the 11th, but they couldn't quite put a definitive date on it, as they all seemed to be like *'ships passing in the night'* which is what a Miss Carmel Whetton stated. Both she, and Rosario's other house mate, a Mr Aaron Fleet, were under the impression that she was more likely out of town staying with friends, maybe found a boyfriend or whatever. Mr Fleet also commented with some amusement, *'We don't live in each other's pockets you know. We've all got our own lives to live and our own separate friends. When we know were going away for a couple of days or something like that, we would leave a post-it note somewhere, like on the fridge, but that's about it really.'*

'So, as you can see it was pretty pointless asking whether they'd heard or knew that she was going off on some work-related business because, for starters, they probably wouldn't have been interested, but more importantly, by the sounds of it any road, she no doubt wouldn't have told them. Perhaps this sense of freedom that the youngsters seem to want isn't all that it's cracked up to be after all.'

'So, what we've got Inspector Mathers is that there are two common denominators here and they're the only things we've got to go on. The first, of course, is that they're both in the medical profession, and do locum work, and the second is that the same message was sent from their phones. Of course, we've got no proof whatsoever, but considering what we know so far with the phone call to the physiotherapist's office and a stranger calling on the agency where Miss Baluyot reports to, it would seem that the same man somehow lured both people into his car under false pretences. We can assume that the man in question is confident, and more importantly very convincing. We need to get a list of hospitals, care homes and any other medical facility that Miss Baluyot was known to have worked in, and we're waiting for the same sort of information from the private practice where our Mr Hackman used to locum.

'We've been told that our Mr Hackman's passion lies with patients who've suffered from brain injuries, whether they're accident driven or some kind of neurological shut down, as it's his belief that with good physiotherapy immediately following the attack on the brain this will ultimately give them the best chance for some kind of recovery. So perhaps, and I guess it's a long shot, but our young Filipino might have had the same specialist knowledge. May I suggest that that's where we should start with our investigation?' Jarvis heard the beeping of his phone, and it signalled a message from the Crown Prosecution Service, 'Gotta go Inspector Mathers, I gotta go. Let's stay in touch yeah?'

Opening the message, he read it with a wide grin plastered all over his face, 'Bail denied. Thought you'd like to know,' as Jarvis grinned at the sight of a yellow thumb stuck up in the air, a simple emoji that said it all.

Jarvis punching the air walked over to the jungle of desks where his little army worked tirelessly, 'Just heard guys, DaCosta ain't getting out before the trial date. And d'you know what, I'd have given anything to have seen that jumped up, smirky face of his squirm like a rat that's just figured it's eaten a shit load of poison,' as cries of 'Wooohoooo,' echoed raucously around the room.

Chapter 12

Having been summoned to meet with the Detective Chief Inspector, Jarvis knew that he was going to be bombarded with a right royal bollocking, as results from him and his team hadn't been the most praiseworthy of late, and now he'd got the added task of explaining why there was yet another missing person.

Climbing the soulless, grey, bare walled staircase to Peter Wolfe's office where, having previously never noticed before, it appeared more depressing than ever as he clomped one step at a time holding wearily onto the banister, even though he knew he would never misread the treads of the bare wooden steps that he'd trod hundreds of times over the years. Standing outside of the pine-coloured wooden door which offered complete privacy for the man behind it, he knocked heavy heartedly until the voice petitioned him to enter.

'Good morning chief, you hum…wanted to see me?'

'Yes, Detective Inspector Jarvis, come in, come in. Please take a seat.'

Jarvis sat on the maroon upholstered seat, crossed one leg over the other and waited like a schoolboy in the headmaster's office, waiting for his admonishment.

'So, Jarvis, shall we dispense with pleasant formalities, especially as you and I have known each other for the wrong side of ten years now, eh? I've been informed that we now have two missing persons on our list, and I need to know what you can give me, because the bosses at the top of the tree are demanding that we give a press release. So, tell me everything you know up to date.'

Jarvis relayed all the information that he'd been given, and the investigations and lines of enquiry that his team had followed, especially in the case of Robin Hackman. He corrected his boss as to the second missing person because she was, to all intents and purposes, not within their jurisdiction, but the main reason that they were apprised as to her disappearance was due to the fact that she was associated with the medical profession too.

'Humph…so these are all the details that I'm armed with when I'm standing up in front of a group of hungry journalists and tell them what…an absolutely big fat nothing. There's no doubt about it, it'll be the most amazing question and answer time in living memory, because the only bloody answers that I'll be able to give will be, '*No comment,*' or '*we're not apprised of any such information at this time.*' This is going to really increase confidence in the police force, don't you think?'

As he was speaking, Jarvis wondered to himself why it was that men that were obviously almost totally bald did that Bobby Charlton look where fine wisps of fairly long hair are combed over to the other side of the head in order to hide a shiny scalp.

'Are you even listening to me JARVIS?'

'Yes, yes of course I am. It's just that well…what do you want me to do, make some stuff up so that it'll look good in the media circus, you know like…'Oh it's okay Mr Hackman's returned home, and it was all a misunderstanding, he was just hiding from his partner for a few days as a bit of a joke. And here's the other funny thing, the nurse that was missing has, by all accounts, flown back to her mum and dad who live in the Philippines as she was a bit homesick, and we've heard from her family that she is indeed fit and well and will be returning to the UK within the next few days.' Is that what you want? Because let me tell you sir, we haven't got any leads to go on, and believe me we've exhausted every angle.

'But see here's the good news and that is we've just received lists of all Mr Hackman's patients that he sees at his private practice, and we're in the process of somehow trying to find patients that he's treated within the last six to twelve months at hospitals and care homes, which isn't easy as I'm sure you can imagine, because some have probably relocated, some died, so the task is positively enormous. And as I'm sure you're aware from the DCI from Siddington Police Station, we're working alongside them trying to find the Baluyot girl using pretty much the same line of questioning. If Sir, you have any useful hints as to what we should do next, then please I'm all ears.'

'I know it's a tricky case Jarvis, and we may get lucky when their photographs get published, but we've got to pull out all the stops otherwise both you and me are going to be retiring a lot sooner than we'd have liked. So…just keep me posted and let's get this sonofabitch.' Before Jarvis had even had the time to stand up, Wolfe picked up his internal phone and was speaking to someone through the mouthpiece.

The descent from the fourth floor of the building to his office on the second was even more arduous than the ascent, but he'd made his mind up about something, and all he had to do was talk to the guys about it.

***

Having persuaded the lads to go for a jar after work seemed like a good idea, and Eleanor had more or less insisted that she thought it was important that he go for a snifter with his buddies in an attempt to offer some moral support, especially in light of the difficult cases that they'd recently been landed with. Before removing the phone from his ear, he promised her that he was going to take her out for a slap-up meal soon and that he'd be as quiet as a church mouse when he came in.

He decided that he'd leave his car at work and find some other means of getting to work in the morning, and whilst walking at a steady pace, Jarvis knew he'd reached his destination as he stepped into a cloud of smoke from the nicotine junkies who were all huddled outside the main doors.

Opening the heavy mahogany doors to the 'Ball and Chain' pub which he and his crew often went for a well-deserved drink and to let off steam, he was completely bowled over by how busy it was in there. Ray, the landlord seemed to have managed to attract regulars and visitors to this once failing watering hole by offering good ale, and food that was home cooked, very tasty, not overly priced and didn't take hours for it to arrive at the table. He also had decided to decorate the pub with paintings and memorabilia in conjunction with its name which would always result in good, humoured conversation whilst waiting to be served at the bar, where chit chat with strangers was the norm.

This was a Wednesday night and if it had been a Friday or Saturday, then this would have been understandable, but the din of laughter, heavy voices mixed with music emanating from the juke box was almost deafening. The usual, dominating football banter, and drink fuelled predictions by die-hard fans being made, *'Yer wah, never…2-0, 'nah, yer orf yer 'ed mate…1-1,'* were prominent amidst the general hubbub of every day events, and the latest smear campaign about the latest dodgy politician. Weaving his way through the throng of people, who surreptitiously moved their glasses above their heads, or behind their backs, as Jarvis extended his apologies, 'Sorry, sorry,' whilst almost pirouetting in order to avoid spillages of the person's tipple.

He spotted Javid first who nudged the rest of the gang to make way in their circle for their boss, 'What took you so long, guv?' the Indian detective sergeant asked whilst taking a thirsty guzzle of his pint of lager.

'As you're already propping up the bar Dean, mine's a pint of Thatchers,' remarked Jarvis as he took a handful of crisps from the almost empty brown wooden bowl that was sitting idly on the bar. 'Ugh, my God…no wonder they're free, bet they're two years passed their sell by date,' whilst looking for a napkin to spit them out onto, finding none, Jarvis had no choice but to swallow them followed by a rather large gulp of his tipple.

They all laughed, 'You're lucky you didn't try the nuts, boss.'

'Cheers everyone,' saluted the Inspector as he raised his glass in the air. 'Cor bloody hell, now that's a nice pint. So…what've I missed? Who've you been slagging off tonight then, eh?'

'No one in particular, just the crooked bastards that we have to deal with every day. But the one great thing that's gone our way is that that wicked sonofabitch didn't get bail, so that's something to drink to,' glugged Dean as he downed the syrupy looking liquid and clinked his glass against Kelly's.

'Let's pray the bastard gets what he deserves then, yeah?' uttered Kelly raising her gin and tonic in the air.

With the drinks flowing and the banter getting more and more light-hearted with cases that they'd managed to close, obviously not giving out names but they each knew which low life villain they were referring to, when Jarvis piped up with the most bizarre statement that the rest of the crew had ever heard.

'I think they should get those lazy, good for nothing bastards out of their cosy little nests, supposedly doing time for crime, and get them sweeping the bloody pavements and streets,' as the explosion of laughter was palpable within the group.

'What the fuck did you say?' slurred Josh.

'Well, stands to reason, doesn't it?' answered the senior detective as he stared at him with hands held akimbo, 'I mean, people are paying good money to local councils to have their streets cleaned, and 'cos leaves from the trees are dropping faster than you shittin' after a curry, why shouldn't they use these low lives to sweep 'em up? I mean they'd be getting fresh air, and we wouldn't have to wait for councillors to find the manpower to do it because you have to kinda agree there's an abundance of it behind bars, so what's not to like about the idea? And let's face it guys, innocent taxpayers are having to put up with slipping and falling on wet leaves when prisoners are allowed to sit in the warmth with every luxury that they could possibly want, plus free courses for this, that and the bloody other, when our hard-working students have loans that they'll be paying back from out of their pensions. No, it's high time that they should be made to put something back into society for the crimes that they've committed and earn the food that's put on their plates.'

The five junior detectives stared, grunted and shook their heads as they realised that their gaffer was absolutely serious, as Josh, who was normally the quiet one of the gang, wiped his mouth after spluttering his lager down the sides of his mouth argued, 'It's not gonna 'appen guv, I mean let's face it how can you let a bunch of pissin' convicts on the streets with brooms and spades in their hands? You can imagine it carn't ya, passers by being bad mouthed, sex starved men wolf whistling at the ladies, and well…I suppose some might like it, but most of 'em will lash out at them and hit 'em around their heads with their 'andbags. And where d'you suppose they're gonna go for a piss, are they going to knock on one of the home owners' door and say, *'Scuse me but I'm a banged up prisoner, and well I'm doing a bit of sweeping up of all these wet leaves so you don't like…erm fall on your arse, and well I desperately need to take a shit, so d'ya mind if I use your bog?'*

The laughter was infectious and not only with the detectives but also with a few of the punters who were standing nearby, as they couldn't help but overhear their chatter and guffawing. One of them had craftily sneaked off to the jukebox and when he returned, he and his mates started singing along with Led Zeppelin's Ramble On, which spurred the police officers on as they raised their empty glasses to open mouths as they used them as microphones whilst singing along enthusiastically to the lyrics. The hilarity that this scene brought, to what was rather a mundane kind of a day, certainly lifted their spirits, and it seemed that most of the pub were joining in with the chanting of the words with arms raised in the air as if it were a football anthem.

Jarvis really didn't want the night or the jocularity to end, but he knew she was right when Kelly declared, 'Guv, we've all had a blast don't ye know, but sure it's time we were gone, so I'm going to say good night to ye all,' as she headed off towards the door, she made a wave behind her back.

Supping their drinks until the bottoms of the glasses could be seen, the other four officers cheerily made their way, following their colleague.

***

Deciding that he'd better have a slash before he started on his two mile or so walk home, he once again weaved his way through the now emptying hostelry towards the solid black door marked Gents. Making his way back towards the door and a quick exit he glanced towards the corner of the polished wooden surface of the bar, where he noticed the figure of a solitary man whom he recognised straight away, 'Luke, is that you?' whilst proffering his outstretched hand, waiting for the gesture to be reciprocated.

Sliding off his bar stool, the man grabbed Jarvis towards him and hugged him cordially slapping him gently on the back, 'Mark, my old friend, great to see you again. I thought it was your lot over there making all that din, but I wasn't going to come over and spoil your night out with the lads. How've you been? It's been a lifetime since I saw you, how's Eleanor and the boys doing?'

'Yeah, it's been too long, but I don't know about you, but I just don't know where the time goes,' thinking to himself that it would be rude not to offer his old buddy a refill, but cursing himself that he hadn't waited to attend to his bladder when he got home. So, he asked the slim man who was sporting black jeans and a black polo shirt with the famous green alligator logo, 'D'you want another one Luke? I know it's a bit late, but we could have one for the road, or do you need to get home to Nancy and Julia?'

'Yeah, I'll have a glass of Rioja.'

'So, half a Thatchers and a large Rioja for my friend here,' requested Jarvis of the barman, 'oh and have you got any crisps well…the non-stale kind?'

'We've got salt and vinegar, cheese and onion, smo…'

'Cheese and onion make that two packets, and a bag of dry roasted peanuts as well, please,' turning sideways to glance at his mate he remarked, 'Not had any dinner, and I guess there'll be nothing in the oven when I get home as I told Ellie not to bother,' patting his stomach he smirked and stated, 'Well…it's not as though I'm going to end up in a special unit for eating disorders, now is it?'

Still not forthcoming in the conversation department the detective continued, 'So, how's work going then? Still at the same place, erm…an accountancy firm or auditing, something to do with numbers if I remember correctly?'

'Yeah, still at Dunstan and Cooke', and as jobs go it's not too bad, I suppose, same old, same old I guess. Did I ever tell you I got a promotion? Mind you it was way overdue, but the extra money comes in useful now that we don't have

Nancy's income.' Jarvis turned askance towards his old buddy, and with a dry inquisitive expression, enquired, 'So, you've at long last decided to keep your wife to the life that she should be accustomed to eh? Good for you. I've been trying to get Ellie to relax more you know, instead of worrying how many paintings she's got to do, and if she's gonna get them done on time, and hum…is she charging too much or too little. Mind you I bloody envy you coming home to delicious smells from your kitchen, what with Nancy's gourmet cooking skills and everything. You lucky sod.'

'You really don't know…?'

'Know what?' Jarvis examined.

'Nancy had a brain haemorrhage about erm…almost two years ago now, and even after four months of hospital rehabilitation she's unable to walk, she never got the use of either her right arm or leg back. But the worst thing of all is that the only way we can get her out of bed is by using a bloody contraption called a hoist, which is the same kind of crappy machine that they use to weigh cattle, for fuck's sake,' reported the slim man sitting aside the police officer sporting his short, mousey brown, spiky haircut.

'Ah Luke, I'm…absolutely gutted man, I really don't know what to say. Will she be able to walk again, d'you think? I mean she must be getting lots of treatment right, even though she's at home. A stroke's not really that big a deal these days I guess, because medicines come a long way don't you think? I know that lots of old people have them, but that doesn't mean that they end up with not being able to do anything for themselves, does it? Aren't you being a bit um…pessimistic about Nancy, I mean…let's face it she's still young, fit and she's got years and years ahead of her. Nah, she'll be fine, and if I remember well that's one of a gutsy woman.'

Taking a long swig of the dark red liquid that was swilling around the goblet shaped glass, Luke cleared his throat slightly before waspishly replying, 'So, you know all about strokes now do you? Can I ask you a question? How many people that are known personally to you have suffered from one so badly that not only have they lost the physical abilities to stand, or feed themselves, but have mushed up shit to eat 'cos they can't swallow properly, and perhaps even worse than that…is when the only words that comes out of their mouths is '*doo na,*' so now tell me that I'm being, what was it you said, erm…oh yeah, pessimistic.'

'Sorry man, I didn't mean to imply that it's not difficult, all I meant was that because she's so young and strokes really affect older people that she'd have a better chance of a recovery. That was all. I erm…. didn't mean any offence,' as Jarvis realised that the alcohol that he'd rather greedily drunk earlier had more or less worn off, and that he was now unfortunately completely sober.

'I'm sorry, I guess I overreacted. So, how's the lovely Eleanor and the boys?'

'Everyone's fine thanks, but we're going through the whole late teenage years stuff now, and unfortunately there's not a pill in the world that'll get us through it, so we sigh a lot and try to keep our opinions to ourselves. Alex still throws us his corny, one liner off the cuff jokes, and their attempts at trying to hide the unmistakeable smells of the adolescent compulsory experimentation with nicotine, and the sweet-smelling aromatic sprays to try and hide the stench makes our home stink like some kind of cheap brothel.

'They've even made endless excuses to walk a dog that we haven't got, and always offering to take the rubbish out every night even when the bin's empty. Eleanor simply laughs it off and constantly reminds me that our two boys didn't invent this stuff, as we did exactly the same when we were their age. Mind you the price of a pack of ten then is nothing compared to what it is now, so we think it'll fizzle out…' the Inspector sniggered at this last remark, 'sorry about the pun, but well…once their pennies run out at the end of the month, they absolutely don't get any more.'

'Right yeah, we've all been through that I s'pose. Want another one?' enquired the slim man, as he tapped the polished counter with a beer mat in tune with the strumming guitars of Mark Knopfler to *'Money for nothing.'*

'Just half for me, ta. Got a long day ahead tomorrow,' came the reply as he guzzled the last of the dry roasted peanuts in his mouth, chewed vigorously, and then brushed both hands together to rid his hands from the brown powdery residue.

'Is Nancy able to go for walks especially in the nice weather and I don't mean physically walking, but are you able to take her out in a wheelchair? Stanton Park is particularly beautiful at this time of year, and it's completely wheelchair friendly, it's got the lake and all the natural wil…' was interrupted before he could finish, Luke acidicly demonstrated, 'I'm well aware what the bloody park's got Mark, but once again I'm going to have to remind you that it's not that fucking simple is it?'

'How so?' pondered the detective.

'For a start off, she won't sit in the soddin' chair without wriggling and trying to get out, and if she does, how the hell am I going to get her back in it if I'm in an open space like that? Secondly, she has no control over her bladder or her bowels, and if she has an accident then she starts howling, and people start gawping at me as if I'm trying to kill her. But the worst of it all is that even though she's not the same person that she once was, or will ever be again, deep down she knows what's happened to her, and the one thing that she would positively detest is that she has no control over what happens to her.

'Of course, I can't be sure, but the worse than useless speech and language therapists claim that her understanding is not impaired, it's just that she can't communicate her feelings and the only way she knows how is to, well…thrash out in anger. Now, you know Nancy, considering all the time we spent together doing school runs, barbeques, school sports days and all the usual run of the mill compulsory extracurricular activities that we as mums and dads are forced to attend, she'd absolutely hate to be a burden to anyone, and she's just so proud, and the thought of losing all control well…I can't imagine the devastation that's going around in her mind, and she's got to hum…handle all of it by herself, despite me or her full time nurse telling her that it's not a big deal. So, Mark to answer your question that would be a big fat no to taking my wife to the park or anywhere else for that matter.'

'D'you know what, I think I'm going to call it a da…' murmured Jarvis, but before he'd got time to finish his sentence, his one-time friend, touched him lightly on the arm and commanded, 'Ssshhhh, I want to listen to this.'

On the flat screen housed in a convenient niche in the bar, the head of a familiar police officer beckoned everyone's attention, as the ticker tape at the bottom announced the disappearance of two members of the public, of which Jarvis was well apprised as to the current information.

'Turn this up,' demanded Luke.

'Good evening I'm Detective Chief Inspector Peter Wolfe from the Stockfield Road Police Station here in Upper Stanton.

'We have had two disturbing reports of two people one, a Mr Robin Hackman, and a Filipino known as a Miss Rosario Baluyot who seem to have sadly gone missing.

'Mr Hackman was last seen on 31st March, and it was alleged that he had gone to a medical symposium, but after lengthy investigations by our officers, we have been unable to find any evidence that he was either seen or known to have attended any such conference within a thirty-mile radius of Upper Stanton.

So, it would appear as though he either didn't arrive at any such meeting, or if he did, he failed to notify either his long-term partner or his family as to his current whereabouts. He's not answering his mobile phone and his family are understandably concerned as Mr Hackman is incredibly close with his mother and sister, and it is so uncharacteristic of him not to notify them or his partner of his location.

'As for Miss Baluyot, she last spoke to a nursing associate of hers on 13th April and she too was meant to have been at a medical conference, and likewise as with the case of Mr Hackman, no details were given as to where this was to be held. We've got teams who are presently contacting hospitals, known conference halls, medical institutes and educational venues to find out if she was included on any list for any symposium which she would have been likely to attend, which I'm sure you'll agree is an incredibly lengthy task and up until now we have no leads to go on.

'The reason for this interruption into your late-night viewing is that we need you, the public, to assist the police to help locate these two people. The photographs that you can see on your screens are the most up to date, and we've been assured by both Mr Hackman's and Miss Baluyot's family that these images are correct, and as you can see there are no obvious identification marks on their faces such as moles, birthmarks, or any other distinguishing features.

'Mr Hackman sports a tattoo of a spider trapped in a web on the back of his left shoulder, and as far as Miss Baluyot's parents are aware she doesn't have any at all on her body.

'We at the Met have been proud in the past with the public's response in cases such as these, and we urge each and every one of you to help us find these two people. At the bottom of the screen you'll see various telephone numbers, and officers will be manning them twenty-four hours a day.

'On behalf of Stockfield Road Police station I want to take this opportunity in thanking you for your continuing support.

'I will now be taking questions from members of the media.'

Ray, the owner of the Ball and Chain held a remote control in his hand and swiftly pressed one of the numbers on the black handset where a whistle was being blown by a man wearing a black football shirt, shorts and black socks, as loud cheers ricocheted around the room from the punters who were still left in the pub.

'So, these two missing people, it's a big deal right?'

'Yeah, it's really bizarre, and obviously the families are extremely worried that something bad happened, because it's just so out of character for them to simply run off without telling anyone,' replied Jarvis as he ran both hands up and down the half-pint glass.

'You've really got no idea where they are, or why they went missing, 'cos this thing about what did he say, they hum…went to a what…symposium, that's really a bit weird, don't you think?'

'I'm sorry Luke but I can't discuss it any further, but I can tell you that what you just heard is, unfortunately, all the information that we have.'

'Okay, I understand. I hope you find them, and quickly of course.'

The senior detective, wishing to side track the conversation, continued, 'So as you're here, I'm assuming that perhaps Julia is sitting at home with her mum, eh?'

'Good God no. We have around the clock care for Nance, and I never go out until she's in bed, that's when I slip out for a couple of hours in the evening, well …. after she's gone to sleep of course. I need this escape, know what I mean, and anyway that's what the nurses are paid for after all, wouldn't you say?'

'Have you given up work, or do they let you work from home?' enquired Jarvis, as he leant heavily on crossed arms on the polished surface of the bar.

'They've been really good to me you know, like if I need time out to see one of her therapists, or she needs to see her GP, and on the very rare occurrence that a nurse hasn't shown up for her shift, well I have to wait for a replacement, but basically, I just do my own thing. My boss assured me that they understood my difficulties, and they were just fine with allowing me to work wherever it suited me, just so long as it got done. But seriously though, I don't know how I'd cope if they weren't able to allow me a bit of slack with regard to Nancy's treatment and ongoing care.'

'Tell me, how do you manage to get Nancy up and down the stairs, have you got a special lift or something, 'cos that can't be easy right, and er…is she able to have a bath and stuff?'

'No, it's impossible for both the first and the second questions. Apparently, with Nancy earning a fair amount when she was working as a legal assistant, and with my earnings, we don't apparently qualify for any contributions towards house adaptations. In fact, we still haven't even got a wheelchair ramp outside of the property which I forgot to mention is another reason why I wouldn't be able to take her out for some fresh air, and that also goes for her being able to sit outside in the garden because I can't bloody well get her over the steps into the back. I've had certificates signed by our GP to say that it's imperative for her mental health that she goes outside, and I've had statements from our bank manager stating that we're just about managing with the mortgage repayments, but the council or whoever's in charge of dealing with this kind of shit are still not willing to budge.'

Forcing a tired smile onto an already perplexed face, the detective turned towards his friend and asked curiously, 'Are you telling me that poor Nancy has to stay in her bedroom for the rest of her life, simply because no one is prepared to foot the bill to get her up and down the stairs? I mean…this is the twenty first century for fuck's sake. But also, when you think about it, isn't this violating her human rights, because no one should be locked away when there's a perfectly simple solution, it's not as though we're in a third world country now is it? Why haven't you been in touch with your M.P. 'cos I know I bloody well would, that's for sure. You've both paid National Insurance and Income Tax all your working life, so isn't it time to recoup some of the benefits that I think are owing to you both?'

'Wow…you're really fired up about this aren't you? I've done the hitting my head against the brick walls and throwing anything that'll smash against the kitchen walls thing, but I guess I've learned to live with the fact that that gorgeous woman of mine is physically impaired for the rest of her life. If it wasn't for the sheer pig headedness of her consultant, believe me she'd still be bed bound upstairs, but thanks to him he called in a favour from one of the A&E consultants and arranged for an ambulance, which had obviously got a stretcher to bring her downstairs, and we turned the dining room into her new bedroom. The idea was that if Nance was brought down closer to the main hub of everyday life, this just might help her to readjust and somehow persuade her that she wasn't forgotten in relative isolation, which is what she may have been thinking by being upstairs alone for the best part of the day. So, she's got a nice little room next to the kitchen, and she's got all of her most loved possessions, framed photographs, pictures on the wall, and she's even got one that Eleanor painted for her shortly after we guys first met.'

'That's good to hear Luke. So, she sits with you and Julia in the kitchen then, perhaps in a more comfortable chair, a bit like a…hum…an armchair that sort of thing? There's got to be something that's actually designed for people who are immobile, because sitting in a wheelchair all day long may get pretty uncomfortable and not good for the posture, I guess?'

Giving his onetime close friend a dismissive flick of his hand, Luke irritably barked, 'Don't you think I've tried, Mark? Godammit, haven't you been listening, all this fucking talk about bloody chairs, of course there are specialist chairs and you'll be glad to know they come in a range of colours,' retorted Luke sarcastically, whilst raising the near empty wine glass to his lips, 'but as I keep bloody telling you, I can't get any financial help from anyone, and all this adaptive furniture you keep banging on about costs thousands and thousands. And as for her sitting in the kitchen with me, oh boy let me tell you I tried, I really did, but she just gets so...' The narrator stopped in his tracks, slid off the bar stool and started swaying with closed eyes as the hypnotic sounds of keyboards, and the harmonic plucking of guitar strings orchestrated by Genesis as the heart-rending 'Afterglow' vibrated around the room.

As he sang the lyrics faultlessly, he was almost trance like as he carried on with the emotional lament.

As the tune slowly wound down and finally came to its crescendo, Luke climbed back on the stool almost metamorphosed from the bitter, angry man that had sat there earlier, into this illuminated figure who didn't seem to have a care in the world.

'What a tune, you remember it right?' Luke quizzed, whilst fixing a penetrating gaze towards the police officer.

Answering as he tilted his head to one side and with a somewhat shame faced look admitted, 'I kinda remember it, but seriously can't remember the name of the band, eighties band perhaps?'

'It's my absolute all-time favourite song from the album *Wind and Wuthering* by Genesis man, and the track that's just been played is called *Afterglow*.'

Gazing at the animated man, Jarvis added, 'Course I remember it, but I wouldn't have got either name if you hadn't have told me. I am, well was...perhaps is more of the truth, a fan of the band, but it's a long time ago since I heard their stuff, you know. Did the song make the charts back then?'

'What the fuck's that got to do with anything?'

'No, no I'm not saying that a tune isn't a great success just because it doesn't make the charts, it's just that I remember songs a lot more when they're played on the radio and given a lot of airtime and stuff. I know, I know...that must sound pretty stupid and a bit juvenile, but that's erm…just the way I am, I'm afraid. I also have to say in my defence, that I'm more of a Gabriel fan myself, so I'd probably be able to name his tunes more than the Genesis ones after he left in, when was it…let's see, probably around 1975?'

The transfiguration didn't last long as Luke started gesticulating with his hands and jabbing a pointed forefinger into Jarvis' chest, and with a loud groan of despair declared, 'You've got no bloody idea what you've just said have you? You see, what you ignorantly fail to realise is that if Gabriel had still been with the band, we'd never have got this incredible sound, and you know what, the words of this will never be understood by the likes of you, because let's face it, you've got everything you fucking well need. Just, erm…listen to the words man, it's about being lost, and having the things that you love and adore taken away cruelly, and in the end, you're left with nothing, nothing except the memories and crucially the worst of it is, everything that you once had, you'll never have again.'

Whilst lowering his gaze to hide his embarrassment and the bizarre nature of the discussion, Jarvis announced to Luke that it was time that he was heading home.

'Yeah, I s'pose you're right, but listen Mark my old buddy…it's been great to catch up again. Let's not leave it so long next time huh?'

'Why don't you come over one night as I'm sure Ellie would love to see you again, and well…she makes a mean lasagne, and she makes her own garlic bread too. How's that sound?'

'Yeah, yeah…let's stay in touch,' Luke reached for his wallet from the back pocket of his faded black jeans, but Jarvis had beaten him to it as he handed over his credit card to the bar man.

'Tonight's on me pal, and I'm really sorry for everything you're going through, but I'm here for you if there's anything I can do, anything at all, just give me a call. You've still got my numbers, right?'

'Thanks mate. I mean it, it was really great to chew the cud, and thanks a lot for listening to me, but I have to say I'm a little bit sorry and embarrassed that you had to witness my little outbursts, but whether or not you agree with me, I think the whole thing just sucks and the people with power don't give a toss about either the patient who has disabilities or the carers of those individuals.'

'You know what I was just thinking about though Luke, as you feel so passionate about this issue and quite rightly so, why don't you do something about it? As I said earlier, contact your M.P., contact local newspapers, and radio and get them to interview you, and you could become a kind of platform for not just Nancy and you, but the thousands of other people that are struggling with the same or similar issues as you guys,' he paused momentarily before he quietly continued, 'well, that's what I think you should do anyway, and I reckon you'd be a great champion for the cause.'

Both men strolled towards the door with Luke trailing behind, muttering inwardly, 'Champion indeed, why don't you just fuck off.'

***

As both men stepped onto the pavement, the detective was somewhat taken aback when the man whom he'd spent a large chunk of the evening with wasn't going in the same direction, especially as they both lived in the same part of town. Turning slightly, whilst sauntering fairly casually on a gorgeous moon lit evening, he noticed Luke walking in lengthy strides with the slight hip hitching that he'd forgotten about, which he'd inherited during a football kick around a few years back.

Opening the door to the driver's side of the deep red coloured Ford Transit Courier van, he stared at his reflection in the rear-view mirror, and mockingly announced with pure venom in his voice, 'Him and his cock-sucking lasagne, and he knows where he can shove his wife's homemade fucking garlic bread. He really is a total wanker and so he thinks you would be good as a champion for poor, poor people who need help with things doing to their houses, and new chairs. Oh, please Mr soddin' Policeman, when did you become so bloody self-important?'

Not caring that he'd had far too much to drink, or even being the slightest bit concerned whether there were any cops on the road, he started the engine, even though he could feel his anger growing which was intensified by the excessive alcohol that was flowing freely through his blood stream.

'I'll show you who's a fucking champion, and it won't be in front of a stupid newspaper or M.P. No, I'm gonna prove to you that I'm a supporter of doing things my way, and you're never gonna find out what it is I've done, well...not until I'm ready to tell you that is.'

Pressing play on the CD, nothing could have been heard from the outside world as Phil Collins's melodious tones diffused through the remaining air molecules all fighting for space.

Driving over the disused, empty car park, he killed the head lamps, went around to the back of the van, opened the doors and removed the two bags that he would need for the next thrilling hour or two, which he was really looking forward to.

Chapter 13

Waking up with a stomping headache, and thankful to the high heavens that it was a Saturday morning, Jarvis, whilst rubbing his forehead backwards and forwards with his fingers, lightly trudged noiselessly down the treads of the stairs one by one as his sensory receptors were set on fire by the smell of fresh coffee and toast that definitely had that distinctive 'left in for too long' aroma. But he really couldn't care less because all he needed were two little white tablets from a blister pack and a cool glass of ice-cold water just to get rid of the mould that someone had planted on his tongue overnight.

'Morning pops, been on the razzle again, have we?' sniggered Alex, as he stood by the sink shovelling cocoa pops or some other quirky sugary cereal into his mouth.

'Very funny, could you just like…let me deal with the hamster that's running around the inside of my skull on his cute little running machine, and then you can throw all the jibes you want at me,' groaned Jarvis as he turned the cold water tap on full blast and began filling the half pint glass.

Casting a shifty glance at the flat screen ensconced neatly in the alcove of the Welsh dresser, he picked up the remote control to turn it off from one of the myriad of cooking shows that seem to control the television world, and replace it with the world news channel, but he was halted by his younger son Andy who quickly protested, 'Aw dad leave it, this is a good programme, and it's not just about cooking you know, they have some really cool guests.'

'Oh well, if you don't want to know what's going on in the world and you'd rather watch these exorbitantly paid 'D' celebrities sit and ogle at so called passionate chefs chopping up bits of celery, onion, whilst grating garlic along a serrated piece of metal and marvelling at themselves as to what an easy, exotic dish they'd just created then knock yourself out. The funny thing is about these stupid programmes is that, even though the wider audience is meant to be following how to make food that's fit only for paradise or for Satan, and as the chefs and guests continually chatter all the way through, how could anyone

179

possibly follow the damned recipe? And the other thing is, if viewers aren't able to taste the grub to see if it's worth making, and they can't follow the recipe, what's the bloody point of putting these damned shows on the telly in the first place?'

'Jeez, you're a real old grouch this morning, lighten up will ya?' declared Alex whilst inwardly finding the whole thing highly amusing.

'Ssshhhhhhh,' moaned the boy's father, 'wait till the pills find where they're meant to attack first, then you can shout all you like.'

His eldest son, as he was already standing by the kettle and the coffee jar, heaped two loaded teaspoons of the bitter smelling granules into a mug with the words *World's Greatest Cop* sprawled on the side of it, filled it with boiling water and added way too much sugar, but he knew his pops would drink it if it meant the demons were finally released from his head.

'Where's mum?' asked Jarvis as he took a sip of the scalding hot drink.

'She's around somewhere, not sure where though,' replied Andy.

As water could be heard filling the cistern once again, the unmistakeable sounds of shuffling slippers announced the arrival of Eleanor.

'Morning darling, did you have a good time last night with the lads, or are we going to hear the same ole mantra, '*never again, never again?* '

'Mum, I wouldn't speak to him just yet, he's got the mother of all hangovers,' warned the thin, handsome face of Andy bedevilled with the cruelty of teenage years, whose pale skin had turned scaly and red possibly due to all of the lotions and potions he applied to rid himself of the hormonal spots.

Ellie found herself in front of her struggling husband and planted a quick peck on his coffee-stained lips, brushed past him and opened the fridge door where she removed a carton of eggs, a Tupperware container with a bright yellow lid, which contained bacon, and plopped the rashers into a black, metallic frying pan where they started to sizzle loudly.

Feeling slightly better after his mini feast, Jarvis humbly announced, 'D'you know this is the first time I've eaten since yesterday breakfast, well apart from some out-of-date crisps and nuts at the pub, so it's no wonder I felt damned rough,' swilling down the last of his breakfast with a gulp of fresh orange juice. He suddenly remembered, 'You'll never guess who I bumped into as I was going for a sla…I mean a pee last night, which is the reason why I'm kinda in the state that I'm in this morning, 'cos I was just about to come home,' Jarvis standing up from the kitchen table and ridding his plate of the fatty rind into the bin, when

Andy sneeringly mumbled, 'Are you going to tell us who you saw or are we going to have to guess by playing charades or by using transcendental powers?'

Playfully pinching his son's cheek, he responded, 'So…as I was saying, I accidentally ran into Luke Ferguson. Hasn't changed a scrap, still looks like he's an advert for recruitment to the armed services, he's very trim even to the point of appearing as though he hasn't eaten a thing in weeks. But it's no wonder though, because he's struggling badly with home and everything, as hum…poor Nancy had a bleed on the brain and she's not doing too good.'

Putting her hand to her face in sheer shock Ellie sorrowfully groaned, 'Oh my God, that's just terrible Mark. When did it happen d'you know?'

'It all came as a bit of a surprise when he told me, and I was like…well, I'd had enough to drink, but I was also knackered and hungry, and to say that he'd dip in and out of mood swings is a bloody understatement, but if I remember I'm almost sure he said that it happened about two years ago.'

'What d'you mean in and out of mood swings?' enquired Alex as his father ran his hand across his throbbing forehead.

'He was just like…oh I dunno, incredibly low because of Nancy's physical impairments which is totally understandable, and then he became incredibly angry because there's only two words that she can say, and don't ask me what they are 'cos I really can't remember, and then a Genesis track came on from the juke box, you know, and he was transformed into this educator of music. He then became so defensive of this bloody song that he obviously chose, and gave me a lecture about Phil Collins versus Peter Gabriel, but he was almost transported into another world and erm…trance like during the whole song. It was weird to see him like this, I can tell you. And then after it finished, he started mouthing off about how no one is helping him financially to get the house kitted out with special adaptations so that Nancy can go out in her wheelchair, or have a shower, and it was almost as though he were blaming the whole of society for what happened to his poor Nancy.'

Eleanor, still seated at the table with her head resting in cupped hands remarked, 'I can't get my head around it. I mean, I know we've kind of lost touch, mainly because we no longer share school runs where we were able to tell each other everything, and the time to nip to one another's house for coffee or lunch had long gone, but it doesn't stop me from feeling as guilty as hell. It's just so sad, and she doesn't deserve this as she never hurt a soul, and I can't ever remember hearing her say a bad word about anyone or anything, so it's no wonder I suppose that Luke's a bit up and down, why wouldn't he be? And it's no surprise really when you say that he's lost a load of weight. Did he say how Julia was getting on, because she and her mum were more like sisters or best friends?'

'Ah…I did ask, but he kind of skirted around the issue and he never actually answered my question, so actually I've got no idea how she's handling it.'

'I don't see much of her now, but the last time I saw her, well…we passed each other on the street, she was going one way and me the other, but the very quick glance that I got kinda shocked me actually. She seems to have turned into some sort of Goth, her hair is stringy and jet black, she'd got piercings out of her nose, lips, and forehead and I doubt she'd even be able to count the number of rings that she's got in both of her ears. Her skirt left little to the imagination, mind you she'd got the most amazing boots with straps and chains, not so sure about the fishnet tights though, 'cos they were like riddled with holes, but perhaps that's what they're meant to look like,' reported Alex the elder of the two sons. 'I've also heard from a couple of my mates that she's the go to girl when you're in need of a quick fix, whether it's an upper or downer, white pill, blue pill or just a quick spliff, shell point you in the right direction. Now that's not something you'd expect from that sweet, innocent little girl that we used to sit in the car with every day going to and from school, know what I mean?'

'Aw…no, you're kidding me right,' exclaimed his father in a somewhat disbelieving but saddened tone, 'how the hell did she get into that evil world? No wonder he wouldn't answer my question when I asked how she was doing. She's still living at home though, right?'

Alex shrugged his muscular, beefy shoulders and shook his head, 'I've got absolutely no idea.'

Eleanor, not having said much for a while, shuffled in her backless fluffy slippers as her dressing gown gaped open, pressed the on button to the kettle once more, and asked concernedly, 'Mark, how can we help these guys? Shall I go and see Nance, I mean…did you ask Luke whether he would like her to have visi…?' and then almost knocking down one of the kitchen chairs she speedily made her way to the hallway and ran up the stairs.

With the three males of the household stumped for something to say as they confusedly scanned each other's faces as to what could possibly have contributed to such a hasty exit when suddenly through the thinly plastered ceilings, they could hear the distinct sound of retching.

'I didn't think mum would take the news this bad,' murmured Jarvis, as he raised his dark eyes to the heavens with a small query creasing his brow.

Andy, the younger, coughed nervously, and with serious eyes glanced at his dad, 'That's not the first time I've heard mum do that, she's being doing it quite a bit recently. You don't think she's got that eating disorder, you know erm…anorexia, do you? I mean…she's just eaten, and isn't it normal when people have that disease, that they chuck it all up so they don't put on any weight?'

'No, you're wrong son. Mum loves her food perhaps even more, dare I say, than I do, and over the years she's managed to be able to eat what she likes, and as you can see, she's still got a lovely trim figure,' as he ruffled his son's short dark hair which had not been gelled into his normal quiff, so for once this made it easier for his father to disturb his fashion statement.

'Don't you think you should go up and see that she's alright?' asked Alex as he cleared the table of the breakfast detritus, rinsing the crockery before loading everything into the dishwasher.

'No, I think every woman deserves a bit of privacy, don't you? It can't be easy living in a house full of testosterone, know what I mean…?' trying to lighten the atmosphere, their father continued, 'she'll let me know in her own time if there's something wrong. But I can honestly hand on heart tell you that she's fine. I think I'd know after all these years if mum was struggling with anything, whether it's physical or if something's upsetting her. So, let's just try and be natural for when she comes down. Why don't we do a few chores around the house, and give her a nice surprise when she comes down? If either of you have got plans this morning, then I'm sorry to say I won't be able to volunteer to be a taxi driver, as I think I should be with mum while she's not feeling too good, and of course, don't forget I've still got booze in my system, now that certainly wouldn't be a good look now would it, if I hum…got hauled in for being over the limit.'

Andy was the first to reply, 'I've got nothing until three when we've got a swim meet down in Kingsmead, and I must admit I got a mountain of homework but that can wait,' and he headed towards the utility room and came back carrying the hoover.

'If you've got revision Al, go for it, because me and the young 'un will tidy the place up a bit.'

'Nah, I'm happy to help and then it gets done sooner so we can all enjoy the rest of the day,' he returned to the kitchen where his father was busy wiping down the granite work tops as Alex got to work cleaning the terracotta floor tiles, plugging his earphones into his phone making the chore more endurable.

With the whining sound of the carpet cleaner and Alex's out of tune singing with the mop being used as a guitar, Eleanor re-entered the busy, domesticated kitchen relatively unnoticed, but the smell of her newly lathered skin and hair, giving off the unmistakeable scent of citrus fruits, alerted her husband of her arrival. Mark spun around from the sink and hugged his wife mumbling into her ear, 'You okay, sweetheart?'

As she pulled away from him, she reached for a glass from the oak cupboard with its brass vintage styled handles, and letting the cold-water swirl around the sink, she filled the glass tumbler. Taking small sips, whilst leaning against the now spotless counter, she glanced sideways to Mark and quietly acknowledged, 'Yeah, I'm fine. Apparently, I've got a touch of irritable bowel syndrome and having the odd bout of chucking up goes with the territory. So, Mr Detective man, what's with the domestic bliss that I've walked into, eh? Is this your way of trying to get back into my good books, which incidentally, you know you don't have to, because I like it when you go out with the boys, as it's important that you let them know that you care and respect the hard work that they do.'

Mark sidled up to her and affectionately put his arms around her slender waist and whispered into her ear, 'You don't have to hide anything from me you know. I saw the bottles of pills in the bathroom cabinet, so are they going to get rid of this IBS thing you've got?'

Peering into his eyes, Ellie casually reported, 'Apparently, they're the bees knees, but I've got to let them really get into my system before they have any real effect. So, I guess its early days yet, so please stop worrying, I'll be fine.

'Are you sure you're telling me everything?'

'Of course I am silly. Anyway, let's get back to what we were talking about before, you know, the Fergusons. D'you think Luke will let me go and see her? Shall I call him, or do you want to? I feel as though we've got to do something, because we've been friends for years and us can't just pretend as though we don't know what's going on. Julia may have gone off the tracks, but that doesn't mean that between us we can't steer her back towards some kind of normality now does it? She was just the sweetest, cutest little girl, and I'll be perfectly honest with you when she was about five, I yearned for another baby and would have

184

done anything for it to be a girl. Can you imagine what a sad household it must be for her to be growing up in, with her poor, beautiful mother not being able to speak to her, or for them to share girly jokes, and your mother not being able to pass opinions about your latest boyfriend, or the new dress that you've bought. Because let's face it, girls need their mums especially in their teen years.'

'I'll give Luke a call, and suggest he and I perhaps go for a drink, and you can sit with Nancy, does that sound like a good idea?'

'That's great, but when you call him, tell him I can come around any time and if he wants a night off, I can come around in the evening, it doesn't necessarily have to be in the day. Now I really need to finish the piece I'm working on as I've got a date that it must be completed by, and I really don't want to let her down as it's a gift for a milestone anniversary.'

Eleanor gave Jarvis a hasty peck on the cheek and moved to the back door, opened it, and made her way to her makeshift studio which was a redesigned rather large garden shed.

Mark reflectively gazed at his wife as she strode across the flag stones strategically placed so that in the winter she didn't need to wade through sodden turf, and it was then that he noticed that her previously tight fitting jeans were hanging off her, and as she was always so proud of her well-toned torso, the shirt that she wore showed no evidence of any curves only the protuberances of her spine.

***

I knew exactly who he was, but this time I had to change my identity as the past two times I'd been a little slack.

This was to be the real catch, my nemesis, and nothing must go wrong. I'd done my homework, knew his routines and so I was fairly confident that this would go without a hitch. He never left the surgery before seven and apart from the old dragon that manned the reception, he was always the last one out of there. Now, whether he was actually treating patients right up until the time he left, well that was a different question altogether. Mind you, he wouldn't have been fucking the old bag, that's for damned sure.

I parked halfway down the adjoining road from the surgery where I knew there'd definitely be no prying camera lens because let's face it with the shitty houses and the even shittier cars, there was nothing worth stealing anyway, so why waste time and money on camera footage?

While waiting, I ate the burger and fries that I'd bought on the way, and even though stone cold now I really didn't care, because I seriously couldn't remember the last time I put food in my mouth. And just as the last ketchup coated splinter of a chip slithered down my throat, I saw the silhouette of the man that I was waiting for cross the potholed tarmac of the surgery car park in long strides, as if he'd got somewhere important to get to.

Wiping my mouth so there was no trace of food that may have deposited itself in my new-found facial hair, and brushing down my clothes, I stepped forward just as the man with deep copper, slicked back hair, dressed casually but smartly in beige coloured jeans and a red pin striped shirt with a navy blue blazer, appeared on the footpath.

He stopped when he saw me, whether out of fear or surprise it was hard to know, but I cleared my throat. 'Ahem…sorry if I startled you, but are you Dr O'Keefe?'

Holding onto the strap of his brown leather man bag that hung from his left shoulder and reaching for his mobile he tried to push past me without answering my question, 'Hold on a minute, I only asked you a question. It's just that if you are the doctor, then I really need your help.'

With that the man turned around and squinted at me trying to block out the strong rays of light emitting from the streetlamp, and asked curiously, 'Look erm…I've had a rather long day and I'm sorry but the surgery is now closed. If you're worried about someone, then the best thing is to either call for an ambulance or if it's not that urgent then take the person to the Accident and Emergency Unit. That's all the help I can offer you, I'm afraid. Now I really have to get going.'

Once again he was on the move, but this time it looked as though there would be no U-turn, and thinking fast on my feet I dug deep, 'Listen Doctor, I know it's late, but this lady needs your help and fast, and I can't possibly take her to the hospital because you see she's kind of a refugee, and well…she didn't want to stay in the detention centre as she thought that something dreadful may happen to her as there was always constant fighting, stealing, and women were definitely not safe you understand? Anyway, to cut a long story short, I was huh…coming home from work late one night and I saw this woman just walking in the rain with just two plastic bags, so doing the gentlemanly thing I stopped to see if she was okay, you know as most people would, and that's when she told me of her plight. Me and my wife we took her in and offered her shelter and food, and well…she's stayed with us ever since.'

'That was really generous and kind of you, and you should be applauded, but I still don't know what you want me to do? I've given you my advice, now if you'll excuse me'.

'No, you don't understand. I can't take her to hospital or phone for an ambulance because she has no national insurance number. She doesn't even have a passport for Chrissake, and make no mistake about it, if she's found without credentials, they'll take her back to the centre, or worse deport her. Now the reason that we need your help is that before she fled her country erm…Iraq, she found out that she was pregnant with her husband's child, but here's the bummer, he died in the freezing cold waters of the Channel, but she thankfully survived. So, all I'm asking is that you come and see her because she's not sure of her dates, but I've a funny feeling she's due to deliver, and believe me when I tell you neither me nor my wife know anything about delivering babies.'

'Oh, I'm sure the maternity unit at The Hamilton General will see that she's alright, and I can assure you from previous experience, having done my training at a few of them around the country, they don't usually check on whether people are legal or illegal immigrants, they're only interested in their medical condition, especially in cases where a woman is going to have a baby. And I can honestly tell you that she'll be much safer there rather than with a general practitioner who hasn't performed a delivery since med school.'

'Oh, come on now doc, surely it's like riding a bike?' I sniggered, 'I'll drop you back here as soon as you're done, or better still I could take you straight home and then you'll have the rest of the evening free. Please…do it for the new life that's about to come into the world. She's already lost its father and well…you wouldn't want more blood on your conscience, would you? I mean, how would you be able to sleep at night if anything happened to either of them knowing that you were asked for help but refused to give it?'

Frowning deeply, he finally conceded.

'This house of yours isn't miles away is it because I really have a mountain of work to do tonight? You see there's a misconception out there that when we doctors leave the surgery at night that that's the end of our day, but in actual fact that's absolute nonsense. So, I will agree to see this woman, but I'm going to make it very clear that if she does go into labour then I'm going to have to call on the midwife who takes care of our patients. Deal? By the way, you never even told me either your name or the young lady's.'

Striding on ahead of the suburban doctor, I opened the passenger door for him, and offered him my hand whilst introducing myself. Forgetting who I said I was the last time someone asked me my name, I figured what the heck, and simply made up another one, 'Billy Wilkes, and the poor unfortunate woman is called Maranatha Kazar, but we call her Martha 'cos it's a bit of a mouthful, if you know what I mean.'

After buckling up and placing his bag in between his feet, the doctor glanced sideways towards me and said, 'The sooner we get going the earlier I'll get home.'

During the drive we didn't exchange any small talk and the silence finally came to an end when he saw where we finally ended up, and then the explosion finally erupted with the usual diatribe I'd experienced with the other two. I, of course, ignored it all, and he had no choice but to follow my drawn-out footsteps when he stopped dead in his tracks as the loud cries for help echoed around the soulless walls of the basement.

Stunned by the obvious betrayal of his good and caring nature he marched back to the main door and started pulling at the doorknob in quite a rage, and having no clear escape route, he began kicking violently at the wooden panels, in some futile act of vengeance. He stopped dead in his tracks when he felt the very sharp stab of my knife within the deep crevices of his bony spine.

'You can shout and stomp all you like Dr O'Keefe but it's not going to do you a scrap of good, so you might as well just listen to what I've got to say. Of course, there is no baby, but it was a good ruse don't you think? No, you're here as punishment for what you did to my very significant other, who, I hasten to say, wouldn't be in the state that she's in today, if you'd only listened to her. Perhaps you could have sent her for a few tests, but instead you decided to fill her body with fucking Aspirin, and then of course she ended up in hospital and came out a mere ghost of who she once was. So, this is payback time and now you'll find out just how inconsequential I can make you feel, just like you did to her, and you're gonna see the benefits of Aspirin, again just like you insisted she take.'*

I grabbed a handful of his blonde, curly hair, spun him round and deftly moved the knife to his throat. Standing there in disbelief he looked at me in sheer terror and cried, 'You're…you're……the husband of hum…'

Eyeballing him piercingly, I screamed, 'You see, you don't even remember her name, do you? You have no bloody idea whose life your crap diagnosis destroyed, but then that's you shitty doctors all over, isn't it? You think you save money by not referring people for specialist opinion, when instead you insist on playing your stupid guessing games, and its people like me who're left to pick up the pieces. D'ya know what? I can't remember the last time you came to see her, or even phoned to see how she's doing.

'So now it's my time to play God, and you're going to do everything that I tell you, because if not, I know where you live, and I know your wife's name, where she lives, and I know where your son goes to school. So, I'd be very careful if I were you not to piss me off.'

I unlocked the door where the stench of human excrement hit me full on as there were no windows or ventilation in the room where Hackman was still chained to his bed, and the Filipino slouched depressingly on the top of her bed in the crumpled stained clothes that she'd obviously slept in.

'Evening to both of you. As you may have noticed there's a third bed in here and this is the man who'll be joining you. I'd like to introduce you to Dr Miles O'Keefe, and he'll be staying with us for a while. You can introduce yourselves after I've gone, but in the meantime Miss Baluyot, I'd like you to set up an IV line,' slinging the bag to her with all the necessary paraphernalia inside, 'and I'd like you to run the drug through him at a regular but slow

pace, because I don't want him to have severe adverse reactions too quickly, as I want to see the benefits of him getting it if you get my drift.'

'But…' the young Asian nurse argued concernedly looking at the small plastic-coated packet of liquid Aspirin, 'this could be fatal for him. No, no, no…I won't do it. I can't. I didn't sign up to be a nurse to kill people, it's my job to look after the sick.'

'Yes, it is. You're absolutely right, so why didn't you do that when you were asked to? Or is it because he's a doctor and the most important person in my life was just another nobody? Is that it? Nah, don't bother answering that, because d'you want to know why? I'm sick of listening to your shit about being on your feet twelve hours a day with nobody caring about how little pay you get for supposedly working all the hours that God sends. And yet, while you sit around on your fat arses moaning and bloody groaning, good people are sent into your care and you can't be bothered to help them with the most basic of care, leaving them to rot in their beds all alone for the best part of the day, with no one to talk to, or console them when they feel lost and forgotten. So, spare me the Florence Nightingale speech and do what you've been asked to do.'

With quivering fingers as she stared at the blade I was holding against the doctor's jugular, she started to tear apart the wrappers where the cannula and the plastic tubing were housed, which eventually would be inserted into the doctor's arm, with the sole aim of feeding Aspirin into his blood stream. With no tourniquet at hand, she sidestepped cautiously to the handcuffed captive, Hackman, who was anchored to the bed, where she yanked a sock off his cold, right foot. She then carefully tied the navy-blue cotton sock around O'Keefe's left bicep as she gazed sorrowfully into his terrified, almost lifeless eyes, as a thick blue vein swelled within his muscular upper arm, whereupon she dejectedly inserted the thin plastic cannula.

Lying on the bed, O'Keefe was too mentally exhausted to fight, and merely closed his eyes as the liquid was transported around his body as I restrained his right arm and leg to the side of the bed leaving him virtually powerless.

I climbed the stairs two at a time, unlocked the door to the dungeon, and left once more. Sitting behind the wheel of the van, I removed the doctor's phone from the side pocket of my hoodie, found the name that I was looking for under the letter O, and messaged his wife with the four words, 'gone to a symposium.'

I then started the engine and headed home.

190

Chapter 14

At his desk, Pettrini could be heard on the phone in the throes of arranging for Dominic Thurston to come to the station and finally reveal information, which he was clearly hiding, regarding the disappearance of his partner, Mr Hackman.

'*Is this a Mr Thurston?*' questioned the police officer.

'*Yes, it is, who's calling and how did you get my number?*' responded the voice on the other end of the phone.

'*Good morning, this is detective Sergeant Nico Pettrini, and I don't think I need to remind you, but you volunteered your home and mobile phone numbers when I last visited you. As you might expect, this is about your partner, a Mr Robin Hackman, but before I go any further, am I right in assuming that you've not heard anything from him since we last met?*'

'*Oh yeah, okay detective, sorry but I hum…hate answering calls where there's no caller I.D. you know, as I'm always being pestered about have I been knocked down by a car, and did I need a good solicitor. And then there's the random call centres with a voice on the other end that is so completely undecipherable, gibbering on and on about God knows what, and well…to be honest with you, I get so bloody angry. Anyway, to answer your question, no I haven't heard from, or been in touch with anyone who knows where Robin is. If that's all detective, because to be honest with you, it's extremely busy here in the pharmacy. So, I'm very sorry but I seriously need to crack on. B…*'

Interrupting the young pharmacist in his tracks, and dispensing with the softly, softly approach, Nico adopted a harsher tone of voice, '*I don't think you seem to appreciate how serious this matter is Mr Thurston, and I appreciate how busy you are, but we really need you to come to the station to answer a few more questions.*'

Nico having to remove the phone slightly from his ear as the volume seemed to have heightened, the pharmacist ranted, '*What now? I can't possibly come now, can't it wait? Look here, Detective Pettrini, this is simply not on. I could, I suppose, if I really had to, make it after we close at half past five but that is the best I can do.'*

'Look let's get this straight, this isn't some invitation to go to a drinks party or the bloody movies, and you seem to forget that we're investigating your partner's mysterious disappearance, and if I may say so, you're behaving rather oddly considering the man whom you're going to marry has been missing now since the end of March. We'd like you to come to the station right now, and if you don't have the means to get here, we can send a car around for you. I'm sure there must be someone that can take over from you for an hour or so?'

'Well, I suppose if you put it like that then you really give me very little choice, do you? I'll be there as soon as I can make arrangements for a locum to take over, will that do?'

'Yes, that'll be fine and thank you for your co-o...' click, signalling the end of the conversation, just before the police officer had the time to finish his pent-up sarcastic gratitude.

***

With Jarvis having made the call a couple of days ago to Luke to ask whether it would be alright if Eleanor could visit Nancy, and as Ellie was having one of her better days, she decided that today would be the best bet, as she didn't know when she'd have a relatively pain free day again in the near future.

Dressing very casually in dark blue jeans, and a gypsy-style shirt hanging loosely over the top, and with her dark, wavy hair hanging over her shoulders, she felt rather nervous at the impending visit. Not that she didn't want to see her once very close friend, of course she did, but she wasn't quite sure whether she'd be able to hide her feelings when she saw Nancy, and how through no fault of her own, had sadly ended up in a wheelchair. Parking as close to the Fergusons' house as she could, she was mildly excited, but equally surprised, that the Victorian style house that she'd been to hundreds of times over the years, hadn't changed a jot.

As she opened the rusted metallic gate, the one thing that did strike her as a sign that all was not as it should be, were the weeds fighting for their eagerly awaited freedom from underneath the previously immaculate York stone paving stones. Nancy would freak out if she saw that her tormentors were winning the battle, as she took immense pride with the garden, and even if she were going out and was slightly rushed, if there was the slightest hint of anything that wasn't invited into her domain, she would viciously yank it out, cursing loudly at the audacity of their invasion.

This brought a wide grin to Ellie's face, as she took her time using small strides up the five steps, which would lead her to the bottle green front door with its colourful obscure windowpanes. Pressing the brass button affixed to the right-hand side of the red bricked wall, she patiently waited for the chiming to end and for the locked door to reveal a face behind it.

Luke finally opened the door as Eleanor tried to hide the astonishment on her face, as the person that stood on the other side of the threshold was certainly a ghost of the man that she had known for years. Instead of the usual well groomed, casual, but smartly dressed man in his late forties, the face that stared back at her was a gaunt, hollow-eyed man, clad in clothes that had once showed off his trim, muscular body, but now merely hung off his lean bones.

Leaning towards the woman who drove his daughter to school and back over the years, Luke leant forward still maintaining his position within the doorway, and put his arms around Ellie's shoulders, commenting warmly, 'Hi there stranger. God it's so good to see you again and may I say you're looking as gorgeous as ever. Come in, come in.'

'Luke is this a good or a bad time, because I can come back, if it's inconvenient?' Ellie remarked, as she combed her hair behind her ears with her fingers.

'No, its fine honestly.'

As Luke closed the door, Ellie made her way to the kitchen and once again she was slightly taken aback that nothing whatsoever had changed, apart from the empty loving atmosphere which used to ooze from within these very walls.

'Sorry but had a bit of a late night last night,' commented the man of the house as he started to load the dishwasher up with empty glasses of all shapes and sizes, and throwing out the uneaten triangles of pizza whilst folding the cardboard box into a neat little parcel, which he discarded into the bin underneath the kitchen sink.

'Bit of a party last night, huh?' asked Eleanor as she held onto the back of a chair with two hands.

'No, I just haven't found the time to clear up for a couple of days; I don't know where the time goes. I'm sure you find that too, huh?'

'Oh, my goodness, not just occasionally but all the time lately, so it's a good job that Mark keeps stupid hours, otherwise I'd have to do more housework.' Both homeowner and visitor chuckled, even though it was painfully obvious that each of them was lying.

'So Eleanor, now that I've found a clean cup would you like tea or coffee or…' side stepping to the fridge he leaned on the integrated fridge door and took out a carton of apple juice that had already been opened, he shook it opened it and smelled the contents. 'Yep just tea or coffee I'm afraid,' as he tipped the contents down the stainless steel sink, opened the door to the back garden and threw the empty container outside.

'Don't worry, I just chuck everything out there, and before I lock up at night, I throw whatever needs to be recycled in the blue bin and whatever's crap goes in the black. Just explaining, in case you think I've turned into a complete slob, as it seems that these days people are bloody obsessed that they're doing their bit for the planet, but to be honest with you, it's gonna take a hell of a lot more than me forgetting to toss the apple juice carton into the Thursday recycling bin.'

'I wasn't thinking anything at all Luke, we've all got our own little quirks, haven't we? D'you know what, I could murder a cup of coffee, black please with one sugar.'

'Shall I take you in to see Nancy now, and I'll bring it in to you?' asked Luke, as he led the way across the dark grey, vinyl floor to the makeshift bedroom that once held a rather large mahogany reproduction dining table and eight chairs.

Not bothering to knock on the door but simply pushing it open with his finger, Luke stepped to one side to allow Eleanor inside.

His wife's bespoke wheelchair was facing towards the window so she could have some contact with the outside world, so Luke eagerly grabbed the handles and started to turn her around so that she could see her visitor, but Ellie interjected very quickly and commented, 'no Luke that's okay, I'm sure Nancy would rather look at the garden than my pokey face. I'll just grab a chair and bring it over to her.'

Before removing items of clothing, bags of incontinence pads and various other personal hygiene accessories off the only chair in the room, Ellie knelt down in front of her old friend, and taking both of her hands in hers she looked attentively and with a beaming smile uttered, 'Aww Nancy it's so good to see you again,' and with that she pulled the chair close. Eleanor, who normally never struggled with conversation, found herself scanning her brain for snippets of gossip or news that might interest the woman who was confined in the chair with its adaptations of an enormous head and neck rest, and with a table affixed to the arms which held quite strangely, or so Ellie thought, bits of Plasticine, a squash ball and bits of paper with pictures of people appearing to make strange faces. At the top of the page Eleanor was able to see the words that the Speech Therapist had obviously printed out in red ink, and instructions on how to do the exercises and the recommended repetitions that must be done throughout the day, in order for the therapy to work.

'Ah, I see you've got some homework then Nance? I must admit I could do with doing some of these facial exercises, might get rid of the bloody sagging jowls and these lines that seem to pop up every time I look in the mirror,' joked the visitor, as she lightly but fondly rubbed Nancy's hands backwards and forwards.

'*Doo nah, doo nah,*' she replied staring into her friend's deep brown eyes.

Ellie was grateful that the small flat screen television was on, as it proved to be a useful distraction in hiding the obvious embarrassment and discomfort that both ladies felt as to how things had so drastically changed since they'd last met.

Leaning in closer to the wheel-chaired woman, almost as if they were to impart some close previously undisclosed secret, Eleanor couldn't help but notice the scent of uncleansed skin mixed with cheap perfume in the hope of a futile attempt to blot out the undeniable body odour permeating off this lady, who was so particular with her appearance, so much so, that she wouldn't be seen dead in the street without making sure that her shoulder length auburn coloured hair, shaped neatly in a bob with a side fringe was exactly how she wanted it to look, and her makeup which was applied thinly, added a glow to her long, angular face, which only a small minority of women were able to achieve without plastering the stuff on like emulsion on walls.

The sad thing though was that the neglect didn't seem to end there, as it appeared to Nancy's visitor that the clothes she was wearing must have been simply pulled out of a drawer and draped on her without caring, or even bothering to ask the lady who was expected to wear them whether the clothes that were chosen for her were acceptable to her, not only for comfort, but also ones that she actually liked. She resembled some kind of bag lady who had to rely on jumble sale or garage sale remnants, as she sat there clothed in trousers which seemed to have been just sewn together without any desire for style or flattery, and they were pulled up so high, denying the wearer the chance to display any evidence of the elegant and petite waist which Nancy had been blessed with, and was so proud of, although it took hours of painful pull ups, push ups and yoga sessions to own such an enviable attribute to a female body.

But that wasn't the worst of her apparel, the cloth was covered with an array of summer garden flowers and was outlandishly matched by a canary yellow coloured blouse, which gaped where the buttons and its holes were stretched to ripping point, revealing pink flesh, emphasising breasts which had been left to just sag, as the supposed main carer of this uncommunicative lady failed to support this important part of her anatomy or her sexuality.

Eleanor remembered seeing her friend wear the vividly coloured blouse before, but that was when it was in the height of summer, and it was trendily teamed up with a pair of cigarette styled jeans, which generously showed off her long legs and trim waist, so different from the way it was draped on her now, being heavily stained with wet patches of drooling fragments of her breakfast which had slithered down from the side of her mouth down her neck and finally nestling in her cleavage.

Looking up to the heavens, Ellie silently thanked the celestial powers that there were no signs of any mirrors in the room, but what did that matter, because even though she'd lost the power of speech her eyesight was still very much intact, and there was one thing about her dear friend, she was no fool, she knew exactly what she looked like, as both their reflections stared back at them from the large patio doors.

'D'you know what I was thinking about the other day, Nance?' asked Eleanor with a hint of amusement as she placed her hand in her friend's. 'When you used to tell me the stories of when you and Julia would have your little dressing up parties, and she would totter around in your high heels with her hands on her almost non-existent hips, swivel her bottom as she walked, and she'd pout at any passing mirror whilst she admired her lips that were slathered with dark red lipstick. If I correctly remember you always used to play that Roy Orbison song, erm…oh yeah, *'Pretty Woman'* as she performed her catwalk performance.'

'Doo nah, doo nah,' this time her tone had gone up an octave, and she had a big, broad smile on her face, which intonated that she did remember and that it was indeed a happy, joyous memory.

'You know I was telling Mark the other day how being with your Julia really made me feel broody again, but only if I could have been guaranteed with the blessing of a girl. She was the gentlest little girl I've ever known, and now that she's all grown up, I can tell you that some of the stories she used to tell me and the boys on the way to school were just pure hilarious.'

'Doo nah?' asked Nancy in a curious tone.

'Well Nance, you know how Julia would get all excited when she thought she had something important to say, you know when nobody else would be able to get a word in edgeways? Anyhow, this one morning we'd just closed the door as your daughter climbed into the car, and as she detached herself from her '*My Little Mermaid*' backpack and Andy strapped her in, and that was it, she was off.

'Last night, I told mummy and daddy that I wanted a puppy, and as it wasn't fair that I had no one to play with at home, they should get me one. Then daddy said something to mummy, so I couldn't hear and anyway mummy got all mad and she went like whoosh, she exploded. She left the kitchen, banged all the doors and then she said that she wasn't going to eat anything because she wasn't hungry anymore because his face was annoying her, and then she stomped up the stairs still shouting at him and said that he must help me with my homework and give me a bloomin' bath, and then she said that he had to do the washing up.

'There was a lot of shouting, but daddy was smiling all the time. Anyway, mummy didn't know I was pretending to be asleep, and she stood at the top of my bed and told me that she wished she could give me a little puppy, but it wasn't kind to him to leave it in the house all by himself while I was at school and mummy and daddy went to work to pay for Billy's food. That's the name that I was going to give him. Then I went to sleep and thought I'd ask for a cat instead. I don't know about the boys, but I was dying to have a good giggle. Mind you I didn't dare as she was deadly serious, her hands were flying all over the place, she was rolling her eyes, pointing her finger, shaking her head, you know like adults do, when they're really excited or angry about something. It kept us in conversation in our house for a long time I can tell you.'

Nancy perseverated the two syllable sounds that were her only form of communication as she laughed heartily, having been reminded of the happiness that all three Ferguson family members enjoyed, in what must seem now to be a long journey into the past.

The door was then pushed open without the courtesy of even a single solitary rap on the wooden exterior, as Luke strolled across the wooden parquet flooring with the fine Bone China cup clattering around nervously in the matching saucer.

'Here you go Eleanor. Sorry it took for ever, but I was looking for a clean mug or cup and then I remembered that we kept these for best in a box in our bedroom.'

'Luke, you shouldn't have bothered, any old mug would have done, but thank you,' whilst taking a sip of the dark liquid which appeared even darker by the pure whiteness of the cup. Ellie grabbed Nancy's two handled feeder cup and offered to give her friend a sip out of the insipid blue plastic spout with its tiny perforations at the top of the vessel, 'Nance would you like a drink? I'm not sure what it is, but I bet you're a bit thirsty, yeah?'

Whilst shaking her head and closing her eyes, the lady in the black bespoke wheelchair declined the offer.

'Are y...'

'Ssshhhh, there's an urgent news bulletin,' announced Luke, as he turned around to face the flat screen that was stood on the chest of drawers, which housed a myriad of framed photographs of varying sizes, half bottles of perfume, topless lipsticks haphazardly and uncaringly strewn on the top, whilst hair brushes, combs, clips and various other sundry items covered the piece of dark, wooden furniture.

'Good morning viewers, we're standing outside the home of a Dr Miles O'Keefe and his wife Mrs Belinda O'Keefe in Sawbridge, just four miles outside of the Upper Stanton area,' the ticker tape running below the head and shoulders voice of the speaker announced that the reporters name was Simon Lane, from the Langdon News Corporation (LNC). A photograph of Dr O'Keefe was highlighted in the right-hand corner of the screen, where the prominence of his short but stylish deep copper coloured hair, dark rimmed glasses and a distinctive gap in between his two front teeth were meant to attract the viewer's attention.

Mrs O'Keefe, whilst standing at the bottom of her gravelled driveway looked directly at the furry long handled microphone, which was greedily thrust in front of her, as journalists circled around like sharks having hungrily trapped their prey.

The first to fire a question was the casually dressed man, clad in khaki army combat jacket revealing a white T-shirt and black jeans, as his unruly, long, dark blonde hair was tucked behind his ears, *'Mrs O'Keefe, Matthew Lyle from The Herald, can I ask you why you've asked everyone to attend here today?'*

The petite, ample bodied, pixie styled peroxide blonde, clad in an expensive, chic ensemble of white classic shirt tucked into a black calf length skirt with black shiny high heel boots making her much taller than the estimated five feet two, and completing the outfit was a short, black suede jacket, spoke directly into the hairy microphone with a mixture of clarity, disbelief and anger, *'As members of the public are aware, there have been two people who supposedly went to some kind of symposium, and somehow failed to return to their homes once it was over. We have also been informed that these individuals were not tracked down at any medical institute, teaching establishment, and in fact there have been no further reports as to whether these two individuals actually ever went to a conference. The reason that I'm here today standing in front of our home, is that my husband sent me a text six days ago with just four words on it, and they were exactly the same as the other two, 'gone to a symposium.'*

The reporter from The Herald pushed his wire rimmed, round framed, John Lennon lookalike spectacles back up his nose with his right forefinger, and continued his inquisition, *'So, Mrs O'Keefe, could you tell the viewers and listeners when was the last time that you saw your husband?'*

'Well, even though my husband and I are separated, we keep in very close contact with one another because we have a son together, and Dr O'Keefe is unwavering in his commitment to our son, both inside and outside of the school gates, and he has never been late or failed to pick him up from his soccer matches. But he did fail, on 27th April. He never did watch our son play in the match, which was incidentally, the semi-final for the under 10's regional cup, and this in itself would mean that my ex-husband would never have missed that game. As neither parent was at the football ground, I was incredibly grateful to the school football coach who took him back to his school, which was closer for me to pick him up, because it would take me a while to get to him as I was in a meeting which, of course, when I found out what had happened, I left immediately.'

Lyle, whilst scribbling frantically in the ring bound note pad proceeded with, *'So what are the police planning to do, Mrs O'Keefe?'*

'Actually, if they're tuned in to this programme this literally will be the first time they're hearing of it as I feel that now they might take my husband's failure to come home a bit more serious than the other two people, as it would seem that they haven't got a clue as to their whereabouts, and quite frankly they don't seem to be doing a fat lot to find them either.'

This time one of the other journalists managed to fire a question, *'So, what you're saying Mrs O'Keefe is that the police have no idea about your claim that your husband is missing? And what were your first thoughts when you received the text message?'*

Mrs O'Keefe responded waspishly, *'The reason why I asked you ladies and gentlemen here, rather than wasting time waiting for the police to act in finding him, is that I wish to appeal to both Miles and the public at large, in helping me to get my son's father back home where he belongs, so I think that answers your first question. As regards the second, I'm sure you'll agree that even though at this time it's unsubstantiated there is no doubt that this is probably the same man that took the other two health workers, and this is when my world went black for both me and my son.'*

Turning away from the media frenzy momentarily she tearfully pleaded, *'Miles, if you can hear me, please come home, as me and Benjy miss and love you very much. Now, if someone out there has taken or knows the whereabouts of Miles O'Keefe, please, please let him go and if he is returned unharmed, I promise you neither of us will press charges, you have my word. My husband is a good man, he's never hurt anyone, and he has patients that depend on him, so please do the honourable thing and let him go, I beg you.'*

After this cry for help from a woman who at first seemed so strong where nothing would unhinge her, she slowly strolled up the meandering driveway with immaculate herbaceous borders nestling in amongst an array of different coloured shrubs, back to her front door. However, she was stopped in her tracks by the journalist from the local news corporation and with microphone poised in one hand and with an air of solemn poignancy simply raised the question, *'Mrs O'Keefe how do you expect the police to react when they see that you have failed to speak to them before you went public with your husband's apparent failure to return home?'*

The interviewee turned abruptly around and peered directly into the camera, and with her chest heaving up and down rapidly, she uttered her response with such condemnation, that the surrounding journalists scribbled vigorously on the lined and unlined pages of varying sizes of notebooks, *'If this is the only way that I can get the police to treat these missing people seriously then quite frankly I'm glad that I came to you people first. They have got to find my husband and the other two who have not been seen for a while now, but what are they doing really? They have no leads, they simply haven't got a clue, and if it takes me standing in front of a camera and talking to you lot, then they're just going to have to accept it. Now, thank you all ladies and gentlemen, but that's all I've really got to say.'*

The snap snapping of cameras continued loudly and with more vigour, as they zoomed in to get even more shots of the lady who was not afraid to bypass the normal routes of officialdom to attract attention for the families and friends of the people who had all seemingly gone to a non-existent medical symposium but had not been seen or heard of since. The lady definitely had spunk, her professional appearance which would be on the front pages of all the nationals would help her gain momentum with the general public of the plight facing the police, which is what Mrs O'Keefe was striving for.

The heavy, austere looking mahogany door closed sharply as the clattering of the letter box signalled to the hordes of journalists still rooted to the ground that the interview was definitely at an end, but as they were still thirsty for more they refused to budge.

'Oh my God, that's just terrible,' exclaimed Ellie whilst glancing towards her friend for some reaction, in the hope that even though dreadfully aphasic, she realised that she was very much part of the conversation.

'Doo nah,' uttered the forty-five-year-old petite woman sombrely.

Luke, being non-committal in any response to this newly shocking news was interrupted during the ensuing silence as Ellie asked thoughtfully, 'So Luke, what do you think's happened to these people that seem to have just vanished into thin air?'

'Hum…I have absolutely no idea, I mean it just doesn't make any sense, does it? But I totally understand why she went in front of the cameras though, and I know you're married to a copper but what are they playing at? They don't seem to have a clue as to what's happened to any of them, which to me sounds completely bizarre. I mean…I'm not really sure what I would do if it was someone belonging to me out there being held by some mad man, you know. For Christ's sake this is England not some Sicilian village where people went missing all the time, but here we are in a small town, barely visible on a map, and we have not one, not two, but three people who apparently all went to some kind of medical conference, and mysteriously never returned.'

'Oh, you're right of course, but it's just so sad, those poor families, not knowing where they've gone, or even if they're still alive. And, don't you think it's a bit strange that they hum…all have some kind of medical background, I mean well…there's got to be some kind of connection, but as to why they've been targeted, that's going to be a tough one for the police to figure out. I, for one, can't stop thinking about them, and every night I say a quiet little prayer for their safe return.'

Nancy voiced in her own authentic way, 'Me too, me too.'

Luke swapping his glare from the small television screen and beaming it now on Eleanor, asked with a peculiar smirk on his face, 'Ahem…Ellie can I get you some more coffee, perhaps a couple of biscuits if I can find any?'

'No Luke I'm good thanks, any more caffeine and I won't sleep for a month,' sniggered the visitor, whilst picking up the two handled feeder cup again trying her best to persuade Nancy to drink something.

Making more small talk with her friend, Ellie after a short while noticed that Nancy was perhaps getting uncomfortable in her chair and asked her if she needed to lie down for a while and rest her back for a bit, and the answer revealed a definitive nod of the head.

Eleanor held her friend's hand in hers, and quietly arose from her chair quietly muttering, 'I'll go find out where Luke is and tell him that you need to have a rest, I won't be a mo'.'

Opening the door of Nancy's makeshift bedroom and momentarily forgetting that the kitchen was to the left, she scanned to the right where she noticed in the rather colourless, cold hallway the dark blue mechanical machine that would have been the means of assisting Nancy back onto the bed. The sight of this piece of equipment that would scoop up this diminutive, proud lady into the air, reinforced to Ellie just how badly she relied on help in all its forms.

Finding Luke at the kitchen table sorting mail into two piles, junk and stuff that needs to be read, he turned around when he heard Ellie's nimble footsteps on the grey, laminated tiled flooring, questioned coldly, 'Everything okay in there?'

'Erm…I think Nancy's telling me that she wants, or perhaps needs, to go back to bed.'

'Well, her speech must have improved since I left the room. Sorry, that was out of order. Paula, her nurse of the day, should be back soon, so she'll just have to wait until she returns I'm afraid.'

'I could help you if you like. I mean…you must have been trained to use the hoist and I'm a very quick learner, honestly.'

'She gets paid to do it, so like I said, Nancy's got to learn to wait for things and that people can't run to her every whim, because let's face it, this is the way that life's going to be for us now,' turning back around to face the piles of paper with pictures of Thai cooking, Balti dishes, huge pieces of cheesy dough smattered with red shavings of tomatoes, whilst getting ready to tear them into shreds. Ellie asked politely, 'Okay, well shall I bring her out here then so she can have a chat with us? I'm sure she'd love that, you know she was always interested in gossip and the latest news headlines,' replied the visitor, as she stood leaning against the previously heavy laden sink, which now lay empty of soiled crockery.

'No, I really don't think that's a good idea, as I think this room reminds Nancy of all the bloody wonderful cooking and baking that she used to be able to do, and to be honest Eleanor, it just upsets her too much, and it broke both of our hearts especially mine, because you see it was all out of my control, and there was nothing I could do to get things back to the way they were. And a couple of times when Julia came home from wherever she'd been and found her mum upset, who d'you think got the blame for her being like that? Ah…well that would be me, and then she'd go up to her room slamming the door so hard that it made Nancy even more angry and then she'd start howling.

'And no matter how much I tried to persuade our daughter to come back down she would flatly refuse, and d'you know why, because then that would mean we'd have to talk and say sorry to each other, but you see that's the cruel part, we've got used to not talking. Here's the saddest thing though, I've not only lost my wife, but my daughter's gone from me as well. Now, does that answer your question, Ellie?'

'Oh my God I'm so sorry Luke, I didn't think…Look, why don't you go out for a bit and I'll wait for Paula to come back, and then she and I can help Nance back to bed?'

'She'll be back in a little while, honestly.'

Feeling slightly awkward and not quite knowing what to do next, she turned and made her way towards the wooden frame of the kitchen doorway when Luke interrupted her bare, cautious footsteps suggesting hopefully, 'Sit with me for a while Ellie, please. I really could do with some company right now…a decent conversation when it's not just me that does the talking. I know our friends and both families are all very upset about what happened to Nance, and they really do care and everything but hum…well, call me jealous or acting like a spoilt teenager, but everyone seems to ask how Nancy and Julia are doing, but guess what...no one gives a shit about how I'm feeling or coping.'

Standing within arm's length of this somewhat mentally battered man, Ellie placed her hand on his left upper arm, muttering, 'Luke, of course I'll stay, but first you have to answer me this, why didn't you let me or Mark know about Nancy before you ran into each other in the pub? We could have helped you all along right from when she was allowed home, if only you'd told us. It's bound to take its toll on you and Julia, what with trying to juggle work, her with exams, and of course the constant worry of not knowing how Nancy's going to recover from this dreadful thing that's happened to her. But you need to know that you don't need to do this on your own, we can help you, if you just tell us how.'

'I'm sorry we didn't let you know but it was all so sudden, and what with Mark's ridiculous hours that he keeps, and you with your art work, well...me and Julia figured we'd be just fine on our own, you know. It was tough at first, but once we'd got the funding for 24/7 care it seemed to be much better, but lately Nancy's mood swings are getting more and more frequent, so that's why I asked my boss at Dunstan and Cooke whether I could work from home some of the time. Thankfully they agreed, but they were adamant that I would have to go in for client meetings and updates with managers, but it's something at least. But the other reason why I felt it important to stay at home more is that the way she is at the moment, as I'm frightened that the nurses won't want to come back, and then she'll have a different one every day, instead of the routine we've got now where the same one stays for five days and nights.'

Gently rubbing her faintly lined forehead back and forth with the fingers of her right hand, she calmly remarked, 'I get what you're saying Luke, and I can only empathise with what you're going through, but perhaps I may offer a suggestion which just might help with her moods. I noticed that the clothes she's wearing are to put it mildly well...not the kind of stuff that Nance would normally wear. I mean, does she ever get asked what she'd like to wear for example, and when was the last time that she had her hair done, or someone put some make up on that lovely face of hers? You remember...she would never put the bloody bins out if she didn't have her face cream on, or her favourite eye liner, and she definitely wouldn't be seen dead without her eyebrows looking perfectly shaped. And let's not forget these cupboards have glass doors, just because she's lost the power of speech doesn't mean that she can't see what she looks like, and these reflections represent a very different Nancy from the one she used to be when she was so happy and carefree.'

Turning the tap on the empty China cup and rinsing it through carefully, and without even looking into her deep brown eyes set amidst thick dark lashes, he remarked, emotionless in tone, 'I hear what you're saying Ellie, and I know the style isn't the greatest, but the clothes that the nurses put her in have to be practical for when she needs to use the loo as the carers have to undress and dress her lower half time and time again, and well it's easier, don't you see?'

Not feeling exactly happy with the response, Eleanor stood with her back against the draining board, 'Surely, it shouldn't be a case of what's easy for the nurses, I mean, well…they're getting paid after all. Couldn't they hum…perhaps offer Nancy two or three outfits every day and let her decide, because she'd be quite capable of letting them know which she would like to wear, and then ultimately she'd be part of the decision process, making it less likely that she feels as though she was some kind of a burden, or incapable of thinking or being able to have feelings. It's no wonder that she gets upset, I mean she's still a beautiful woman Luke, both inside and out, but you need to make her feel wanted and loved.'

The man with the short, mousey coloured hair with black deep set eyebrows, and rather sallow skin, leant on the sink and cradled his head in his hands, 'Oh my God if it was only that easy Eleanor. You see some of the nurses will do just that, you know, ask what she'd like to wear but others complain that it's too much to ask of them to help her into a skirt because of the rolling backwards and forwards on the bed to pull it up…blah blah blah. And don't forget of course,' Luke tapped at the side of his temple, 'Nancy's no fool you know, she knows which of the nurses do the job for the love of it, but she's also aware of those who just want the pay cheque at the end of the week. And those she's not very fond of believe me she can make their life hell,' where a tiny, tired smile appeared at the corner of his mouth, 'and sometimes it feels as though I'm a bloody referee in a boxing ring for fu…I mean for God's sake. But here's the thing Eleanor, I've got work to do, and when this is going off big time I just have to get out for a while, and then I get the backlash from work, because I'm not answering my phone, or because I'm not at my desk where I'm supposed to be. It's all a soddin' big fat mess. And d'you know who I blame, that shittin' rehab unit who was supposed to be giving my wife therapy for her recovery. They're crap, the lot of 'em.'

'How can you blame them? That's hardly fair, Luke. I mean to say…I guess they did the best that they could, considering they're working with NHS budgets, and doubtless they would have suffered staff shortages, illness, qualified people leaving because they are dissatisfied with working conditions etc., I mean that's just the way it is, isn't it? But I'm sure they all tried their best. Tell me about her speech therapy, because I noticed on her wheelchair table that she's got exercises to practice, so they must have treated her at some point.'

'Don't even get me started. Okay…erm…when she left intensive care and was admitted to the rehab unit it was all peachy you know, she had a timetable from Monday to Friday with therapy slots from eight in the morning until five in the evening, and she'd have treatment from all of the disciplines. So anyway, once we saw the therapy charts, both me and Julia were very excited that she was going to get some rigorous treatment, and one of the psychologists that we met while we were in intensive care, suggested to me that it was vitally important that me and Julia both played a part in her recovery you know like to help with her mood swings which would apparently be a roller coaster ride, give her lots of encouragement, praise, hope, that sort of thing.

'Anyway, I turned up for the sessions, and believe me I was never late, in fact I was always way too early. But check this out, possibly five or six times out of ten a nurse, or a ward clerk or some other person who wasn't a therapist would tell me that the therapy wouldn't be happening on that day because someone didn't show up, or they had a bloody meeting to go to or, now this is the belter, they'd doubled booked. I can't tell you how angry it used to make me feel because time was getting on and all the time the doctors and therapists kept talking about a window post stroke, and after that time limit then it was doubtful whether there'd be a full or even partial recovery.'

Eleanor leant into him slightly and put an arm around his shoulder, picked up a wine glass from the drainer and requested with a hint of a curious smile, 'D'you know what? I'd love a glass of wine if you have it of course.'

Standing up and moving towards the fridge, he opened the door whereupon he grabbed a bottle of Chardonnay that was standing up with a plastic bottle stopper in it, and on removing it; Eleanor noticing that it was practically empty laughed and said jokingly, 'I certainly don't need to be afraid of drunk driving, that's for sure.'

Emptying the bottle of the colourless liquid into the freshly washed glass, Eleanor protested, 'No, no, no Luke, if you're not having one then we'll just share this one. I wouldn't have asked if I thought I'd robbed you of your last drop. Go on…you take it, please.'

Initiating the act of sitting down, Luke made his way to the table with the half empty glass in his hand and placed it on a coaster bearing a colourful scene of horse riders clad in red jackets.

'Honestly no, it's far too early for me, besides I've got a lot to do today and so much to catch up with tonight, so go on enjoy it. Cheers.' Luke tapped his small bottle of water that was already sitting on the pine kitchen table against Eleanor's wine glass as they toasted one another.

'Hum…now I can see why you're a little bitter towards the people that were supposed to be getting her strong again, but that was then, so now isn't it time to move forward and help Nancy as much as you can? Do they still come to see her, any of them, you know…the therapy teams?'

'I try and talk…' Conversation having been stalled as a key could be heard sliding into the keyhole whereupon the door was opened and two red handled shopping bags were left on the floor as the woman with the black buttoned up mac, and the flat, sturdy looking lace up shoes turned around after closing the door with its colourful obscure glazing. Taking her coat off and hanging it with a kind of precision onto one of the brass hooks, she began whacking it with her hand in a bid to rid it from any foreign particles that may have attached themselves to it, and finally she pocketed her keys into her black shoulder bag.

Picking up the bags with the yellow egg carton sticking out from the top of one of them, she sauntered along the hallway whose walls were lined with mounted portraits of landscapes and family members, bearing a constant reminder of happier times, and entered the kitchen, where noticing the sight of another woman sipping out of a wine glass appeared to take the wind out of her sails.

Noticing the nurse's obvious disapproval of seeing alcohol being drunk so early in the day and with a stranger other than his wife, Luke very quickly tried to quell the unsubstantiated feelings of disgust that were emblazoned across her plump cheeked face. 'Hi Paula, this is Eleanor Jarvis, a very close friend of mine and Nancy's. We used to take it in turns to do the school runs with Julia and her two sons.'

Extending a hand towards the seated woman, the nurse merely uttered in an indiscernible tone, 'Pleased to meet you,' averting her glance swiftly but rather abruptly towards Luke she asked, 'How's Mrs Ferguson? Have you offered her a drink since I left, because you know I'm worried that she's not getting enough fluid?'

'Of course we have, but you know what she's like, it's difficult to get her to drink enough no matter how much we coax her. But anyway, she needs to get back onto the bed as she's getting a bit fidgety, so if you could do that, then that would be great.'

The middle-aged lady, clad in a pale blue nursing tunic with her ID badge clipped securely onto her side pocket, and with both arms entwined underneath her ample breasts, requested with an air of sarcasm and disdain, 'So how long ago then did she ask to go back to bed? I mean wo...'

Eleanor, who sensed that the nurse was most put out by the fact that her patient had to wait for the hired help to assist her back to bed interrupted enthusiastically, 'I can help you if you like. I mean...you just tell me what to do, and I'll do my best not to get in the way. I'm a fast learner, and I guess an extra pair of hands would be quicker for you.'

'You just carry on sitting there, I'll be fine on my own thank you very much,' answered Paula dogmatically, as she scuttled along to Nancy's room.

Luke and Eleanor glanced at each other guiltily, and breaking the momentary lapse of rather uncomfortable silence, Luke tittered boyishly remarking in hushed tones, 'Well, I guess that told us, eh? If she could have done, she'd have put us into detention. Anyway, on a more serious note where the hell was I?'

'I asked you whether she was still having therapy.'

'Yeah, anyway after most of her sessions were a complete bloody waste of soddin' time, I then received a letter from the discharge planning team that they needed to see me in order that arrangements could be made for her to leave the hospital. I was summoned exactly three months after her admission, and there were all these bodies around a conference table, and I was politely asked to sit at the top where I could feel all their eyes peeled on me. There was her consultant, a member of each therapy team, neuropsychologist, senior nurse from the discharge team and a social worker. Honestly Ellie, I felt as though I was on trial, it was the most intimidating moment of my life.

They each in turn had their say, and huh...in a nutshell they told me boldly, and I can honestly say with hand on heart, quite mercilessly, that she'd had her stint at rehab, and it was now time for her to move on, and what they really needed to know was where I felt that she should go. Nursing home for the rest of her life, or back home? I wanted the earth to open and swallow me up as I couldn't believe what I was hearing, as they were all nodding with each other in agreement saying that there was nothing else that they could do to help my Nancy, a forty-one-year-old woman, who was a wife and mother. Of course, I was quiet for a minute or two, as they patiently scrutinised my face waiting for me to agree to their apparent wisdom.

Well, I just sat there and as I looked around the table at their fucking, sorry Ellie, smug faces I kinda lost it a bit. The consultant, seeing that my face didn't bear the usual traits of hum…gratitude or elation that finally my wife was being set free, merely rambled on about how the swift action of the paramedics and finally his team, had in fact saved her life, and unfortunately, not everyone pulls through after having had a brain haemorrhage or a clot, but…hopefully in the years to come, there'll be a lot more research into finding ways to reduce both temporary and permanent physical impairments. So, once again I just sat there staring around the room where one of them started to get a little uncomfortable with the tense atmosphere, as the blood was over enthusiastically flowing in her cheeks and neck, whereupon she used her notebook as a handheld fan to cool herself down.

There were a couple of members around the huge table who couldn't or wouldn't look me in the face, and merely sat there with bent heads, and another one was getting on my nerves, as she continually tap-tapped the manila folder in front of her with her stupid pen. The social worker, who was obviously a Muslim, and wore the familiar dark blue hijab which matched her trouser suit then decided to speak. She had the most beautiful, shaped eyes, and flawless complexion, who had a voice that was soft and full of empathy, and I remember her words exactly, even though they were spoken nearly two years after the event. '*Mr Ferguson, my names Farha Nasvallah, and I've been appointed as your social worker. I guess what Dr Harding is trying to say is, that we can't keep patients here on the rehab unit for ever, because it's not only unfair for them, but it can be incredibly dangerous as they can contract nasty hospital infections, and I don't need to tell you, but this then means that not only are they so unwell they can't get out of bed, but also a lot of the rehab that they've undergone has to begin again, and so it's like a vicious circle. Now, I'm sure Dr Harding meant to tell you that just because your wife will no longer be on the unit, this doesn't mean that her rehab therapy stops here.*'

At this point, it was quite laughable as everyone around the table automatically seemed to adopt the nodding dog syndrome, you know the stuffed ones that you used to find on the back ledge of cars, and all grinning from ear to ear as if miraculously their minds and hearts were suddenly guilt free, and that I'd be, albeit reluctantly, happier upon hearing this blackmail for my wife to be released from their care, when I absolutely knew she was miles away from being ready. *'So, the main reason that we're all here today is for each therapy member to give their professional opinion as to where Nancy would be best suited. There are excellent care homes, nursing homes in your area, and of course you'd be allowed unlimited access to visit her. I...'* the brochures of the homes that she was about to hand to me unfortunately didn't make it, 'D'you know where you can shove those? My wife is forty-one years of age, and you're telling me that all of you in this room are happy for her to spend the rest of her life in some old people's home, and I'm certainly not being disrespectful to the residents who live there, but she wouldn't get much mental stimulation, now would she? I mean is that what you're telling me, because if it is, then I'm out of here, until you can all come to your senses and take me and my family seriously. Have you any idea of the dreams that we had, and you're all just sitting there happy for those dreams to die? Let me ask you something, what are you all doing sitting around here talking to me about what she can't do, instead of treating her so that there'll be activities that she bloody well can do? What is she doing right now, any idea? I'll tell you where she is, she's in bed as usual, like every bloody time I come and visit.

'And, for what it's worth, every time I've been invited to join in a session with you people I've been left waiting, sometimes more than a bloody hour, only to be told that it's been cancelled for one stupid reason or another. So, you tell me, how can these poor people in your care recover, when you're all sitting on your holier than thou arses, no doubt staring at computers, sending e-mails, going on a training day, or an in-house meeting, without giving the treatment that you all promised to give? Aren't you all just a little bit ashamed of yourselves? I'm going to tell you this just once, Nancy is not going anywhere until she can eat proper food and drink liquids, that don't have that crappy bloody wallpaper paste added to it. Oh, and has it never occurred to any of you that this might be the only thing that she's got to look forward to, or don't you even care, because I suppose, she's just another number to you people.

'Well let me tell you she's my wife, and the mother to our daughter, and d'you know what...I'm not listening to any more of this shit, so give her some real therapy and then you can call me when she's ready to come home, but I have to warn you, don't give me any excuses that you need an empty bed so some other no hoper is going to spend twenty four hours a day rotting away, and with that Ellie, I stood up, and almost knocked the chair over, I then opened the door and slammed it shut.'

'Oh Luke, that's just terrible, I mean…I've never heard anything like it. I mean, to think that they even entertained the idea of a nursing home is just unthinkable. Why didn't you make some kind of complaint about the poor therapy that she was receiving?'

'I can't even tell if it was good or bad, because no matter what time of the day I went to see her she was always in bed. When I asked one of the nurses why this was, one of them said, whom incidentally I saw on many occasions, that it was because it was easier to leave her on the bed because she was, using the two fingered rabbit eared quotation marks, '*Badly incontinent, and we haven't got the time to keep getting her back on the bed every time she needs changing.*' So, when I wasn't there, I actually don't know how much real intensive therapy she was having on a daily basis, which I'd been promised when the discharge planning nurse phoned to let me know that Nancy would receive a further month of rehab, as that was what everyone around the table that day had agreed on.

Running her index finger and thumb along the stem of her drained wine glass, Ellie asked quietly, 'What the hell did you say when the nurse told you the reason why Nance was in bed so much? I think I'd have smacked her one Luke, I really do. That's just bloody shameful and disgusting it really is.'

'Tell me about it. I went to see the ward manager who sat me down in her office as she gave me the spiel about lack of nursing staff, and the ones that they did manage to get for the shift were all struggling with bad backs, and if I didn't know before now well…working on a stroke unit is hard work. She then looked at me over the rim of her glasses as they'd slipped onto the end of her nose, and asked me if I wanted to make a formal complaint? She almost begged me to, because, she said, the more complaints we have, the better our chances are of getting more staff. Can you believe that?

'They actually wanted people to complain about the lack of care that the patients that they're entrusted with, were receiving. That's when I made my mind up. I wanted her home with me and Julia, and we'd see that she got some therapy at least, and if they honoured the promise of sessions at the house, then it was better for her to be with us, rather than rotting away in a bed away from the people that she loved. That's it really,' declared Luke ruefully as he rubbed the back of his neck with his right hand.

'But I notice that the drink that I helped Nancy with, that's thickened right? So, does that also mean that she's not able to eat regular food then?'

'Yup. The speech therapist comes every so often and trials her on different stuff, as well as going through some of her facial exercises, but so far, she's still on the same regime of food and drink that she was on whilst she was in hospital. Absolutely nothing has changed. And, going back to her kicking off when she's in here, I think it's because she can see and smell all the foods that she's not allowed to have, and this is what makes her so angry, you know.'

'That would explain it I s'pose. I mean…I guess anyone would go a bit crazy if they can't eat what's being cooked for everybody else only to be served up with something that's mushed up like baby food.'

'Yeah, well there you have it, and people wonder why I've become such an angry son of a bitch, sorry.'

Using the arms of the pine kitchen chair to push herself up into standing, Ellie announced, 'Luke, I wish I could stay a bit longer, but I really have to go, but I'll come and see Nance again soon, honest. But you must promise me that you'll call if there's anything that either me or Mark can do to help, and hand on heart, it would be lovely for us to be close again. Also, don't give up on her. These medics, and therapists are not always right you know, and I guess it's a bit of a cliché, but miracles can happen. And for what it's worth, I strongly believe that our destiny lies in God's hands, so my advice to you is, go and see your GP and ask to be referred to a different set of therapists, you never know…a change in style of treatment, and new faces might be just what she needs. Nobody should be allowed to say, he or she will never walk again, or speak again, only God can, in my humble opinion that is.'

Luke also stood up and remarked, 'Thanks a lot Ellie for coming, it means a lot to both me and Nance,' and with that they both stretched out their arms and hugged each other briefly.

Standing in the hallway, the visitor stopped to look at one of the many photographs on the wall, 'Aww Luke, look at this one. D'you remember where this was taken. Oh, listen to me, of course you do. By the way, I'm ashamed I haven't even asked how Julia's doing. I'm sorry you must think I'm a heartless so and so.'

Gazing at the mounted and framed 8x10 photograph of both of his girls, Luke pensively muttered, 'Oh I remember exactly where this was taken. Julia was in a three-day netball tournament in Kenilworth and so we decided to stay at a Bed and Breakfast place so we could watch the whole thing. She was a really good goal attack, I think, and this was taken at a local beauty spot called Crackley Wood Nature Reserve, it was an amazing place. You and Mark should take the lads some time, they'd love it.'

'You're joking, aren't you? They wouldn't be seen dead with us now, as it's not cool, you know. Mind you, if we tempted them with somewhere a little more exotic, then I'm sure they'd drop the teenage thing, you know, that all parents are just fuddy duddies. So how is she then, Julia I mean?'

'Oh hum…well, she stays mostly at her friend's house these days. You know what they're like, she goes out to do her homework with one or more of them, and because I keep banging on about not leaving it too late to get the last bus, she just decides it's safer to stay the night. I don't mind, at least I know she's safe.' The small change could be heard jangling around as he jiggled the coins with both hands thrust deep down inside his pockets.

'Yeah, course. Give her my love, okay? I haven't seen her in such a long time, I bet I wouldn't recognise her these days.'

They waved to each other as she closed the five barred metallic gate, and Luke, after shutting the front door, leant his back against it, sighing heavily, and realising what it was he had to do next.

Chapter 15

'He's here,' signalled Pettrini to Detective Das, as he picked his jacket up by the collar from the back of his black mock leather chair.

'Want some company, Nic?' he asked, as he also grabbed something more formal to conceal his rather informal looking shirt, as there were some sort of exotic birds flying all around the fabric.

'Right let's go. See if we can get something out of this bloke, eh?'

'Shall we go and swing by the boss's office, I've gotta hunch he just might want to listen in?'

Both men headed towards the door of Jarvis's office which always remained open, as their boss felt that even though some of the men had different titles, they were in fact all doing the same job, despite the pay grade, thus the open-door policy made it more of a congenial place to work.

Neither detective needed to knock as the Inspector noticed their approach and immediately beckoned them into his office with a hastened retracting of his index finger, 'What's up chaps?'

'Thurston's here guv. D'you want to come along and see what he's hiding?'

'I sure d...' the beeping of his internal phone disrupted the end of the detective's answer, 'Scuse me a minute, I guess I'd better get this. You go ahead without me, drop me a text when you know which room you're in.'

Scowling waspishly down the mouthpiece, Jarvis demanded, 'Yes?'

'Detective Inspector, its DCI Wolfe here. Have you seen the news this morning?'

'No, I was late leaving the house, and to be honest I was in the mood to listen to a CD I've compiled with a mixture of 70s, 80s an...'

'I'm not bloody well interested in what your musical tastes are, godammit. We've got another missing person, but this time the wife decided that she'd rather go straight to the press rather than talk to the very people that are entrusted with not only her care, but each and every one in our community, because, um...this is the best part, she doesn't think that we've taken the cases of the other two missing people seriously enough. So, Detective Inspector Jarvis, got anything to say about that, have you?'

'Sorry sir, bu…'

'My office now Jarvis,' and with that, the discourse was at an end, as the officer on the receiving end of this shocking new development dropped the hand set back onto its cradle.

Once again climbing the dull, grey staircase whilst desperately seeking to figure out how he was going to defend both himself and his team as to why this woman, whoever she was, decided that the best course of action was to humiliate the force in such a public manner. Mind you, there's no law against not going to the cops first after all, is there, well…not that he was aware of anyway. Before he knuckle rapped on the gaffer's door, bearing the oblong shaped brass plate, slightly marred with dark spots and thin vein-like lines, as a result of old age, his phone spewed out a message bearing one word and one number, *Room 5.*

'Come in Jarvis, barked the Inspector in his white long-sleeved shirt, as the light from his desk lamp reflected on the three shiny pips lying side by side on his epaulettes.'

The TV screen was on, and with the remote control in his hand, the chief inspector pointed it at the frozen picture of a woman in front of a media frenzy, and pointed to a chair where Jarvis would unmistakeably have a prime viewing spot, not that this was going to be pleasurable by any stretch of the imagination, but he'd have to sit it out, nevertheless.

Listening to the woman pour her heart out to the hungry wolf pack was not easy listening, and Jarvis was getting pretty fed up with the incessant negative comments that were emanating from his boss's mouth.

'Right Jarvis,' as he pointed the grey, slender remote control towards the screen, where the figures suddenly disappeared. 'What the bloody hell is going on? Have you any leads on the other two, the erm…physiotherapist and the girl?'

'No, we've got nothing as yet, but right now, where I should be is listening to an interview with the partner of Mr Hackman, the physiotherapist which you so correctly remembered is his job title.'

'Well, I'm telling you that you're going to go around to see this Mrs O'Keefe and find out from her any more information that she hasn't already given to the public at large. And let me advise you Jarvis that you go cap in hand, subservience in large doses, and I don't need to tell you that I don't want to hear that you've torn into her for going to the media first instead of coming to us, d'you hear me?'

'I'd really like to see what Thurston's got to say first, he might be able to give us something, and then we'd be able to pass onto the doc's wife that we've got a positive hunch as to where her old man might be.'

'Remind me again who's running this show detective Inspector. Now I'm sure whoever's in the interview room with this fag...I mean partner of the missing man, that they'll do a sterling job. So, without sounding boring and repeating myself, I need you to go there now, and the minute you get back, I expect you back in here and report everything that she's told you. Got it. But erm...before you go Jarvis, could you let me in on a little secret and tell me what you've been doing to find out where these people have vanished to, because let's face it, up until now you've been rather hum...scant in giving me any reports. No, strike that last comment, I haven't had any details written or otherwise as to what you and your team have been doing since the first man failed to return home. So, what've you got?'

Jarvis, already having arisen from his chair ready to bolt, gingerly lowered himself slowly back down, where crossing his legs and folding his arms, he tried to hide the high rising tension running right through him, 'No, you're right Chief Inspector, I haven't had much time to send you blank pieces of paper, because that's what I would be giving you, absolutely nothing, zero. And it's certainly not for the want of hard work as the lads have been working double shifts, and there isn't a bloody door that we haven't knocked on in the areas where both Mr Hackman and Miss Baluyot lived, also suffice to say, there isn't any one person that we interviewed that was known to both.

'We've had squad cars randomly driving around day and night around vacant buildings, warehouses to see if there are any unusual sightings, but nothing. We've even interviewed Hackman's clients and spoken with nursing colleagues at both the agency where the Filipino nurse is employed, known as the Phoenix Specialist Nursing Agency, and the wards and care homes where she's done shifts, and again nobody was even aware that she'd gone missing, because hum...well let's face it, she's a locum and doesn't normally do the same shifts at the same place every day. I guess, a bit like Hackman, she fills in at hospitals and care homes where they've got staff shortages and sickness issues, and this is the problem that we're up against, there's absolutely no common denominator between both cases. Now, especially...' Jarvis found himself pointing to the empty black TV screen, 'with this latest one, this really is going to put the spanner in the works.'

'I'm assuming you did the regular appeals to the public and all that?'

'Yes, of course we did, and it goes without saying that our officers are chasing up anything that we can get of interest, but you know the score, there's always the jerks and the crank calls, most of whom have some kind of an axe to grind against us, and some of them are actually stupid enough to believe that we're gonna take them seriously.' The Inspector flicked through the loose pages ensconced within a manila folder, found the relevant page with its scribbled pen markings, repeating, 'The guys at Siddington station went around to speak with the young lady that received the text message from Miss Baluyot, a Miss Philippa Nugent, a twenty-seven-year-old nurse who works at the same Agency. But here's the thing you see, Philippa said that before she'd gone to work on the last day that she was seen, Rosario told her she'd got a date, and never mentioned anything about going to a conference of any description. So, if she was lying then the multimillion-dollar question is, why? Doesn't make any sense, does it?'

Wolfe, whilst tugging at his cuff sleeves commented with his familiar raspy voice, 'Was that all she'd got to say? Did this Baluyot woman not give any details as to what the bloke looked like, I mean…we know what women are like when they get chatting about a new fella that they've met, they tell each other everything, don't they? Did she not even mention where her and this bloke met, no photo on a phone sent from the Filipino to her mate about what she thought, you know like…did the friend think he was good looking, too fat, too scrawny, too many tattoos, rings through his nose that sort of thing?'

'Nah, that was all we got, I'm afraid. Rosario's parents who're incidentally still in the Philippines have also been contacted, and the last time they were in touch with their daughter was via a face time phone call on 11th April, and her mother said that her daughter never mentioned anything about a new boyfriend or being asked to go to a medical conference. And she also told Detective Constable Moore from Siddington that they would have been ecstatic if Rosario had told them this, as that would mean that she was doing so well, considering she'd never left her home country before, and especially with her being such a shy, unconfident kinda girl. Moore also spoke with the other flat mate, known as…oh here it is, a Mr Aaron Fleet, who informed them that he only saw Rosario on a handful of occasions during all the time that they all lived together, because all three house mates worked at different places, and all had unusual shift patterns. We checked this guy out and he'd got no previous criminal charges. So, as you can see sir, it's a clear-cut case of pissin' in the wind.'

'I hear you, but I can bet my year's salary that I'll be getting a visit from the Chief Superintendent before the day is out, and I'd better be able to tell him that we've got a plan, and a route out of this mess. There's one thing that I'd like you to do, and that is that you take a WPC with you when you go to visit this O'Keefe woman, and then you're gonna take a visit to the GP's medical practice and interview all employees there. The public are already getting very twitchy, and they don't like to hear us banging on and on about them having to use extreme caution when going out, telling all and sundry where they're going, what time they left the house and what time they're due back, get my drift? And Jarvis, I don't need to tell you this, but there'll be no excuse this time if there's nothing on my desk within the next thirty-six hours, do I make myself clear?'

No more words were exchanged, no polite handshakes forth coming by either officer as the Chief Inspector was nervously cradling his head in hands staring blankly at some paperwork as Jarvis made his way to the door.

As he closed the door behind him, he leant against the back of the door with his eyes lowered towards the floor, not really looking, or thinking of anything, he simply needed to be trance-like for a few moments, where his brain could disengage itself from everything good and bad.

Holding onto the finger smudged black, shiny banister whilst descending the stairs with cautious long strides, his phone pinged deep within his jacket pocket. Stopping midway on the staircase, he opened the message, and it read quite succinctly, 'Trial starts day after tomorrow, let's nail the bastard.'

He smiled and suddenly felt feather-like as he trod with an air of upbeat lightness down the rest of the grey stone steps whilst punching his fist in the air, 'End of the road for you DaCosta, you fucking low life.'

Having reached the second floor, Jarvis pulled open one of the double doors that led to the Incident Room where his diligent officers were huddled over computers searching screens and peering at photographs that beamed boldly up at them. Thanks were relayed to the providers of information of things that they'd thought they'd seen, with half-hearted promises that they would be contacted again if they were needed before finally re-iterating that there would be no reward money.

'Listen up guys,' announced Jarvis, as the officers slowly congregated around him like infant school children about to be told a story by their teacher,

'Just had a brief from the man upstairs, who's to put it mildly, crapping himself about the O'Keefe publication to the media about her husband not having been seen for six days. So Kelly, I want you to come with me as we're going to have to dish out the mea culpa by the bucket load, even though we've done nothing wrong, but we've got to get her trust, otherwise this whole damn thing is going to explode in our faces, and the next thing you know we'll have local residents marching up and down the streets with great big bloody placards saying that we're useless shits, and we'll have rioting outside the station.

'Are Nico and Javid still in with Thurston, by the way?' scanning around the room, there were shrugs of shoulders, and blank faces each peering at one another in the assumption that someone would know where they were, 'Dunno guv, haven't seen 'em for about an hour, so I guess that would be a fair chance that that's where they both are,' reported Turner as he perched idly on the side of his desk.

'Okay, I'm sure they'll report back when they get back here, turning briskly around and heading towards his office where he went to retrieve his jacket, where he swivelled around on the spot, and pointing in the air with his index finger, as if he'd just remembered something important, he elatedly boasted out loud, 'Oh yeah…DaCosta's trial starts the day after tomorrow, so save the date and the time, because we'll be out celebrating when that sonofabitch gets banged up. C'mon Kelly better not keep the good doctor's wife waiting, eh?'

***

As both detectives entered through the meandering, gravelled driveway of Mrs O'Keefe, they both glanced at each other askance, with Kelly emitting a long, high-pitched whistle, 'Well there's no doubt about it, your GPs certainly earn a fat lot more than us, that's for sure. D'you think she'll mind if we park this clapped-out piece of shite behind her posh BMW?' Not waiting for an answer, the female officer did anyway. At the top of the two semi-circular steps which led them to the black front door with all its shiny brass furnishings, they gazed around at the luscious wealth of greenery that formed the boundary of the extensive property, but this was prematurely interrupted as the door opened.

'Yes?' asked the short, blonde-haired lady as she stared with an almost blatant sense of hostility out of her steely blue eyes.

Jarvis and Donnelly both held their ID badges at eye level, where she responded, 'Come in detectives,' whilst opening the door wider for them to gain entry.

Waiting for the thud of the door shutting off the outside world, both officers peeled their eyes scantily around the wealth of rich deep colours that covered not only the floors but also the walls of the expansive hallway. Antique, gold sprayed frames hung delicately, proudly displaying pictures of white swirling waves devouring small fishing boats, whilst the carcass of some poor beast was being stripped to the bare bones within the wilds of southern Africa, as the viewers' eyes were being drawn to them by the innocuous lighting that shone above them.

With the sound of the clip clopping of backless mules on the stone floor, both Jarvis and Donnelly stood aside to let Mrs O'Keefe pass, and with her face set in a hard and expressionless mask, she simply retorted stonily, 'Follow me if you would, officers.'

Thoughts being momentarily interrupted by this brusque command, the senior officer smiled sweetly and quietly sauntered behind her into what would undoubtedly be another opulent, interior designed room, where the owner more than likely spent endless hours turning the hundreds of pages from the colourful magazines in an attempt to emulate the ideas that were portrayed on the glossy pages.

Being led into the ivory-coloured kitchen with its black oyster marble tops, the doctor's wife pointed to two bar stools, which were uniformly placed within the islands seating area.

'Coffee, tea or a cold drink perhaps?' she asked, with a drawling accent, laden with a spoonful of contempt.

'I'm good,' replied Jarvis.

Sergeant Donnelly shook her head slightly and responded, 'Nah, haven't long had one, but thanks for the offer. If I change my mind, I'll let you know.

'So…what do I owe the pleasure of Her Majesty's finest visiting me, rather than patrolling the streets looking for people that suddenly have gone missing? Or are you simply here to give me a right royal ticking off for what I've done, instead of me going to you people with cap in hand asking for help?'

The elder detective took the lead and replied, but before he did, DCI Wolfe's orders clawed at his power of speech, 'No, not at all, Mrs O'Keefe. You're quite within your rights to do whatever it is you want to do. Both Detective Sergeant Donnelly and I are here merely on behalf of the force to offer you the assurance that we'll do everything we can to successfully re-unite you and your son with your husb...'

'If you'd given even a modicum of attention to the interview Inspector, you'd know of course that we are no longer married,' retorted the petite, blonde lady with a voice that was even more hostile than the devilish look that she cast.

'I'm sorry Mrs O'Keefe, but I don't think questioning the effectiveness of my memory as to what was or wasn't said at your press release is going to be very helpful at this point. Whether you are, or indeed no longer married, does not escape from the fact that you went on local television stations and announced that your former husband is in fact missing. And perhaps more importantly, let us not escape from the one indisputable fact that he remains the father of your son, irrespective as to whether or not you're still a couple. So, I hope we can move on, and with your help we may be able to learn a little bit about your ex-husband, which may give us a few clues as to where he may be.'

Kelly pulled out her notebook and pen from her black shoulder bag, and clicking the top of the pen she was now ready to jot down aspects of a man's private life whom she'd never met before.

'I know you said that Dr O'Keefe was last seen on 27th April,' whilst studying both police officers, the casually attired woman, clad in a silk looking baggy blouse sitting atop multi coloured hareem style trousers, once again rudely interrupted the flow of the detective's words. 'I never said he was last seen on that date, Inspector. I seem to remember that I said I last spoke to him on that date, so hum...d'you see the difference?'

Jarvis, whilst trying to keep his voice at a constant measured tone, refusing to rise to the bait of this bitter tongued woman, asked sourly, 'So, was that early in the day, last thing at night, could you tell us when exactly?'

She turned her right wrist towards her and glanced at the quirky but doubtlessly fashionable watch, as she responded, 'I know exactly when it was. It was at exactly seven fifteen in the morning, because I needed to remind him that it was his turn to pick Ben up from his football match, or practice, one of the two anyway, and I wanted to make sure that I got hold of him before he went to the surgery, so that he couldn't make the excuse that he'd conveniently forgotten, or his phone had run out of battery, you know...the kind of lies that you men make all the time, just to get out of duties that involve the kids or the house. I'm sure you've pulled a few of those out of the hat in the past, eh Inspector?'

Inspector Jarvis found himself silently uttering a prayer to the gods in the sky, '*Just a word, if you wouldn't mind…I know you know that I want to put my hands around her throat, but please I beg of you, don't let me do it. I'll do anything you ask of me, I'll start to be nice to people, and I could start to do some voluntary work if you like, help more around the house that sort of thing, if you can just stop me from wringing the life out of her,*' and smiling blandly he simply enquired, 'So when did you last see him then, or when was the last at the surgery, assuming that you'd already been in touch with his co-workers at the medical centre before you erm…decided to go public?'

'I saw him on the Saturday 24th April when he took Ben out for the day, and if my memory serves me well, they went to London, sightseeing and what have you, because Ben had got to write a story on something that he really likes and finds interesting and that happens to be The Tower of London. So, Miles thought it would be kind of cool if they both went, and Ben could take some pictures of the Beefeaters and the tower itself of course. They also wanted to do the usual touristy things like a boat trip along the River Thames, nip on and off undergrounds and then to finish it off Ben's dad treated him to see the Lion King. I was obviously in bed when they got home, but Miles made sure that Ben went straight to bed, which is where I found him the next morning, absolutely spark out.'

'You never answered my question, Mrs O'Keefe. Did you speak to anyone at the Centre about your ex-husband's whereabouts before you contacted the media? I'm anxious to find out because he may have confided in them that he was going somewhere for a couple of days without wanting to…shall we say alert you as to his whereabouts. You have to admit that at times, we all want to get away for a while, sometimes on our own, or with a close friend. Don't you agree that this could in fact be the case?'

'How many more times do I have to tell you? He wouldn't have left Ben at the bloody soccer pitch when I'd rung him to remind him that very morning that he'd got a match, he's just not like that Inspector. He is also very well aware that our son is a bit shy and nervous, and the very idea that Miles would fail to turn up at a given time is completely out of character and quite frankly out of the question. It was the soccer coach who stayed with him until I was able to get there myself, and for that I will always be in his debt.'

'Right. Mrs O'Keefe did your husband tell you of anyone that's been badgering him lately, or perhaps someone that's got an axe to grind. Do either of you have any problems with the teachers or the kids' parents at the school? You don't need me to tell you, as I'm sure you're very well aware that jealousy amongst school kids can have a knock-on effect with mums and dads, and sometimes sanity takes a back seat, and instead of the various parties talking things through like sensible human beings, ugliness seems to take over.

'We've had cases where windows have been smashed, dog excrement shoved through letter boxes, hateful, nasty messages pasted on front doors and all because a child decided that he'd make up some story about a kid that had done nothing wrong except to get a better mark than him in the weekly spelling test. So, if you can think of any recent spat that either your son or your ex-husband may have mentioned, then we'd really like to hear about it.'

The lady of the house perched lazily on the edge of the bar stool, rested her hands on the island as the bracelets on her left wrist jangled noisily, churlishly remarked, 'My husband is an educated man Inspector, and brawling around a school playground is hardly becoming of a doctor or his estranged wife, and perhaps more to the point, he would never jeopardise my son's popularity with his friends as a result of some degrading confrontation with any parents, regardless of their background. Now if there's nothing else, I have things that I must be getting on with.'

'Please bear with us a little while longer, Mrs O'Keefe. Both Sergeant Donnelly and I would be very grateful if you could let us have the names and addresses of any close friends of his, whether associates of both of you when you were a couple, or since your separation. Also, it would be very useful if you could let us have details of any groups or clubs that he was a member of. Now, we could wait for them here if you wish, or you could call either myself or the Sergeant here later on in the day. As I'm sure you'll appreciate, the sooner we have this information, the quicker we'll be able to find out if anyone from these groups of people either know his current whereabouts, or have been in touch with Dr O'Keefe.'

The lady elegantly slid off the stool and went into an adjoining room and returned clutching a leather-bound small note book and opened the relevant pages and read out the names that Jarvis had requested.

'Here we are, and correct me if I'm wrong, but you haven't asked me the current address where he's now living, but then I'm assuming when you heard the news that you'd have made it your business to find out, but just in case you need a reminder it is a lovely little mews house and it's 64 Prince Albert Grove,

Little Buckleden, which is about six miles outside of Upper Stanton. Now, Miles still plays badminton, and he is part of a league, but don't ask me how often he plays because I haven't got a clue. The name of the club is Shelton Sports Centre and this is on the main Richmond Road.

'He also plays a few rounds of golf, again I haven't got a clue how often, but he mainly plays with two of his buddies whom he graduated medical school with. One of them is Bobby Gibbons and the other is Sean Gulliver,' she passed the notebook across the island to Sergeant Donnelly who jotted down the phone numbers.

'The other question I'd like to ask you is presumably you've been to his house to make sure that he's not there?' asked Jarvis.

'Of course I have, I'm not some stupid bimbo you know who'd go around reporting that her husband is missing when all the time he could have been shutting himself away in the house? Seriously Inspector, have the decency to show me a little bit more courtesy, and if I may say so, respect.'

Running his fingers through his blonde fringe that had somehow re-routed itself across his eyes, and whilst grasping for the right words, even though it was increasingly evident that this was not likely going to happen anytime soon, he remarked, 'You'll be surprised Mrs O'Keefe that when something like this happens, people forget to look in the most obvious of places, so once again forgive me if you think that the question was, how shall we say…insensitive?'

'I'm not people Inspector and suffice to say that even though we're no longer together, I'm absolutely terrified that something bad has happened to him. You can answer me a question now if you will, what are you going to do next to find out where Miles is?'

'Well, obviously we're going to check up on those names of friends that you've kindly given us, and we'll check up on the golf club and the sports centre to find out if they've got records of dates he was last seen there. I'd also very much like to have a set of keys to his house so that we can get a feel of what things may have gone missing, or if there's any evidence of a scuffle that sort of thing. Or, if you'd prefer, you could escort us if you're in the slightest bit apprehensive as to handing over the key to us. If this were to be the case, then you may be the best person to clarify as to what things if any, may be missing like hum…you know items of clothing, have all of his toiletries been cleared out, and perhaps more importantly, if you know where he would normally keep his passport, then that would give us a clear indication that he definitely hasn't left the country, well not legally that is.'

'I think that would be the best idea Inspector, we could go now if you'd like?' this was the first time that this petite, casually attired lady had shown even the slightest modicum of a positive approach to the detective's line of questioning.

'That's very kind of you Mrs O'Keefe but there's one last question that I wouldn't mind putting to you if I may? Since you and your husband decided to go your separate ways, has Miles begun another relationship, well…one that you know of? I guess what I'm getting at is, if this turned sour, have we got ourselves a case of a scorned lover perhaps? And it goes without saying that this could be either male or female?'

This suggestion was met with her usual embittered, acidic tongue as she quipped, 'I hardly think so, Inspector. Even if he was in the throes of some romantic tryst, the circle of people my ex would have associated with would not have gone to such lengths, just because she'd been dumped. Notice how I use the pronoun 'she' officer, because if you think for one minute that Miles is gay then I can assure you he was and remains one hundred percent heterosexual. And…just for the record, he wasn't seeing anybody because even though were no longer an item, we're still friends, for the sake of Ben, and we'd always agreed that should the marriage fall apart, then we'd move hell and high water to make sure that our son wasn't going to suffer because of our decision to untie the knot so to speak. No…that idea is definitely out of the question.'

'I understand what you're saying,' Jarvis stated, having listened patiently whilst nodding his head imperceptibly, 'but you know these days, there's hundreds of these so-called dating sites, and by and large the parties involved in setting up arrangements to meet up are generally a well-kept secret. That's the only reason why I asked, believe me. We have to explore every avenue as I'm sure you'll understand. You see, crime solving is very much like crossword puzzles, in that even though the readers have been given a clue, it's not until you've tried various letters to fill the boxes that you actually find the word you're looking for…d'you see?'

Lowering her eyes, and touching the sparkly oyster eyes in the island's marble counter, Mrs O'Keefe muttered almost contritely, 'That's quite an analogy Inspector, and I guess I understand, but it's well…understandably very upsetting for little Benjamin, as he keeps asking me when he'll see his daddy again,' and retrieving a tissue from the side pocket of her baggy harem trousers, she dabbed the corners of her eyes and blew her nose gently, adding, 'and d'you know the worst thing, I don't know how to begin to answer him? The teachers and pupils at his school have been very supportive, but you see that's not enough for a nine year old, now is it?'

Standing up and pushing the bar stool noisily away with the back of his legs, Jarvis remarked softly, and with an air of unmistakeable sincerity, 'Thank you very much for your time Mrs O'Keefe, and needless to say if you hear anything then here's my card,' he removed the card from his jacket pocket and laid it on the cold mottled marble surface, 'and as you can see, it has numbers of both my direct line and my mobile. It goes without saying that as soon as we hear anything, and I mean anything, we'll be in touch straight away.'

***

Silence ensued between the two detectives, and the only sounds to be heard were the clunking of the car doors and the rattling of the security chain as the austere black door closed itself from inquisitive prying eyes, leaving only the vision of an imposing property, majestically concealed behind its fortress-like gates, with its Latin name of Veritas blazoned on a brass plate.

'Well, d'you think I behaved myself adequately, Sergeant Donnelly?' enquired the Inspector sarcastically.

'Don't know about that now sir, but I guess you did al…'

The electric guitar chords rapturously resonated from the Inspector's phone, and recognising the caller ID he winked at Kelly and said, 'Gotta get this, it's Nico, and it's probably an update about Thurston.'

'Hi Nick, please for fuck's sake tell me that you've got some good news for us?'

'Hi chief, we've been round and round the bloody Wrekin and we've got some info but not much that we can put out a photo fit of the bloke that's for sure. There's no doubt about it though he's scared shitless, because as you can imagine our mystery man threatened that he'd do serious damage to Mr Hackman if Thurston was found squealing like a pig.' '

'Go on then, make mine and Kelly's day and tell us what you do have, as we've just spent a gruelling hour with Mrs O'Keefe, and believe me if we don't get some results and bloody fast, then her first and only broadcast for an appeal for help ain't going to be her last, that I can assure you. And I'll bet my sodding pension that she'll give our Detective Chief Inspector a call by the end of the day about our behaviour,' turning to the right, he glanced towards the driver and grinned sneakily.

'Thurston was able to give us something about the bloke's appearance though, he claimed that the guy sported a black goatee, but he also felt that this may have been dyed, because it was almost jet black, and yet his eyebrows were a light brown colour. Also, when he handed over the drugs that the mystery man had demanded from him, he had to take his sun glasses off to read the instructions as to how to administer them, and as he did this, Dominic managed to get a quick look at the colour of his eyes, and he said that they were the most amazing shade of blue he'd ever seen, almost well…fake like. So, this might mean that the fella probably wears these coloured contact lenses that you can buy almost at any optician, or so I'm led to believe anyway.'

'What were these drugs that he wanted?' asked Jarvis as Kelly had to sound the horn of the Volvo as a vivid red coloured Mini cut her up. 'You stupid bastard ya,' she roared.

'I can see our lovely Irish gal has found herself an enemy on the road, eh? Tell her to wash her mouth out,' snorted Javid, whilst Jarvis mockingly reminded them, 'You're on speaker phone lads, and from where I'm sitting, she doesn't look like a happy bunny, so I'd be careful what you say.'

'Sorry Kel, only joking. Anyway, going back to the drugs thing, this is a really weird shopping list from a so-called kidnapper of three people. He demanded that Thurston give him Aspirin, but not in tablet form, which is what's sold over the counter. He insisted that he only wanted the sort that could run through the system intravenously. He demanded a pile of incontinence pads, bandages, and obviously all the paraphernalia that you need to run IV drugs through.'

Staring out of the windscreen, Jarvis noticed how fast the black clouds were forming, hiding any evidence of where the sun had been earlier, frowned and responded inquisitively, 'Why the fuck would he want this stuff? I mean, hard core pain killers like Tramadol, Morphine that I could understand, but this just doesn't make any sense, does it? Did Thurston give any indication as to why this bloody nutter wanted this stuff?'

Javid responded with a serious sound in his voice, 'The only thing that our chemist was able to tell us was that if someone takes Aspirin especially in this form, then complications such as severe headaches, dizziness, and vomiting could occur, but perhaps more importantly, Thurston told him that if he didn't administer the drug correctly the result could end in a fatality, and guess what the reply was, *'Don't worry, I've got someone in mind who's in the know about this sort of thing, my friend.'* I mean he's absolutely gutted that he just kinda handed everything over to this maniac, but he felt that he really didn't have a choice because of the threats that he'd made to Robin.'

Jarvis questioned glumly, 'Did he offer anything else, piercings, scarring to the face, tattoos that sort of thing?'

'Nah,' Nico replied, 'other than of course the description of his clothing, which was a bog standard black, long sleeved hoodie, trackie bottoms, but he did notice that when he went back to his bike, he could swear that the man had a bit of a limp going on, but erm…because his mind was understandably elsewhere, he couldn't say which leg was the dodgy one.'

'I guess we've found out why he needs the services of a doctor then haven't we, so he can dope up our Mr Hackman with all kinds of shit, but the million-dollar question has got to be, why the fuck would he want to do that? Anyway guys, nice work, and could you get the report typed up and take up to his highness on the third floor, as he's got his Y-fronts in a right old knot, meanwhile me and Kelly are off to Green Street Medical Centre to talk to a few of the staff. And just so you know, we managed to get the names and addresses of his sporty friends that he hangs out with and the names of a golf club and the sports centre where O'Keefe spends some of his time. I've also told his missus that someone will pick her up, as she's insistent that she wants to be there with us when we search her ex's house, so erm…we'll have a briefing when we get back, and we can sort out then who's doing what. So, see you guys later.' Click.

Chapter 16

As Jarvis fiddled around with the air conditioning knobs on the dashboard, and as the cool air blasted out, the Irish detective bellowed out, 'Feck me sir, if you're too bloody hot take your soddin' jacket off, or just open a damn window why don't ya?'

Arriving outside of the Medical Centre, Jarvis suggested, 'Let's park on the roadside here, see if we can find anything useful.' Whilst signalling left, Sergeant Donnelly reversed the grey Volvo in between two parked cars and the detritus left behind from a shedding cherry blossom tree.

As Kelly aimed the fob at the engine automatically locking the doors, she glanced upwards, whilst pointing her finger towards the rather overweight pigeon, 'Don't you be shittin' on the car while were gone.' Jarvis just shook his head and sniggered, 'You're unbelievable you know that?'

They split up as they scouted around for any visible or obscure cameras, signs of broken glass, blood stains, a glove, hat, or some other piece of clothing that may have been dropped. But they both agreed that even if they were lucky to find anything, there was no guarantee that it belonged to the almost middle-aged doctor.

Poking underneath piles of leaves with the toe cap of her well-worn Chelsea boot, Sergeant Donnelly quipped, 'Absolutely feckin' nothing.'

Jarvis made his way into the neatly tarmacked car park without responding to his sergeant, whilst all the time scanning around for tiny cameras that may give some much-needed answers.

The automatic double doors swished open where they finally got what they wished for, as the tiny little aperture sprang into life. 'Ahhh, finally. At least we've got something that might give us some clues, we'll pick the tape up after we've spoken to a few of the staff here.'

Stepping across the flat, weatherproof mat, there was the familiar sight of row upon row of black plastic-coated chairs with bodies planted in them all waiting obediently for their name to be called out by the receptionist who smugly held their fate in her hands.

Both police officers strolled towards the front desk where they were greeted by a very attractive thirty something old woman, whose broad, beaming smile proudly revealed a mouth of sparkling white teeth. Her Afro-Caribbean hair had been hidden by a colourful blue and gold coloured head wrap which was made even more eye catching by the long dangling ear rings that draped down to her chin line. Her blouse and trousers were quite cleverly and elegantly chosen as they were of the same blue colour as her turban, and it was blatantly obvious that she took great pride in her appearance.

Seated behind a teak-coloured table and peering at a computer screen, she stood up and hailed, 'Mrs Webster Room 3, Mrs Webster.' The Inspector smirked inwardly as he was finding it quite amusing, especially in doctors' surgeries, as people that were waiting to be called usually had a head in a magazine, or a book, and as soon as a name had been called they would be compelled to peer over the top of it, inwardly guessing what was wrong with the person being summoned.

The Naomi Campbell lookalike bade them good morning and enquired as to whether they were here for an appointment. Having for what seemed like the umpteenth time that day, they dug out their wallets revealing little Perspex photographs of themselves bearing their names and status.

'Pleased to meet you detectives, I'm Mrs Vivienne Tucker. How may I help you?'

Inspector Jarvis inquisitively asked, 'Is there somewhere a bit more private that we could have a chat d'you think?' as a second lady slipped behind the tidy, efficient desk and placed her dark brown leather handbag underneath it.

'Mary, could you manage the desk while I speak to these two officers, please?' Vivienne asked, with a very subtle hint of a southern European accent.

'Of course, Viv, take as long as you like,' the prim grey haired lady replied reassuringly.

Both officers followed the long-legged receptionist who sashayed past the eagerly awaiting patients where they were persistently turning wrists over and surreptitiously glancing at strategically placed clocks, to make sure that all the hands on the timekeepers were in the same position.

Vivienne knocked politely on a door that didn't display either an engaged or vacant sign, and without there being a response to the rapping on the wooden surface, she gingerly opened it and briefly peered inside before opening it up fully for all to enter.

Inviting them both to sit beside a desk which was host to an old-fashioned sphygmomanometer, stethoscope, and a hideous looking metallic contraption that must have been used to probe into people's ears, Jarvis skimmed around the room in idle curiosity. On the counter beside the wash basin there were the familiar jars of cotton wool balls and a couple of tourniquets, and then of course alongside the one wall was the light blue examination table with a matching roll of paper lying in readiness on the end.

Opening a window slightly, to rid the air of some of the highly potent cleaning fluids, Vivienne then sat and joined the detectives.

'Am I right in thinking officers that your visit has got something to do with the recent appeal by Mrs O'Keefe?'

'Yes erm…Miss, Mrs…I'm afraid I was only able to catch your first name on your desk.'

'It's Mrs Tucker, Inspector,' as she erotically crossed her right leg over her left whilst resting interlocking palms on the top of the dilapidated old wooden desk.

'Okay, very well Mrs Tucker. We are indeed here to ask you a few things about Dr O'Keefe if that's alright. So…if you may remember on the broadcast that you obviously saw, Mrs O'Keefe was absolutely adamant that the last time that she had heard from her husband was on 27th April and this was verified again to us this morning. Sergeant Donnelly and I would like you to tell us when Dr O'Keefe was last present here in the surgery, or what might be even more useful to us would be if you could give us a list of names of the patients whom he saw on the last known day of his treatments, whether it be here at the clinic or perhaps home visits.'

'Hum…well I don't have a problem giving you the information that you need, but…wouldn't that contravene some kind of ethical guidelines perhaps? I mean it goes without saying that we should all do whatever it is that needs to be done to find out where he is, but I'm afraid that I'd have to check with one of the other senior partners before I can give you that information.'

Fiddling around with a small, sealed sachet of a sterile bacterial wipe, the Inspector nodded his head and reiterated with a tone of sincere concern, 'I absolutely whole-heartedly agree with everything you've just said, and of course you need to check with your senior colleagues. My other question would be is, have there been any patients that you know of that could have been using threatening behaviour, or put the heebie-jeebies up the good doctor, either more recently, or even perhaps within a longer time span, shall we say…about a year, year and a half?'

'Oh gosh I can honestly swear that I'm not aware of anyone who would either wish harm, or more importantly cause harm towards him,' answered the black receptionist as she straightened her back forcing her shoulders back slowly, 'but then I s'pose…a bit like you guys and your profession, we don't normally tell each other everything, now do we? I mean, if we happen to be in the staff room together, which is a rarity I can assure you, or if we go out for a drink or a bite to eat which is even rarer, we would just stick to run of the mill topics, like the weather, who's got a holiday booked, that sort of thing. We don't pry into each other's lives Inspector, especially when we're not invited to do so.'

The Irish detective clad in a plain, cornflower blue blouse with the two top buttons undone, revealing a dainty, small diamond studded crucifix, chipped in, 'We understand fair enough what you're sayin', but like, there must have been patients at one time or another who've caused aggro, especially if they can't get an appointment, or if the wrong diagnosis is made, d'ya not think Mrs Tucker?' Inspector Jarvis snidely kicked his colleague in the shins and raised his eyes to the heavens in a subtle attempt for her to stop the Irish brogue.

'Well obviously we get irate patients, but mainly that's saved up for us. In fact, we get it all the time,' the receptionist started gesticulating with her hands whilst mimicking some of the clients attending the clinic, *'D'you know how long I've been holding on this soddin' phone waiting for an appointment? It's a bloody disgrace is what it is, I mean I could be dead by now!'* And then nine times out of ten when we ask the person on the other end of the phone could they please tell us what the nature of their ailment is, d'you know what they say? *'Mind your own bloody business.'* So, I've got a choice, I either offer them an appointment that day or I make 'em wait. I mean, don't get me wrong, the situation's far from ideal but we can only offer an appointment when there's one available, right? So, I suppose in answer to your question Inspector, these people blow hot and cold, but mainly they're good eggs, you know. No, the more I think about it, there is no way that anyone would want anything bad to happen, especially not towards Miles at any rate.'

Reflecting inwardly with humour on the conversation that he had had with Javid just a few days ago on the same topic of who would be granted an appointment and who'd have to wait, he needed to refocus before replying.

'How long have you known Dr O'Keefe, Mrs Tucker?' asked Jarvis, 'and could you tell us a little bit about him, for instance…was he good with patients, did you ever know him to lose his temper, did he show up for surgery on time, or…did he have to shoot off during the day for issues unrelated to work that you're aware of, that sort of thing?'

Pulling her chair even closer to the table, and with elbows resting heavily on the old wooden desk, she replied candidly, 'Oh my word that's a lot of questions that you want answers to Inspector. Right then…' she began almost matronly, 'again, this is just my opinion of him, because I don't know a damn thing about him out of surgery hours. I mean he could be for all I know an…erm Jekyll and Hyde character, but joking aside, he seems to be a really nice guy and he's very popular especially with the female patients of all ages as they'd always ask to see him, and when the caller hears that he's fully booked up, you can honestly hear their sighs of disappointment.'

'Was he a flirt then would you say,' requested the Inspector, resting folded arms on the table.

'Not in the slightest, well not openly anyway. He just, oh I dunno…made everyone feel special, whether they were a lithe eighteen-year-old blonde, or a ninety-year-old who was crippled with arthritis. You see, I sincerely think he didn't give a damn about the time allocated for each patient, because the way he saw it was that well…these people wouldn't be wasting their time sitting in a dingy room, where people were coughing and spitting into handkerchiefs, scratching some possible skin infection, unless they were desperately needing help of some kind. And let's not forget, this might mean reassurance about a lump or a mole that maybe considered insignificant to the untrained eye, or more often than not, in the case of a patient who's incredibly frail or afraid, and well…they might just need a friendly ear, d'you see what I mean?'

All three people in the room turned their attention to the sound of the lashing of the rain pounding against the window pane, when Sergeant Donnelly broke the spell with, 'So, Mrs Tucker, if there's nothing else that you think we need to know, then we look forward to receiving that list, and in the meantime, if we could perhaps speak with the other members of staff, perhaps in between them seeing patients, then that would be marvellous.'

And so, painstakingly, the two detectives listened attentively to what the other members of staff at the medical centre had to say, and found themselves repeating the same mantra at the end of each conversation, '*If there's anything that you can remember, no matter how insignificant you may think it is, then please contact us, and here's our card where you can contact us, either at the station or on our mobile phones.*'

Dashing hurriedly to avoid the rain as they made their way back to their car, Jarvis turned around as he heard a voice hailing them together with the sound of hurried footsteps, and catching hold of her throat whilst gasping for breath, she recounted, 'Sir, I'm sorry to hold you up, but I'm not sure whether this will be any good to you or not, but you see I've just remembered something.'

Jarvis opened the rear passenger seat for Mary, whom they recognised from the reception desk when they first arrived. 'Right hum...Mary, isn't it? How can we help you?'

Both officers turned their heads to hear what the lady, clad in her emerald green twin set, neatly decorated with a string of costume jewellery pearls, had to say. Whilst patting her bottle dyed chestnut hair making sure that no strand had escaped from its perfectly coiffed, tightly curled style after her sprint, she reported, 'The last time that I saw Dr O'Keefe, well...the last time any of us saw him, it was my turn to lock up the practice as I was on the late shift, and I was last one out, and that's when I saw him standing outside of the gates, and he was talking to a man in a red van, not a big van you know, like the ones they use for moving house with, but a little one that are used by decorators or florists, that sort of thing. Anyway, obviously I had to turn my back towards them to lock the building, and by the time I'd got to my car there was no sign of either of them.'

'Mary, what time was this, can you remember?' asked the Irish detective.

'Let me see, I have to stay at the surgery until seven in the evening, just in case there are any emergencies, and of course after that, well patients have to use A&E services, you see. So, I guess, after I'd locked all the offices up, spent a penny, got my coat and everything, it would most probably be around 7:15. Yes...it would definitely be about that time, I'm absolutely sure.'

'Did you hear anything at all like for instance raised voices, shouts for help or a scuffle, anything like that?'

'No, because I would definitely have gone to see what was going on as, well...I've been known for being a bit on the nosey side,' she covered her nose and mouth with her right hand as she tittered, and as neither police officer responded to this rather amusing comment, she continued with her narrative, 'but the one thing that I did hear was the sound of two doors closing.'

'You're sure about this Mrs…?' enquired the Inspector, noticing the gold wedding band.

'Duggan, and yes I'm one hundred per cent sure as both doors seemed to close almost at the same time, but not exactly if you get my drift, it was merely a split second, that's all.'

'You said that it was a red van, is there anything else about it that you can tell us? For instance, did you manage to get the number of the registration plate, or did it have a roof rack or any other distinguishing details? Did it look new or battered about? Was it loaded with workmen's tools, that sort of thing?'

'I'm afraid I didn't notice anything like that, I mean…the sides of the van didn't have any windows, that much I can tell you, so I wouldn't be able to see what was in the back now, would I? It certainly didn't have a roof rack of that I'm certain, and from where I was standing, it didn't look to be an old crock, the roof looked kinda shiny to me, but then again it could have been the streetlamp reflecting the light on to it, making it look good, you know what I mean?'

'Okay Mrs Duggan, now I want you to think carefully. Did you see what the man was wearing, or tell us anything about what he looked like? Did he have long hair, wear glasses, fat, thin, and I know you weren't standing close to either of them at the time, but if there's anything that you can remember about him, we'd be very grateful for your help.'

Folding her arms under her ample bosom and with a slight rocking motion, she reported cautiously, 'Don't forget Inspector, I didn't have a long time to see anything, but let me see…he, the man that was talking to Dr O'Keefe that is, had his head covered with one of those hoodie things that all the youngsters seem to wear these days, and it was definitely a dark colour, black, navy blue I guess, but other than that I couldn't really see very much, because he had his back to me.'

'Ah…I see, but the van was definitely red in colour of that you're absolutely certain? Was it a scarlet red or a darker red a bit like hum…red wine?'

'It was dark red officers, there's no question in my mind whatsoever on that score.'

Both Sergeant and Inspector glanced at each other as the elder of the two shrugged his shoulders slightly in a silent motion of suggesting that there was nothing else that they were going to glean from this impeccably attired lady, who was probably close to retirement age.

'We're so grateful for you coming forward with this information Mrs Duggan, and if it's okay with you, I'll be sending over an officer to see you with photos of various types of vans, and if you could kindly take a look at them and see whether you could identify which model you think you saw. But also, in the meantime, if you should think of anything else that may be of interest to us, we'd be grateful if you could contact us,' as the lady in the back seat of the car gingerly opened the car door and carefully hid the two business cards into the side pocket of her skirt.

'So, we now know that our guy drives a dark red van, and we already know that he wears a dark coloured hoodie, so once she's identified,' Jarvis crossed his fore and middle fingers, resembling a good luck gesture, 'the type of red van, then we can check all the garages, rental agencies for recent acquisitions. So…well it goes without saying, that we need this info sooner rather than later.'

Scanning across at her boss from the steering wheel, Donnelly suggested eagerly, 'I'm not doing anything tonight I don't mind going back. I could get a load of printouts and take them round, because as you know they don't close until after 7:00 pm so that'll give me enough time, so it will.'

'Thanks Kelly, perhaps you could take Dean with you and then the two of you could perhaps make a night of it and go to the pub after for a swift half,' quipped the Inspector.

'Fair enough, we could do that I s'pose,' grinned the Irish Sergeant.

***

Unlocking his front door, he could hear the sounds of people clapping raucously as a male voice tried to make himself being heard over the din, *So it's over to our panel of judges. Felicity, what did you think of our amazing Finn and the adorable, fluffy Husky called Ali?'* and with that Eleanor appeared in the hallway, with tousled hair as if she'd just woken up, sporting multi-coloured baggy trousers coupled with an oversize shirt.

'Hi sweetie, you're home early tonight, aren't you? Is everything alright?'

Sliding slightly in his stockinged feet across the uncarpeted floor, he folded his wife into his arms, 'Sorry I haven't been around much Ellie, but things have been a bit manic lately,' combing her hair with his fingers away from her face, as he planted a solitary kiss on her bare lips.

'Yeah, don't worry honey, I've been hearing about it all on the T.V. and the radio, pretty scary out there at the minute, eh? Anyway, are you hungry because I'm sure I could rustle up something from yesterday's leftovers?'

'That's not something that we say very often in this house, especially with the two human dustbins, where are they anyway?'

'They've been and gone, you know what they're like. Alex is swatting at someone's house, and our younger son is kicking, throwing or catching a ball on some playing field somewhere. So…what's the verdict, to eat or not to eat, that is the big question?' teased the Inspector's wife.

'Actually, I'm bloody starving, but don't go to any trouble, I'll have whatever's going. Are you going to join me?' asked Jarvis as he followed his wife into the kitchen, and headed for the pine wine rack which sat rather neatly on top of the fridge/freezer where he pulled out a random bottle of red without even checking the label as to how old it was, where it was from, whether it was dry, fruity, or full bodied, as truth be told, he really couldn't care less, he just felt as though he needed a drink. Pulling open the kitchen drawer where potato peelers, garlic crushers, scissors and all the other must haves that modern kitchens were equipped with, he picked up the corkscrew, ripped open the seal on the unopened bottle, sucked the blood from the paper cut wound that the metal packaging had bestowed on him, and with a loud pop the cork was eased from the bottle. Taking two glasses from the Welsh dresser he posed the question, 'D'you want one honey?'

Stirring a heavily spiced concoction in a black cast iron pot with a wooden spoon, and without even bothering to turn around she yawned and mumbled softly, 'Yeah sounds good to me. Mind you, our quack says that I'm not supposed to drink, because apparently alcohol doesn't mix very well with all the bloody tablets that he's given me, but d'you know what, sod it, I'm having one. After all you only live once.'

Pouring two large measures into balloon glasses, and handing one to his wife, he sipped the warm red liquid and immediately felt it soaring through his blood vessels, as he exhaled a loud, 'Aaahhh, that's nice. So, are you feeling any better hon? I mean you look okay facially, but you look as though you've lost a lot of weight, and let's face it, you haven't got much to lose, have you?'

'Oh, stop worrying Mark, I'm alright. Once these pills have had a chance to work, I'll get my appetite back and then I'll get my love handles and my big fat belly back. Anyway, enough about me I went to see Luke and Nancy like you suggested, and I can't tell you how bloody tragic it is to see her like that. It's hard to take in you know that one day you're fit and healthy and the next thing you know something out of the blue changes your life for ever. I mean…she's so young for her to be dependent on other people and not being able to speak must be the shittiest thing ever.

'Can you imagine not being able to ask for something to eat or drink, or not be able to choose what clothes you'd like to wear, and the sheer embarrassment and frustration at seeing the person you're talking to, just well…trying to fathom out what the hell it is that you want to say? Doesn't bear thinking about really, does it?' as she wiped the corner of her eyes and sniffled loudly, blaming it on the onions that she'd peeled earlier.

'Aww, honey,' as he sidled up towards her and put his arm around her waist, 'I know life sucks sometimes, but you know we'll be there for her as long as she wants, and of course Luke. Speaking of which, how was he when you saw him?'

'Honestly…? I erm…found him rather hard work to talk to, he's just so…angry, yeah that's exactly what he is now that I've said it out aloud. He blamed the hospital for allowing her to be discharged before she could walk or speak, and the fact that she can't swallow compounds his hatred for all the people that treated Nancy when she was in The Hamilton, and I really think he blames them for her being wheelchair bound. The look in his eyes actually made me a little fearful of him at times, almost as if he was ready to hit out at me, I mean…of course he wouldn't, but oh I dunno…there's some kind of hidden rage going on inside that head of his.'

'Did he talk to you about what Julia's up to? If you remember, I think it was Alex, who said that…um she looks a bit slutty and stinks of de ganga man,' as Jarvis did his best at imitating the Jamaican patois and puffed on an imaginary spliff being held in between his fore and middle fingers.

Giggling at her husband, Ellie rested the wooden spoon on the green ceramic rest, shaped in the form of a large leaf, turned to face him and responded, 'The only thing he was willing to tell me was that she didn't spend much time at home these days as she always seems to be spending nights at friends' houses, and he claims he's okay with it because, as he says, at least he knows that she's safe and isn't catching the last bus home, or getting into a cab on her own. I didn't ask about her school life or anything like that, because it was clear he kinda wanted to steer clear from any conversations about his daughter, so in other words…back off.'

'Was he even pleased to see you, and hum…how long were you there for?' Reaching over to the neatly arranged plate rack where she pulled one out, and opening up the over door where she placed it in so that the food would stay warmer when she'd dished it out, turned to her husband and commented, 'I think he was more shocked than pleased when he opened the door to me, but he welcomed me in and yet I kinda got the feeling that conversation was really strained you know, considering the four of us used to spend quite a bit of time together, but I guess no one's to blame are they? I mean…once kids become independent of their parents, like going to and from school it's only natural that the mums and dads go and do their separate things. I spent a good oh…an hour with Nancy, and I could tell that she was excited to see me, but also slightly embarrassed about the way she looked. I mean, God knows when she last had her hair washed, and I know that she can't have a bath or a shower yet, but surely the nurse who must be getting paid a fortune for living in, could well…wash it over the sink, I mean…I've done it hundreds of times. And seriously, don't get me started as to the bloody clothes that she was wearing.'

'Did you mention any of this to Luke?'

'Of course I did, but he just made excuses saying that the nurses didn't have the time to prance about looking for clothes, and that she was hardly going to be in a fashion line up any time soon. I even offered to go shopping for her, like you know…if he felt that her clothes no longer fitted her, because I know how Nance likes to dress, and she would certainly never have been seen in tats like I saw her in today, but he didn't want to take me up on the offer, so I let it go. I met the nurse, huh…Paula I'm sure that was her name, she seemed nice enough, a bit matronly if you get my drift and,' sniggering before continuing, 'I think she thought that me and Luke were having a romantic afternoon. I mean, you should have seen the look that she gave us because he offered me the dregs of a bottle of wine, and I'm not kidding when I say there were probably a couple of mouthfuls. It was actually quite funny.' Ladling the garlic-laced bubble and squeak with rashers of bacon onto a heated plate, and placing it onto the island where Jarvis was seated, she asked, 'So are you any closer to finding these missing people?'

Using the glass, stainless steel topped salt and pepper shakers, he lavishly applied both to the steaming fare on the oval white plate, and whilst blowing on his loaded fork he reported, 'As a matter of fact we did have a bit of a breakthrough today. I and Kelly were just about to leave Green Street Medical

Practice when one of the receptionists came out to the car and told us that she thinks she saw a red van parked on the roadside outside of the practice, which coincidentally was the last time that he'd been seen at work.

'She also said that she saw Dr O'Keefe talking to a man who was dressed in the same clothes that the partner of the physiotherapist, who you may remember is also missing, described when we interviewed him. It's not much to go on, but let's be honest, it's the best that we've got right now, so we're going to have to use all the manpower we've got trying to find out who was driving that van. We'll pull out all camera coverage on all of the surrounding roads in the hope that we get lucky, so I'm not sure how many more evenings I'll be home in time to sit down for dinner with you and the lads, and believe me I'm really not happy about that, but I can't ask the lads to do long hours if I'm not prepared to make sacrifices myself.'

'Don't you remember when we first got together, and you said, that if you managed to rise up the ranks, then being home in time for evenings out, parents' evenings at schools, and all the rest of the extracurricular stuff, could never be guaranteed. So…,' as Ellie reached across the island and tenderly took his hand in hers and stroked the back of it, 'it never made me angry back then, and I can guarantee you it won't upset me now. It's like I always said, I'm not just married to you, I'm married to your job and everyone in it, and I guess that includes the criminals too.'

'Tomorrow's not going to be much better either as it's the start of the trial of that young woman whose body was mercilessly beaten black and blue, but d'you know what, I'm rather looking forward to the judge reading him the riot act and to see the look on his cocky, smirky face when he's sent down for what we all hope will be a bloody long time.'

Chapter 17

Driving away up the leafy suburban road in his old Peugeot, Jarvis felt strangely odd in his starched white shirt buttoned to the neck, a tie which he felt would suck the last few molecules of oxygen from his lungs, and the encroachment of his driving skills due to the tight-fitting trousers and jacket of his navy blue suit, all attributed to him being in a tetchy mood. He found himself loudly honking his horn over the most trivial of reasons where, ordinarily, a disgusted *'You stupid jerk'* would have placated him, but not this morning as his nerves were as taut as his stupid tie.

Entering the second floor of the Stockfield Road Police Station via the cold, bleak staircase, he was met with wolf whistles and cries of, 'Ooh wee, 'my, my, don't we look smart,' as Sergeant Carmichael went one step further and quipped, 'Is there something that the missus should know about?'

Inspector Jarvis motioned towards his office, and without glancing towards any member of his team, he retaliated with, 'Behave you lot, never seen a bloke in a suit before?' displaying a boyish, broad grin on his face.

Not needing to go through his usual routine of hanging up his outdoor gear, he slid into his office chair, turned on his computer to check for any messages, and announcing to himself that there were none that couldn't wait, he went back outside to have a brief handover with his crew.

He sat on an empty desk in front of a white board where the photographs of the two missing males and one female, with dates and times of their last known whereabouts, and a street map denoting all three addresses and places of work, all strategically placed, demanding everyone's undivided attention. Noting that there was a new addition to the now colourful wall, he put his thumb up in the air and directed his gaze towards Sergeant Donnelly, 'So she was able to come up with the goods then Kelly, eh?'

'Yeah, it took her a while, but she was sure right enough that she identified the exact one that she saw. I've called a few places in the area where there've been recent rentals and sales, and I've also checked all the names against criminal records data base, and so far, we've got absolutely feckin' nothing.'

'It's early days yet, and we may have to widen the net to around a fifty-mile radius, but we also mustn't count out the possibility that he borrowed it from a mate. In the meantime, has anyone come up with a plausible reason why this guy's taken these three random people. I mean, as far as we know none of them knew each other except perhaps our Mr Hackman and the nurse, Miss Baluyot,' pointing to their photographs he continued, 'because as we now know these two were locums, so…their paths may indeed have crossed, but to the best of our knowledge, and the interviews that have been conducted, they don't seem to have bumped into our Dr O'Keefe. But there's absolutely no doubt in my mind that their professions have something to do with why they're missing in action. Anyone got anything to add?'

Javid cleared his throat, 'Ahem, well it's just a theory of course, but well…my gut's telling me that somehow these three were involved in the treatment of a patient that went horribly wrong, and this is the bloke's way of retribution. We're still trawling through shifts at The Hamilton and a few of the local nursing homes where we know that Hackman and the Filipino nurse had previously worked, and all we need now is a break, placing the two of them at the same place within the same time zones.'

Holding on to the back of a chair with both hands, the Inspector responded, whilst sighing heavily, 'Let's look at what we do know, and that is that Thurston gave us the heads up about what could happen if the intravenous Aspirin is administered, without medical supervision that is, but did he manage to say what sort of illness that it's needed for? I mean…it's obviously not for a relative or a buddy, because why wouldn't he just go the same route that all of us do and make an appointment at his local surgery? I think we can all agree on one thing though and that is it's certainly not a coincidence that after the mysterious man gets his grubby hands on the sweeties, that O'Keefe goes missing.'

Detective Sergeant Turner looked puzzled as he crossed his legs and with arms folded questioned the Inspector, 'D'you wanna know what I reckon? I think the doc gives a wrong diagnosis, tells whoever goes to see him to go home and take some Aspirin, then the shit goes down. The person then gets admitted to hospital for treatment, and this is where the nurse and the physiotherapist come in. And you know what else I think? The Aspirin is for O'Keefe because somehow, he screwed up with the cause of the person's illness, and more importantly the end result.'

Heads were nodding around the Incident Room with Detective Sergeant Pettrini applauding vocally, 'Josh that's really not a bad shout you know, and it really kinda fits in with the big question as to why these three people, who all have medical backgrounds, have mysteriously disappeared. Yeah, if I were a betting man,' the rest of the crew all laughed loudly, 'okay, okay, so you all know I'm too mean to spend the money on stupid things like that, but I must say, I've got to agree with our man here, that he's definitely on to a winner. I mean…when you think about it, it makes perfect sense, well as far as the random selection process goes, that's for sure.'

Inspector Jarvis stood once more, stepped towards the white board whilst pointing towards the most recent photo of Miles O'Keefe and reported almost matter of factly, 'Right, so…if what Turner's saying is the case, and I have to admit that I can't think of a more plausible account as to why he's chosen these three unconnected people, then it's imperative that we check through all of the doc's patient records and establish those who were prescribed Aspirin, and details of those who were hospitalised, which would then hopefully lead us to the association of Hackman and our young Filipino nurse. Kelly, I'd like for you to try and get a uniform to assist you in trawling through information regarding the hiring, leasing, or buying of new and second-hand vans, as per identification from our receptionist at Green Street Practice.

'The other thing guys…as you're all aware, I'm trussed up like I'm off to some kind of soddin' red carpet affair.' Wolf whistles echoed through the Incident Room once more as the previous heavy tension was eased, albeit for a short while. 'Anyway today's the day that our poor Eva's trial is heard,' and almost silently all eyes in the room focused unblinkingly at the image of the black and blue, hideously swollen face and torso of the young girl who was beaten within minutes of her life, 'and Timothy Slattery from the CPS and Nina Bartholomew, Eva's attorney, have both suggested that I attend, so that Miss O'Connor can see a friendly face in the court room. Hum…hopefully this will set aside any fears that she may have that we're not doing everything we can to make sure that she remains safe and that we uphold our promise to stand by her one hundred percent. Now let's all go about our business, and I'm contactable of course should you need anything, and before I go to see the sonofabitch get nailed, I'll bell the gaffer upstairs and let him know what were up to, so at least for the time being he can leave us the hell alone.'

The officers seated around in no particular order arose, and in turn muttered, 'Go watch him squirm guv,' 'Good luck Sir, and the same to Eva,' 'Let's see that low life DaCosta try and wriggle his way outta this one eh?' And with that they were slowly dispersing back to their little lairs as the Inspector held his hand in the air, and retorted, 'Great work guys, and Josh, excellent perceptive thinking, but let's hope you're right.'

With this, Inspector Jarvis left his team to make the phone call to Chief Inspector Wolfe as to the up-to-date progress, and at the end of the five minute barrage of strong, almost threatening conversation with the last sentence being, 'Well don't just stand there with the phone in your hand, get knocking on doors man and do some proper police work for a change. You're not going to get anywhere by wasting precious time talking to me now, are you?'

Slamming the receiver down onto its cradle, Jarvis uttered into the stillness of the air, 'Go fuck yourself,' and with that he walked out of his office and headed to the stairwell at the back of the second floor offices.

***

Inspector Jarvis managed to find a fairly decent parking space not too far from Chingford Crown Court, which was a good half hour's drive from Upper Stanton. He entered the dark, concrete, outdated 1960s car park, pressed the dispenser to get a ticket upon receipt of which the red and white barrier majestically arose in the air and allowed him entry. Retrieving a handkerchief from his jacket pocket, grateful for his mother's wisdom, *'Never leave the house without clean underwear and clean handkerchief'* and making his way to the exit, he placed the cotton square across his nostrils to eliminate the stench of stale urine, vomit and other bodily fluids which seemed to have been absorbed into the molecules of the concrete, grey pillars. Whilst concentrating on finding fresh air and inwardly congratulating himself at the speed he was able to achieve at running down the stairs, and without once touching infested hand rails, he almost fell over a badly stained sleeping bag, which must have been dropped whilst the sleeper had been caught in some kind of illegal or amoral act, and he'd had no choice but to simply leg it, leaving his worldly possessions behind.

Standing at the foot of the steps leading to the rather dark red-bricked building with its darkened windows, he was witness to what could only be described as an entourage of fans of the accused on trial, Lenny DaCosta, as they stood stubbing out cigarettes into the ground, pulverising them around and around to shreds of insignificance with the balls of their feet. He then spotted the petite, almost girlish stature of the young lady, who had claimed a large chunk of his mind since he first met her that dreadful night at The Hamilton General Hospital.

As he watched her, he could see her trying her best to make her way through the track suit clad mob, and doing her damnedest to block out the jeers and heckling that she must have known were directed only at her. It was then that he knew he'd made the right decision in coming today, even if it was just to see her rejoice that at long last justice was not only going to prevail, but it was her day and hers alone.

From where he was standing, he was pleasantly surprised to see her dressed in a very smart maroon coloured trouser suit, with her hair styled in a kind of French pleat, to which there was no doubt in his mind that she would have been coerced by her very clever lawyer, Ms Bartholomew, to reveal as many wounds as she could, which in turn would have a greater impact on the hearts and minds of the jurors as they heard the sordid evidence.

She didn't seem to ooze confidence, but then again, he noticed that she didn't hang her head low with shoulders slumped as she did each time that Jarvis went to see her. No she was giving off a message that said to the world, '*This is my time now, no matter the outcome, this is for me,*' which, let's face it, was quite an achievement, considering she was entering this well-known building, which had held court over some of the most barbaric, hideous crimes over the last few decades, and that's when he noticed something very strange indeed.

For some unknown reason which he couldn't fathom out from where he was standing, Eva stopped in her tracks, looked to the left of her, presumably in response to her name being called out, and then she bent down and picked something up from the ground. Making his way up the stairs, Jarvis could clearly see that the man whom she'd glanced at looked very intimidating with his bald head, heavily tanned obese frame, and sporting a very expensive looking dark pin striped suit, coupled with a brilliant white shirt, as he dragged his right forefinger across his throat. Eva slowly unravelled the white piece of paper that had been thrown at her feet, and it may have been because of the high heels that she was wearing that caused her to stagger slightly, but it could also have been the words that were written on it, but she merely dropped it in her bag and went inside ready for the security check that she would be enforced to go through, before she met up with her counsel.

Inspector Jarvis having gone through his own scrutiny by the uniformed officers and placing keys, wallet, watch, phone and anything else that may have bleeped through the scanners onto a grey plastic tray, went in pursuit of the young innocent victim and her prosecution attorney, who was known in the trade as 'the lioness,' as she would never settle for anything other than going for the kill, especially if her client was a woman. He saw both ladies with bowed heads, and with a real quickness of stride, and from where the Inspector was standing, it certainly looked as though whatever they were discussing there seemed to have been some kind of disagreement brewing, as arms were being flung out in the air, and fingers pointing at one another, and that's when he heard the door bang shut as they both disappeared from the busy, noisy corridor, where the clip clopping of shoes on stone floors echoed throughout the building.

There was a red leather couch positioned quite close to the soundless, windowless room, where they were no doubt thrashing out whatever issues they now found themselves up against, so Inspector Jarvis sat hunched forward with clasped hands folded on the knee of his crossed leg, and patiently waited for the women to emerge.

The first to appear was the impeccably dressed attorney in her official looking dark grey skirt suit with a light grey blouse underneath as she flicked fingers through her mousey coloured shoulder length wavy hair and mounted her black leather bag with its wide strap onto her left shoulder and walked with purposeful strides in black leather shoes. She noticed the Inspector sitting patiently with an obvious air of curiosity and simply raised her eyes to the heavens as she shook her head slightly, with Eva following close behind like the lamb obeying the shepherd, and even though she knew that the Inspector was there, she either couldn't, or wouldn't, glance in his direction.

Jarvis had a very bad feeling about all of this, and whilst slowly walking towards the doors of court number three, his stomach was sending bullet-sized acid jets through to his digestive system.

With everyone in their places, the Inspector decided he'd sit almost at the back, so he'd be able to gauge some of the expressions of not only the jurors faces, but also those of the spectators as they heard and saw evidence that was put forward as to the heinous crime that had been committed towards the young strawberry blonde haired girl. It didn't take him long, however, to see the accused in the dock, clad very smartly in a black suit, crisp white shirt and a red striped tie and his hair was swept up into his usual fashionable top knot, and even though his goatee beard had been trimmed his deep olive skin would not go unnoticed. There was no doubt in the Inspector's mind that the man who was seated behind a Perspex partition with two police officers stood to attention behind him, looked even more smug than he did the first time Jarvis had seen him being interviewed at Stockfield Road Police Station.

Silence was ordered by the usher, who with black austere gown, seemed dwarfed amidst the opulence of solid oak benches and the spectators who were ensconced in them.

'All rise,' and then with equal volume pronounced, 'This court is now in session.' The judge entered from her chambers through the walnut-coloured door, closed it noiselessly behind her, and with lightweight tread made her way up the few stairs to the bench and the rather majestic red oak wooden chair with its rather lush green leather seat, where she would be forced to listen to the gruesome account of the trial that she was about to preside over. After finely tuning the collar and the sleeves of her official black gown, the proceedings were about to begin.

As law advisers, defendant, plaintiff and spectators all began to sit down, only the words of the judge resonating in the stillness of the air were heard, 'Could you please ask the jury to come in?'

A teak-coloured door slowly opened where twelve members of the public meekly sauntered in with eyes fixated directly in front of them. There was no turning of heads, curious to snatch a glimpse of who did what to whom. No, they simply sauntered in, found a seat on the wooden benches and focused all their attention on the diminutive but powerful woman clad in a black robe with an emerald-green blouse underneath, giving her a more feminine allure rather than the austere drabness of the obligatory gown.

As the proceedings were about to continue, Inspector Jarvis found himself transfixed to the backs of the impeccably dressed Ms Bartholomew, and the transformed smartly attired Eva. He still couldn't dismiss the notion, however, that something was seriously not right, as their deep-rooted discussion seemed to continue with their heads bent towards each other, and not being able to see what the lawyer was reading, she merely shook her head and turned to face the plaintiff, gently placing her hand on her forearm.

'Is the prosecution ready to deliver its opening statement?' enquired the solitary figure cloistered at the head of this rather imposing room, amidst the surrounding symbolic sculptures which lay voiceless, having held witness to some of the most macabre cases of the last century.

'Your Honour, permission to approach the bench?' voiced the erectly poised Nina Bartholomew, as mumbled voices from the spectators were silenced, as they desperately tried to figure out what was going on.

Inspector Jarvis kept a beady eye on the DaCosta crew as they were easily distinguishable, and there was absolutely no doubt in his mind that the mob of the accused knew exactly what was transpiring as they nudged one another in a somewhat futile attempt to hide their amusement as to what was unfolding.

'Order, order,' bellowed the usher.

The judge, who was jokingly known to law enforcement officers as The Fiddler as her surname was Fiegler, apparently due to her German heritage, was intently listening to what Nina was obviously pleading for. Jarvis figured that she'd more than likely petition for a motion of some sort or another, but obviously the counter pleas from the defence lawyer who was shaking his head vehemently and waving his arms in the air, made it all the more evident that he was having none of it.

With elbows resting on the wooden surface, Judge Fiegler brought her forearms up, cupped both hands and formed a steeple with her fingers, thought long and hard before she came to her conclusion, and ordered the lawyers back to their seats to await her response.

With a no-nonsense tone, she informed the now silent congregation, 'Ms Bartholomew your motion is denied. Thank you, members of the jury, you are now dismissed.'

With almost mirroring precision, the twelve members chosen randomly from post codes around the county exited in the exact same way as they entered, and undoubtedly, the more curious of the selected few would have been disappointed that they didn't get their chance to witness a gory, newspaper-worthy trial, where when it had all ended, they could have boasted to their mates in the pub that they were responsible for putting the monster away. Others may have been slightly annoyed that they'd have to return to work the following day, but there could be no doubt whatsoever that as soon as they'd left the historical, architecturally eye-catching building that they would all convene in a coffee shop or pub to discuss what could have caused this incredibly dramatic unfolding of events, especially as their silence was no longer compulsory.

With all eyes now on the person whose voice would finally assuage fears and guesses as to what had transpired, the usher retorted in a very commanding way, *'Court is now dismissed.'*

The next announcement ordered all those present including law enforcement officers and those in the spectators gallery to *'All Rise,'* as the judge stood from the bench and with her black gown billowing into the air strode towards her chambers, and as the sound of her door closing reverberated through the air, noise emanating from DaCosta's mob was deafening, with loud cries of 'W'oo hoo and 'Yesssss' exploding around the now emptying court room. Inspector Jarvis sat firmly in his seat with his hands clasped tightly around the back of his head, not quite believing what he'd just witnessed, but what really made his blood boil was the sight of the defendant in deep embrace with the man that he'd witnessed at the top of the stairs outside of the court who obviously was responsible for Eva's change of heart. DaCosta glared in the direction of the Inspector and with his right arm raised in the air, and with fore and middle fingers raised in a V for victory sign, with his head held high he arrogantly strutted past uniformed officers towards the exit sign.

The detective, still not being able to grasp the events of the past hour, was one of a handful of people left in the room where justice was supposedly rolled out to those that deserved it, but not this time. Journalists rushed past one another ready to print off the story ready for the editor's desk, sketch artists were packing up their black and white etchings, as Eva trudged her way back up the stairs past the Inspector once again, averting any eye contact with the man who did his best to right the wrongdoing and abuse that she'd suffered.

With briefcase in one hand and an empty Starbucks coffee cup in the other, the prosecution attorney made her way up the bare wooden steps towards the exit when she stopped where Jarvis was obviously waiting for her, and desperately waiting for the lady to unravel the events leading to her clients change of heart.

'Jarvis, what can I say but I'm so sorry, but unfortunately, my hands were tied.'

'What the bloody hell happened? We'd got it in the bag. I mean…I honestly thought we'd got enough to nail the sonofabitch.'

Knowing that the detective would want all the nitty gritty details, Nina handed over to him the note that was clasped tightly in her hand, sighed and murmured apologetically, 'This should tell you everything you need to know Inspector.'

With dark rimmed reading glasses at the ready, he put them on and slowly unfolded the white piece of plain paper and as he read the bold handwritten words in block capitals, he removed his specs and read *'DROP THE CHARGES OR NEXT TIME YOU'LL GET WORSE COMING TO YOU.'* Remonstrating loudly, not holding anything back, and not caring if anyone could hear him either, 'That fucking piece of shit. I thought something had happened on the steps outside, but I couldn't be sure, I mean I was close enough to see something wasn't right, but not close enough.'

'Well…it doesn't matter a damn now does it, whether you did or didn't see anything, because it's finished now.'

Scrutinising the woman standing opposite him and raising a questioning eyebrow he couldn't help himself for asking, 'Couldn't you have asked for a closed court trial, or perhaps a change of jurisdiction, you know…' whilst holding the note up in the air with his thumb and forefinger, 'because of blatant witness intimidation?'

'Oh believe me I bloody well tried, and it caused a right fracas with Digby the Shitby because he said that his client would have been disadvantaged, as his ageing mother who apparently has a serious heart condition, wouldn't be able to attend if the trial were to be moved, and check this out…she might not live long enough for her ever to see her precious son again. And then to top it all, our precious defence counsel started to cite human rights violations if we went ahead with a different court. But you know what…it didn't matter anyway, because Eva had already made her mind up, and I could have stood in front of the bench all soddin' day and night, and she still wouldn't have budged.'

'So, that's it then I s'pose, well…until the next beaten up naked woman appears on a bench outside of The Hamilton General?' grunted the detective inspector as he dug his hands deep into his trouser pockets and produced a set of keys, held together by a claret and blue key chain bearing a lion and the letters AVFC, 'Yeah, I guess so,' replied Nina, as she started to mount the final steps to leave the court and return to her office. 'Let's hope and pray she can rebuild her life again, eh?'

With that both officers of the law parted company.

Even Jarvis' favourite Joy Division song, *'Love Will Tear Us Apart'* couldn't blow away the blues on his drive back home to Upper Stanton. He'd made his mind up he wasn't going back into the station as he couldn't face re-living the day's sorry outcome, so he was going to call it a day, go home and spend some quality time with Eleanor as he'd not been at home much lately.

Leaving his battered old Peugeot on the roadside, he noted that his wife's deep red coloured Mini wasn't on the driveway, and feeling as though he'd had the stuffing knocked out of him for a second time in a day, he sluggishly strode up the neatly laid block paving, put the Yale key inside the lock of his front door, and silently sighed that within these walls, and albeit for a short while, he'd be free from the faces of the demonic monsters that paraded through his very soul.

Entering the hallway with keys clanking into the ceramic dish on the hall table, his shoes kicked off and jacket hung lovelessly on the brass hook which swung loosely from the weight of his outer clothing, serving as a constant reminder that this was just one of the many jobs around the house that needed doing. He called out his wife's name even though he knew no sound would reverberate back at him, and sauntered slowly to the garden shed which had been transformed into her den where she could escape from all the males in the household and do whatever the hell she liked.

Unlocking the bolt to her haven that secured her most private and intimate thoughts, and where she was allowed to let her imagination run riot, the only signs of life in there were the images that bounced off the canvases as the explosion of light beamed onto them.

It suddenly dawned on Jarvis, as he stood with hands on hips peering closely at the paintings in front of him, that he hadn't seen much of his wife's latest work and he found himself in awe of her ability for the creation of the scenes that seemed to come alive right before his eyes.

She never spoke much about her work, never demanding either praise or criticism, and he would never dream of prying, but these latest pieces were deep, almost as if she were somehow trying to tell a story that he felt deep down he wasn't invited to know about. Perhaps she was trying to tell him something, but as usual, secretly chiding himself, he was always too goddamn busy fixing everybody else's lives, and his own family had to make do with the leftovers.

Closing the door behind him and securing the metal padlock once again, he pocketed the key and took his phone out of his dark navy-blue suit trousers. Standing on one of the paving slabs that meandered from the kitchen door to his wife's sanctuary, which were laid after Ellie slipped badly on a bitterly cold, icy February morning he typed, *'Hi babe, Where are u?'* and alongside he posted the yellow face with furrowed eyebrows with thumb and forefinger resting on his chin, known as the 'thinking face' emoji. Before he'd even crossed onto the next stepping stone the familiar ping announced, *'Out for a walk xx'*

Opening the door to the Aga heated kitchen and firing up the kettle into life, he found a mug in the scrupulously tidy cupboard and smiled as he read the worlds sitting idly under the face of a laughing pink piglet's face, *'The world's best copper.'*

As the water was boiling, and having taken the green top milk from the fridge, he remembered the faces of his two sons as he tore the wrapping paper with dancing Santas all over it. They were definitely into their teens, but that morning they'd acted as though they were about seven or eight years old, as apparently they'd had no help from their mum and they'd simply gone on line and ordered it, and even though they knew they'd be up for a clip around the ear for buying it, they also knew that their dad would see the funny side. Whilst stirring the tea bag and pressing it against the side of the mug before dropping it into the spoon rest, he texted Ellie again, *'D'ya want me to join U?'*

He figured she must have had her phone in her hand the whole time as her response was even faster than the first one, *'No, I'm good thanks. See you when I see you. Xx'*

Bewildered as to what was going on, he decided he'd leave her alone, drink his coffee, treat himself and dunk a couple of ginger nuts and let his team know where he was.

He knew that the jobs around the house were piling up, so he figured he'd surprise Ellie when she got home and have them all done, so he decided that now would be as good a time as any. He was about to get the step ladders out of the adjoining garage to fix the cable for the satellite dish that had come away from the outside wall, when the guitar strings from 'Paranoid' exploded through the air waves and noting that the caller ID was that of Javid Das he lay his tool box back on the shelf and responded with a sense of grateful enthusiasm, as he hated DIY shit, 'Jav, what's up my friend?'

'Sorry to bother you guv, but I thought you'd want to know that a woman has just been in touch and she said she'd had a bit of a weird conversation with a bloke who needs her help with his son who's finding it difficult to swallow food.' Glancing around the neatly stacked piles of tools which Jarvis couldn't ever remember using, he quipped rather sarcastically, 'And hum…why would I find this to be of particular interest to me?'

'Ahem…' the detective sergeant coughed nervously, 'the woman in question is a speech and language therapist and what with the missing three people being medically trained one way or another, she felt she needed to get in touch, as she felt that the caller was a bit of a weirdo, but a clever one…you know?'

'Anything else to go on?' asked the Inspector as he perched himself on the edge of his work bench as he ran his free hand alongside the smooth surface, and inwardly smirked with pride that it was in the same condition as when he bought it, no chisel marks, no splodges of paint, nor any signs of pliers used to remove nail heads that had missed the intended target. In fact, after years of being stored in the garage there were no tell-tale signs of it ever being put to use at all.

'Not much except a name and address, and she lives in an area called Barmford which is about nine miles out of Upper Stanton and…'

'Who've you got going with you, Jav?' pondered Jarvis, almost willing the other detective to say that there wasn't anyone available, as his afternoon hadn't quite panned out the way he wanted. Making his way back to the main part of the house having heard his sergeant's response, he recommended to Das that he pick him up from his house as the caller's address was in his neck of the woods.

Trying to lay to rest the fear that lay within the crevices of his mind that something wasn't quite right with the love of his life, Jarvis threw the dregs of his now cold coffee down the sink, made his way to his bedroom where he got out of the stuffy suit that he had felt obliged to wear that day, and put on a pair of dark brown chinos and a light brown linen shirt. He made his way to the hallway again where he slipped on his oxblood-coloured loafers, put on his old faithful Marks and Sparks black woollen jacket and retrieved his keys once more.

He heard the tooting of the horn, opened the door and spotted Sergeant Das in his newly acquired second hand Volkswagen Passat parked on the opposite side of the road. Opening the passenger door and bending his six-foot frame, not wishing to repeat the same faux pas that he did the last time he clambered into it, which left an indentation in his forehead that seemed to hang around like some kind of birthmark, and saluted his colleague, 'Hey Jav.'

'Guv. Hope I didn't mess up your afternoon or nothing?' quizzed the slim, but athletically built Asian detective as he sprang the engine into life by turning the ignition key.

'Nah, you're fine, you know the saying…best-laid plans and all that. And anyway, you actually did me a favour, 'cos you got me out of some shit that needed doing around the place, and well…not only would I have made a dog's bollocks out of it, but I wasn't in the bloody mood either, because of the shitty day at soddin' court.'

'Christ yeah, we all heard it on the local one o'clock news. That creep walked, didn't he? What the hell happened boss, I mean…she seemed to be so positive about her time in court, did someone get to her perhaps?' he enquired, as he pressed the windscreen washer button, and watched the miniature boomerangs from the oak tree that he was parked under glide across the windscreen.

'Oh, she was got at alright, good and stinkin' proper. She was shaking like a leaf as she was scared shitless, and there wasn't a darn thing anyone could do or say that would change her mind. She was determined to drop the charges. According to Nina Bartholomew, Eva kept repeating over and over again that she couldn't bear the thought of being terrified for the rest of her life, having to look over her shoulder to see if there was some nutter who would smack her over the head, or leave her for dead again. She just walked out of that court room, and I swear that she saw me, but I don't honestly think she could bear to look me in the eye.

'So, we'll just have to hope and pray that that fucker Latino gets caught using or selling dope, or with his trousers down again, because we'll get the sonofabitch someday, somehow and that is a promise Jav.' The detective Inspector glanced momentarily at his message provider on his phone, and finding it empty, slapped it heavily on the dashboard, and hurling a *'Tch'* into the air whilst adding, 'Anyway, that was then and this is now, and we've got to find these missing people.'

Sensing the Inspector's frustration, Javid asked quietly, 'Everything alright boss? It's just that you seem a bit hum…pissed off.'

'Nah, I'm alright. Just need to sort some things out that's all.'

'At the next roundabout take the third exit onto Caldwell Road'…not waiting for the annoying voice on Satnav to finish directing the car to the correct address,

Jav merely uttered two words which when said with the right emotion can speak volumes, 'I see.'

'You have now reached your destination…71 Denton Avenue, Barmford.'

'Oh well, looks like we'll soon find out whether we've at long last got something to get excited about, or whether she's just some kind of Agatha Christie addict with an overactive imagination,' commented the Inspector as the seat belt clicked and whirred away into freedom.

As they parked outside number 71, it looked as though it was a fairly new build, and like most new dwellings that have been squeezed onto an empty rubber stamped plot of land, developers show very little interest or enthusiasm as to the legacy they leave behind. As row after row of red bricked houses are uniformly built side by side, almost mirror images of each other and with a drastic shortage of housing, people were being forced to buy the products of soulless and spineless, architects.

Walking up the black tarmacked driveway that was lined with terracotta planters housing evergreen shrubs, miniature conifers, and two bins lined side by side bearing the house number in thick white paint, the two detectives stood outside the front door with its obscure glazing showing a pattern of swirling black lines, and waited for the doorbell to be answered.

The chiming of the bell resulted in the raucous howling of a dog and from where the two men were standing it didn't sound like it was of the small, fluffy variety. As the door partially drifted open, the lady who appeared to be in her thirties with jet black hair swept off her face with a bright red scrunchie neatly keeping her pony tail in place, was stooped in between the door and its frame, as she was trying to convince the canine that the intruders didn't need to be eaten alive.

Both detectives removed their IDs from their wallets as the senior man introduced them both, 'Good afternoon Mrs Walker. I'm Inspector Mark Jarvis and this is Detective Sergeant Javid Das. We'd like a few words with you if we may in connection with the telephone call that you made to one of our officers this morning.'

Trying her best to keep the slobbering mutt under control, she grabbed him by his black studded collar and pointed with her forefinger with its bright blue painted nail, and bellowed, 'That's enough Monty…be quiet,' and finally, 'Go to your bed. Now,' and with that the animal who was more than likely twice the weight of its handler, shook his head in disgust and deposited his slathering saliva all along the side of the wall, where it slid down onto the wainscoting.

'So sorry about that detectives, but you won't believe this but he's a pure softy, and I must apologise for the smell but you see well…when he's over excited, he has a tendency to fart, which apparently is a common trait amongst Boxers.'

All three adults sniggered as the tall, slim lady clad in a loose khaki coloured jump suit opened the door wide open and beckoned, 'Please gentlemen do come in.'

She led them through a narrow passageway that claimed its title as a hall and invited them into a cosy, tidy but obviously lived in sitting room. The furniture was a mishmash of colours and fabrics but with the displayed pieces of contemporary art work, everything seemed to be cleverly put together, making it feel welcoming to all who entered.

'Can I offer you tea, coffee or perhaps something cold detectives? Please…please, sit wherever you like.'

'I'm good thanks Mrs Walker, I've not long finished my lunch,' responded the senior officer.

Sergeant Das shook his head, removed his notebook and pen from his black linen blazer, and politely refused, 'I drink far too much caffeine as it is, but thanks for the offer.'

'So 'began Jarvis, 'you rang the station today and spoke with one of our officers about something that you think was quite suspicious and which may be relevant in helping us with one of our ongoing investigations.'

Melanie Walker sat down in a pastel green cosy chair which was perched adjacent to the light coloured stone fireplace where a wealth of framed black and white, and coloured photographs lined the shelf and the hearth, each one having their own private story to tell.

'Yeah, it was actually really weird. I'd just got home from seeing one of my patients at his home. I'm erm…a speech and language therapist by the way, and I guess it was around 5:30 when this man called. He said that I'd treated his son who had both aphasia and dysphagia…'

'Sorry,' interrupted the sergeant, 'I'm not sure if I heard those two words correctly.'

'Ah yes, of course, let me explain. Aphasia is where someone has communication difficulties due to either an acute illness such as a traumatic brain injury, or a long term condition such as Parkinson's or Motor Neurone disease. Now, dysphagia is the term used for someone who has swallowing complications, and once again this can include a huge range of patients, but nowadays I see more and more elderly people with this condition who sadly have Alzheimer's or dementia.'

'Ah, I see,' muttered the detective as he flicked the page of his notebook over, whilst scratching notes hurriedly with his pen.

'Anyway, when I asked the man how he got my number, he seemed very hum…hesitant in replying. You see, what you have to remember is that Rainbow House, the…the practice that I belong to, well we're all very, very strict on not giving out numbers, especially over the phone, and I know that none of my colleagues would have divulged this without getting in touch with me first. So, like I said his response wasn't automatic, it was as though he had to think of a reply, you know? It seemed like ages, but I reckon it must have been about after oh…perhaps ten seconds when he said he got my details on the web. Of course, that started alarm bells ringing because I'm not listed on line, and to be perfectly honest with you I've no need to, as I've got a waiting list as long as your arm with patients being referred by clinicians at The Hamilton, GP surgeries, nursing homes, etc., etc.'

'Did you find anything else suspicious? I mean…were you able to keep him talking for a bit, you know?' asked the Inspector whilst studying the woman sitting opposite from him, noticing her round face, and high cheekbones which looked as though they could have been cosmetically enhanced, and her recently applied deep pink gloss on perfect shaped lips.

'Well, yes, mainly because I was really intrigued as there was definitely something off about him. I asked him how old his son was and how I could help him, and then he said the child's name was Sean and that he was nearly eight, and because he'd had multiple sclerosis from infancy his swallowing was getting worse. But you see, when I asked him what he meant, he was quite flippant in his reply and said almost monotoned, *'Well being a speech and language therapist I thought that was stating the bloody obvious. It's because he can't eat his food and hasn't been able to for three days now.'* As you can imagine that kinda did it for me, so I said why on earth haven't you taken him to A & E or to your local doctor's surgery, and before he'd got time to give me an answer bloody Monty started growling and getting upset at something he'd heard outside. So, I went to the window and literally inched the vertical blinds apart, and that's when I saw a bloke in a red van staring at the house, and I could see he'd got a mobile in his hand and well…he must have got spooked, because he instantly removed the phone from his ear and drove off like a bat out of hell. This wasn't what set the dog off, and to be honest I never found out what that was, but for once being a pain in the arse most definitely paid off, and if the information helps with your case of the missing people, then it'll all have been worth it, won't it?'

The junior detective stopped his pen from dancing around the page and anxiously sought a reply to his question, 'I don't suppose Mrs Walker that you managed to get a licence plate of the van that he was driving, or notice any signs on it like you know…Bob the Builder that sort of thing? Were there any dents in it,' and with that he got up from the deep grey chic sofa and wandered over to the window. 'So from where I'm standing, and as you say he was parked across the road, I guess it's doubtful if you could give us a description of him, but perhaps he was close enough that you could give us colour of his hair, did he wear glasses, or have a beard?' The therapist got up from her chair and joined him at the window and not wishing to pull the blinds completely away leaving it bare, she twiddled with the beaded chain and pulled them away slightly, but enough that she could point out exactly where the van was parked.

'Can you see the house with the boring net curtains, and the monkey tree in the garden, that's number 36,' pointing with her index finger, 'right there, well that's where he was parked. So, as you can see, even though I suppose I could have seen the registration plate fully my brain didn't engage quickly enough that this could have been the guy on the other end of the phone. D'you see what I mean? And even though it left me feeling a bit oh…shaky I guess, something inside,' pointing to her right temple with forefinger, 'sent an alarm bell ringing, and as I said he shot off like a bullet from a gun but I managed to get the letters S and V, and there were definitely the numbers seven and nine, but I'm afraid I honestly haven't got a clue as to the order of either. As for the bloke driving, well I can honestly, hand on heart tell you, that he wore dark glasses and a hoodie, and I wouldn't be able to swear this on oath, but I don't think he appeared to be a big man, just kinda well…normal build I s'pose.'

***

Fuck, fuck, fuck. How the hell could you have been so bloody stupid? beating the steering wheel heavily over and over again, and then resting my pulsating forehead against the coolness of it, trying to erase the scene of the woman trying to peer at me through some bloody stupid blinds. Did she think I was stupid?

Slamming the door of the van and stomping heavily around the disused car park of *The Tanner House*, kicking large stones, broken pieces of glass into the air, and indeed anything that got in my way.

Making my way around the back of the crumbling ale house, I slowly removed the blue cord from around my neck where the key was nestled for safe keeping, and unlocked the padlock which secured the bolt of the main exterior door. Striding purposefully past the old wooden bar, I heard the clumping of a stool as it crashed to the floor, as the abandoned room was engulfed in blackness, and headed towards the basement.

Hearing the familiar clunking of the metallic bolts, the heavy fire door screeched open. After groping around on the left-hand side of the wall for the switch at the top of the stairs which would spring new life into the bare bulb as it swayed limply from a long dark flex, finally erasing the darkness that had begun to hurt my eyes, I could hear the echo of a faint, panic cry for quiet, 'Ssshhh…he's…'

The stairs creaked and groaned as I made my descent.

Everything was how I'd left it; both men slouched on beds staring at the badly stained ceilings, and the Filipino nurse fiddling around with a pump that controlled the drug that was swirling through the doctor's veins. I slumped heavily onto a battered, badly stained mushroom coloured armchair, whilst drumming tunelessly on its arms with my long, slim fingers with nails bitten down to the quick, as I grinned coldly and emotionlessly enquiring sarcastically, 'Sleep well, everyone?'

Looking at the three beds lying side by side it made me chuckle inwardly, 'cos it really did look like a bit of a hospital ward, and it was all thanks to my sheer cunning lies that I'd managed to get them at all. Calming down a little now, I remembered the act of charity and kindness by a local hospice who'd donated one of the beds for my poor dying mother, as I tearfully told them over the phone that it was her wish to die at home. I vowed that I'd promised to look after her as she drew her last breath, but the saddest thing of all, as I broke down theatrically, was that I just didn't have the means to fund a hospital bed *and it was something that she desperately needed, I added, especially in her hour of need.*

Of course, I had to repeat this story three more times to different charitable organisations where each convincing tearful performance of a plea for help, resulted in not only beds being delivered but also pillows, linen, duvets and the assurance that should I need anything else at all, then please…please let us know. At the end of each telephone call, I was told that I was a very brave and caring man, and that my mother should be proud of me.

Coming out of an almost trance-like state, I had no choice but to direct my gaze towards the words that were cascading out of Hackman's mouth, 'Look you've had your fun, you found a way to get us here, now just let us go before something terrible happens to one of us. I mean…if I don't take a few steps soon, or hum…use my arm soon, my muscles will get even weaker and then I won't be able to move them at all. And if you're any kind of a human being at all, you'd at least let me use the bucket like the other two do, you can't keep treating me like a caged bloody animal.'

'No shit, Sherlock. Let me think who that could remind me of, not being able to move her muscles that is, let me see now…her name is on the tip of my tongue. You know, you really are an arrogant prick, just listen to yourself, because you're damned sure not listening to me, and it's blatantly obvious that this little hum…retreat is teaching you absolutely fucking nothing.' Realising that his plea was having no effect, Hackman buried his face in his free hand despairingly.

I produced the plastic carrier bag with a bit of food and two bottles of milk and water and slung it uncaringly on the bed that wouldn't now be taken up by the fourth person who caused him wrong. With eyes that seemed to have sunk further into their sockets and lined heavily with black rings underneath, O'Keefe murmured almost inaudibly, pleading, 'Please…please, end this now. We've told you that we'll help you in any way we can, so now just let us go. Have you thought about what's going to happen to you when the police find us? You'll go to prison, and then who's going to look after your relative, friend or whoever the hell she is?'

Springing out of the chair at a speed akin to a greyhound out of a starting block, I strode backwards and forwards whilst cupping both hands on the top of my head and then found myself hovering over the doctor as my hands gripped the side rail of the bed whilst shaking it violently, shouting, 'If ONLY you'd done what you were supposed to do, then none of this needed to happen, but you didn't did you? ANY OF YOU.'

The short, jet black haired Filipino's body was shaking uncontrollably as the tears ran down her face and neck as she knelt on the cold, stone floor with both of her hands in a steepled, praying position, and with eyes closed she silently beseeched her maker for help.

I crouched down to her level, and with a piercing look into her sorrowful deep brown eyes, I shouted angrily, 'Stop with the bloody bleating will you, it's a bit late for that don't you think? Now get the fuck up and give these two clowns something to eat.'

'Leave her alone, can't you see she's upset?' protested the lanky physiotherapist.

'Oh, upset is she, well she didn't seem too upset when she left her patients to shit and piss in their beds because, as she put it, they had a nappy on, so they'd be alright. Didn't give a fig when they ended up with pressure sores did she, oh no, just said they'd heal with a bit of cream. So, forgive me if you think I'm being a bit harsh, but let's hope the same thing doesn't happen to you while she's looking after your so-called needs.'

I'd had enough for one day, but before I headed for the outside world again, I issued them with a kindly reminder, 'You might not be aware but I have all of your mobile phones and it would be very easy for me to send pictures of you in your…shall we say little holiday camp, so do as I ask and don't try anything foolish because even though your folks at home will be glad I suppose that you're still alive, but hum…I'm not so sure they're going to like what they see.

'Oh, and just so you're aware Miss Baluyot, the bag of the IV Aspirin has been marked with permanent marker with the dosage that should be given every day, so I wouldn't try and try and meddle with the dosage because I'll know. So, you see, you worthless pieces of shit, you may have thought you were dealing with an amateur when I asked you to come and join me, but as you can see, you couldn't be more wrong. Before I leave, I'm going to give you all one piece of friendly advice, and that is…I wouldn't test my patience if I were you. Toodle pip.'

Passing by the bar, I sat on an old wooden stool and stared into the mirror that lined the back wall where reflections of beer pumps and glasses lazily hanging upside down peered back at me. Pulling the small Dictaphone out of my rucksack I clicked the tape into position and pressed play as I fed the words into the machine, 'Inspector Jarvis…I've been meaning to speak to you about three people who don't seem to have turned up at various medical conferences…'

Chapter 18

On the drive back from Melanie Walker's house, both detectives felt a surge of adrenaline flow through their veins as they silently felt a sense of self-congratulatory relief that they'd managed to get a modicum of a breakthrough.

'We've got to track down this bloody van. I think the only way that we're going to get a quicker result is if we go viral, because maybe…just maybe someone may have loaned it out as a friend, you know *'Can I borrow a van for a couple of days just to move my kid into rooms at her university. We don't need to do it officially like, you know informing insurance companies, we can do it just as mates,'* that sort of thing. Or has someone had their van nicked and didn't report it because they perhaps haven't had it taxed, or had no MOT and didn't want to report it, knowing that the owner may get slapped with a fine?'

'Yeah, they're certainly possibilities alright. But at least now we've got a couple of letters and numbers to be going on with, and no matter how long it takes, we're just going to have to track it down, because there's no doubt about it, someone, somewhere has seen this bloody van,' replied the young Asian detective, 'erm…home or station guv?'

Jarvis bent his wrist towards him and quickly scanned the time, 'I think I'll call it a day, but I'm contactable should anything come up. And you…isn't it about time you went home at a decent hour?'

'I'm alright thanks guv, when I get back, we'll trawl through the lists we've got from DVLA and also hire companies again to check against the info we've got. The other guys are still going through medical records showing who O'Keefe prescribed Aspirin to, and cross checking their names with The Hamilton General and a few of the surrounding hospitals,' reported Das, as he drummed his fingers against the steering wheel waiting for the traffic lights to turn green.

'I trust you and the other guys to do whatever it is that needs doing, and I'll call the chief and tell him we need some media coverage as to details of the van.'

Carefully easing his six-foot frame out of the car, the Inspector sluggishly sauntered towards his driveway where he stopped and cupped his hands around his face whilst peering into the passenger door window of his wife's Mini that had been reversed onto the driveway. He didn't know what he was looking for specifically, it was just a copper's instinct kicking in, whilst secretly hoping and praying that there were no giveaways as to why she had lied to him.

He flicked the lights on in the main hub of the house where all was clean and tidy and no sign that any recent meal preparations had taken place. Light rays from wall lights in the sitting room were escaping from the partially opened door where all he could see was the head and backs of both his sons as they sat against the coffee table with huge headphones on, as the words 'bang, boom,' sprang out with red lights dancing around the flat TV screen, mimicking gun fire and explosions, wiping out the imaginary goodies and baddies during a highly addictive game that they enjoyed playing on Play Station.

Jarvis merely shook his head amusingly, as he could never fathom out the attraction of such violent fantasy. But still, he figured, at least they weren't hanging around the streets, drinking illegal booze and smoking dope with ne'er do wells, pissing off people in quiet neighbourhoods who insisted constantly that they needed more of a police presence, otherwise the scourge will just get worse.

He quietly tiptoed around the boggle-eyed teenagers, hypnotised by the running, hurdling characters jostling briskly across the screen where he stood in front of them, whilst jokingly blocking their visual path.

'Daaaaad...wh...' exclaimed both Alex and Andy in unison.

'Hello to you too...and thanks for asking, but I'm very well thank you,' quipped the Inspector.

'Sorry pops, but I was just in the middle of zapping him,' sniggered the younger of the boys, Andy.

'No, you weren't, I'd have shot off your bol...'

'Okay, okay, you guys, I think I get the picture. Where's mum?'

Alex was just placing the heavy, black head set on again with its great big air cushioned earphones, declaring 'Dunno...she might be working, or she may have gone up to read.'

The teenagers' father joked on his way out, 'keep the noise down,' and went in search of his wife. Peering through the kitchen window rather than physically making a trip to her makeshift studio, he noticed that the place was in total darkness, and so he headed towards the staircase and made his way to their bedroom.

Sitting up in bed, and with her dark brown tousled hair hanging seductively around her shoulders, she started to remove her dark blue-rimmed reading glasses, placing them on top of what seriously looked like a pile of travel brochures. Jarvis sat on the side of the bed and curiously picked one up randomly, flicking through colourful pictures showing sailing boats idly cruising through deep blue waters, trains meandering around luscious green mountain sides, and water fountains lit up by luminous fairy lights, 'Going somewhere nice, are you?' he asked sarcastically.

'Hi sweetie,' pushing heavily on the mattress with both hands so that she was sitting upright, 'when did you get in, I didn't hear you?'

'Just…literally about five minutes ago. Have you all eaten already because I must admit I'm bloody starving?'

'For once the lads didn't have much going on after school, so we had an early dinner. I've left you some nice broccoli quiche, and there's some vegetables left in the Pyrex dish, and there should be a couple of pieces of garlic bread left unless of course someone else beat you to it. All you need to do is whack everything in the microwave. Oh, and there's also some grated Parmesan cheese in a little yellow Tupperware container…if you want it that is.'

Stroking her concealed leg tucked away underneath the brightly coloured, silky smooth duvet cover, Jarvis gazed into his wife's deep brown eyes and asked quite sombrely, 'El, what's going on? You have to tell me. I know you weren't out walking today because I was here, and it was all meant to be a bit of a surprise like. I just thought we could have spent a bit of time together and perhaps go to The Hatters or somewhere for a bite to eat, or a walk in Leyton Park where we could have chilled out for a couple of hours. So…where were you? I mean, you don't have to tell me, because well…I'm not your jailer or anything, but erm…I have to know why you lied to me.'

Pushing the thin red straps of her flimsy cotton vest back onto her shoulders, she reached out and lovingly clasped his hand tightly within hers, and stroking it gently she replied pityingly, 'Oh Mark I wasn't lying to you. Look, I did go for a walk, but I wanted somewhere more than side streets and shops to take my mind off things, I just needed open space with trees, benches dotted around where I could just sit and think and let the world pass me by, you know. And to be fair to me, you didn't say you were coming home to see me, did you?'

'So, what's all this about then?' as he flopped a brochure labelled, '*City Breaks'* down heavily on the far side of the bed.

'I've been toying with the idea for a few weeks now, and I just feel as though I need to get away for a while, especially after seeing poor Nancy practically housebound. But don't worry, nothing's been finalised yet, but well…I've been thinking life's too short, and it's just something that I feel I need to do.'

Jarvis begged with pleading eyes, 'But…couldn't we do this together? I know now isn't even remotely possible, but can't you wait until this case is over, and I've got so much leave to take, we could well…make it an extended break, plus the boys are now old enough to look after themselves, so…' cupping her face in his hands, 'we could make this a kind of second honeymoon.'

'Look it's a really lovely idea, but I've been talking to Bea recently and well, you know she's having a hard time with that wanker of a husband of hers, and quite frankly she's had enough. So, we just ran the idea past each other, places that we might like to see, and quite frankly honey, it would be so lovely to have a bit of girlie time for a change, especially as we only really get to see each other at Xmas.'

'Why didn't you tell me you were so unhappy? Is it me, the job…. what? I know I'm not here enough for you or the boys, but it's not forever, and I've got a good feeling that we'll nail this sick bastard soon, as we're getting a few leads, and there's absolutely no doubt about it, but he'll slip up sooner or later.'

Ellie crawled out from beneath the duvet and knelt behind him cradling him towards her whilst kissing the top of his head as she lamented, 'Oh darling, you're the most perfect man anyone could wish for. Of course, I can't say the same about the job, but then I knew that when I married you. And as for the lads, they're working hard at their exams and apart from clearing mud from rugby and football kits, they're pretty good as teenagers go, and as they've got their own mates, I feel as though well…they know I'm here, but they don't need me any more in the way they used to, apart from opening my purse for a hand out for something or other.'

'Are you saying you're lonely, because if you are, I can take early retirement, and to be quite frank with you, why not? Just bring the inevitable forward a few years, we'll manage alright. I'll get a fairly good pension and you could sell the odd Picasso, and bingo…we're sorted.'

The Inspector found he was angry at himself for not turning his phone off especially at this point of the conversation, ping. 'Sorry El, won't be long,' and placing it against his ears, he slowly arose from the bed announcing, 'Jarvis.'

'DCI Wolfe here. I just wanted to catch up with you at the station, but your officers told me that you'd decided to make an early day of it. Look…if you're not prepared to put in the commit…'

'Excuse me sir,' imploded the Inspector, 'we've all been working flat out on this case, and this is the first time I've seen my wife and kids in a couple of days. You get to see yours every evening I take it…sir?'

'Er…sorry Jarvis, but I've got top brass breathing down my neck, not to mention the bloody media. So…have we got any major breakthroughs yet?'

Standing, staring at one of Ellie's still life paintings on the wall outside of their bedroom, he reported unenthusiastically, 'The creep tried it on with a local speech and language therapist, but thankfully she saw through his pathetic charade, and she managed to get two digits and letters of the van's registration plate, so we've got everyone working on it.'

'Good…I'm glad to hear it. All annual leave's been suspended for the time being, and that comes right from the top. Anything you need from me to expedite matters…? I'm sure we could loan a few uniforms, but Jarvis, listen, this case is dragging on, and we've still got three people missing, and I don't need to remind you that the longer they're unaccounted for, the weaker the chance is of us seeing them alive.'

Side stepping along the wall, and with a beaming smile, as he peered closely at the four people in the framed photograph, and it was this happiness and familial closeness reflecting back at him that somehow left him feeling a real sense of sadness for the families and friends of the missing health professionals.

'Of course, chief, I understand everything you've said, but there's one thing you could do and that is ask for help from the public regarding the van. We know what make it is, colour and now we've got a possible lead on a partial plate. Somebody out there may have seen one parked outside of their house, or up the road, or your typical window stalker may have spotted one that drives past at the same time, I mean…we've closed cases before with less to go on, so why not Lady Luck give us the wink on this one?'

'I'll get onto it first thing in the morning, and hopefully coverage will go out at lunch time.' Jarvis broke the stifled silence that ensued sighing deeply, 'If that's all chief, well then, I'd rather like to get back to my family, if you don't mind.'

'Hrumph…yes of course Jarvis, give my regards to your wife, and I'll see you at the station tomorrow.' Click.

Stepping slowly into the bedroom, he quickly noticed that his wife had got back into bed and had resumed her flicking through colourful pages contemplating as to which would be the best place to fulfil this new dream of hers.

'Sorry about that El, it was the boss. Look erm…I'm going to take a quick shower and then we can talk about this later, okay?'

'Yeah, go ahead, but don't forget about the quiche, I mean…didn't you say you were starving to death?'

Chapter 19

Julia once again found herself standing within the small but serviceable porch, ensconced within a red brick archway, and inserting her key inside the brass Yale lock perched underneath the rather colourful, cathedral-like stained glass windows, as she finally opened the bottle green painted door.

Pocketing her keys in her faux leather bomber jacket and peeling the rucksack off her shoulders, she dumped everything on the floor as close as she could to the door, almost in readiness for a quick escape. She didn't need to stop and peer at the happy family framed photos that adorned the walls in the hallway because they were all stored in her childhood memories where everything was good and everyone was happy and her mum was well…mum, able to talk, feed herself and do all the things that every parent teaches a preschool kid. And yet now, everything had been cruelly stolen from her and from her daughter.

'Hi…its only me, Julia,' the young teenager announced fairly loudly, where sauntering towards her was a rather pleasant looking middle-aged lady clad in a pale blue nursing tunic displaying an ID badge which was clipped securely on her side pocket. Her regulation blue trousers together with her flat, black shoes, cruelly stole from her any signs of femininity, and managed to emphasise just how petite she really was.

'Hi, Julia. I'd forgotten it was Thursday, oh…and just so you know, you've just missed your dad,' folding her arms, whilst keeping her ample breasts aloft, 'and he never said when he'd be back. Mind you, he's in and out at different times of the day lately, so I never bother to ask him anymore.'

'Oh…that's okay. I'm not here to see him anyway, I'm here for mum,' flicking her thumb towards her mother's bedroom. 'So, tell me, how's she been?'

'Yeah, she's not doing too badly at all. But you know that physically she's the same, but at least today she's done much better with eating, and thank goodness she's drunk a bit more than usual, but…' wagging her forefinger whilst making a tut tutting sound as if scolding a naughty child, 'she's still a bugger about having her food pulverised to a pulp, and she always fights me when she

269

has her drinks thickened, but there ain't nothing I can do about it, 'cos orders are orders I guess, eh?'

Scratching her right forearm underneath the black, slightly frayed jumper, as beads of sweat dappled across her upper lip, Julia ranted, 'So…is she never ever going to be able to eat proper food again? I mean is nobody bothered in giving her a chance, or even gives a rat's arse as to what she wants? When was the last bloody time that someone actually came to see her and tested how she coped with proper soddin' food? Am I the only one that gives a shit that she probably thinks we've all put her on the rubbish skip and that we couldn't give a fuckin' toss as to what she really wants?'

'Now wait a minute young lady, there's nothing that I or the other nurses wouldn't do for your mum and believe you me she's getting the best care in the world, so don't you go round sayin that we don't care, 'cos you couldn't be more wrong. And just so you know, because let's face it you're not around very often, but your mum's speech and language therapist was here the other day, and she said that Mrs Ferguson isn't strong enough yet to tolerate solid foods, and well…me hands are tied ain't they?

'I could lose my job if I were to take it upon myself to go against their strict instructions, but let's face it…it's a step up from her having to be fed from that God awful tube that she had to put up with, for months and months. So, you see, you might not think it, but she's really come on leaps and bounds, despite what you may think. I know your dad thinks exactly the same as you, but it is what it is, and as much as you don't like to hear it, we have to just carry on until your mum is strong enough to try normal food and drink. But she'll get there, just 'ave a bit of faith.'

Thinking that she may have spoken a little harshly, she sidled towards the daughter of the household and draped her arm around her shoulder as the youngster stood staring out of the kitchen window where it seemed that the memories from happy times in the back garden reflected back at her. There was so much life when the sun beamed down, and even more when it became a carpet of pure white snow. Grandparents, aunts and uncles were frequent visitors as clouds of smoke billeted out from the rust-infested barbeque that her father had insisted would not only stand the test of time, but was good for the next thousand fat-injected sausages. Her mother's hard toil of creating summer harvests of the finest colourful plants, twisting, turning, climbing around the several blossom trees that lined the elegantly shaped lawn were the envy of not only the

270

neighbours but anyone that graced through the back gate, revealing the family's small, yet idyllic piece of paradise.

Slowly removing the friendly, contrite arm from her skinny shoulders, she turned and faced the older lady, and with an air of sincerity proposed softly, 'Look, why don't you go and have an early night…me and mum will be fine? In fact, it's been such a long time that I had her all to myself, and I know that she won't be able to talk to me or answer my questions, but I'll know what she's trying to say to me. The funny thing is…' snorted the only child of the Fergusons', 'it'll be a bit like a role reversal. You see, when I was no more than a baby, apparently, well according to mum and dad, I used to jabber on ten to the dozen with absolutely no pauses and no one had got the faintest idea what I was trying to say.

'But you know what…they went along with it and pretended that we were all having this really wicked conversation, and that they understood everything I was saying. I heard this story time and time again when I was growing up, so…when you think about it logically, it's my turn now to do something kind for her, don't you think?'

'Oh…I don't know,' replied the petite, stocky nurse whilst frowning heavily, 'if I get found out that I've truanted well…I'll probably lose my job.'

Peering closely at the employee's badge which was still perched on her tunic pocket, the teenager scoffed, 'Truanted? What are you…12? Look, no one will ever know, and if anyone from your agency calls here wanting to speak to you, I'll just tell them that you've gone to the shops to buy some milk or summat. Now seriously Mrs Corcoran, do me a favour and go, go to the pictures or the pub, or play some cards with your neighbours, or just do whatever it is that you like to do in your spare time, and I promise you…' ending the conversation with a zipping gesture across her lips with her forefinger and thumb.

'I'll do it but with one condition, and that is well…if you get into trouble, or you need help of any description, then you promise that you'll call me, otherwise it's a definite no, understand?' as she side stepped into the laundry room taking clothes out of the wicker basket and started flapping them into the air to rid them of any post tumble dry wrinkles, cleverly negating the necessity of the burdensome chore of ironing.

'Just leave it, now go.'

'Okay, okay, I'm going,' and with that she grabbed her orange plastic shopping bag with its white advertising letters brandished on the side from one of the arms of the pine kitchen chairs, and with the squeaking of leather soles plodded across the laminate flooring towards the front door, as the teenager displayed a rather churlish, somewhat self-congratulatory smile, opened and finally closed the front door.

Not even waiting for the sound of the thump and rattle of the letter box from the closing of the door, Julia opened the fridge door and eyeing the brown oval eggs from the side of the door quietly removed four of them. Finding the bread bin right next to the black shiny kettle, she raised the lid and removed slices of wholemeal bread from the cellophane wrapping.

Flicking the switch on and hearing the bubbling sound of water boiling, she removed two plates, two cups and saucers from the oak-coloured cabinet and cracked the eggs on the side of the clear, oval Pyrex dish.

Chapter 20

'We interrupt this programme to appeal to the public for any information with regard to the whereabouts of a red Ford Transit Van which we believe is somewhere within a ten-mile radius of Upper Stanton and could possibly have been used in the abduction of three missing people. Now it would have been better if we could let you have the full registration plate, however, we can advise you that the numbers seven and nine and the letters S and V are included in the identification of this vehicle.

'We would like anyone who may have seen a van with these numbers and letters, irrespective of their order, to please come forward as soon as possible and to contact Stockfield Road Police station at 01768 500300.

'We will treat any information as highly confidential, so don't be afraid to come forward, no matter how insignificant you think the details may be.

'Thank you for listening and for lending us your much appreciated support.'

'Okay folks you heard the Chief Inspector so let's all keep our eyes peeled and let's find the red van. Now, it's over to our regular Tamla Motown slot and we're going to kick it off with the gorgeous, sexy, Queen of Soul, Aretha Franklin and my personal favourite, 'I say a little prayer for you.'

Timothy Reid was singing along as he fiddled around with metal parts underneath the bonnet of the dark blue Discovery when his boss, Geoffrey Pearman marched in with a sense of urgency, 'Hey, Tim I've just been listening to Radio Diamond, and they're appealing for any information on a missing red Ford Transit van and I remember we had one booked in, but there's no records of it ever having been picked up. The registration plate seems to match the one they're looking for, well...let's put it this way the letters and digits that they broadcasted are included in the one that we have entered in the log in book, but when was it picked it up and by who? Any ideas?'

Tim, whilst wiping his greasy hands on an already dirty rag and placing both hands on his hips covered by dark grey overalls, looked round the car port heavily laden with all makes and models of vehicles needing some repair, or an up to date certificate of road worthiness, for some inspiration which would jog his memory into action. 'I remember seeing one about oh…six or seven weeks ago, and if I remember correctly, I think it was Jason that worked on that one, literally just before he left us.'

'Well the dates would match the one that we've got recorded, but I don't know why we haven't got any sign-out details. I've asked Miriam on the front desk, and we all know she's got the memory of an elephant, but she's absolutely one hundred per cent certain that she didn't log it out, so that would also mean that we wouldn't have been paid either. So…where'd it go?'

The noise of power tools, banging of metal against metal, the shrilling ringing of the phone in the supervisor's office together with the constant interruption of the over excited DJ in the middle of tunes, both old and new, forced the young mechanic to speak louder than usual in order for him to be heard, 'I guess the only thing you can do is to call Prentiss himself and see if he remembers anything. I've got his number if you need it, not that we stay in touch anymore, but just so you know.'

'Okay, thanks Tim. I'm sure I've got it in the office because I've still got his employment file, hoping that one day he might come back.'

Mounting the steps two at a time, Geoffrey opened the wooden door with the sign 'Manager' embossed in red capital letters displayed in the centre. He opened the dour looking, grey metallic filing cabinet and with fore and middle fingers he skipped through the manila folders until he found the surname, 'Prentiss' followed by the name with which he was commonly known, 'Jason.'

Not even bothering to sit down, he punched in the eleven digits of the last known phone number of the former employee.

'Prentiss,' the raspy voice declared.

'Hi Jason, this is Geoff Pearman. How's it going my man?' the manager of the auto repair garage asked cheerily.

'Good thanks, Geoff. Job not too bad, and the one good thing is that since my travelling time to and from work has almost halved, I get to see more of the kids,' chuckling good humouredly. 'So, her indoors doesn't seem to be quite so grumpy, either with me or them. So…everyone's a winner, eh?'

'That's great, Jase. So, I bet you're wondering why I called right? Well, I don't know whether you heard the plea from the local police at Stockfield Road, but they're looking for help in trying to find a red Ford Transit van that they believe may have been used in abducting the three missing health care workers. Now, I know that we had it in the workshop because we've booked it in, but here's the problem, there's no record of it ever having been collected and there's no documentation as to what repairs were made, and indeed we have no receipt of any payment having been made. I spoke with Tim and he kind of remembers you working on a vehicle very similar to the one that the cops are looking for. My question to you is…do you remember anything about it? If it helps to jog your memory, Tim reckons you worked on it about six weeks before you left us.'

The silence on the other end of the phone prompted the question, 'Jason, are you still there?'

'Yeah…just thinking, you know. Now that you mention it, I remember, well if it's the same one that is, that the van was losing oil badly, and the brake pads were a bit worn, and when I'd finished working on it, I parked it on the road outside, because there was nowhere else to put it as the forecourt was jam packed, and I couldn't swear to it, as I'm a typical bloke, you know not very observant an' all that, but I definitely don't recall seeing it there the next morning.'

Sighing, almost out of relief, the manager of A-Z Car Repairs, scratching the back of his head, pleaded beseechingly, 'I don't s'pose there's any way that you'd remember the license plate number Jase?'

'I never told you while I was with you guys, well…just in case I got into a shit load of trouble, but here's the thing, every car I fixed up I took a photo on me phone, a bit like a trophy if you like, and sort of like a reminder of what a bloody brilliant mechanic I am,' snorting loudly whilst searching through his self-acclaimed memoirs, 'got it!' he exclaimed excitedly.

'Okay, just so you know…I'm definitely glad you didn't tell me what you got up to, so we'll forget all about it if you could forward this on to me, but before you do, can you read the license plate out to me?'

'Sure. It's definitely the right colour and the model and reg is…S769 VES.'

'Thanks sport. I'll bell the cops and let them know. Oh…and Jase,' sniggered Geoff, the manager, 'if ever you need a longer ride to work, give me a shout, as there'll always be a job for you, you know that don't you, but there would be no more photo shoots, understood?'

Both men snorted at one another and then hung up.

Chapter 21

Inserting the key into the front door, Paula Corcoran, still feeling as though she'd committed a serious crime, was somewhat relieved to see the coat belonging to her patient's daughter having been thrown lazily on the floor, was thankfully lying in the same place. The only thing that had been moved was her rucksack, but she silently prayed, at least she hadn't run out on her mum and left her on her own, as it was obvious that Mr Ferguson had gone out even earlier than normal as his coat wasn't where he normally hung it, and the pewter dish where he normally discarded his keys was empty.

Removing her arm from the second sleeve and hanging it up by the hoop sewn inside the collar, she was amused, and her heart gave a little skip as she heard the melodic sounds of music, which seemed to be coming from Nancy Ferguson's makeshift bedroom.

Deciding that she would surprise them both with an early wake-up cup of tea, she tiptoed towards the kitchen, and whilst waiting for the kettle to boil, she cleared up the remnants of their girlie evening together. The young teenage girl had obviously made herself some scrambled egg as the saucepan bore the tell-tale signs of the dried congealed substance around the bottom half of the aluminium pot, and she found herself cursing silently that she'd never get it clean and wished Julia had cooked the eggs in the microwave instead.

Rather than waste time trying to clean it, she simply submerged the pan under the tap and squirted red soapy liquid from the bottle that was always found underneath the sink. Removing the three cups from the pine cupboard above the sand covered marble countertop, and opening the fridge, she grabbed the green top milk from the shelf on the door, plopped a tea bag in each cup and finally dropped a tea spoon on each saucer.

Knocking on Nancy's door and with no sound emanating from either lady, she opened the door slowly and smiled broadly, as mother and daughter were still both fast asleep with the teenager's head resting on top of her mum's stomach, whilst holding tightly onto her hands that were clutched together on top of the bed.

Paula quietly edged towards the bed, not wanting to scare either of them, gingerly placed her hand on Julia's right shoulder tapping it affectionately, whilst whispering into her ear, 'Morning sleepy head, I've made us all a nice cup of tea.'

Not waiting for a response, the care giver glanced across at the woman lying very still in the bed, and even though it was still fairly dark in the room, she was able to see her face as the early morning light cut through the gap in the curtain like a dagger, and moving even closer, she saw with horror the spittle congealed around her mouth, as her eyes stared unblinkingly at the Artexed ceiling.

Paula shook Nancy's shoulders with more vigour than she had her daughter, but there was not the merest hint of a flicker of the eyelids that covered those deep brown eyes, and putting her nursing skills into overdrive she felt for a carotid pulse, and leaning towards her patient's neck she placed her fore and middle fingers against the carotid artery but no pulsating thumps could be felt.

Stepping around the bed to where the teenager lay, knowing that something was dreadfully wrong, she did the same thing, and that's when the piercing scream was loudly emitted from her mouth, but it felt as though it couldn't be heard amongst the subtle instrumentals and heart wrenching words from 'Afterglow' that were emanating from the tape deck.

The middle aged nurse couldn't stand it any longer, and ran through the front door crying and punching in the three nines for emergency services where a torrent of words flowed from her quivering mouth as she finally managed to make her desperate plea for help.

She couldn't go back inside alone, so she sat on the front step leading up to the front porch with her arms wrapped around her stomach, as she tried in vain to gain a little comfort from the warmth that was trying to make its way through her cold racked body, when a man crouched down in front of her. Feeling quite stunned by the man's presence, she turned towards him with frightened eyes whilst shaking her head slowly from side to side lamenting, 'It's my fault…it's all my fault. I never should have agreed to it.'

Moving quickly from the bent position, the stranger eased himself up to where Paula was sitting and gently taking one of her hands in his and patting it comfortingly, he sympathetically replied, 'What is it that you think you've done? I'm sure you've done nothing to be ashamed or afraid of, and well…' brusquely interrupted from finishing his attempt at consolement by the piercing sounds of sirens and the blinding flashing lights of both the police and the ambulance as they punctured the early morning stillness of this quiet suburban road.

The ageing, balding, paunchy stranger helped the emotionally distraught nurse to stand up, and as she entered through the bottle green door for the second time that morning, the police officers followed her inside and finally into the room where the two women were to be found.

Without thinking, Paula knocked on the oak-coloured door before entering, and before she was able to step over the threshold, she was taken aside by a WPC who tried to calm the nurse by suggesting that they have a cup of tea together, whilst the other officers and paramedics got on with their jobs.

An A&E doctor had gone with the ambulance when the report came in that there could possibly be more than one fatality, and it didn't take him long to report to the attending police officer that indeed both women were dead.

A call was put through to Jarvis' team, and just as Josh Turner was spooning in some sugar in his first infusion of caffeine, quietly cursing the person on the other end of the internal call, he quickly responded to the incoming message.

'Detective Turner, its Sergeant Shields at the front desk. I've just had a call from one of our squad cars, and there's been confirmation that two bodies have been found dead in a house in Eddington Sands, a…' scavenging around picking up bits of paper until he found a blank one from his normally tidy desk, continued with his characteristic monotoned Birmingham accent, 'the house is Number 23, Trinity Road, and the householder's name is Ferguson.'

The young black detective put his own needs on hold, started to write swiftly on a yellow post-it note, and seeing Pettrini had also made an early start to the day, beckoned him over whilst grabbing his jacket from the back of his chair, 'Hey, Nick come on let's go…we got a call about two dead bodies.'

Snatching up the cold, dried piece of toast and tearing it apart with perfectly formed incisors, Pettrini strode across the dull, grey carpeted floor, 'Okay Josh, where're we off to?'

'Eddington Sands, about eight miles north of here. Mother and daughter apparently found early this morning. We better let Jarvis know, but we can call him from the car.'

Descending the stairs two at a time, the men soon found themselves scurrying through the front entrance where it was obvious that for some reason the night howlers had been in overdrive as there was rather a loud racket as the alcohol and other substances that had been drunk, snorted, sniffed or injected had weaned their way out of the users' blood streams, who were all loudly demanding that they be allowed to go on their merry way as they'd done nothing wrong.

Winking at Sergeant Shields and raising a thumb in the air, the officers marched towards the car park adjacent to the station and decided to use Turner's dark maroon Vauxhall hatchback.

Driving through the main Upper Stanton High Street, Pettrini started to punch in Jarvis' number on his Smartphone, but was very quickly interrupted by Sergeant Turner, 'If you're thinking of calling the boss, I think it'd be better when we knew a bit more, you know. I mean we don't even know the victims' names yet, so better hold off till we get there.'

As the screen went dark, Pettrini pocketed his phone, removed his glasses, and cleaned them with the bottom of his shirt, 'Have we got anything to go on apart from the fact that there are two dead bodies?'

'The only thing I can tell you is that the call was made to the emergency services this morning, and two females were pronounced dead by a medic who accompanied the paramedics. That's all I can tell you, but until we get there there's no point in us speculating on any of the sordid details.'

***

It was difficult to park outside of the victims' house as there was still a huge presence of emergency vehicles, so they found a spot in a nearby cul-de-sac and quickly made their way to number 23 Trinity Road.

Making their way through the narrow hallway, both men glanced at the walls which adorned, almost shrine-like, framed photographs all bearing the happy, proud faces of two adults and the girlish grin of a young girl which was obviously their daughter. Scenes of frolicking on a beach, riding bicycles in woodlands, licking pink candyfloss off long wooden sticks underneath a Ferris wheel and even outside a famous theatre in the capital advertising 'Mama Mia', showing the obvious glee of both mother and daughter. These imprints revealed the once happy family that seemingly had now been ripped apart.

Raising their ID badges in the air so that all attending police constables could see that they'd got every right to be there, both detectives made their way to where the bodies were lying in the hope of trying to establish what, when, and possibly why this tragedy had occurred.

Turner approached the slim, middle aged man who was pocketing his stethoscope into the pocket of his dark blue scrubs and packing up the rest of his medical paraphernalia into his emergency bag. The detective introduced himself whilst extending his hand, 'Detective Sergeant Josh Turner, and this is my partner DS Nico Pettrini. Can you tell us what's happened here, Doc?'

'Hi, Dr Joe Brewster from the Hamilton General. Well, there's no question that both females are deceased, and from my initial findings I think the woman in the bed, identified as Nancy Ferguson by the live-in nurse that found her, more than likely choked to death, and I can't be sure...at least not until the post mortem, but I would hazard a guess that the young girl, a Julia Ferguson died of a drugs overdose. She's definitely got tracking marks on her arms, and as there were signs of bile congealed at the corner of her mouth, and also a fair amount on the bed clothes, and I can only assume that whatever drug she was taking, well...she unfortunately took too much of it.'

'In your opinion Dr Brewster, can you define what time they died, and are there any obvious signs of trauma, struggles or anything of that nature that could have led to the deaths of either of the ladies?'

Waiting for the medic to answer, who was hastily signing forms attached to a clip board, 'No, but as I say, we'll know more when the coroner opens them up. I gave you what I consider to be their immediate cause of death, and from the state of rigor, I can only hazard a guess that they died somewhere between ten and midnight last night. Now, if you're asking me whether foul play was a cause of death, then it would be unprofessional of me to completely rule it out. I'm afraid that's all I've got for you. Now...if you'll excuse me, A&E will be back to back with patients that could have gone to a local pharmacy, or taken their so called ailments to their GP but no, they seem to enjoy sitting around for up to four hours, and none of them will budge until they've been seen as a matter of urgency,' the doctor used quotation marks in the air as he uttered the last three words.

Raising his hand in the air in an empathetic gesture, Turner muttered, 'No, that's fine doctor, and thanks again for your help,' directing a swift nod of the head in the direction of the Italian detective they left the scene where the two ladies silently lay and stepped into the kitchen where a WPC was consoling a very fractious middle-aged, uniformed lady.

'Why don't you go and make the call to the boss Nico, and I'll have a quick mooch around just to see if I can find anything?'

With mobile already in his hand, Pettrini stepped into another room completely away from the kitchen and he found himself turning a brass door handle which opened up to a modest sized sitting room, revealing a beautifully lacquered parquet floor, and an ornate fireplace, with the customary Victorian tiles decoratively positioned either side, complementing its authenticity. Aside from the ever popular Van Gogh replica of his 'Sunflowers' and a gilt framed mirror hanging over the fireplace, the room appeared somewhat sterile to Nico, and as he looked around, he spotted the cushions that seemed to have been strategically positioned with almost obsessive precision on an over indulgently sized sofa. There was absolutely no indication that anyone had sat in this room for a long time, no lingering smells of perfume hung in the air, no footprints on the wooden floor, no books, magazines, newspapers, no remote control for the TV adorning the nest of tables, in fact there was no evidence of family or friends ever having gathered within the confines of this loveless, barren room.

'Oh, hi guv, sorry to disturb you, but me and Josh were called out to a house in Trinity Road, Eddington Sands, where two female bodies were found earlier this morning, we do...'

'What...erm...what number house is it?'

'Twenty-three, boss.'

'Oh shit...the family name is Ferguson, isn't it?' asked the Detective Inspector nervously.

'I believe so, yes. I'm sorry guv to be the one that's given you the bad news as it's obvious that you know them, but just to let you know that SOCO are here, and obviously the house has been cordoned off until we know more about the cause of death. The nurse who found the body is here, and we've arranged for a female uniformed officer to sit with her until she's calmed down a bit. As you can imagine, it would be very difficult to get any sense out of her at the moment, so we figured it'd be best to wait until you get here.'

'Okay, I'll see you when I get there,' as there was no need for Nico to give his boss an address, Jarvis abruptly ended the call.

***

Trying to focus on the road, but finding it almost impossible, as not only had Eleanor gone away on a trip as she'd planned without him, but how the hell was he going to break the news to her? Did he wait until she'd decided to come back to him, or did he risk spoiling her chance of a bit of freedom, which is what she claimed she was desperately in need of? Depressing as the morning was turning out to be, he knew that whichever path he decided to go down, it wouldn't be an easy one.

His black thoughts were interrupted by his phone bleating out noisily, and using hands-free with the loud speaker on, the words reverberated around the inside of the car, 'Sorry guv, but thought you'd like to know…' sounded the deep, husky tones of Detective Sergeant Carmichael, 'we've just had a call from a repair garage and they think, well they're almost a hundred per cent certain that they had the red transit van in for repair.'

Slamming the wheel in frustration as to the time that had been wasted, he waspishly asked, 'So what the hell took them so bloody long to let us know?'

'I'll find out soon enough because I'm heading out there now, oh and I'll be taking Kelly with me. So, let's hope we're getting lucky at last, yeah?'

Emitting a sarcastic grunt, the Inspector paused slightly before answering, 'I'm not counting my chickens that's for sure. And just so you know, I'm on my way to a house where I'm almost a hundred percent certain that I know the owners, and who are now, according to Nic, corpses. Listen Carmichael, let me know how you get on, will you?'

Approaching the address that he knew so well, the Inspector couldn't quite make sense of the scene that was surrounding the house that was always filled with laughter, and people coming and going with requests of, *'Come back soon, you know you're always welcome.'* And that was the thing, every one that stepped across their threshold was indeed treated more like family than mere friends.

There were the obvious emergency response vehicles, a couple of vans bearing the names of local media stations, and a myriad of onlookers, who no doubt on questioning, would all have seen something, however, none of them would have anything worth listening to, except pure speculation, which he figured was nothing more than human nature. Scanning around, he saw the bloodhound from The Herald newspaper with his familiar mop of shoulder length unruly curly hair, scruffily dressed which he liked to think was his trademark, and his John Lennon round-rimmed glasses. It always amazed Jarvis as to how journalists, especially this one, got to hear about news almost as fast as the police. Grimacing sourly, the Inspector slowly shook his head, as he was certainly not in the mood for any kind of confrontation with this clown.

Parking a fair distance away from number 23, he allowed the silence within his dilapidated old car to completely envelope him as he slowly leant his head against the coolness of the steering wheel, trying to assimilate in his mind what could have happened, and how he was going to maintain his composure when he stepped over the threshold.

Chapter 22

Detectives Carmichael and Donnelly seemed to drive the five miles from Upper Stanton to Maskill Road in record time, not really looking forward to a plethora of excuses as to why no one from the company had contacted Stockfield Road Police Station as to the possibility that they had indeed had the van within their possession all this time.

The gym loving, muscular Carmichael, with his fashionable shaved head, garbed in his characteristic checked shirt parked in front of the garage, where the sounds of up-to-date hits could be heard blaring loudly from speakers, as workers sang out of tune with botched up chorus lines. Sparks could be seen flashing from welding guns, and cars were seen being lifted up high in the air with jack stands where mechanics hovered underneath the raised bonnet searching for clues as to a diagnosis, similar to humans being opened up by surgeons.

Turning the engine off, Carmichael glanced over towards Kelly, and he was quietly taken aback as to how naturally lovely she looked today, and wondered whether it was the deep shade of maroon of her leather jacket that showed off her black curly hair and how her sea blue eyes seemed to glisten. He didn't fancy her though, as he was hooked up with Molly with the expectation of a bundle of joy on the way. Still…it didn't hurt to look occasionally at eye candy, now did it, he reassuringly told himself?'

'Now Kelly, you're not going to go off on one in there now, are you?' he asked jokingly.

'Why would ye even tink I'd do such a ting? Don't you know I'd never embarrass ye at all,' quipped the Irish detective.

'Behave Kel,' as they both headed to the door marked, '*Reception.*'

Pushing the heavy glass fronted door open, Carmichael waited until the mature lady behind the wooden desk had finished dealing with a young twenty something male, clad in baggy trousers which hung low enough to reveal the name of a top designer's name on the rim of his underwear, topped off with a hat which could have been worn by any one of the seven dwarfs in the famous Disney cartoon.

'Hi, there Miss…or is it Mrs Holman?' glancing swiftly at the name badge on the lady's lapel, 'I'm Detective Sergeant Carmichael, and this is Detective Sergeant Donnelly,' swiftly flashing their ID cards at the rather bemused looking receptionist, who dabbed rather nervously at the side of her nose with the tissue that she'd just removed from the box strategically placed at the side of her desk. 'It's Miss Holman, now how can I help you officers?'

'Is the manager around for us to have a quick chat?'

'Erm…' looking around her shoulder towards a wall which was decorated with a huge whiteboard with vehicle numbers and names beside each one, presumably the identity of the mechanic that was dealing with a specific car, she calmly reported, 'His name's not on the board for today's works so I'm guessing he's in his office,' she picked up the receiver for the internal phone and pushed three digits. 'Geoff, sorry to bother you, but there's two detectives here to see you,' putting the phone back on its cradle she declared reservedly, 'He'll be out in a minute. You can sit over there if you like,' pointing to a red imitation leather sofa which had the customary Ikea coffee table in front of it with magazines of the latest models, all showing off their flashy interiors, listing benefits of having the biggest engine, information as to fuel consumption and the deals that could be struck, if a person committed to buying it within a certain time frame.

Having just sat down, a door leading to the main hub of the repair section opened, and in marched a tall, extremely slim black man, who was clad in a red polo shirt bearing the name of the garage in big bold white lettering above black combat trousers, no doubt the surplus of pockets proving to be extremely useful when working on the shop floor.

Proffering an outstretched hand to both detectives, he shook his head slowly in apparent sympathy, 'Officers, I can't tell you how sorry I am that you've had to come all this way, when I know that you're very busy, but I've given all the relevant information that I can give you.'

'Thank you for seeing us Mr Pearman, but we need to speak to anyone who can perhaps give us details as to who picked the Transit van up, and also it would be very useful if we could look at any CCTV coverage that might identify the person who collected the vehicle.'

'Ahem…' nervously clearing his throat slightly, the manager smiled awkwardly, 'but you see that's the thing, no one seems to know anything about who collected the damn thing. And I know it was parked on the roadside, but even so its baffling as it seems to have completely vanished off the face of the earth.'

'How far back did you check the coverage of the cameras?' asked Donnelly.

'I think I told you that the mechanic that worked on the van no longer works here, but he vehemently remembers driving it onto the roadside, as there wasn't enough room on the front car park where the other vehicles are parked ready for collection. He also remembers handing the keys over to Stephanie over there after he'd parked it.'

'Well, you must have records of who paid the bill or even when it was paid, so could we see your invoice records please? We can wait over here if you like.'

The manager paced swiftly across the mushroom-coloured lino floor in pursuit of the officers' request.

Both detectives side glanced at each other, and call it a female intuition, but Sergeant Donnelly happened to glance towards the plump, middle aged woman, who after tearing the pristine white tissue into strips cradled her head in her hands.

Kelly casually stepped towards the desk and approached Miss Holman, who sported the same red uniform shirt as her boss, but she noticed, there was a noticeable absence of any jewellery. No rings on any fingers or in either ear could be seen, but there was a very small Timex watch which was held together with thin plastic-coated straps decorating her chubby right wrist.

Sergeant Donnelly winked at Carmichael, who took the subtle, yet obvious hint, and decided he'd go in search of Pearman, as she had a hunch that this timid woman, who clearly liked working there, had something to tell, and…most likely hadn't imparted it to her boss.

Leaning towards the woman and resting both arms on the wooden surface, the detective tried to engage her in casual conversation in the hope of putting her at ease, and began by asking, 'So…erm…Stephanie, is it okay if I call you by your first name?'

The nervous woman nodded slowly, as Kelly continued, 'Have you been working here long? I bet you see all sorts coming through those doors, eh? I think if I were working here, d'you know what I'd do, I'd…well, have a little game and see whether the vehicle that's being picked up matches that of the owner. You know like, a bloke walks in wearing a cravat, now would you suspect that he was picking up the small battered mini or the Jag that's parked right next to it? Have you ever done anything like that, I mean…it would help to pass the time of day I s'pose?'

The woman on the other side of the reception desk looked startled at this suggestion, as she retorted defensively, 'You have no idea how busy this place can be. I have people shouting at me over the phone asking if their bloody car is ready to be picked up, I have blokes who stand in front of me sighing, and tutting and looking at their posh watches demanding that their stupid car be brought out to the front immediately. So, just so you know, I bloody well wouldn't have the time to play a silly guessing game, and even if I did, I certainly wouldn't stoop to playing something that didn't engage my mind, especially as I frequently am able to finish the Times crossword!'

Pushing herself up into standing from the desk and taking a step backwards, the detective sergeant raised her hands in the air and said contritely, 'Oh Miss Holman, please forgive me, I really didn't mean that you were sitting behind the desk twiddling your thumbs all day, or idling your time away with flicking through Agony Aunt columns. But…there was a reason that I gave you that scenario, it was to see whether on the day that the red Transit van was picked up, you could remember or be able to give a description of the man or woman who laid claim to it.'

The receptionist seemed to struggle in knowing what to say, but finally the words seemed to gush out, almost as if she were confessing sins that she'd held within her very soul for an eternity, and desperate for someone to finally absolve her.

'It was me…I let him have the bloody van and it wasn't him I was supposed to give it to,' she exploded as her shoulders quivered and red blotches appeared on the bare flesh of her cleavage. 'It was so busy and he…he just slammed his fist down on the desk while I was on the phone, and I remember there were two or three other fellas waiting to be seen who got angry that he'd jumped the queue, and so I asked what was the registration number and the make of the car, and I told him the cost of the job, and before I had chance to tear out the invoice, he was gone. He grabbed the keys from the desk and threw a hundred quid, all ten-pound notes, down here right in front of me, and the next thing I know the cheeky sod just marched out!' Her arms were all over the place as she recounted the scene, 'Bloody cheek of him he just marched out. Am I going to g…?'

'Take it easy now Stephanie; let's take this one step at a time, eh?' Pointing to the comfy red sofa Kelly suggested, 'Why don't we sit over there…and then you can tell me all about it, nice and calm like you know? Shall I ask someone to make you a cup of tea or something?'

'No…no I don't want anyone to see me like this, please…don't,' rising from the black swivel office chair, she stepped around the desk and followed the detective to the visitors' seating area.

Gently placing a placatory hand on the distraught woman's arm, the detective continued, 'You said that you weren't supposed to give it to this fella, what did you mean by that?'

Retrieving a tissue from her trouser pocket, the receptionist dabbed at her eyes, and with a trumpet sound blew her nose, and replied in a rather mournful voice, 'Well, you see he…he, I mean…when someone picks up a repair job, they're supposed to offer some form of identification, driver's licence that sort of thing. Well, it stands to reason though doesn't it, we can't just give keys away willy nilly to anyone that walks in off the street, now can we? Anyway, when I asked him ooh…it must have been at least three times, well then he lost his temper, good and proper I can tell you, and then he slammed his fists on the table and said that he'd just started with the company and it wasn't his fault if their HR department hadn't got around to getting his ID badge.

'One of the other men in the queue had a go at him and told him to mind his manners, and that he should have waited in line like the rest of them. Well then he had a go at him and told him to shut the f*** up, and roughly snatched the keys, an…an…and then he threw the cash on the desk and marched out so quick, it was like in them films when someone's robbed a bank.'

Crossing her left knee over her right, and leaning in even closer to the receptionist, who thankfully had seemed to calm down, as she continued with verbosity and dancing animated eyes, 'Anyway, that's…that's when I knew it couldn't have been him that owned the van, because that bloody bossy bloke from the company that it really belonged to called me up and asked when it would be ready, and oh my…' but her new found stoicism didn't last very long as she continued her account of the conversation and let out a funereal wail, 'he…, he said that it had taken far too long to repair and that it wasn't good enough. He even threatened to take his business elsewhere, and still shouting he said that he'd be 'aving words with the manager. I didn't know what else to do, and I don't know why I said it, but I just told 'im that the soddin' van, well…I didn't swear at him did I, I mean I would never do that over the phone to a customer now would I? But…anyway…I told him it wasn't ready and that the parts were taking for ever to be delivered.'

Composing herself once more, and flicking off particles of white tissue paper off her black pleated trousers, she quietly asked the Irish detective, 'Have you ever wished officer that you could turn the clock back? Because believe you me I do, 'cos then I would have told him the truth and then you wouldn't be 'ere would you, and you might have caught that bloke that's taken them poor people, oh………' and then the door opened slowly, and with frightened eyes she looked towards the two men, but the narrator quickly lowered her gaze as she couldn't bear to look at her boss knowing what she'd done.

Not wishing to interrupt the flow of dialogue between both women, the men busied themselves in searching through computerised records, but there was no doubt that their ears would be pricked high into the air, as they didn't want to miss any snippet of information as to what had actually happened to the van.

'So, Stephanie…there's a few things that we need to know on the back of what you've just told me. Firstly, what's the name of the company who the van really belonged to, and could you give a brief description of the fella that picked it up? Was he tall, short, fat, thin, did he wear glasses, have any snakes or dragons drawn on his body, that's the sort of thing we'd like to know about. Oh…and if you could remember what he was wearing that would be really, really useful, and I know that it was a while back now, but anything that you can give us would be grand.'

A rather large crease furrowed across her forehead, as she stammered her reply, desperately trying not to let her boss have any more reasons to loathe her for what she'd done, 'I don't even need to look up the name of the company 'cos it's up 'ere all the damned time,' pointing her right index finger to her temple, 'it's called, 'Finnegan & Son,' and I'm pretty sure their address is somewhere on the Maskill Road. The guy who runs it is known as Marcus Finnegan, and I'm sure his son is called Seamus. He's nice the young fella is, he'd never speak to me like that, because he's got a bit more respect than 'is dad.'

'Thanks so much for that Stephanie, and by the way you're doing really well. Now, what can you tell me about the man that picked up the van?'

'Aw, I dunno now. I was in such a kerfuffle, but I can tell you that he was wearing one of those hoodie things and it was definitely black, oh and yeah…he'd got really weird green eyes, almost as if they were a false colour, d'ya know what I mean? They were too green, I mean…I've never seen anything like them before, they were like the colour of marbles that we used to play with when we were kids like. Can't remember seeing any of them tattoo things, nor I don't think he were wearing glasses, but as he was rushing out, I could have sworn I saw that he had a slight limp, but that just might be my imagination running away with me. Is that the kind of thing that you're looking for Sergeant?'

'Considering you said that you wouldn't be able to give us anything, you've given us a lot to be going on with, believe me. My last couple of questions are; when were you going to let Mr Finnegan know the truth about what happened to the van and secondly, what did you do with the money that he threw down on the counter?'

Nervously touching her cheek, and turning her head in the direction of the two men, placed her hand sideways at the corner of her mouth to block out the reply, and whispered, 'Well I was hoping that the bloke would have just put the van back where he found it, and I know it sounds a bit stupid now, but I honestly feel that there's good in everyone, and that he'd see sense, feel sorry for what he'd done and simply return it. As for the money that he threw at me, well I had no choice, did I? I put it in the petty cash and if there were ever any questions as to where it had come from, well…I'd just tell 'em that someone left it as a tip because they were so pleased with the work that was done.'

The manager had obviously overheard this last statement as he looked across at his dependable right-hand woman with his mouth wide open, and whatever words were about to be emitted were temporarily stalled as the loud shrill of the telephone demanded his attention, 'A-Z Car Repairs, Geoff Pearman speaking, how may I help you?'

Quickly removing the pencil from behind his ear and finding a bit of paper on the receptionist's desk, he began jotting down notes, with the occasional murmurings of, 'Uh huh…uh huh…yeah not a problem, we can do that for you.'

Sergeant Donnelly rose from the sofa, and as she did so she bent down to retrieve her bag and jacket, and with her outstretched arm she thanked Miss Holman for her time, paused and uttered quietly, 'We'll be in touch with you shortly so that you can meet with our sketch artist to see whether he could possibly make a picture of the man that you said picked up the vehicle. So, please don't make any arrangements to go anywhere for a while, understood?'

As she was about to saunter towards the desk where both the other detective and the manager of the garage were standing, she felt a hand grasping onto her arm, and with fear in the woman's eyes and with a tremulous voice, she asked nervously, 'Sorry officer, but am I going to be arrested for erm…helping a criminal, because I've heard about cases like that before, you know on the news like and in films,' and Sergeant Donnelly couldn't help but raise a smile, as she replied, 'Well I'm not going to lie to you Stephanie, you've certainly made our life a lot more difficult by not coming forward sooner with this information, but no, I can honestly say that there will be no serious repercussions as to your let's say…neglect in informing us of the events that you've just told me about. On the other hand, you can feel proud that you've been able to remember so much, considering the heat of the moment and his behaviour towards you. So, I think the best thing we can do is move forward with this information and see if we can find him and the transit van in question.'

The smartly dressed, perfectly coiffed woman stood still, almost statue-like, not knowing whether she should yet approach her boss who might issue her with her marching papers, or worse, perhaps give her a proper rollicking in front of the detectives, which in her mind would have been worse than death itself, so she remained perfectly still until she knew the coast was clear.

Donnelly sauntered towards the two men, and motioned with her head to the side door, as she suggested matter of factly, 'Could we go somewhere private do you think?'

'Yeah, of course…through here,' suggested the softly spoken manager with just the merest hint of a Caribbean twang.

As the door of the office marked '*Manager*' clicked into a closed position behind them, Kelly imparted the sorry saga to both men, and with all three exchanging glances at one another in sheer, utter amazement, that the short, middle-aged woman in the other room, could inadvertently be responsible in aiding and abetting a bloody kidnapper.

Mr Pearman shook his head and studied both detectives just for a moment, before commenting, 'You couldn't make it up, could you? I mean…how long did she think she could keep fobbing off the decorating company with lame excuses as to why their van wasn't ready? And not only that, but now I've got to somehow explain to them, who just so you know, have been trusted clients of ours for years, as to what's happened to their damned van. Not to mention the fact that I'm going to have to pick up the bill for a replacement, which will of course mean my bloody insurance premiums are gonna go through the roof.'

Reflecting that nothing was fair or indeed straight forward, Kelly gazed towards the thin, handsome face of the obviously annoyed manager, and almost pleadingly requested, 'Mr Pearman, I get that you're pissed and quite rightly so, but cut her some slack, eh? I mean…we all make mistakes and God knows she's made a galactical one, but you're not going to fire her are you, 'cos despite this naïve error of judgement, I guess she's a good egg wouldn't ye think?'

'Sergeant,' the man began, 'there's no way I'm going to let her go because I honestly don't know what I'd do without her. She's never late, she's always here later than she should be, never had any problems with the money side of things, so I can only assume that this bas…, sorry…geezer must have really riled and put the fear of God into her, that she thought she couldn't come to me at the time. But to cover it up like that well…I can only assume that this has been rolling around and around her brain since it 'appened. But d'you know what? I think I'm going to install an alarm button under her desk, so God forbid that anything like this happens again, she knows that either me or one of the lads in the garage will come and help her out. I s'pose she's a bit vulnerable out there all on her own, and I guess it's partly my fault that I never thought about it before now. So, rest assured officers, as long as this garage remains open Stephanie will always have a job here.'

'Okay, that's good to hear that she'll get a second chance, but now…we're going to have to move on and visit these Finnegan lads, because it seems to me that someone in that company let the man know where the van was being repaired. When we do find him though, I'm not sure his boss will be so lenient, do you?' Carmichael remarked, as both detectives bade the good hearted manager farewell, and said that they'd be in touch with any further information.

***

Inspector Jarvis knew the time had come for him to leave the tranquillity of his car and approach the blue and white cordoned taped area surrounding the house that held so many cherished memories when the children were smaller.

No sooner had he crossed the street when he was approached by Matthew Lyle from The Herald, with his cross body bag hanging tightly across his chest, with no doubt a recorder hidden somewhere about his person, when he asked loudly, 'Can you give the people of the neighbourhood reassurance that the scenes that we're witnessing is not a murder investigation, Inspector?'

'No comment,' replied the blonde Inspector.

Following in hot pursuit, the reporter continued with alarm in his voice, 'Don't you think you owe these people some sort of comment? How are they going to be able to sleep at night knowing that there might be a killer at large?'

'No comment.'

Even though he tried his best not to pay any attention to the drones of monotonous voices the cries of concern and bewilderment could be heard, *'Oh my God such a nice, caring family,'* *'What d'ya think has happened, huh?'* *'It ain't right being murdered when you're asleep.'*

Jarvis kept moving, but he couldn't help but wonder why there were so many children there in Superman pyjamas holding onto their favourite teddy bear for dear life, clearly excited about all the flashing blue lights, when surely they should have been getting ready for the start of the school day.

And just when he thought he'd escaped the hurling questions that were being fired at him, one bloke came within spitting distance of him when Jarvis was almost sick as he caught sight of the dried up cornflakes, or whatever cereal the man had eaten for breakfast, which had taken residence in his unkempt ginger beard, as he slobbered disgustingly, *'You need to tell us now, is this some kind of terrorist attack, you know like some kind of Russian nerve agent, 'cos we've got a right to know, and we ain't leaving here till you tell us the truth.'*

At the sound of that one word 'terrorist' the so-called worried neighbours turned into an ugly mob, all waving their arms in the air whilst shouting profanities, oblivious as to the children that could hear them.

'Get this lot away from here now, and that's an order,' Jarvis bellowed to the nearby uniformed officer.

'Alright, alright...go back to your homes now, let us get on with our job,' echoed the young constable.

Slowly but surely, even though speculations were still being deliberated on, the crowd started to dissipate.

'Aw mam, can't we stay a bit longer, we're gonna miss the best bits,' quizzed the excited children.

'Nah, yer've got to go to school now, but just think you'll be able to tell all yer mates and the teachers about it, and yer may even get a gold star or summat for being here when it all happened.'

With the sudden realisation that the young, innocent witnesses would be the heroes of the class, they skipped jauntily to where their uniforms would be waiting, and this time no doubt there would be no need for parental persuasion as they dived into them.

Stepping into the hallway, which he'd done more times than he could remember, Jarvis refocused his attention as to the reason why he was here, as a slight shiver ran through him.

Moving cautiously into the hub of the house he was met by Sergeant Pettrini who reported in a fairly light voice, desperately trying not to let the nurse, who discovered the bodies overhear him, 'I've hum…spoken with the medic who accompanied the ambulance, and well he's almost sure that the one woman, the older one, died of choking, and the younger one it would seem died of an overdose. He reckons that the time of death, well…that's to say the levels of lividity, and rigor mortis, suggest that they both died around nine or ten last night, but again he stressed that it's up to the coroner to make the call. However, he was pretty sure that the timeline wouldn't be too far out.'

Nodding his head slightly towards the distraught nurse, who was cradling a dainty China cup, Jarvis politely asked, 'This is the lady who found the bodies I take it?'

'Yes guv, a Mrs Paula Corcoran.'

'Right, ah…My wife came around to see Mrs Ferguson a couple of weeks back, and she said that she'd met one of the nurses here, and she definitely fits the description that Ellie gave.'

Scrutinising his boss somewhat, the Italian Sergeant coyly asked, 'So guv who are these people, and how…if I may be so bold as to ask…do you know them?'

'Now's not the right time Nic, later perhaps, eh?' turning away from his colleague, Jarvis removed his phone from his black woollen jacket and sauntered towards the living room where it was profoundly quiet unlike all the noise that was emanating from the other rooms on the ground floor. Using speed dial, he scrolled down until he reached the letter L and pressed the phone symbol, and after only ringing out once, the no-nonsense, expressionless voice declared that he was not available to speak to anyone, and that he would promise to call back when he was available. Inspector Jarvis used a rather informal tone, as he didn't want to leave a message saying that his wife and daughter had been found dead and somehow spook the guy, but he merely asked if he could call him back as a matter of some importance.

Making his way back into the kitchen, Jarvis asked the WPC if he could have a few words with Mrs Corcoran, and so sat himself down on the pine kitchen chair previously occupied by the female officer. The pale lady, whose shoulders were raised almost up to her ears, sat there listlessly, simply tinkling a teaspoon against china whilst effortlessly stirring the honey-coloured liquid around and around.

'I'm Inspector Jarvis, Mrs Corcoran, and I'd just like to ask you a few questions, if you're up to it that is?'

She took a sip and swallowed deeply before murmuring quietly, 'Yes…I s'pose so.'

'I believe you worked for Mrs Ferguson, is that correct?'

'Yeah…ever since she came out of the hospital, ooh…must be almost three years now, I really can't remember the exact time.'

'That's fine. Now can you tell me everything that happened since the last time that you saw Nan…Mrs Ferguson?'

As she had finished her tea, she now rocked the empty teacup backwards and forwards between her clasped hands, and nervously answered the tired looking detective with bags underneath his eyes. 'It must have been about half past seven I guess, and as it was Thursday, Julia, that's erm…Mrs Ferguson's daughter, the one that's in there,' with salty tears in her eyes she moved them in the direction of where the deceased lay, 'you see she only comes in on a Tuesday and Thursday like, don't ask me why, but I reckon it's got something to do with 'im,' staring coldly at the framed photo of a man that was hung on the wall between the fridge and the cooker.

'Sorry for interrupting Mrs Corcoran, but you sounded rather hostile when you mentioned 'him'. Am I right in thinking that it's Mr Ferguson that you're referring to, and why the angry tone in your voice? Did you not get on with him or something?'

'No, it's not that so much. I mean…he was great when she first came home, but lately he's been acting really weird, never really speaks, and I don't know whether it's because they've had words or something, but well…when Julia comes home, it's almost as if she's waiting and watching for him to go out before she'll even think about coming through the door. I don't know what 'appened, as this used to be such a pleasant place to work, considering everything that 'appened to that lovely, lovely woman. Such a crying shame, that's what it is, alright.'

Smiling awkwardly, the Inspector encouraged the petite lady sitting across from him at the round, pine kitchen table to continue, 'Please carry on, and try to remember everything you can from last night till this morning.'

'Yeah as I was saying, it must 'ave been about half past seven and Julia came in really quite chirpy you know, lovely girl, except I don't like all those tattoos, and why anyone would put rings through their nose and lips is simply beyond me. I mean they look so ugly, and I really can't get it through me head why someone would want to wear black all the time, especially as she's…I mean was a really pretty young thing, but then I s'pose everyone dresses like that now, don't they?

'Anyway, she said that it was time that she looked after her mum without anyone else being there, given that there might come a time when she'll have to do it in the future, and she'd like to prove to her dad and herself that she'd be able to do it. Also, she said that it would be nice for her and her mum to be together as she hadn't had the chance since well…you know she came back from hospital like. So, I wasn't 'appy about it I can tell you, but she insisted and said that she wouldn't tell anyone about it at the agency, and that it would do me good to 'ave a night off. I insisted that I could just stay in my room, and promised I wouldn't interfere with either of them, but she was getting a bit antsy you know.

'So well, in the end I thought what harm could one night do? I mean, he'd be home in a few hours anyway, so if she got stuck with summat then he'd be able to help her. Realising that she wasn't going to take no for an answer, I got my bag and coat and left them to it at about quarter past eight, and when I come back, this is what I found…' trying to quell her tears, she covered her nose and mouth with a white handkerchief that she'd taken from her tunic pocket.

'Mrs Corcoran, when was the last time that you saw Mr Ferguson?'

'Ooh…let me see. He'd already gone when I got up yesterday morning, so he must have left really early because I get up around six thirty, and I know he was in late the night before because I 'eard him around half past one in the morning.'

Nodding slowly with mutterings of 'Uh huh, uh huh,' Jarvis continued, 'and you didn't see him at all this morning? Didn't you think that was strange, I mean…as you said, he always comes home in the evenings despite the lateness of the hour, and yet if he did come home, then surely he would have seen his wife and daughter well…lying there?'

Narrowing her eyes almost as if she hadn't heard the question, she eventually replied, 'I did tell you that he's been acting a bit funny lately, didn't I? Well he goes out at different times of the day and never comes home at the same time either, and to be 'onest with you, I've been wondering if he's got another woman, because when she first left the hospital he was always here, especially when it was meal time, just to make sure that she ate and drank something,' nervously running her hands down the thighs of her dark blue uniform trousers, 'but lately…oh I dunno, it's almost as if he doesn't care. And I'm absolutely certain that she, erm Mrs Ferguson knew it an' all.'

'Tell me Mrs Corcoran, during this time that you say that Mr Ferguson was, in your opinion, acting how shall we say…out of character; did he alter his appearance at all? You know, did he wear different style clothing for instance, or wear a beard, change his hair style that sort of thing?'

'Funny you should ask that question because I used to get so much laundry from him like nice work shirts, and I always used to wash and iron about three pairs of trousers each week, but now there's 'ardly anything in the basket. Mind you that's not really surprising because he lives in those track suits, and 'im being the age he is too! I mean my 'usband wears 'em, but only when we've finished for the day, you know when we're watching telly in the evening, 'cos he says they're really comfy to just be lazy in. But he wouldn't be seen dead wearing a gct up like that in the street, I mean what would people say?'

Jarvis forced a rather artificial smile whilst carrying on, 'Anything else that you noticed was different about him lately?'

'Well, when I first met him he always had his hair nice and trim almost like a solider, you know neatly cut and short, but nowadays he seems to almost have a different colour each week. Like last week, it was peroxide blonde, weird for a bloke I thought, but then I'm not paid to comment on people's hair now am I? Oh…and the other thing I noticed was that his ey…'

Jarvis' phone, even though it was on silent, vibrated inside his jacket pocket, 'Excuse me Mrs Corcoran I'd better get this,' noticing that it was Sergeant Carmichael whose name appeared on the screen.

Pacing swiftly away from the table with phone held tightly against his ear, he once again found himself surrounded by the quietness of the sitting room, whereupon he wearily asked, 'What's up Dean?'

'Sorry guv, I know you're pretty tied up, but we've found out some interesting stuff about the van. I'm not going to get into all the details, but it was delivered to the repair shop known as A-Z Car Repairs by a man called Roger Wallis, who works at a decorating firm in the name of Finnegan and Son. It took us a while, but we found out that his van broke down just after lunch time that day, and by the time that he'd dropped it off for repair, he figured he'd call it a day. Anyway, that same night he met a few of his buddies at the local pub known as The Bird In The Nest and he was telling them what a shitty day he'd had and told them about the problems with his van.

'So then Wallis, that's the name of the bloke, nips to the loo, and a bloke walked in, who he said he recognised, but he only knew his first name, and then this other geezer spurted out this sob story about having a hard time of it lately, what with his mother being sick and in order to look after her he had to give up his job and was living hand to mouth with minimal pickings from the state. Anyway, to cut a long story short, this fella said that he needed a van as a matter of urgency, just to pick up an electronic bed, you know…the kind that they use in hospitals, and he didn't have the money to pay for a hired van, and did Wallis know of where he could get one.

'Being a little worse for drink, and not really thinking about what he was about to do, Wallis told him that he'd just dropped one off for repair, and if he called the garage and pretended to be him, then he could borrow it, but only for a couple of hours. He then gave him the receipt for the drop off of the van, which obviously had the name, address of the repair shop, and that's why it was never picked up by the decorating company.'

Running the palm of his hand across his creased brow Jarvis murmured, 'Jesus Christ, it bloody well beggars belief, and all this time we've been running around chasing our soddin' tails. Didn't this Wallis guy think that it was a bit weird someone asking for a van while he was having a slash? I mean was he that drunk for pity's sake?'

Inspector Jarvis stood up from the oversized floral sofa and pacing swiftly across the wooden floor, asked Carmichael suspiciously, 'Did this Wallis man give you a name?' dreading inwardly the name that was shortly going to be revealed.

'Name's Luke guv. But, he never got to ask him his second name as he left the pub almost immediately and Wallis has never seen him since.'

As his heart beat faster, he stared in the mirror and caught the reflection of the named man reflected back at him from a portrait that Eleanor had painted as a birthday present for some milestone birthday.

'Good work Dean, but I gotta go,' as Jarvis silenced the phone and slipped it back into his pocket, and that was when he heard the thunderous tones of his DCI, 'Where the hell is D.I. Jarvis?' he bellowed.

Standing in the doorway of the kitchen with his hands in his pockets the Chief Inspector gazed all around at the scene that was unfolding before his eyes.

'Can someone enlighten me as to what's been going on here?' as he wagged his thumb in the direction of a plethora of white suited bodies with faces hidden behind masks, all carrying black, heavy duty cases containing equipment essential in commanding answers as to how, what, and why events led up to the beginning, middle and end to this bizarre and fatal story. 'And is it too much to ask why none of you had the brain cells to inform me as to what the hell happened to this mother and daughter? Because you see officers, I had to find out from a local bloody news flash. So…anyone got anything to say, well?'

Jarvis moved towards the back door and stepped out into the damp, spring morning where their footsteps left a trail of prints in the dewy grass.

The Chief Inspector deftly followed, and both men moved in the direction of the picnic bench where they heaved themselves onto the wooden seats, which gave rise to a rather loud groaning sound, as the garden furniture complained of the weight that it was now being burdened with.

'Okay Inspector, I'm listening.'

Jarvis told his boss that finally they'd found some invaluable information regarding the red transit van, and that they were sure it was the one that was used in the unlawful detention of the three missing health care workers. Jarvis also informed DCI Wolfe that the elder of the two ladies was Mrs Nancy Ferguson, and the younger her daughter, a Julia Ferguson. He also told him that he had known the family for years, and that he'd tried to contact her husband and the father of his daughter, a Luke Ferguson, but so far his phone was going straight to automated answer mode.

'So, do you think there's some connection in what's happened here and with the guy that's taken these people?'

Jarvis stood up and stepped towards the old doll's house that stood at the back of the garden, which was screened by an overgrown Buxus hedge, desperately seeking a safe distance between him and the outspoken, bullying figure who was increasingly getting under his skin, as he feared that if he stayed a minute longer having to listen to his derision, he'd have no choice but to punch his lights out.

So, with the phone in his hand he pushed the button marked 'E' and tried to call his wife, but for the second time that morning, it was obvious that no one wanted to answer his call.

***

Running now faster and faster, feeling as if the walls of my heart would cave in, not only due to lack of exercise, but also at the sight of the two most precious people in my life who were now unable to draw in oxygen that would keep them in my world.

Driving around not knowing where I should go, I found myself almost in a robotic state outside of the empty garages that sat idly behind my mum's house, and just sat there, now empty of all feelings as the words of the treasured anthem 'Afterglow' bounced off the cold, opaque windows as I wrote the names of my lost beloved ladies underneath a giant heart on the damp glass.

Don't you know both of you that I adored you, and now my life is worth shit, there's nothing left for me anymore as all our dreams are dead and lifeless, just like you my two precious angels.

Gazing longingly at my childhood home, I knew there was no other choice, but not here, which was the home of so much laughter, as my father cracked his corny dad jokes, and we all loved playing charades, which was not only a weekly favourite, but was also considered to be a treat for all of us.

No, no I couldn't do it, not to my mother.

So I drove again with my right foot almost glued to the accelerator as there was no doubt in my mind where it was that I wanted to be, and I needed to get there as quickly as I could just in case I changed my mind that was now spinning out of control.

I knew that I'd parked in the perfect spot, and one that I'd always used when as a family we would come here on sunny days and even if it was cloudy and drizzling we would still visit here just because we all loved it so much, and it meant Julia could run, do her gambols, handstands and anything else that meant she could turn herself upside down. Meanwhile, me and Nancy would walk hand in hand, and speak if we wanted to, or just remain silent with only thoughts that would swirl around in our heads, and almost instinctively we both would know what the other was thinking. But that was then.

I opened the glove compartment and deposited a note on the grey driver's manual, opened the driver side door and quietly closed it. Leaving the van and glancing over my shoulder, I suddenly realised that I'd left the keys in the ignition, but then laughing out loudly, where there was no one around to hear me, I thought…so what, if it gets nicked, it's not a big deal, 'cos it ain't mine anyway and I won't be needing it again now will I?

Chapter 23

With everyone at their desks bright and early the following day and with all reports typed and given to DCI Wolfe as requested, Jarvis stood in front of the white board once again, but this time there was a new photograph pinned up on it, and it was one that he was very familiar with.

'Okay everyone, as you can see the latest addition to the board is Luke Ferguson who, as you all know by now is the husband of Nancy Ferguson, who was found dead in her bed yesterday morning, as well as the body of her daughter Julia, who was found at her side. As you have probably been made aware, I have known the family for years, and I have tried so many times that I've lost count, to get hold of Mr Ferguson, but as yet he still hasn't returned my call, and as the house is under 24-hour surveillance, he hasn't tried to return there either.

I know for a fact that his mother, a Mrs Olive Ferguson is still alive, and he's also got a sister, a Mrs Jacquelyn Monahon, the addresses of which will be e-mailed to you when we're finished up here. Dean and Kelly managed to find out what had happened to the Transit van and the events leading up to why no one came forward with any information, which leads me to the next line of enquiry. Javid, how are you guys getting on with searching through medical records and the possible link with O'Keefe and doses of Aspirin being prescribed?'

Detective Sergeant Das, whilst casually leaning against the corner of his desk, flicked the pages of his notebook and announced dryly, 'Well, I guess we know who we're looking for, because one of the patients that was given Aspirin for a suspected bad headache was a Nancy Ferguson, and cross-checking hospital records, she was admitted with a stroke. So, I figure before we nail this Ferguson guy, we need to go further through all documentation and find out whether our Mr Hackman and our Miss Baluyot treated her whilst she was on the ward.' With that he left, picked his keys up from his desk and grabbed the jacket from the back of his chair.

'Listen up, while we wait for confirmation from Das, we need to find Ferguson, so…Donnelly, you and Turner go and have a chat with his mother, and you Carmichael, go with Nico and go check out whether his sister has seen him, or if she's got any idea where he might be, any special place that perhaps he and the family liked to go together, or even just on special occasions that sort of thing. Meanwhile I'm going to the coroner's office and see what the actual cause of death was, and I've asked for help from uniforms to ask around the neighbours who may have seen anyone in or around the property at any time after around eight thirty, which was when the nurse left for the day. Let's catch up again before the end of the day. Thanks everyone.'

Swiftly pacing towards his office, he once again found L on speed dial and tried Ferguson once again, '*Luke this is Mark Jarvis. I really need you to call me back as soon as possible,*' pocketed the now silent phone, and hastily pulled his coat off the top of his desk and made his way to the stairwell.

As he was expected, Jarvis was ushered into the office alongside the mortuary where the coroner had the report waiting for him, 'Thanks for seeing me so quickly, Dr Spencer. So…what did you find?'

'We'll start with Mrs Ferguson. Not sure if you know, but she'd had a stroke on the left side of her brain thus resulting in hemiplegia of both her right arm and leg, and I would hazard a guess from the damage to the precentral gyrus of the right hemisphere, that this lady had severe difficulty with swallowing. I found a congealed mass of food which was pooled inside the trachea, which as you may or may not know, is the main airway to the lungs, so therefore, if this is blocked well…even though you're not medically trained, even you can guess what the outcome is.

'Suffice to say though, even if she did manage to swallow the food without difficulty, she would more than likely have ended up with yet another extremely severe complication, known as aspiration pneumonia, and this would, in my most humble of opinions, have involved hospitalisation, and I would say, given the severity of the stroke that she sustained, it would have been almost impossible for her to pull through.'

Picking up the next buff coloured folder marked 'Julia Ferguson' with a series of numbers annexed to the initials, he leafed through the pages until he reached the right one, cleared his throat slightly, and continued, 'Now, with regards to the younger of the two, seventeen year old Julia, this was definitely an overdose, and from the toxicology reports it was heroin and there were also traces of Ketamine. She has tracking down both arms and, in both feet, so it's obvious that she's no virgin to this kind of drug abuse.' With this Dr Spencer scratched his head which seemed to awaken his unruly mass of greying, curly hair, whilst throwing the case notes onto the already overloaded desk, 'Why? Why do they bloody do it, what…just so they can forget for a few hours about the world and the shit that's thrown at them, only to wake up and find that the crap is not only still there, but it's even worse than they imagined, because they end up not being able to function at all. For what? I'm sick of opening up all these young bodies when they've got so much to live for, and yet they simply want to suck the oxygen out of their very souls. Fucking tragic, that's what it is.'

Inspector Jarvis had to agree with everything that he'd just heard, but over the years it seemed as though he became impervious to this kind of death, as the war on drugs was being lost, and the monsters supplying the stuff were stealing a generation of young hopefuls who were being somehow brainwashed that the crap that they flooded their bodies with was after all…just for a bit of a release from the strains of life.

There were no laughing moments though when the body had expunged these toxins from the blood stream, as they usually ended up with no job prospects, a broken family life, a life of crime simply to feed their addictive habit, and finding themselves sleeping in shop doorways on filthy duvets with plastic bags full of emptiness, and then there's the pitiful, woeful looking dog at their side to keep them from what, a fate worse than death, as if they hadn't inflicted that knowingly on themselves.

But this time it was different, having stood at the doorway to Nancy's makeshift bedroom just hours ago whereupon seeing both mother and daughter in their final embrace, made him sick to his stomach.

***

Jarvis felt a wave of blackness swell over him as he walked the short distance back to his car, and even though he tried he couldn't get the idea out of his head that things just didn't add up.

He didn't need to be back at the station because the guys knew how to get hold of him with any up-to-date information, so he drove until he ended up back in Eddington Sands. Parking in exactly the same position as he did the day before, and still trying to get his head around what happened, he glanced towards a house that was three doors away where he noticed the twitching of net curtains that once had been a snow white colour but were now an ageing dirty grey and yellow.

With nothing to lose, he strode towards the red brick house to see whether whoever was peeking through the thin, laced fabric had seen something the night before last. There was no doorbell, no knocker so he had to just flick the letter box open and shut several times, but he was sure that the person inside knew he was standing outside.

His heart stopped when the door was opened by a frail, elderly lady, who was clad in a pair of grey trousers with a heavy elasticated waist, coupled with a cream shirt tucked inside and buttoned up to the neck, and a black knitted cardigan draped around her shoulders. Reaching into his pocket, Jarvis slowly removed his ID badge and showed it to her whilst she studied him fleetingly, 'What is it dearie? How can I 'elp you?'

'Ahem...' Jarvis coughed somewhat nervously, 'I'm Detective Inspector Jarvis and I'm from Stockfield Road Police Station, would it b...'

'Come in, come in. I don't get many visitors I can tell you.' As the Inspector closed the door gently behind him, she sauntered slowly with walking stick in her hand and asked him quite loudly, 'Can I get yer a cup of tea or something Inspector? I've got some nice jam tarts if you want one.'

'Please don't go to any trouble, Mrs erm...'

'Cleary, dear. Mrs Marjorie Cleary. And it's no trouble at all, you just sit yerself down, and I'll put the kettle on.'

The ginger tom cat obviously liked the sound of human voices, in presumably this very lonely household, as he sidled towards the six foot detective, and with his tail in the air and his back arched, purred contentedly as Jarvis stroked his soft fur with his long, slim fingers, 'I was just wondering Mrs Cleary, did you know the family at number 23 at all?'

'Well yes, I did as a matter of fact. Before she was taken ill, that lovely lady Nancy used to do bits of shopping for me, and she'd always knock the door during silly weather like if it were too hot or too cold, to see if I needed anything. Ooh she were lovely,' and with that she used the tea towel that hung limply from the back of the rather outdated kitchen chair, and wiped her eyes.

'Is it true that they're all dead, detective? I mean...I don't mix with a lot of 'em around here 'cos all they want to do is gossip, but I were talking to a Mrs

McMenemin from across the road, and she said that all three of 'em were found dead in the 'ouse.'

Glancing around the stark, antiquated kitchen with its floral wall paper now showing no obvious signs of what flowers were etched on it, a plastic curtain of multi-coloured strips hung from the outside door, presumably in a futile effort to stop the onslaught of flying bugs, and as the small lady looked out onto her garden she smiled whilst she watched the birds that she diligently fed and watered hopping around the greenery.

Jarvis smiled at the sheer honesty of this diminutive, extremely pleasant elderly lady, and replied, 'I must tell you Mrs Cleary that that's not actually correct. Sadly, Mrs Ferguson and her daughter's bodies were found, but not Luke the husband. The reason that I came to speak to you is that well...sometimes people find it difficult to sleep, so I was merely wondering if perhaps that on the night when all of this happened, did you perhaps hear or see something that might help us with our enquiries?'

'I always go to bed at the same time around ten o'clock and I guess it's because I'm not very active anymore, but I always wake again around midnight. Mind you, it doesn't help that the street lights seem to get brighter and brighter, or is it in my imagination, and what with me arthritis in me wretched shoulders, I can't close the curtains properly you see, so I s'pose it's me own fault that I can't sleep no more. Anyway, I'm waffling again. Actually, I did hear a door slam and then squeaky hinges of a gate, you know how they sound when all someone's got to do is put a bit of oil on them.

'I mean if my poor Vic were alive he'd be out there quick as you like, oh no he couldn't put up with that noise every time someone went in and out. But I guess that's the way of the world isn't it, no one's got time anymore to go fixing things, and most people don't do they, I mean repair stuff, 'cos well they just go out and replace the broken things with new ones? Oh dear, 'ere I go again...so sorry officer. Any road, I couldn't be sure because there was that bloomin' dog a couple of doors down barking like anything, but I could have sworn I heard someone kind of wailing like, but as I say, me 'earing isn't brilliant. I bet you think my body's falling to bits don't ya love?'

And with this she gave a rather croaky, hacking chuckle, 'Anyhow like I was saying, I went to have a peek out of the curtains and I thought I saw someone walking quite quickly, well these days everyone walks faster than me I s'pose and I guess that's all I can tell you. Another tart...sergeant, wasn't it?'

'No just the one's enough for me but thank you Mrs Cleary. When you say that you heard loud squealing noises well...am I right in thinking that it was someone outside and not inside a house, and did you see anyone that you think was responsible for making these noises? Did you get a glimpse of anyone in the road at this time, like what he or she was wearing, was the person tall, short, fat, thin, anything at all?'

'Ooh no dearie, nothing like that but...he kind of walked as though he might have hurt his leg or something like that any road. Perhaps I should have gone out and lent 'im me stick,' as she accidentally clanked the cup rather loudly onto the saucer, the ginger tabby, not being used to sudden noises, jumped lithely onto her lap.

Jarvis smiled affectionately towards this delightful lady as he asked his final question, 'Are you saying Mrs Cleary that perhaps this man had a limp of some sort?'

'Yes, that's it. I know 'im at Number 23, you know its terrible isn't it, but I always seem to forget their surname, but he sort of walked with a bit of a hop if you like, but never that bad. Perhaps like me its worse when he's stiff or if it's about to rain. Don't ever get old officer because believe me at times it can be a right nuisance.'

The Inspector arose from his chair, and Mrs Cleary pushing hard on the table in an effort to stand, but as her hips groaned loudly, the detective put his hand in the air and said, 'Please don't get up. I can see myself out and thank you again for your kindness and for being so helpful. And I'm so sorry for disturbing you. Here's my card and if there's anything that is troubling you, please give me a call. Bye for now Mrs Cleary and please take good care of yourself.'

As he closed the door shut, the metal cover of the letter box rattled swiftly before it silenced itself.

***

Strolling towards the blue and white cordoned house where two uniformed police officers stood outside with hands clasped in front of them, Jarvis asked one of them for the key to the house that he'd been inside more times than he could remember.

Stepping inside once more in such a short space of time, he couldn't shrug off the constant niggling feeling that something didn't sit right about this whole sad story.

He stood in Nancy's bedroom which was now bereft of all noise and life, and simply tried to mull over the final moments which only the four walls bore witness to. He noticed the tape deck that was sitting on the chest of drawers where tracings of dusting powder were the only evidence that the SOCO team had rampaged through the room just hours before. He pressed play, and then out poured the lyrics and melodramatic sounds of the song that somehow had a powerful, mystical control over Luke.

Jarvis pressed the stop button as he couldn't bear to hear it again, certainly not now, and not with the mournful words that held such despair and loss.

Leaving the room, he then made his way to the stairs where he stood at the bottom, and while holding on to the dark varnished banister, he started to climb the thirteen treads as his feet thudded noisily on the wooden steps disturbing the quiet serenity of the house. Pushing open the door at the top of the stairs revealed a spartan, white bathroom with a deep blue tiled floor where there was an obvious lack of female wares as each surface laid claim to shaving goods, aftershave, and a solitary comb that lay on the windowsill.

Grey fluffy towels were neatly folded, no signs of taps that hadn't been turned off properly, toothpaste and brush still in the plastic tumbler on the corner of the basin. Moving along the hallway, he opened cautiously the next door and hanging from the brass handle of the deep mahogany wardrobe revealed the occupier, as the blue striped tunic hung limply from the wired frame of the hangar. Closing the door quietly, he found himself outside of the room that he was most interested in, pushing a tired smile onto his face, he quickly scanned the sign printed on a metal plate, resembling those used to name streets, roads etc., bearing the warning, *'Adolescent in residence, do not come in unless I say so,'* and adorned underneath was the face of a cute Pug puppy encased on what appeared to be a postcard.

Even though it was obvious that no one on the other side of the white painted door would answer the knock that he imposed on it, he did so anyway, and on entering, the Inspector found himself staring at the magical square of walls and floor that oozed the secrets, dreams, passions and hopes of the young girl that he'd once known.

Every conceivable surface was festooned with childhood memories from smiling dolls, sombre-looking dolls, teddy bears, and the white pasted, red lipped, orange haired clown that Jarvis found to be hideously nauseating, but much loved by the world at large. A slight shiver of fear ran up his spine as he looked around and figured that all of these memoirs were most probably in the same place as the teenager had left them, as they perched majestically, and as she closed her eyes at night, these would be the reminders of the love and happiness that went into each and every acquisition. Bookshelves sat above a desk where not only the compulsory curriculum literature by Shakespeare, poetry by Wilfred Owen and Keats, French and Spanish dictionaries were housed, but also magazines where skinny models in the most up-to-date fashion adorned the covers.

A full-length mirror was positioned between the bed and the window where roller blinds covered the rain splattered pane of glass, as the figure that peered back at Jarvis was the youthful, happy, carefree girl holding her wooden backed hairbrush in front of her like an imaginary microphone as the famous, adulated faces gazed down at her from her walled shrine.

He pulled open the doors to the pink coloured built-in wardrobe, and with blue latex gloves gently made his way through the fashionable clothes dangling from the metallic rail. Still not sure what he was searching for, he crouched down and searched through the piled-up boxes where once new shoes resided, and carefully lodged behind them away from the outside world and its prying eyes, he discovered a pink book with a silver clasp on the front where two words embossed in gold were displayed, *My Journal.*

Snapping the lock open, and with slight tremulous fingers, slowly flicked through these privately written confessions, some of which were written in a child's hand until the script of a teenager was visible, not only in the words used, but also the content seemed to have lost its loveable innocence. Inspector Jarvis, whilst feeling increasingly guilty for prying into this young girl's innermost secrets, sighed deeply and groaned as he reached the last entry, whereupon he lowered his head, as the book with all its silent, hidden secrets thudded to the carpetless floor.

***

Chapter 24
Present Day

Having sat down for what seemed like hours, both Jarvis and Noel Deacon, the journalist interviewing the retired detective, were in need of a drink of some kind, and so following a winding path edged with almost threadbare branches to the water's edge of the manmade lake where it stopped abruptly, they found themselves in the claws of a pub called *'The Weavers Arms.'*

With the warm, autumnal sun dipping in and out of the white puffs of cloud, they walked around the side of the hostelry and found an outside table.

'What's your poison?' Noel asked as he made his way to the bar.

'Half a bitter, and any chance of something to munch on, you know like scratchings, bag of cheddars, well…anything really. I know I shouldn't, but what the hell.'

Waiting for Noel to return with the drinks, Jarvis checked his phone and chuckled at the quirky little message, *'Gotta dog yet?'* with a yellow emoji of two fingers crossed. Slapping the phone back onto the wooden bench whilst trying to find the right quip to send to his son Alex, the clinking of glasses and the sound of the packets of crisps thrown onto the table diverted his attention from the thought of a four legged mutt that, let's face it, part of him wanted, but the other part made him think that he'd got places to see and go to, and yet…

'Cheers and thanks,' mumbled Jarvis.

'So, I kind of think I can guess the ending, but…you're not going to leave it there, are you?' demanded the inquisitive journalist.

'No, not at all,' taking a long sip from the pint glass, the retired detective continued his narrative.

'There's no question that the journal was the eureka moment in the investigation because you see, both I and everyone else had, due to the fact that there was very little other evidence to the contrary, decided that it must have been Luke that was guilty of murdering the two women. DS Das found the evidence from the hospital that both the physiotherapist and the nurse had actually treated Nancy whilst she was on the ward in The Hamilton General, and of course we already knew that Dr O'Keefe did in fact prescribe Aspirin for Mrs Ferguson, which would have given Luke the motive to start his sordid revenge in the first place. So, as we now had this evidence it seemed to make sense that we had our guy and needed to find him fast.

'But well, you see…I knew I had to get back into the house, because as I said earlier, there was something niggling me, just swimming around and around in my head, and I couldn't shift it. There was something oh, I don't know off, none of it sat right, know what I mean. Just think about it, if he'd gone to all that trouble to seek justice for what he felt was maltreatment of his wife knowing that if he was caught, he'd end up behind bars, why then would he go and kill them? It just didn't make any sense, and that's when I decided I'd go and see if there was something that we'd missed.

'And there it was, in black and white. Julia had made daily entries since she was old enough to write, and as I sat there reading back from the date that her mum became sick, it became evident that she wasn't coping emotionally. On her sixteenth birthday, which was I suppose almost eighteen months after Nancy suffered the stroke, Julia went out with her mates, and it was then that she met some bloody bloke who said that he knew how to give her a good time, and to paraphrase from her journal, *'Can't remember a fucking thing about last night, got completely wasted. Don't even know what his name is, but I think we shagged, and I'm certain I took something, don't know what it was, but oh my fucking god, was it good.'*

'It was pretty obvious that she'd experimented with some kinda shit, and neither was she in the slightest way upset about having no control over what she was doing, or worse, who was doing what to her, because she wrote in capital letters and then underlined them, *'I need some more of whatever it was I had last night, 'cos I can't remember feeling as carefree in a long time, and for a short while I forgot just how shitty my life is right now.'*

'Then it became clear that she was using regularly and was hooked, as she used the letters C and H with a smiley face each time that she scored, and I guess that was the beginning of her drug habit.

'Reading the last two weeks of her missive, it became abundantly clear that seeing her mum struggle with life was the reason why she turned to chemicals, as she heartbreakingly wrote these words, and believe me when I say that they'll remain with me up here for a very long time,' pointing his forefinger to his temple.

'Mum, we used to have so much fun together, and with you not being able to talk to me or laugh with me is killing me. I don't know how to help you, and for me that's the worst thing, because I know that you hate being who you are, not being able to talk, walk, put your make-up on, but I think the worst of all is that it breaks my heart to see you not eating proper food, which you used to love. I mean, let's face it mum, you loved food more than me or dad and you really could shovel it away. Talking of dad, he's really getting on my nerves, he doesn't listen to anything I say, and I can't bear being in the same room as him anymore, and I know that he's not treating you like his wife, and that's killing me too. I know you can understand things even though you can't speak, but I don't live here anymore as he threw me out. I guess he found out that I've been taking C and H, and he can't handle that, but I guess he's right not to, because in a way he's not only lost you, but he's lost me too. I don't know how to get out of this hole that I've got myself into, but I promise if you try to get better then I'll clean my act up too.'

Opening the crisp packets up, both men took a handful and crunched loudly, as neither of them would have been able to hide the strained, croaked voices if they were to utter a word.

'The words that followed on the night they were found dead were not really a surprise, '*Mum, you and I are going to be together for ever now in a much nicer world, where we'll be able to dance and sing again, because I know if there is a God up there, then he'll make sure that you're well again, and you won't ever have to suffer anymore'* and she drew an enormous cloud with both of their initials inside a red heart and an arrow piercing through it.'

'Oh my God,' commented the journalist disbelievingly, 'she knew exactly what she was doing when she gave her mum the food, didn't she? D'you think that she made her mind up that night, or was it something that she'd thought of doing for a long time? Oh man...' circling his forehead with the tips of his fingers, perhaps unknowingly in an attempt to erase the words he'd just heard.

'I guess we'll never know, will we?'

'But what did Luke have to say, I mean I suppose you eventually tracked him down and the three missing health professionals?'

'I'll get us another drink and I'll fill you in with the last bit of the damned sorry saga.'

Chapter 25
Two Years Earlier

Locking the house with the young teenager's journal safely tucked away in the pocket of his jacket, the Inspector made his way back to the station where the mood in the incident room was, to say the least, sombre.

Once again standing in front of the white board where photos of the head and torso of a number of people, and maps of possible sightings where the three missing people may be holed up, were safely held in place by a plethora of multi coloured pins and string, in the hope of trying to make some sense of the only clues that they had.

'Got a minute, guys?'

With the slamming down of phones, chairs scooting around having been pushed away too vigorously, his trusted colleagues crowded around ready to hear what the up-to-date news was in the investigation, which not only seemed to be unending, but with the passing of each and every day, the hope that the three missing innocent victims would be found alive and well, dwindled with increasing speed.

Perching on the side of a desk directly underneath the information board, Inspector Jarvis held the pink journal in his right hand and tapped it with the fingers of his left, 'Guys, we now have evidence that Luke Ferguson did not kill his wife and daughter, and that it was in fact Julia, the daughter who somehow took it upon herself to commit some kind of mercy killing, and then she, not wanting to live without her mother, committed suicide by overdosing on cocaine and Ketamine. Now, it goes without saying, that we need to find Luke and fast, because a neighbour who was having a hard time sleeping, spotted someone, and in my humble opinion it's got to be him leaving the house at around midnight, the night that the Ferguson women were last known to be alive, according to the latest post-mortem results.

'I know that you're all aware that Luke Ferguson and I are very well acquainted, and I can tell you that this is not the family man that I knew, but what I am certain of is that he is not capable of murdering these two women because they are his life. However, my biggest concern right now is that he is now a bitter, desperate man and I'm seriously worried what he might now do.'

Sergeant Das then stood and addressed the other detectives, 'We tracked down his mum and his sister and they haven't seen hair nor hide of him for about a month. According to Ferguson's sister, a Mrs Jacqueline Monahon, Luke has never been the same since his wife came home from hospital. He became moody, short-tempered, blamed everyone for his wife's physical impairments, but more importantly, he kept on insisting that someone should pay, not for what they did to her, but for what they failed to do.

'His sister also said that she spoke to him several times and tried to convince him that what had happened to Nancy was not some malicious act, but an unfortunate act of nature, and that no one was to blame. Apparently, she didn't see him again after that, and he refused to answer her calls. So, she thought she'd give him time, and like always, once he'd cooled off, he'd be back in touch. Likewise his mother, Olive, knew that something was bothering him, but she said that he was never one to listen to advice, always got the hump over the merest trivial things, so he talked and she listened.

'I did, however, ask her whether there were any favourite places that he liked to go to with his wife and daughter and she said that he loved to walk beside the river when Julia was little as she could ride her bike there without any fears of busy roads. She also said that they liked to visit the big stately home on the Monsanto Estate because they had beautiful grounds which kept Nancy happy, and a bit of a petting zoo which was Julia's absolutely favourite thing that she enjoyed the most when they went out as a family.

'Thanks for the update Javid,' commented Jarvis, forcing a tired smile onto his face, 'did you by any chance mention to Olive the reason why we wanted to see her son?'

'No, because well I couldn't tell her when she was on her own, so I thought we'd best arrange for her daughter to be there together with a Family Liaison Officer. So I could arrange that if you want, or would you like to do it as you're senior officer?'

'Yeah I'll get on to it straight away before the DCI issues a press statement, and it goes without saying that it'll break her heart when she sees her son's face all over the media. But now we've still got to answer the burning question which is, where do we look for him? So, on the back of what Olive told you as to his favourite places to go, let's get some bodies down by the river bank and some to the Monsanto Estate in case he's holed up in a shack, or outbuilding somewhere. And I also think it would be a good idea to carry on scouring through vacant buildings, around a ten mile radius from here, to see if the victims are being held in one of them. I know uniforms have been thorough, but they're in one of them I'm damned sure, because let's face it, where else could they be? I'm going to talk to his employers, and see whether they can give us anything to go on. Stick with it guys, we'll find them and him, and without stating the bloody obvious, we've bloody well got to, haven't we?'

***

Jarvis having parked his battered old Peugeot in the busy car park of Dunstan & Cooke's, which was considered to be the most upmarket in the field of accounting and auditing firms in Upper Stanton, sniggered waspishly as he sauntered past the named parking space of Chief Executive Officer where the bold and imposing warning that anyone who dared to park in the white marked rectangle would end up paying a heavy fine to the tow company to re-possess their vehicle.

Entering the reception area that fronted the modern, spacious and bright office block where floor to ceiling windows allowed the morning and afternoon sun to radiate through, Jarvis announced, 'Good morning, my name's Inspector Jarvis and I'm here to see Mrs Amelia Pritchard.'

'Do you have an appointment sir?' enquired the slim, well-dressed young man who appeared to be in his twenties, glancing at the proffered ID badge.

'No, I'm sorry I don't, but it's quite an urgent, sensitive matter, and I can assure you that if it wasn't important that I speak with Mrs Pritchard, I wouldn't be standing here now, would I?'

'Of course, sir. I'll see if she's around,' and with that he picked up the phone and pressed just one digit and spoke rather shyly into the mouthpiece, responding with 'Right I'll show him to your office.'

'She…'

'Yes, I heard,' and not waiting for the young man to get to his feet, Jarvis was already following a sign which signalled the way to where the CEO would be waiting. The young man swiftly overtook him, and the detective couldn't help but raise a smile at the suited man, who instead of wearing smart shoes, decided on the fashionable, comfortable look of white trainers, as he knocked on a pale blue door with the name plate, 'Mrs Angela Pritchard' etched in white lettering onto a black, shiny plate.

Waiting for the voice behind the door to acknowledge the two knuckled rap, the young man opened the door, and with a rather theatrical outstretched arm, he invited the detective in to meet with the lady, who had control of everything and everyone within the elegant building.

'Thank you Sean,' announced the lady who was now hastily stepping in her fashionable, stiletto-heeled navy-'blue shoes towards the Inspector.

'Please take a seat, detective,' pointing towards the beige, high backed leather chair.

'I'm very glad that you could see me at such short notice, and I'll try not to take up too much of your time. I'm here to ask you a few details about an employee of yours by the name of Luke Ferguson. I really need to know if there are, or were, any places that he and his colleagues used to go to, that you're aware of, you know…perhaps days out as some kind of team building exercises, or venues that perhaps you all used to go to unwind, that sort of thing. Was he close to any employee in particular, and if so, could I please speak to that person?'

'Right Inspector, that's a lot of information that you want, so let me try and tell you everything I know about Luke. Firstly, I don't know whether you're aware, but we had to let him go about two months ago. You've no idea how it pained me to do it, and well…just so you know, I'm not in the habit of letting staff go, but you see he was becoming more and more difficult to get along with, losing his temper and causing a terrible negative atmosphere in the office. He was late with meeting deadlines, and some of the companies that he had on his books were making complaints about the standard of his work, so as you can imagine, he was costing the company dearly, as his clients chose to go elsewhere.

'Believe me when I say detective, I don't believe in kicking a dog when he's down, because of his home situation and the like, but he left me with no other choice. As far as places that he and the other guys frequented, well I'm afraid I've got no idea, except of course that they used to go for a quick pint now and again at the Fox and Feathers, and we use a company called Stand Tall, who organise corporate events, but that won't really be of use to you as we've never used the same venue twice, so I'm not sure it would be worth the time and effort in contacting them. The same could be said for Christmas parties, you see we usually overnight somewhere at a hotel, but as I said before, we never go back to the same place if we can help it that is.

'There was a guy that was probably his best buddy, but he moved on a couple of years ago, and it's anyone's guess if Luke still keeps in touch with him, but other than that as I said, he didn't have much time for anyone towards the end.'

Jarvis responded after some deep, reflective thought, 'Very well, thanks anyway. Oh…before I leave, this looks as though it might be a new building, how long have you been here, and erm…where were your previous offices?'

Twirling the pen around in forefinger and thumb she gazed around the room with pride almost as if she'd built it herself brick by brick and responded, 'Thank you Inspector, it's nice, isn't it? It took us a while to find the right one so when this one came up we knew we were on to a winner, and…'

'So you moved from where?' glancing swiftly at his wrist watch.

'Oh sorry, but it's still very new, us being here, but we moved about 18 months ago, and the address of the old one is the Finchley Estate, on Cotterill Road, d'you know it?'

'Not really, but I can find it,' and with that Jarvis stood and once again they both shook hands as the Inspector made his way to the door.

Striding through the open plan office towards the reception area, Jarvis patted his pockets to make sure that he'd not left anything behind and strode briskly to the car park as the importance of time was at the forefront of his mind.

***

Scanning through the A-Z map of the area, which he always kept in the glove compartment, Jarvis was soon able to find the main contact roads to the Finchley Estate which took him all of about 15 minutes.

Parking the car in the disused car park and looking straight ahead he found the name above the office block where the names of Dunstan and Cooke still stood high with pride, even though the ivy had gathered pace up the austere grey walls and had started to wrap itself around the name plate.

Striding through the cracked tarmac where roots of the nearby oak tree could be seen tearing the once jet black surface into a mound, Jarvis was amazed that somebody hadn't made the most out of the empty land and turned it into a parking area of sorts, or a businessman who could make money using cheap labour for a car washing service.

With virtually no glass left in the surrounding wooden frames where single holes with spider threads running through them could be seen as local kids who, using the same worn-out idiom that they'd got nothing better to do, hurled projectiles of all shapes and sizes at the glass frames as some kind of glory target practice.

Jarvis held onto the blue wooden handrail where the elements had deprived it of its paint and climbed the five steps to the entrance of the building, and as he held the thick 10 mm metal chain within his fingers that held the double doors completely sealed, he was utterly convinced that short of firefighters' equipment, these would remain impenetrable even for the most bored layabout.

He found his way around the back, where he found more proof of adolescent boredom with hundreds of trodden down stub ends, empty Coke bottles, squashed lager cans and a hell of a lot of graffiti as he sniggered to himself that actually the spelling wasn't that bad.

Jarvis was now convinced that this was not where Luke or the victims would be found.

Lethargically sauntering back to his car, Jarvis could hardly concentrate, as his mind was swamped with the plausible whereabouts as to where his one-time friend would be holed up.

Glancing at his phone briefly whilst checking his phone for messages that he'd perhaps missed, and finding that none had been recorded, he decided that he'd go home as there was nothing much else to be done. He figured that in his own comfortable surroundings, his thought processes just might kick in again, so turning the key in the ignition and putting the car into first gear, he started the journey home.

Chapter 26

Hanging his coat up on the brass coat hook in the spacious hallway with its walls bearing the green colour that was so enamoured in the Victorian era and with the terracotta tiles, Jarvis never really appreciated how lucky he was that the home he and Eleanor had made together could hold such warmth and love. But then again he had always thought the same about the Ferguson household.

Alex was just leaving the kitchen with a piece of Pizza in his hand ready to shovel into his mouth when he spotted his father, 'Hi pops. You're early, everything okay?'

Not waiting for his answer, the youngster sauntered into the sitting room where, no doubt, the latest game that he was playing on his play station would have been put on pause.

Jarvis followed him and putting his head around the door, sighed heavily, and responded, 'Yeah, all's good. How're the exams going? You must be nearly finished by now, eh?'

'Not bad ta, just got a couple of orals to do for French and German and then it's a big fat waiting game until August when I guess I know what my fate's going to be, like…University or I s'pose I'll just get a job at Macs until I can figure out what I'm gonna do next.'

Leaning his head against the coolness of the side of the door, Jarvis did his best to placate his son's negative feelings, 'Aww come on now Al, you know you've worked hard and no matter the grades you know that me and mum love you, and that you've done your best, and no one can deny that you've really worked your arse off, so do me a favour and give yourself a break huh? Anyway, is Andy around, 'cos I need to talk to both of you about something, and I don't want you to hear it from one of your mates.'

'Yeah, I think he's in his room. What's up, it's not mum, is it?'

'Nah, I mean as far as I know she's having a good time with your Aunt Bea but the last time I spoke to her she said that they were having trouble with Wi-Fi so she might not be able to keep in touch daily,' and fairly content that he'd been able to con his son with his half-hearted response, he called up to his younger son, and when failing to respond, the Inspector climbed the stairs and knocked on his door.

As all three males stood in the warmth of the kitchen, Jarvis couldn't help but notice how grown up his sons were now. Both the elder and the younger sons had matched him in height, and now it was simply a contest as to who would end up being the tallest.

Andy, not knowing what was going on, impatiently asked, 'What's this all about dad? Are you and mum splitting up, is that it?'

'No, no, no honestly that would never happen, not to us two that's for sure. Listen lads this isn't gonna be easy, but it's about Nancy and Julia Ferguson, and I'm afraid to tell you that they…erm, well they were found dead in their home late last night.'

'Oh my God, so that's what the rumours were about and why there was so much gossiping going on around the school. I mean kids were like huddled together and some of the girls were crying you know, so I knew it wasn't just a case of some nerd getting suspended. Dad what the fu…sorry, hell happened?'

Jarvis sat down, but both teenagers remained standing with arms crossed and heads visibly lowered turning slowly from side to side in shock and bewilderment, as their father talked them through what had happened to their childhood friend and mother.

'Wh…where's Luke dad, I mean he must be feeling pretty shit right now? Shouldn't we call him and ask him if there's something that we can do for him, or something like that?' asked Alex innocently, as he pulled the chair from underneath the table and sat opposite his father.

Slowly massaging his forehead back and forth, the father of the two youngsters calmly explained, 'Well that's the problem lads, I've left loads of messages and so far he's not responding. There's obviously been a press release asking for him to contact the police and for anyone who knows or has seen him to call us at the nick, and that's why I've been able to come home early for once, as there's really not much else I can do right now, except pray I s'pose.'

The usual boisterous, familial sounds that bounced off the walls in this main nucleus of the home had been obliterated and slowly complete stillness engulfed the air until Andy, barefooted, silently left the room, where the only sound that could be heard was the door of his bedroom closing quietly, almost out of respect for the news, which he was no doubt digesting alone in his private lair.

***

Lounging idly in the sitting room after he'd eaten a concoction of food that normally he would have turned his nose up at, but after the human dustbins had filled their bellies, this left him with very little choice.

Not able to concentrate on anything especially on the television and not wanting to self-indulge on his favourite tunes, he decided he'd call Ellie again, and if that failed, he'd email her. She was due to come home soon, and he vowed to himself that nothing would prevent him from picking her up at the airport.

Raising the mug of scented tea to his lips. Inwardly cursing his wife for suggesting that drinking swill that tasted distinctively of perfume could be considered as a positive component for instilling calm to the mind and body, and after several nauseating attempts, he decided that the best place for it was down the drain. So, he poured himself a large balloon glass of his favourite Rioja which, he figured, would offer far wider remedial effects, especially given the events of the last 48 hours.

With his phone almost glued to his hands these days, he prayed silently that the famous guitar strings signalled that it was Ellie that was calling him, but gazing at the screen it was Javid, but the name identifying the caller sent waves of coldness through his body.

'Evening boss, sorry for tearing you away from whatever it was you were doing, but we've just had a call from the East Burnam police force.'

'They've found the van?'

'Yeah…, but I'm afraid to say they've also found Luke and I'm sorry to say it's not good. He was found in a secluded spot, on Pigeon Bay, close to a place called Old Hownston, and he was discovered by some local lads who hang out there after school.'

Clearing his voice with a short cough before responding, 'Any ideas as to what happened?'

'Well, the paramedics managed to resuscitate him at the scene, but unfortunately, he died in the ambulance on the way to The Prince Albert Royal Infirmary in the nearby town called East Moreham. The Detective Chief Inspector over there has asked the pathologist for a speedy review of the body, but from what the detective told me who was at the scene, he'd obviously overdosed on Aspirin, if you can bloody believe it, as there were two empty bottles of the stuff next to the body.'

Sliding his fingers up and down the stem of his glass, Jarvis struggled to draw a deep breath as his throat was so dry, but the words managed to escape somehow, 'Did he leave a note or anything?'

'He did leave a message sealed in an envelope addressed to you in the glove compartment, and they're sending it across, but other than that we've got nothing else. Maybe, he'll tell us in the note where the three hospital workers are.'

'It's a possibility, but I doubt it very much as I've got a nasty hunch that when he saw everything that was his world dead in their home, then it's extremely doubtful that he even gave them a second thought. But there's always hope. Have we got anything at all from patrol cars who're scouting around empty buildings, and we've also got to contact all security firms that are used to patrol these units, because time is now of the essence now that Ferguson is no longer around. I don't want to state the blindingly obvious, but who's going to keep them alive with food and water now, as the only person who knew where they are is dead, well…assuming that they are still alive that is? We're really running out of time now Jav, and boy if we don't find them soon, we'll be vilified by everyone out there, and I guess rightly so.'

'Okay, boss we're on it, and rest assured everyone's working flat out until we find something.' Click.

Swirling the red, full-blooded liquid around the glass, he took another long swig, but somehow, he'd lost the need for calm to flow through his veins, and instead he needed a large dose of an adrenaline push, so he went back into the kitchen, turned the kettle on, and made himself a large mug of coffee.

Using speed dial on his mobile he pressed J for Josh Turner and asked him if he could give him the numbers for Ferguson's mother and sister, and even though Jarvis knew it was a long shot, it was something he had to explore. He figured that as he'd met both ladies before at get-togethers at the Fergusons, they might be able to talk to him not as a policeman but as a sort of friend. He was also well aware that tonight of all nights might not be the most ideal time to make a call of this nature as by now they would have received the police visit which every human being dreads, but right now he didn't have the time for sympathy because he needed to know whether either of them might be able to remember some relevant places in Luke's past that just might throw some light as to where the three victims were being held so, he figured to himself, this was to be the most important phone call he was about to make for a long, long time.

With neither woman able to offer Jarvis any clues that they hadn't already checked, he decided that he'd tidy up a little bit before his wife was due to come home the day after tomorrow, and then nip off to bed and see whether sleep would visit him in the night, or was it going to be a case of constant turning and thumping of pillows.

Chapter 27
Present Day

'Is this one of the main reasons that you decided to give it up early, even though you huh…clearly were an extremely honest cop, which let's face it is something quite rare these days, given the erm…forgive me for saying, but all the bad press you guys seem to get?'

'Yeah, this was a particularly bad time, but not just for me you understand, but for the rest of the team.'

'Earlier this morning when I first met you, I asked you whether you and your wife were still together, but you never answered me. Now, it's obviously not got anything to do with your professional career, but well…our readers still like to get a taste of the personal aspect of whomever it is that we're writing about.'

'No, you're right I didn't tell you, because there's no really easy way of telling you,' replied the retired detective, 'but I'll try my best now. Ellie didn't leave me to go on holiday with her sister Beatrice because she didn't love me anymore, she went to try and enjoy a bit of the world that she'd never seen before, whilst she still had time. You see Noel, my darling wife knew that she'd been given a death sentence, and she did everything she could to hide this from me, because she knew that if I'd known, then I would have given up the search for the three victims, not focused on Eva O'Connor or trying to nail the bastard DaCosta for disfiguring her for the rest of her life, and Ellie being the saint that she was, could never live with herself. You see, what most people never knew about my lovely wife was that she was the most selfless person that was ever born.

'She was diagnosed about six months previously with pancreatic cancer, and as you may or may not know, it is rapidly progressive, and the prognosis is very poor in almost all sufferers. She also told me that she didn't want the boys to know, as they were both heavy into exams, but what she failed to realise was that inwardly we all figured something was wrong, because of all the pills she took, and the increasing times that we found her snoozing on the sofa at odd times of the day, which was just not like her because she had an incredible zest for life. The thing that I'll never forgive myself for, especially as a bloody detective, was how come I didn't know? I mean I saw all the medication in the cupboard, and I believed her when she said that it was fucking irritable bowel syndrome, but why didn't I suspect something wasn't right when I noticed how much weight she'd been losing?

'I mean, I've read up a bit about IBS but it's not that big a deal in the great scheme of things, so no I guess as usual, I put my wife's needs second to this bloody job, and for that there can be no forgiveness, because I'll never have her back by my side, and I'll just have to put up with her memories.

'So, why don't you put that in your article and see then whether your so-called intellectual readers think that I'm such a smart cop, heh…?'

The young journalist didn't quite know what to do to appease the hurt and guilt that the detective sitting in front of him was being demonised by, and if the person opposite him had been a female he'd have reached out and clasped her hand in his, but he hardly knew this man, and he just didn't feel comfortable giving solace in a physical way.

'Look I'm sorry, and we don't need to go on if you'd rather call it a day. I mean…we could finish it another day if you'd prefer?'

'Nah, I'm okay. Let's get it done and then perhaps with everything finally off my chest I can start really enjoying my retirement, because let's face it two years ago was the mother of all years.'

Sipping the dregs of the almost empty pint glass, Jarvis wiped his mouth with the back of his hand and continued his narrative, 'It was confirmed by the pathologist that Ferguson had taken a massive overdose of Aspirin, and even though it wasn't the drug that killed Nancy, to him it was, because if O'Keefe had never prescribed it, then she wouldn't have been bed-bound and Nancy would have still been the woman that he married twenty years ago. So, I guess he felt that he would seal his fate in exactly the same way. We'll never know of course, but why would he choose that drug and not say hum…Paracetamol?'

'What did the note say, assuming you got it of course?' enquired Noel, who was carefully folding an empty crisp packet into neat little squares.

'It didn't say much at all except that he was sorry.'

'I can remember vaguely that the three missing people were eventually found, but I'd like to perhaps revisit it again for our readers, to well…reinforce to people that despite all the negative feelings towards the Met, you guys never give up. I guess the other thing that the general public must be made aware of is that you guys don't do a nine till five job and with everything that you've just told me, you don't switch off, even when you're at home especially with the phone constantly going, and cases always swirling around your brains.'

'It was only thanks to a construction firm that had bought a disused pub called The Tanner House, which is about a mile or so from the notorious area of Denton Heights that they were actually discovered. Needless to say, it was not only a huge relief to them to be able to start the renovation, but also to us that the hunt was finally at an end. It goes without saying that they were in a pretty bad state, very dehydrated and weak. Thankfully though, a leaking pipe was the main source of their water, and because Rosario, the Filipino nurse, was the only one of the three who wasn't handcuffed to a bed, she was able to catch the water in one of the plastic bags that Luke had chucked on the floor, and with a teaspoon that he'd also left for them to use, she was able to spoon-feed the water into their mouths.

'Archaic I know, but it was through her sheer tenacity that they all survived. Unfortunately, they spent a long time in hospital, and both men needed extensive physiotherapy, especially Hackman, ironic as it may seem, but apparently no permanent damage was caused. As both men had severe pressure sores, they did, however, need plastic surgery, but the skin will heal itself eventually, even though they may be left with some scarring. A lot of the praise, however, needs to go to Dominic Thurston, the pharmacist and partner of Hackman, because you see, he must have guessed that Ferguson wanted to cause someone harm or even a fatality with his request for IV Aspirin, and it was all thanks to his incredibly quick thinking that he deliberately gave Ferguson the wrong dosage of Aspirin.

'Apparently, according to the experts, this was the reason why O'Keefe didn't sustain any long-term cardiac problems, but he's been advised to get checked on a regular basis. Even though Miles didn't suffer, thankfully, from any cardiac or neurological complications, which is what Ferguson wanted, or so it would seem, he was just extremely weak and terribly withdrawn because he felt enormous guilt over what he'd been accused of. And, as he said to me during our conversation, he did misdiagnose Nancy, and he will regret for the rest of his days that he didn't listen seriously enough to her complaints of constant raging headaches that she'd had for a while, and to satisfy her and him that there was nothing sinister going on, he is in no doubt whatsoever that he should have requested a brain scan, and if he had done that, then this nightmare would never have happened.

'Quite bizarrely though, the good doctor actually apologised to me for causing so much disruption to the police when he knew that there were an awful lot of crimes that were happening on a daily basis, and perhaps hundreds that had gone unsolved, and he felt increasing guilt that this was all of his doing.

'As for the young nurse, unsurprisingly she left the UK, and nobody's quite sure where she went, but after being mentally scarred with everything that she went through, it wouldn't surprise me if she didn't leave the profession.

'So, there you have it. That's about everything I've got to tell you.'

'There's just one more thing I'd like to ask and that's about Eleanor, your wife. How long from when she arrived back home from the holiday with her sister did you two have together? Because I can't imagine with everything that was going on, how you managed to carry on at all. And of course the boys, they were stripped of their lovely mum at such a young age.'

Rubbing his hand across his chin back and forth, he finally managed to answer the inquisitive, yet seemingly empathetic journalist, 'Well she came back a few days after we found Ferguson's body, so even though it was a rubbish time, I could at least give her some of my time. We had a few good laughs about the cruise that she and her sister Bea went on, and even though she hated not telling me the truth, she honestly felt that she was able to have time for herself, and something that was important for her was to share childhood memories. She was later admitted to a local hospice as the pain became too unbearable, even though I wanted her to stay at home, but she felt that it wouldn't be a very good idea to have such disruption in the household, especially with the lads embarking upon the most important time of their lives. Again, it just proved how selfless she was because there was never any question that she would want to spend the last few days at home, but what did she do, she put her needs secondary to her family.

'Anyway, she died three weeks afterwards but she was in my arms when she did pass and both boys were at her bedside. She looked at ease, and before the end she was able to say that she wasn't frightened, and she made the lads promise that whatever it was that they did with their lives, that they must never forget that happiness was the most important thing, and not how much you could earn in a month. She also made all three of us promise that we must always remain friends, and even if we did have a falling out we must laugh it off and move on, and then the last words that came out of her mouth was that she loved us. And then she was gone. But you see that's what she wanted, and that was to leave this world with her three men at her side.'

Both men paused wondering which one would break the silence.

'Anything else you need to know? For instance do you want to know what happened to Lenny DaCosta, because that was something that managed to bring a smile to my face during probably the worst year of my time on this planet?'

Chapter 28
Two Years Earlier

It was a lovely day, so Jarvis decided to walk to visit his mum at The Chestnuts Nursing Home where she'd been a resident for the past three years.

He wasn't looking forward to the visit because he would have to knowingly lie to her and tell her that everyone was fine, which is the one question that she did remember to ask at each of his visits. He figured there'd be no point in telling her about Ellie as he doubted very much if she'd be able to understand the meaning of what he'd said, as her mind was slowly being decimated by Alzheimer's, for which there was no known cure.

The double doors whooshed open on his arrival, and he headed towards the reception where he duly signed the visitors book logging in the time of his appearance. He used the lift up to the second floor as the stairs were off limits due to safety measures for its clientele who may wander off the dementia ward, thus potentially finding themselves with broken joints at the bottom of the stairwell, or in an unknown environment outside of the support network within which they were cared for and protected.

Scanning around the scarcely populated dining room in search of his mum, he was not overly surprised that she wasn't there, as more often than not he found her in bed with claims from those who were supposed to be looking after her that she'd refused to get up, or even more bizarrely, that she'd been up first thing and demanded to go back to her room. As she was very restless in the childlike cot, Jarvis asked one of the nurses politely whether it would be possible for someone to assist her out of bed so that they could spend some time in the garden as it was such a beautiful day.

Wheeling her out in her wheelchair as she'd now lost the power of her legs, Jarvis sat on a wooden bench with the brass plate bearing the names of Mary and Fred, as she sat opposite her son.

Conversation was at best scant with the usual repetition of phrases about her husband who'd just visited her, but who had in fact passed away twenty years earlier, or that she needed to go back home urgently to put the washing on the line so that it'd be dry before teatime.

Jarvis always found it very difficult to tear her away when she's on a ramble, so he'd have no other choice but to simply let her get on with it, leaving his mind to go on a trip of its own. As the doors leading from the dining room to the garden were open, he could see the television which seemed to be on twenty-four hours a day, and there on the screen appeared a very familiar face. Whilst keeping a close eye on his mum, he went closer to the screen to try and hear why the cameras were zooming in to a face that he'd never forget.

The reporter from the local news channel was standing on the bottom step outside of Chingford Crown Court, and speaking into the furry microphone she announced with an almost applauding tone, 'I'm standing outside of the Crown Court here at Chingford, and sentencing has just been passed by the Honourable Justice Mrs Flint who has sentenced a Mr Leonard DaCosta for a period of twenty five years for the murder of a Christopher Connelly, and the attempted murder of a man named Michael Mulligan, both formerly from Greater Manchester. Evidence was given as to the horror story that lay behind the door of a house in Denton Heights, Upper Stanton which is a well-known haven for accessing Class A drugs.

'Officers described the scene as one of sheer carnage where both bodies were found having sustained severe injuries, and it was further revealed that Mr Mulligan was treated by one of the officers whilst they were waiting for the emergency medical services to arrive. Testimony was also given that there were further arrests at the scene for possession of illegal drugs and for attacks on police officers. During the trial Mr DaCosta attested that he had not used drugs knowingly, but when arrested and after having undergone routine toxicology tests, large amounts of both Cocaine and Marijuana were found in his blood stream. The accused, whilst testifying in the dock, claimed that his drinks must have been spiked saying that this was an unforgiveable act of betrayal by his so-called friends. He was found not guilty of intent to supply Class A drugs, as there was no hard justifiable evidence to support this, and indeed, the accused denied ever having seen or known about the supply that was found at his residence.

Whilst summing up, The Honourable Justice Flint said that DaCosta was fortunate that he was not being sentenced for the murder of two people, and this was due to the incredible hard work by Officer Quinlan that Mr Mulligan survived at all, even though he is still in a critical state. She also said that Mr DaCosta's time in incarceration was going to be a long one, and she strongly suggested that he use this time to reflect on the damage that he'd caused to the family of the deceased. She also said, in quite a flippant tone it has to be said, that where he was going there would be no chance of anyone spiking his drink with illegal drugs, therefore, he could rest assured that he'd be safe from their harm.'

Jarvis couldn't help but snort loudly when he heard this as he uttered a loud rebuttal of, 'Lying bastard.'

To which his mother shouted, 'What's that you say, dear?'

Listening now even more intently, as the microphone was rudely thrust into the face of one of DaCosta's victims from earlier on in the year, which brought back sad memories to the Inspector. Melissa Harding-White from the local NST broadcasting station continued her interview. 'Miss O'Connor, I believe that you were unsuccessful in your recent legal battle to get justice for your injuries that you claim were sustained at the hands of the now incarcerated Mr DaCosta. Have you got anything to say about today's judgement?'

'Firstly, I have to say that my injuries were not fictitious as you seem to be alluding to, they were very real. As you can see from the parts of my body that are visible to the outside world, they are indeed as a result of that monster's vicious attack on me. And what I would like to say to all the women out there is that no one should tolerate abuse of any kind. No one should be robbed of the voice telling others of the mental and physical violence that's hurled at them by people who can only be described as evil.

'No one should be left with stark evidence for the rest of their lives as to the sheer horror and degradation that was bestowed upon them, being left only with the image looking back at them in the mirror. No one should be afraid to leave the house for fear of reprisals lest the victim be bold enough to report the crime. No one should be treated this way, nor left with the memories that will haunt them for the rest of their lives. But you see I've been through all of these things, and with the help of incredible close friends, and professional bodies, I've been able to move on with my life. It was thanks to all of those people that I have opened a counselling service which will operate twenty-four hours a day, where someone will always be there to listen to your story.

'Thankfully, I was fortunate enough to have had someone in the police force who listened to me, and who never for one single second gave up seeking justice for me, and it was his and my hope that this evil man would be locked away for a very long time. I will be haunted by my own body for the rest of my life, but unlike that maniac I have my freedom. In fact, that very kind policeman was there for me every step of the way, as were the medical staff who helped to patch me up, well on the outside at least, and suffice to say without them well…I'm not sure I could have carried on living. This kind Samaritan knows who he is, and I want to thank him from the bottom of my heart for all the hours that he listened to me, and for giving me advice and the inner strength to do the honourable thing. Sadly, I buckled at the final hurdle because, you see ladies and gentlemen, this Satan of a man Lenny DaCosta, and his vicious henchmen, overpowered me mentally with their vile threats, and I wish now with all of my being that I'd listened to the advice that the professionals were giving to me.

'That was then, and this is now, and I can tell you that I'm overjoyed to hear that this man won't be out for a very long time, and for the time being anyway, women will be safe knowing that he's now off the streets. The last thing that I wish to say is that these devil-like creatures deserve to be punished, and believe me when I say that one day, we victims will be the victors.'

One journalist interrupted a rather lengthy, silent pause with only the sounds of the clicking of cameras filling the void of sombreness, as shards of lighting bombarded around the diminutive Eva, almost giving her a saintly halo, asked, 'I'm Vanessa Pendleton from The Langton Chronicle, and may I express my personal thanks to you for highlighting the plight of so many females who are fearful for their lives, and it is wonderful to hear that you have come through your ordeal seemingly a stronger person. We read in the local and national newspapers almost on a daily basis the torrid stories of females of all ages, creed and colour being abused in some disgusting way or other. Can you confirm that anyone, regardless of who or what profession they are in will be allowed the services that you offer, and more importantly how can our viewers get in touch with you?'

'Thank you, Vanessa, and the answer is of course yes. It doesn't matter who you are, what you do, where you live, you will be given free professional advice and a friendly, empathetic ear. And should you wish to take your case through the judicial system, then each and every one of our advisers are trained to guide you through this and they will be able to contact the relevant authorities, and *we'll be with you throughout your ordeal. Our charitable organisation is called 'Voice for the Silent.' All calls are free of charge, and there will be complete confidentiality with each and every cry for help that we receive. The number to call is 07223 278922. So, ladies out there don't wait, don't become a punching bag or frightened to speak out, and please if you're out there listening to this, just remember that you're not alone in the chance for freedom which is your absolute right as a human being.'*

As her face disappeared from the screen, Jarvis found himself once more in front of his 92-year-old mother, and with a beaming smile on his face, and a slight watering of his eyes, he was now able to turn his complete attention on the memories that she was sharing, despite him having heard them countless times before, but he really didn't give a damn. Perhaps something worthwhile did come out of his job after all.

Walking home from seeing his mother, and for the first time in a long while he felt in a good place, so he figured that now was the right time. He removed the cassette tape from his jacket pocket that had been closeted there since the three medical workers had been found after he'd removed it slyly from The Tanner House as he felt that nothing would be gained by putting it in with all of the other evidence, as no one was on trial and never would be. He slotted it quickly but carefully into his Walkman whereupon the deceased man's voice began to course its way through Jarvis' auditory canal.

'Mark this is me, Luke. I know that you and I have been friends for a long time, and when you listen to this, you'll no doubt have worked out that I'm not the man that you once knew.

'It's best I s'pose if I start from the beginning. I guess it all started after I realised just how all of our dreams had been broken and torn apart by Nancy's illness. We weren't the family that once laughed, ate together or went on weekends away to the seaside.

'Of course, it wasn't just the sadness of seeing the love of my life lying there totally dependent on everyone for absolutely everything that she needed. And I never once regretted giving up work for her, well…that's not strictly true, you see I actually got fired, which to be honest with you was the last fucking straw. You see, I ended up having to get a second mortgage on the house, and of course there were the fees for round the clock care, council tax, household bills, and of course still having to pay for a teenager still at school, but even that wasn't the worst of it.

'I knew erm…that Julia was having a hard time. I mean Nancy wasn't just her mother, they were like sisters, or best friends, they were so bloody close, sometimes it made me jealous just like a soddin' child. The trouble is that the closer they became, the more I felt as though they were pushing me out. So, now just ask yourself this, how could a husband and a father even think in such a pathetic way, eh? And yet, this is the man that you allowed to drive your children to school, so perhaps in an odd way I'm not the only fool now, am I?'

'Anyway, Julia seemed to change almost overnight from a little, happy, carefree schoolgirl to a moody, bad-mouthed teenager who came home when she felt like it, and when she did it was obvious that she wanted to be anywhere…just so long as it was far away from me. It's not as though we argued a lot, in fact she never spoke to me, well…apart from when she needed money for clothes, make-up and soddin' tattoos that she insisted she must have. But you see, even that wasn't a trigger point to do what I did. No, it was when I knew for sure that she was using drugs, which meant that I'd not only lost my wife due to a wrongful diagnosis, but also I was losing my daughter to a force of evil that was so destructive that it would eventually suck the life out of her, which kinda leads me nicely into what finally sent me over the edge.

'It was the day that I read in the newspaper that that monster DaCosta got off scot-free, and I knew then that his filth would still be supplying on street corners, making sure that the Julias of the world would get their fix, and she certainly wouldn't have had the cash to pay for it, so it doesn't take a genius to know how she did manage to get the shit that she smoked, snorted or injected.

'So, the more she used, the worse our relations became. She'd virtually quit school, even though all the time I thought she was going on a daily basis hum…supposedly getting ready for her A levels. Ha! She certainly had me fooled, didn't she? Anyway, she eventually came home less and less, presumably because she needed to be close to an easy fix when her body craved it, so she only came home on Tuesday and Thursday evenings for just a couple of hours, and even then, she insisted that I not be in the house when she arrived.

'Mind you, I can't particularly say that I wanted to see her either, as her appearance had changed beyond all recognition, and she certainly didn't resemble the daughter that I'd known and loved since she was born. Her hair was dyed jet black, she wore nothing but black clothes, jeans with holes in them and chains that you'd use to hold a plug in place dangling everywhere, as if she was some kind of groupie in a heavy metal band. Her face was thick with make-up, and you couldn't see those beautiful blue eyes as they were heavily made up with the black shit that she put on them. But not content with all of that, oh no...she had to make herself even more scary looking with piercings in her eyebrows, nose, tongue and those were the only ones that I could see, and God only knows which other parts of her body she decided to mutilate.

'So, you see Jarvis there was nothing else to be done. If O'Keefe had treated Nancy's constant headaches with some degree of concern and not just send her away with the idea that a packet of over-the-counter pain killers would end her problems, then Julia wouldn't have had to witness how her mother was suffering and she wouldn't have gone into a massive downward spiral, ending up as a low life junkie. Then of course we come to the other two, Hackman and Baluyot who also didn't treat Nancy with the respect that she deserved, refusing to give her even a chance. So, what else was I to do? You have to see Mark, someone had to pay for what they did to my family.

'That's about it, except one last thing. That night when you saw me in the pub and me kind of went off on one about that Genesis song, well I guess now you've probably guessed why. It wasn't the music you see – it was all about the words. Phil Collins was singing about my life, and the death of dreams.

'By the way Mark, I really did enjoy our friendship, but I now know that's dead forever, and who knows...our paths may not cross again in this life, but maybe in the next, eh?'

Chapter 29
Present Day

Having spent the day idly not doing very much and with the house eerily quiet with the lads now having gone to start new chapters of their lives at different universities, Jarvis found himself pushing back the niggling little to do list further into the crevices of his mind.

He knew that today was the day when Noel would be heading off to London for the big event that he hoped would give him a leap up into the big players' league of journalism. The retired detective had been invited, but he felt that this should be a time when Noel was with his own kind enjoying the quiet anticipation that each and every one of the hopeful, eager participants could share with one another.

Apparently, the award ceremony was going to be broadcast on a relatively unknown station, but nevertheless he could access it if he wanted.

He'd told his lads about it, and the very idea that their father could be the subject matter of a possible winning contestant of such a prestigious award made them feel so proud of him, which is why they were both rather surprised and somewhat nonplussed as to why he didn't accompany the young man. Perhaps even worse though was that both of his sons were quietly concerned that after their mother's death, their normally affable, sociable dad had decided to just shut himself away.

Jarvis had done his best to learn to cook by following the usual cookery lessons on leading television channels, and he'd even followed recipes which he'd torn out of magazines that lined tables in the doctor's office or the dentist. But having failed miserably, he nowadays used the popular meals for one concealed in little trays in the freezer department of any supermarket which he was pleasantly assured would give him sustenance within about four minutes by whacking it in the microwave.

He would always mix up a salad or boil up a few vegetables to bulk up the meal, and even though he knew that the meals were very plain, and it has to be said, lacking any real recognisable taste, he was happy with his lot, as he really couldn't be bothered with all the measuring, or the adding of spices and sauces that some of the recipes demanded. Of course, there was also the added bonus of cooking this way, and that was by using the disposable little polystyrene trays, there was very little washing-up involved.

Having thrown away all of Eleanor's supposedly insomniac remedies, he'd now resumed his nightly intake of a glass or two of the dark red Rioja that was his favoured tipple when the day had closed its doors and the long dark night surfaced.

The time of the broadcast was set to be 09:30 pm, so after throwing the single plate and the few utensils into the dishwasher he sauntered into the sitting room where he sprawled out onto the three-seater multi-coloured sofa, placed his drink and phone on the small walnut side table cleverly strategically placed at the side so that he didn't have to reach too far. Holding the remote control in his hand, he set about finding the channel that would hopefully reveal the man who had taken a small portion of the detective's life and tried to portray to the world the highs and lows of the job not only with having to cope with accepting the avoidable loss of life, both in a professional and personal capacity of the young and the old.

Having surfed through the myriad of channels on his TV, his search was finally at an end. The leggy blonde with hair styled in a French pleat, dressed in a long, flowing gold coloured gown, standing next to a dark haired, handsome, thirty-something-year-old, dressed smartly in a James Bond-like tuxedo, welcomed guests and viewers from around the globe to the twenty third award winning ceremony of The Journalist Of The Year.

The cameras were zoning in on various contenders and a commentator for Channel 161 who was hosting the event managed to put names to some of the hopefuls whose images filled the TV screens. Jarvis put his glasses on that were hanging limply from a blue chord around his chest as he didn't want to miss even the merest glimpse of his now close buddy, well that's how he now thought of him because, as he silently admitted, he'd never opened up quite so much to a complete stranger in his life before.

In a very strange, bizarre way he was rather nervous about whether Noel could or would win. Unlike awards given for the best film, or the most successful song of the year, the general public would not know anything about the content of the piece of journalism that had been submitted for this highly acclaimed accolade. I guess the writers themselves would have some kind of inkling as to who and how many entrants there were, and hazard a guess as to who the possible winner would be, but the public at large would have no idea, or so Jarvis suspected anyway.

Before the event, Noel had suggested that even if Jarvis didn't manage to find the channel, or even if he did and he couldn't be bothered to watch it, then he would text him the final result.

As with most award nights there was so much waffle and behind the scenes documentaries about how a particular contender had come from a really bad background, managed to get themselves out of slums despite all the adversities that life had to throw at them, and general tear-jerking attempts that were meant to sway public opinion in their favour.

Struggling to keep his eyes open after more than an hour and a half glued to the screen where winners of one category or another were seen weeping as they grasped the gold plaque which bore the shape of the open pages of a book, he succumbed to sleep. The announcer started to introduce quite animatedly how it was an absolute pleasure and quite a humbling moment of her life to proclaim the winner of the 'Most Aspiring Journalist of the Year,' and that without further ado she'd like to introduce Joey Bellamore, the winner of the Golden Pages Award for bestselling novel in 2021 to present this year's award.

'Thank you very much Suzy, and it's a pleasure to be here with everyone, this evening. I guess it's never easy being a panellist on one of these awards as they must receive hundreds of excellent pieces of work, so it is my absolute pleasure to announce that the winner of this year's award for journalism goes to…'